PAWN:

A FAIRY TALE

CALLIOPE MORE

ISBN: 979-8-218-75885-1
Cover design by: Nora O'Neill
Printed in the United States of America

For the ones who still believe in fairy tales.

And for the family members, friends, and educators who encouraged my dream

of being an author. Thank you for falling down this rabbit hole with me.

Meer

The Bad Tooth

The Labyrinth

The Giant's Hut

The Nameless Forest

Conchae Marie

Pins & Needles

Shepherd's Landing

Nacre Coast

The Living Garden

Come, hearken then, ere voice of dread,

With bitter tidings laden,

Shall summon to unwelcome bed

A melancholy maiden!

We are but older children, dear,

Who fret to find our bedtime near.

Lewis Carroll, *Through The Looking-Glass, and What Alice Found There*

CHAPTER 1

JANUARY 17

MY PARENTS SUGGESTED I wait to see my older sister's body.

Perhaps *instructed* is a more accurate way to describe their tone, gentle and firm. "You've been through an ordeal, Alice," they told me. "It's better to take things slowly."

I don't begrudge them for it. I don't want to break down like I did a week ago in the hospital, where I screamed nonsense, except for when I begged for Evie. But she was already gone.

When I breathe, my black dress restricts my ribcage. My mind is as vacant as the white ceiling of the viewing room. I can't shake the feeling that the walls are closing in on me. This room is too much like the hospital ward: cold, stale, and unnaturally sterile.

I remind myself that the sharp scent hovering in the air is the ill-disguised reek of formaldehyde, not disinfectant.

It's not the same. You're not there anymore. It's over.

I curl my fingers into fists until my nails press into the

bandages covering my palms. The biting pain of the still-healing cuts underneath the gauze clears my head somewhat.

The room is too large for the gathered mourners: my parents, Evie's friends, and Willow Creek's tiny Asian community. My maternal grandparents did not come.

I can count the number of times I have seen them on one hand. Over the years, their visits from Hong Kong have dwindled to infrequent calls. Maybe it has something to do with their constant arguments with my parents.

My conversations with them are civil, if brief, since my parents get tired of translating. Mom and Dad didn't teach me and Evie Cantonese because they thought speaking English would help us "fit in" at school. I didn't question it. I wish I had.

No matter how distant I may feel from my grandparents, they should have attended Evie's funeral.

Why didn't they?

I force my face into a blank mask as the line to my sister's casket shrinks. I try not to dwell on who might be judging me in this instant: *Look at her. She's not even crying. How heartless.*

I'd rather appear indifferent than lose control. My grief is not theirs to see.

At my side, Evie's best friend, Mikayla Wong, steps forward. I move with her.

Mikayla could have already paid her respects with Hailey Zimmerman and Khalil Qureshi, Evie's other friends. Instead, she stayed with me. Her self-assured presence steadies my breathing somewhat.

She brushes a couple pieces of her self-cut choppy black bangs out of her eyes. It's normal to see her in dark colors, although it is unusual for her to wear a dress. I wouldn't be surprised if her parents forced her to buy it solely for this occasion. They're also probably the reason that she removed her less funeral-appropriate jewelry. Only her bracelet, a silver band with an adjustable chain, remains on her wrist. I have never seen her without it.

I force my attention to the casket: a sleek mahogany box decorated with white flowers.

Mikayla's lips hardly move when she whispers, "She would hate this."

Across the room, my parents' gazes weigh on me, reminding me that it is our turn to pay our respects.

Together we peer into the casket.

Surrounding Evie's body are keepsakes from people who have already paid their respects: a pendant with a golden coin, a yellow origami crane signed in cursive, a blue jigsaw puzzle piece, and a jade charm.

Stop stalling. Look at her, my inner voice insists. *It's the least you can do.*

The first thing I notice is the pallor of her skin. Evie spent about as much time outside as I spent doing homework—so, a lot, especially during lacrosse season. She often teased me that I was as pale as a ghost.

The freckles on her cheeks have faded, perhaps covered by makeup. She would look like she's sleeping—recuperating from a sickness, maybe—except that she's entirely too still.

I swallow the bile at the back of my throat and force myself to focus on her lips, which the undertaker positioned in a faint upward curve. It is a poor imitation of her smile with none of her living warmth.

I wish this were a dream. I want Evie to wake up. I imagine her grin, her voice: *It's only a joke. I would never leave you, Al.*

Evie will never be older than seventeen. I won't hear her

announce her return home from school when she drops her backpack and lacrosse bag by the door. Her painting supplies will lie unused next to the commissioned watercolor pieces she didn't finish. She won't go to community college with Mikayla like she planned—not that Mom and Dad approved of it.

Why am I torturing myself by thinking about her future? Hypotheticals meant something to my starry-eyed sister, but not to me. *Would have, could have, should have.* None of it matters because it won't happen.

Mikayla leans forward and places a palm-sized mirror—with an ornate ceramic frame that she carved herself—in the casket. She gave the mirror to Evie as a twelfth-birthday gift, and Evie displayed it on her dresser for years.

Coldness hits my gut. I have nothing to offer my sister. *How could I have failed at this, too?*

I grip the edge of the casket to hide my shaking, bandaged hands. The cuts on my palms sting, reminding me of all the painful unknowns I face—especially *The Incident.*

Pain throbs in the back of my head, like it always does when I want to cry but I can't.

This is all *madness.* There is no other word for a loss that collapses your entire life.

Beside me, Mikayla steps back. That is my cue to leave my sister behind and join my parents. Instead, I linger, eyes fixed on Mikayla's mirror.

I see a shade of scarlet so violent that my eyes water. As I study the reflection, it becomes clear I'm looking at roses—otherworldly ones, with petals that appear sculpted. Their edges blur like ink in water, swaying even though no air is circulating through the room.

My eyes drift upward. The flowers on the casket are white lilies. Not red roses. Yet the reflection of the roses in the mirror does not shift. Maybe there's something wrong with my glasses, although nothing changes when I adjust them.

A saccharine scent rises from the red roses, overwhelming the bitter reek of formaldehyde.

I hunch over the casket, drawn by their magnetism. A thrum like distant music beckons to me, urging me to reach out. To grasp a handful of beauty for myself.

My arm extends toward the closest rose.

Then bristling, dagger-sharp shards overtake my vision.

I stagger back, clammy hands clutching my chest. The bandage on my left palm unfurls. The room tilts. When I blink, red roses burn in my retinas. My breathing sounds far too ragged and loud.

"Alice?" Mikayla says. Her gaze darts toward the mirror in the casket. "Is everything okay?"

It's stress and grief, making you see things that aren't there, I tell myself. I force a weak smile.

"Sorry," I say. "I thought I saw something, that's all."

I make my way to my parents until two people approach me. I recognize them as Evie's other friends, Khalil and Hailey.

Khalil's eyes are the same warm brown as his skin, and are glossy in the funeral home lights. He blurs into all the other mourners in funeral black.

"I'm so sorry for your loss, Alice," he says. "I know that Evie is in a better place now."

I've already heard those words countless times today. They mean nothing to me. They mean less to Evie.

My mind dredges up the darkness of a half-remembered night. *Searing pain. Pleading. Screaming.* My breath catches.

"She was one of the kindest, most creative people I've ever known," Hailey murmurs, bringing me back to the present. "I miss her so much already."

Her eyes are tinged with red. She fidgets with the sleeves of her black dress. Nestled in the curtain of her coppery hair is a preening peacock earring whose gemstones wink in shades of blue, violet, and emerald. Unlike Mikayla, Hailey did not deign to remove her more ostentatious jewelry.

An acrid tang rises in my mouth, threatening to choke me.

Khalil clears his throat, bringing my attention back to him. "If you need anything, just let us know," he says.

"Thank you," I reply mechanically. "I will."

My thoughts pursue me as I walk to my parents. *You were too rude. You should have smiled.*

My mother greets me with a brief hug and a wan smile. Her hair is pulled back in a taut bun. She applied her makeup precisely, but I know where the shadows beneath her eyes hide. A tear traces down her cheek. I don't wipe it away. She wouldn't want me to, not with all these eyes on us.

My father folds me into a tight hug. I wince.

I've never thought of Dad as old, but there are wrinkles around his eyes that were not there before the funeral. Before *The Incident.*

"We're all here now," he says, "with Evie."

His low, smooth voice snags on her name, as if he meant to say something more.

This is the last time the four of us will be in the same place together.

I bow my head, my eyes stinging, and wait for everything to be over.

I hope that time comes soon.

CHAPTER 2

MARCH, TWO MONTHS LATER

ADVANCED PHYSICS IS a terribly inconvenient time to be losing my mind.

I am developing a hands-on experiment with mirrors for Willow Creek Elementary School students. At least, that is what I am supposed to be doing. I can't concentrate when the three mirrors on the black lab table are reflecting unearthly visions.

A serpentine maze of thorny hedges.

A hexagonal hall of glowing glass bottles.

A bloodred castle on the horizon.

It's nothing, I tell myself. *You're imagining things.*

I can't bring myself to believe that anymore.

I must be hallucinating from stress. Or sleep deprivation. I haven't had a full night of rest since…no, I don't want to think about it right now. I *can't*.

I lean back from the lab table, focusing on the shuffle of winter coats and squeaking shoes on the slush-stained floor of the classroom. My high school's heating system always struggles to adjust to the cold Michigan weather. Although it is mid-March, snow sticks to the ragged grass outside the window by my table.

My physics project partners are Khalil Qureshi and Ethan Bradford, teammates on the Willow Creek High School traveling soccer team. Their red varsity jackets are identical except for the word *Captain* emblazoned on Khalil's.

I don't look at Khalil. I have avoided him since Evie's funeral in January. It's not that I dislike him. He's polite and empathetic to a fault. If I weren't the teacher's pet of Mrs. Johnson, then I'm sure he would be.

No; I'm just afraid that he might bring up Evie.

On the opposite side of the lab table, Ethan lounges on a stool. A mechanical pencil spins between his fingers.

He raises a thin blond eyebrow at me. "The Missile is coming this way."

I roll my eyes at the nickname that is based on our physics teacher's first name—Melissa—and her ruthless grading style. I don't understand why people disrespect her so much when she only pushes us to do our best.

"Don't call her that," I say.

Instinctively, I search for Mrs. Johnson in the classroom. She wears a heavy plum-colored shawl over a knit sweater. She moves between the rows of lab tables, chatting with students about their project plans.

Ethan points his pencil at the mirrors. "So, do you guys have any ideas for these?"

Khalil's head lifts. He has been staring intensely at the mirrors, although he cannot see what I can. The March sun spills through the window behind him, paling his warm brown skin and dark curly hair by a few degrees.

"Nothing yet," he says.

While he and Ethan chat, my gaze drifts to the third mirror. It still shows the dim hall filled with glowing glass vials. I squint, trying to make out the contents.

The luminescent bottles vibrate abruptly. I jump.

Ethan pokes at the mirror with his pencil. His heavy-lidded eyes flick to me. "I thought you asked for different materials, Alice. I don't want to work with these."

I grit my teeth. What he really wants is for somebody else to pick up the slack. As far as he's concerned, life is all about finding shortcuts. Not that I can do much about it. If I complain, he'll make me look uncooperative…or worse, incompetent.

"If you have to do all the work, you will become better at it," my mother often reminds me. "The others only hurt themselves. You understand that success is the best revenge, Alice. You always come out on top."

I relax my jaw with some effort. I shouldn't be bothered by the likes of Ethan, and if I am, then I'm above showing it. I make my voice cool and clipped. "I don't control our materials. Mrs. Johnson has the final say."

Ethan's scowl turns into a smile. At least, I think it is supposed to be a smile. It's closer to a grimace. That's not surprising, since he's dealing with me: Alice Lee, the infamous goody-two-shoes of the eleventh grade.

"You're her favorite," he says. "She'll give in for you."

For the millionth time, I wonder why Ethan took this class if he isn't willing to challenge himself like the other juniors and seniors here.

At fifteen years old, I'm younger than most of the juniors. Yet I'm no less driven than anyone else in this classroom.

I glance across the lab. Mrs. Johnson is making steady progress toward our lab table. Her eyes meet mine.

Think, Lee. We need to tell her something about our project.

But when I gaze at the three mirrors on our lab table, laid side by side, the scene in their reflections has changed.

The mirror in the middle shows an image of a round cherrywood table. Movement flickers in the left mirror as a man with a black mustache materializes.

He looks about fifty, with a balding head and a paunch. Walking into the central mirror, he covers the table with a red-and-white checkered tablecloth, then sets out silverware and a blue vase.

His elbow jogs the vase. It tips off the table. I tense, waiting for it to shatter.

Instead, it stops halfway to the floor and quivers like an arrow in a target.

The man huffs and puts the vase back on the table. He raises his head.

As if on cue, a woman emerges in the mirror on the right. She resembles a hen with her red ruffled blouse and pleated golden skirts. Her rosy cheeks, mass of dark curls, and toothy smile remind me of the dolls that Evie and I owned as kids. She carries a basket on her arm.

Like the man, she walks into the central mirror. As she approaches the table, she spins, skirts swishing. She bows to him. They lay out a spread of bread, fruits, and vegetables from her basket. Their movements are precise. Choreographed, even. I am fascinated by the sight.

Until, in perfect unison, the two march arm-in-arm from the table. Toward me.

Their empty black gazes fix on me. Their lips stretch into unnaturally wide smiles.

Although their mouths do not move, I hear words,

high-pitched and scratchy. *Welcome, Alice. We are waiting for you.*

Through the pounding of my heart, I form one coherent thought.

My hallucinations have never spoken to me before.

A chorus of raspy shrieks echoes through my head. With horror, I realize it is laughter.

"Stop," I whisper. My breaths come fast and uneven. "This isn't real."

Join us. You will never want to leave.

I press shaking fingertips to my ears. "Leave me alone."

You are our honored guest. Just like your sister.

They laugh again. Darkness fuzzes at the corners of my vision. The laughter keeps going and going and—

I sweep my arms out. "STOP!"

My breath shudders. For a blissful moment, everything falls still.

"Alice!" someone exclaims.

I'm yanked backward by a pair of strong hands.

A wave of cold erupts through me. My eyes fly open at the sound of shattering glass.

The mirrors overlap in a twisted mess of shards on the tiled floor—where my feet would have been if Khalil hadn't pulled me away.

Ethan, shielded from the fallout on the other side of the table, stares at me.

"What was that for?" he demands. "You broke our materials!"

The rest of the students have gone silent. Mrs. Johnson's boots click loudly on the floor as she hurries toward us.

She raises her voice. "Everyone, continue working. Do not move from your stations until the glass is cleaned up."

Slowly, chatter rolls through my classmates again, although many are still staring at me. I turn away.

"Alice?" Khalil asks. He studies me with a slight frown. "Are you okay?"

"Of course I am. Why?"

"I said your name three times just now."

I'm saved from replying when Mrs. Johnson arrives to sweep up the mess with a broom and dustpan. Her hefty cat-eye glasses make her owlish eyes appear even larger as she surveys the three of us. "Are any of you hurt?"

We answer in the negative.

"All of you, check the bottoms of your shoes for glass." She meets my gaze. "Alice, when I'm done here, I'd like a word with you."

"Of course," I say. Nausea roils in my gut.

How much of my "episode" did Mrs. Johnson and the rest of my classmates witness? I can already imagine the whispers: *Alice Lee was talking to herself in Advanced Physics. She's really lost it now.*

I don't need to give anyone another reason to shun me.

"Alice, seriously, are you okay?" Khalil asks in a low voice.

I smooth my scowl over before it shows. I'm not in the mood to say what I don't believe: *Yes, I'm fine. I'm just in a hard spot.*

"You already asked me that," I reply.

"Well, your teeth are chattering."

I fold my arms tightly, trying to summon any scrap of warmth. "It's cold in here."

It's part of the truth, but not all of it. Every time I escape a hallucination, I'm engulfed in an unnatural cold. I feel like I'll never be warm again.

"I know things must be hard for you right now, with your sister…" He clears his throat, tugging on the sleeves of his varsity jacket. "I miss Evie too. If you ever want to talk about it with someone, I'm here."

He has the formula down, I think bitterly.

The acknowledgement of the mourner's difficult situation; the connection to the lost loved one; the offering of condolences and/or a confidant. Everyone substitutes different names—different lives—into this formula.

But I'm only being cynical. Khalil was one of Evie's best friends. They met in the fifth grade when they were paired up for a presentation about a book they both disliked. Both extroverts, they gladly struck up conversations with strangers in cafés or concert venues.

Still, I can't talk about *The Incident* to him…or to anyone, for that matter. I shove down the confused darkness that has tangled my memories for the last two months.

He can't know. I don't even know.

"Yeah," I say. "Thanks. I'll remember that."

Mrs. Johnson finishes sweeping up the glass and beckons me over. I gladly obey. Together, we walk to her desk, which is surrounded by faded diagrams of magnetism, thermodynamics, and kinematics. I catch a few classmates craning their necks in our direction. Some are packing up their belongings even though there are still three minutes until the final bell.

Mrs. Johnson asks, "Can you tell me what happened, Alice?"

To delay answering, I trace the scar that wraps around the knuckle of my thumb. It is the largest scar I received during *The Incident.*

"It was an accident," I say.

Her blue-gray eyes bore into mine. "Is that all?"

"I don't know what came over me," I confess. "I didn't mean to break the mirrors."

"You usually handle lab materials with more care."

I wince. "It won't happen again. I promise."

"It's a good thing that Khalil reacted quickly to the situation. I know he's been experiencing some of the same difficulties as you in recent months."

I suppress the urge to laugh. I doubt he's been having hallucinations of nonexistent creatures and places every time he turns around. During those times, I black out from reality. It's like I step outside of time and place altogether, with nothing to anchor me.

"Khalil was quite close to Evie," she continues. "Perhaps you could talk to him sometime and compare your experiences. It might help you…process."

"Maybe," I say cagily.

"You're a good student, Alice. Inquisitive. Determined."

Inquisitive. Determined. Mrs. Johnson so rarely hands out praise that those two words alone almost drown out her last sentence: "In light of your sister's tragedy, I understand that school is not easy for you, but work done while distracted…"

"…Is no work at all," I finish.

This is one of her favorite sayings, frequently parodied and parroted by the other kids in my grade. Mrs. Johnson isn't necessarily likable, but her strictness helps us succeed.

Her voice cuts into my thoughts. "Are you all right, Alice?"

I stiffen. I haven't guarded myself against the question even though I've been asked it countless times since Evie's funeral.

"Yes, I'm fine," I say.

She taps her fingernails on her desk. "You don't have to take your troubles into the lab, remember? Once you come in here, you're entitled to a fresh start. I want you to remember that."

I wish I could trust in her words, but no number of

assignments or lab reports will distract me from my grief...
or the hallucinations that haunt me in reflections every day. I
have a sinking feeling that they will only worsen.

"I will," is all I can say.

Mrs. Johnson smiles: a rare expression for her. "Tell you
what, Alice. You can come on Thursday during homeroom
and complete the project with your group. I'll assign you different supplies—maybe not something so breakable. And I
won't penalize any of you for late work."

My knees nearly buckle in relief. That's more than I
deserve. "Thank you so much, Mrs. Johnson. I really appreciate it."

"You're welcome." She waves me out as the final bell rings.

When I emerge from the school, Mikayla is waiting in her
beloved red truck, which she named Lucy. Even through the
rolled-up windows, I can hear the rock music blasting from
halfway across the parking lot.

Dozens of stickers and decals cover Lucy's back windshield,
most of which relate to obscure bands or sarcastic slogans. On
the bumper is a long white streak from the time a car scraped
against hers. Her parents wouldn't pay to fix it—not that she
cared. "It's part of Lucy's personality," she claimed.

I knock on the passenger window. Mikayla unlocks the
door without looking up. She sprawls in the driver's seat,
scrolling on her phone.

"Hey," she says as I climb in. "Did you get on the wrong
side of the Missile?"

"Don't call Mrs. Johnson that," I say automatically. "How
did you know?"

When she raises her head, jeweled planet-and-star earrings sway from her ears. She molded them from clay and painted them to match her silver bracelet. Her leather jacket, Doc Martens, and heavy black eyeliner give the impression she's going to crash a concert or beat up someone in a back alley. Maybe both.

She turns the key in the ignition. "Wasn't hard to guess. You never take so long to get out of class."

"I wasn't that late."

Mikayla squints at the clock on the dashboard. "Your margin of error is thirty seconds. A minute, tops. Not five minutes. And you usually don't look like that when you get out of class."

"Like what?"

"Like you've disgraced four generations of your ancestors."

"Very funny."

There's no hiding anything from Mikayla, like it or not. In the time it takes me to relate what happened, we're well on our way home.

"She's giving me a chance to make up the project," I say. "She won't take off points for turning it in late."

That reminds me. I open my backpack and rummage through my calculus and physics textbooks, three notebooks, my laptop, a binder, and…

My fingers close on a dark green planner. I flip to Thursday, two days from now, and scribble, *Make up group project*.

Mikayla coughs. "You were saying about Mrs. Johnson?"

I put my planner away. "Sorry. Anyway, she wasn't angry at me. Maybe disappointed…but she gave me another chance."

"Hmph. Sounds kind of insensitive to me."

"Insensitive? Why?"

"We just passed the two-month anniversary of Evie's…" She falters, staring straight ahead.

Death. The unspoken word is like ice-cold water inside my lungs.

Mikayla and Evie were best friends, although that term doesn't seem strong enough to describe the bond they had. For days after Evie's funeral, when neither Mikayla nor I could sleep, we called each other and talked until our voices gave out.

She helped me through the worst of it that first month, but I can't tell her the real reason that I'm always tired and preoccupied. She wouldn't believe the apparitions that plague me every waking hour.

Mikayla presses on. "She told you that you were distracted when you're still mourning your sister."

"I made a mess of broken glass."

"It's not that big of a deal. Don't let her tell you how to feel."

I stare at the ornaments hanging from her rearview mirror. They are all in the shape of iconic world landmarks. The Great Wall of China knocks into the Eiffel Tower as the truck rolls over a pothole.

"I'm fine," I say.

"Alice, please. You'd say you were fine if you got hit by a car."

"Are you saying that I'm less than open about my emotions?"

"I *know* it."

"Like you're one to talk."

Mikayla smirks. She opens her mouth to reply. Then, her head snaps to the rearview mirror.

Her eyes widen. Her grip on the steering wheel goes slack.

Lucy careens to the right. The tires screech against the curb, flinging us against our seatbelts. I yelp.

Mikayla snaps out of her trance. She yanks the wheel to the left, letting loose a string of colorful curses.

Behind us, somebody lays on their car horn. Mikayla flips them off and floors the accelerator. Soon, we're out of sight.

"Sorry," she says, her brow furrowing. "I thought I saw something."

"It's a wonder you passed your driver's test on the first try," I say, trying to ignore my jack-hammering heart. "Someday you're going to get in trouble."

"For what?"

I raise my eyebrows. "Causing road rage."

Mikayla brushes her choppy bangs out of her eyes. "Nah. No one will catch me. And if you don't get caught, then it didn't happen."

"Is that what you thought when you ran into the police that one time?"

She jabs her index finger at me. "Emphasis on *one time*. You'll never let me forget that, will you?"

"Your parents won't either."

She snorts, but a slight edge creeps into her voice. "Evie and I didn't do anything. We were just in the wrong place at the wrong time."

A couple of minutes pass in tense silence.

I glance in the side mirror to make sure the car is not following us. But the mirror no longer reflects the road. Instead, I'm met with the image of an oval-shaped lake. I grip my backpack as if it is a weapon. With everything it holds, it might as well be one.

At least the lake is placid. Its banks are surrounded by a fringe of dark grass. The colors of the water shift between hues of green. At the center is a spot of dark, likely the deepest part of the lake. It's almost beautiful. Almost harmless.

Then the lake caves in along its middle, collapsing into a semicircle.

No…it didn't cave in, I realize with a wave of nausea.

I fix my gaze on the road ahead, my heartbeat fluttering in my chest. I don't want to see how closely it is watching.

Because it's not a lake, but an unknown eye, blinking at me.

The water is a filmy lens over the green iris. What I mistook for water weeds are veins. And the pupil is a dark epicenter that pins me in my seat until I can't breathe—

"Here," Mikayla announces.

She pulls into our neighborhood. All the lawns are covered with stubborn frost. The Wongs' pale blue house sits directly across the street from my family's chalk-white home.

The Wongs moved into the neighborhood when Mikayla was seven years old. As soon as my parents found out that Mr. and Mrs. Wong were also from Hong Kong, they struck up a friendship. The Wongs speak both Mandarin and Cantonese; when they are with my parents, they converse in Cantonese.

Mikayla understands Cantonese for the most part but does not speak it well. She doesn't know Mandarin at all. At least she has some experience with her parents' cultural heritage, though. Mom and Dad raised me and Evie to speak English, claiming we'd fit in better that way.

Perhaps it's not too late to learn Cantonese. Still, the thought of starting from scratch daunts me. No matter what, I'll always be behind the people who are native or heritage speakers.

Mikayla parks in my driveway. "We're back."

"Thanks." I sling my backpack over my shoulder. I open the passenger door—or try to. Mikayla hasn't unlocked it yet.

She rests an elbow on the steering wheel. "Alice, what's going on with you?"

"Nothing."

"You look like you've seen a ghost."

Close but not quite.

I try to smile. "Well, you know…it's hard to be alone with my thoughts these days. I have to keep busy."

"There are better coping mechanisms. Try doing something that makes you relax. Like daydreaming."

I scoff lightly. "I like to stay in the real world, thanks."

"The 'real world' isn't always fair to people."

"It moves fast," I admit. "But I can keep up."

Unlike Evie, who immersed herself in fantasies where time did not exist. I used to wish I could live in those fantasies too. I was always racing from one test to the next. From one award to another. But I've found that I like keeping busy. It gives me a sense of purpose. A tangible goal. If I am always working toward something, then the guilt of not doing enough can't catch up with me.

"It wasn't fair to *her*," Mikayla mutters.

I don't have to ask who she's talking about.

I press my lips together. Mikayla was Evie's best friend, but she doesn't understand what it was like to live with a sister who was half present at any given time. Evie was the sole person who could have understood my predicament with our parents. Yet she perpetually lost herself in her head—a place that I couldn't reach.

I don't know how much Mikayla knows about that part of Evie's life. Regardless, it's no use reliving the past; I can't change it.

"I've never found escapism useful," I say. "I'd still have to deal with my problems once I came back."

Mikayla shrugs. "Maybe. But it's a good way to practice for the real escape." She adjusts the ornaments on her rearview mirror, untangling the Colosseum from the Sydney Opera House.

"You're still taking your gap year?" I ask. "I thought your parents didn't want you to go."

She smirks. "What makes you think I asked for their approval?"

Lisa and Peter Wong may be strict, but Mikayla is equally stubborn.

"Fair enough," I reply.

The idea of her traveling alone on a trip meant for two sends a pang through my chest.

Perhaps Mikayla has the same thought. Some of the humor leaves her face. Her hand falls to her silver bracelet.

"She wanted to visit France the most, you know," she says quietly.

That doesn't surprise me. Evie, the romantic she was, loved French. It was the one AP class that she didn't put up a fuss about taking. It was also the only AP exam that she scored above the minimum passing grade on.

Mikayla straightens, a fierce expression on her face. "Well, I'll do it for her. I can't wait to get away."

I think about the empty house that awaits me.

"I don't blame you," I murmur.

She hits a button, unlocking the passenger door. I start to open it.

"Hey, Alice."

My hand pauses on the handle. I look at her. "Yes?"

Her head tilts a little as she surveys me. Her choppy black hair brushes the right shoulder of her leather jacket.

"You know that you can talk to me about anything, right?" she says, her voice softening.

But I can't, I think. *You don't see what I see.*

I don't paste a smile on my face. She'd call me out on it. Instead, I roll my eyes, mock exasperation seeping into my words. "Of course I do, Mik."

"Just checking." She grins. "Okay, get out, freeloader."

CHAPTER 3

THE FIRST THING I notice when I enter my home is that the entryway light is on.

I press my back against the door. My pulse ratchets. My key digs into my palm.

Every morning, I am the last person to leave the house. My father works unpredictable shifts at the hospital, and my mother leaves early for the bank. That makes me responsible for turning off all the lights.

I am certain that when Mikayla picked me up before school, I stepped out of a dark house.

My entire body goes cold. I feel like the eye in Mikayla's car mirror is still following me.

Someone has been inside my house. They may still be here.

A home invasion was the first theory that the police devised to explain *The Incident*—until evidence suggested that it was nothing more than a freak accident. A tragic accident, but still an accident. Case closed.

But what if it isn't?

I peer around the corner, past the hulking shapes of

furniture in the living room. The light in the hallway leading to my and Evie's rooms is on. A yellow glow emanates from the crack beneath Evie's door.

A shadow moves across the floor. My breath goes shallow.

I've always dismissed ghosts as superstitions. Yet the irrational thought crosses my mind that my sister has returned to haunt me...

"Alice?" a familiar, high-pitched voice says. "Is that you?"

The tension ebbs from my shoulders. I approach Evie's bedroom and open the door. A lump rises in my throat. I haven't been in here since *The Incident*.

The shattered glass from that night is gone. That isn't a surprise. After the police deemed the case a freak accident, my parents reorganized the space from top to bottom. They cleaned the fragmented glass from the carpet and mounted a new mirror on the wall.

The mirror's presence burns in my peripheral vision. I haven't been able to look in mirrors for weeks. I'm afraid of what might stare back at me. Besides, I can guess at my appearance: sunken cheeks and eye bags that are barely hidden by my glasses.

Evie chose a bright yellow color for her room when we first moved in, much to Mom and Dad's chagrin. On the wall above her violet-colored bed is a garden-inspired mural resplendent with tulips, roses, and daisies. She painted it herself. It matches the daisy-patterned lamp on her bedside table, which bears a long crack in its shade.

Three pillows are arranged in a row at her headboard. A throw blanket is folded diagonally over the corner of the mattress. On her desk, paintbrushes, pens, and pencils are separated into unstained jars. Canvases are stacked in neat arrays. Looking at the scene gives me a sense of vertigo. This version of Evie's room is completely at odds with who Evie was: a whirlwind in a human body, always moving, always free.

On the other side of the room, my mother steps away from Evie's bulletin board, which is populated with the few photos that weren't ruined two months ago. She is dressed in a smart navy blazer and skirt. Her pin-straight hair, like mine, is brushed across her shoulders.

I am often startled by how much she resembles Evie. Both their faces have the soft geometry of round cheeks, full lips, and wide noses. While that composition suited Evie's personality, nothing about my mother can be called *soft*.

Her expression, as always, is a stern line. She surveys the key clenched in my hand. "I heard you come in the door."

Her Cantonese accent is faint after twenty years of living in the U.S. If I listen closely, I can hear the slight rise and fall of her tone, placing stress on syllables that English doesn't emphasize.

"I…I didn't know you were getting back from work early," I say.

"What was that? You're muttering."

I repeat myself.

"Oh, I'm not. I had to return home because I forgot my laptop charger. I was about to leave." She bustles into the hall.

I follow her, wondering why she was in Evie's room. My parents tend to talk around Evie, rather than about her. Still, their grief runs as deeply as mine. Sometimes I catch Mom in the garage, going through countless boxes of my sister's paintings. She studies each piece of art for minutes at a time, tracing the brushstrokes. I'm not sure what to make of it.

Mom retrieves her large black handbag from a stool at the granite kitchen island. As she fiddles with the zipper, she asks, "Did you have a good day at school?"

This is her foray into the standard question-and-answer exchange that we've had since kindergarten.

I lean on the smooth counter and give the answer expected of me. "Yes, it went well."

"Good. Did you get any grades back?"

"I received full marks on my physics test last week."

"Good work. I'm not surprised. Are you continuing the doctor's exercises for your hands and wrists?"

I resist the urge to shove my hands into my pockets. I focus on the blue china vase that occupies the middle of the kitchen island. Mom hasn't replaced the lilies in about two weeks, and the white blooms have long since shriveled. I should have done it for her, but I can barely cling to my normal routine.

"Yes," I say in a falsely bright tone. "I don't think I need to continue them for much longer. I'm not in any more pain."

"What about the emotional exercises?"

Although those exercises are technically for my mental health—meditation and the like—she prefers to call them *emotional* exercises. Perhaps she does not want to admit that anything is wrong with my mind. Well, neither do I.

I tell her what she wants to hear. "They're helping as expected."

Mom scrutinizes me. Her hands pause on the zipper of her handbag. Her eyes soften a fraction. "Are you eating enough?"

"Yes."

In all honesty, I have no idea. Since Evie died, eating has been a mechanical process.

"There's some leftover mapo tofu in the fridge. You can heat it up for dinner. Did Mikayla drive you home from school today?"

I bite my tongue to avoid saying, *She always drives me home now.* "Yes."

"I'm glad. I will thank Lisa and Peter when I see them next."

"She's still planning to travel during her gap year," I blurt out. I'm not sure why I choose to volunteer that information. It interrupts the usual flow of our exchange.

Mom blinks at me. "Is that so?"

I nod. My throat is thick.

"I know Lisa and Peter don't approve," she muses. "But I think it's good for her. She will spend less time with her head in the clouds. Get some real-world experience. You don't need to travel, though. You already are learning the skills you need to be successful, here in Willow Creek."

She rests her hand on my shoulder.

I glance up, startled. Usually, she is more reserved with displays of physical affection.

"You know what to do," she says. "Study hard…"

"And work harder," I finish.

She smiles. The expression is slightly weary. "Your father and I are thankful that we do not have to worry about you."

I bow my head, unable to stifle a smile. It's difficult to please my mother at the best of times. For days after this, when I doubt myself, I'll remember her words.

She straightens. "I have to go. There's still a lot of time left in my day."

"Right." I chide myself for feeling a stab of disappointment. I rarely see her outside of her work, especially since Evie died.

"I'll see you later. Goodbye, Alice. I love you."

Before I know it, she has taken her handbag and shut the front door behind her. I'm reminded of how she's like me: always moving as fast and as far as she can.

"Goodbye, Mom," I say to the dust motes that float up

from the carpet. I heave my backpack onto the same kitchen stool she used for her bag.

A shrill meow from the living room breaks the weighted quiet. I instantly know who it belongs to. I pad out of the kitchen.

Trophies are arranged in a neat line on the fireplace mantel. The majority of them have my name on them for piano recitals, archery, and Science Olympiad. Three of the awards belonged to Evie. She won them on the high school lacrosse team.

Maybe she'll receive an honorary trophy for her senior year season. My gut tightens at the thought of putting it on the mantel.

Mrow! The sound is more insistent this time. My gaze is drawn to the end of the row of trophies, where a fluffy shadow perches. It is out of place against the robin's egg blue wallpaper.

"What are you doing, Dinah?"

My tabby cat, of course, doesn't answer. She peers at the hardwood floor. Her black-smudged ears flatten against her head. Her pale blue bow-shaped collar glints. Evie picked out that collar.

I pinch the bridge of my nose. "Don't tell me you're stuck."

Mrow.

"If you're not too scared to jump up there, then why are you too scared to jump down?"

I resign myself and stand on tiptoe, holding out my arms to my cat. I quell the temptation to look at the flickering shadows in the trophies' reflective surfaces. Hallucinations have already surprised me one too many times today.

As I reach for Dinah, she leaps down from the mantel. She dashes across the floor, skidding around the corner. The door of Evie's room is still half-ajar. Dinah bursts through it.

"Dinah!" I call, charging after her. "Get back here!"

I push into Evie's room. My cat weaves between the legs of my sister's desk. She leaps onto the nightstand. Her tail knocks into the cracked lamp. I wince when it thuds to the floor, along with one of Evie's framed watercolors.

Great. Another mess I'm responsible for today.

I lunge for her. She dodges and runs headlong toward the mirror. I brace myself for the collision.

But it doesn't come.

I blink. Dinah is nowhere to be seen. The room is eerily still.

Where did she go? She must be hiding somewhere.

I move forward—then stop in my tracks.

Although I am standing in front of the mirror, it does not show my image. Instead, it reflects a darkness as pure as ink.

I squeeze my eyes shut. Cold sweat slicks the back of my neck. It's another hallucination. It has to be.

When I open my eyes, the darkness remains.

As I examine it more closely, I realize that it is actually a narrow tunnel. I cannot tell where it ends.

A soft, floral scent reaches my nose. Violets, perhaps. As I breathe it in, a lilting melody drifts from within the tunnel. The song makes my blood hum. I lick my lips, tasting citrusy sweetness.

I feel dizzy. Not sick, but exhilarated. Like I am once again seven years old, playing with Evie in the meadow behind the local tennis courts. We used to hold footraces, most of which she won. Still, she made a wreath of dandelions and crowned me with it. We laughed until it hurt.

The meadow no longer exists. It was plowed and turned into another wing of the tennis courts parking lot. The song evokes the same pang of loss that I experienced as a child, knowing that flowers had once bloomed where white lines painted asphalt.

I blink back tears and spot a faint glow in the distance.

Your destiny awaits, a voice in my head whispers. *Come.*

My vision blurs. My fingers skate along the drywall. Some part of me warns that if I cross through this doorway, I won't come back.

The warning is overpowered by the promise of a past that no longer exists. The music—so sweet, so soft—draws me forward as if in a trance.

This is not like my hallucinations. It is much kinder. Gentler. It is an invitation that I accept as I step across the threshold into the darkness.

Curiosity killed the cat. Evie's teasing voice echoes in my mind.

"But satisfaction brought it back," I murmur to no one.

CHAPTER 4

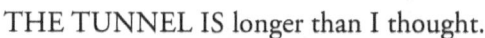

THE TUNNEL IS longer than I thought.

I trail my hand along the wall, then recoil when spiderwebs tangle on my fingertips. With a shudder, I shake them off and quicken my pace. Around me, shapes form hulking shadows. Furniture, maybe? The musty air settles on my skin in a way that puts my teeth on edge.

I can't tell how much time has passed when I finally approach the glow I'd seen from the doorway. It turns out to be a lightbulb with a silver chain dangling within reach.

I yank the chain. Incandescence flares in my face.

"Gah!" I stumble back, blinking the spots from my eyes.

The ceiling appears disproportionately high compared to the doorway that I came through, but that must be a trick of the light.

The tunnel opens into a large, boxy room. Musty-smelling aisles surround me. Each aisle contains antique wooden shelves of leathery books and decrepit trinkets that confuse the eye. My hands itch to put the mess to rights.

I take a step forward. My foot knocks against a bulky, tarnished key, sending it tumbling a few feet away. It flops over once, twice. Then, I spot a flash of white that looks like… wings? I can't tell for certain because in the next instant, the key vanishes behind the shelf at the end of the aisle.

The shelf contains a scarecrow-thin doll with white skin, auburn hair, and beady black eyes that seem to follow me. I walk past the shelf and search for the key, which is nowhere to be found. It probably fell into the floorboards.

When I step back, I notice the doll on the shelf is missing.

In its place is a letter opener, roughly the same height as the doll. Scarlet ornamental flowers twist down the hilt of the blade, along with vines that curl like claws.

How did I mistake a letter opener for a doll? Perhaps the shadows are playing with my vision…or, more likely, I need a new prescription for my glasses.

Disconcerted, I move on to another shelf. This one holds all manner of well-worn books. I peruse some of the titles. *Of Cats, Cabbages, and Kings* is an illustrated nursery rhyme. *Oars and Leeks* is a comedy book. I can't figure out *Muchness: A Field Guide to the Whatchamacallit*. It must be for kids.

In another aisle, I smile when I spot a teapot shaped like a tabby cat. It resembles Dinah.

Wait. Where is Dinah?

My head snaps up. Whatever enchantment settled over me now slips off, leaving me cold with worry.

Dinah is the reason I came through the doorway in the first place. If I lose her, Mom and Dad will be furious.

"Keep a handle on her. You're the only person she'll obey," Mom has told me more than once.

That wasn't quite true. Dinah adored Evie, too. In fact, she was Evie's seventh birthday present. Unfortunately, Evie rarely emerged from her daydreams long enough to remember Dinah's needs. Over the past few years, I've stepped into the role of caretaker instead. I can't let anything happen to my cat now.

"Dinah!" I call.

No answer.

I hurry down the dark aisles, finally reaching a long, moth-eaten counter that is bordered by sills of various bottles.

I skid to a stop. The hairs on my forearms prickle.

On the counter, a dim lamp illuminates a chipped, steaming mug. Cautiously, I press my fingers to the ceramic surface, then wince. It's scalding hot.

Someone has been here recently.

On the wall nearby is a clock crafted from wood and bronze. Although it ticks in a steady rhythm, no hands adorn the clock face. On a perch underneath the number six, a slumbering cuckoo bird tucks its wooden head under its wing. Its chirruping, hypnotic song—the song I heard from the other side of the doorway—is broken by snores.

I glance behind the counter. Piled on a chair is a fluffy white wool coat. On the tabletop, knitting needles protrude from a pyramidal pile of yarn. Someone's unfinished project, no doubt.

"Curiouser," I murmur, "and curiouser."

On the edge of the counter is a stoppered glass vial. It holds a clear solution shot through with streaks of iridescence. I turn the vial around. It has no label.

"Are you going to pay for that?" a gruff voice asks.

I scream and flail backward, knocking over a display of bottled ships and leather shoes. Dust kicks up from the floor.

When it settles, I realize that what I mistook for a wool coat is actually a ewe. The spectacles perched on her nose magnify her rectangular pupils. Clasped in her hooves are knitting needles.

For a heartbeat, we stare at each other. Blood roars in my ears.

This cannot be real.

The ewe points to a sign by the counter. It reads: You Browse, You Buy. Then she points to the larger sign above it: Shepherd's Landing: Artifacts, Oddities, and Unspecialties.

"You browse, you buy," she huffs. "Caaaan't you read?"

She draws out the *A* sound in a bleat.

"I didn't see it," is all I can think of to say.

"Baaaah! That's no excuse. Know-nothing!"

I bristle, and some of my fear melts away. "If it's so important, then you should put it at the door."

"What door?"

"That door—"

I break off. In the direction I came from, there is a solid wall. No tunnel looms in the shadows. I swallow hard.

"It can't have disappeared," I whisper. "That's impossible."

The ewe bleats softly, "Haven't heard that word in a good while. It's got no meaning *here*." She taps a knitting needle against her scruffy chin. "You're the first to come to Meer in a while. The usual travelers are hiding in their own world. They're scared to provoke the darkness."

Meer. That name sounds familiar. I wonder where I've heard it before.

"Where am I, really?" I demand, whirling on her. "Who are you?"

She sniffs. "I am the Sheep, the owner of Shepherd's Landing—the only shop in Meer."

That means even less to me.

This is a dream. There is no other explanation for why I am mincing words with a ewe.

I glance at the crooked, dusty walls of the store. "Wonder what prompted my subconscious to come up with this," I mutter.

The Sheep jabs her needle in my direction. "Don't you dare take credit for building my shop! You have no claim over it."

I decide not to antagonize her while she's holding pointy objects.

"I suppose you built it yourself? It's…" I struggle to supply an appropriate adjective. "Quaint."

"I didn't build it."

"Then who did?"

"The Lost Queen did," the Sheep says. "She created this world, Meer…and she made the gaaaame."

The way she draws out the last word is strangely ominous.

"What game?" I ask.

She blinks at me over her spectacles. "Meer is everything that is, was, and ever will be, and it is many things that have not happened or never will happen. Just as many things that can or cannot be, or should or should not be, are or are not."

She must have misheard me. A simple question did not merit such a nonsensical answer. Although…I wonder who the *Lost Queen* is.

"That's not what I asked," I say. "What do you mean?"

"Why, what a question! Do you always mean what you say?"

My brows knit together. "Of course I do. Why wouldn't I?"

"That's a poor way of doing things. You may as well say what you mean!"

"But I do that, too. It's the same thing."

"It's not the same thing at aaaall," she bleats derisively.

Her knitting needles click in a tempo that reminds me of a Chopin piano piece I played a few days ago. I watch them, half-hypnotized.

"Are you going to buy that secret?" she asks.

I blink. "What?"

She points to the vial of iridescent solution on the counter. I'd forgotten about it. It gleams faintly in the lamplight.

"If you don't like your secret Lukewarm, I have Hot, Cold, and Juicy in stock," she offers.

"I don't know if I want to buy that."

I've had enough of secrets, bottled or otherwise.

"You have to buy something," the Sheep insists. "Every newcomer does."

If I buy something, maybe she'll stop bothering me.

I fold my arms. "I'd rather browse some more, if that's all right."

"Nothing is all Right. There's also Left, Up, Down, and of course, Sideways and Diagonal."

"I beg your pardon?"

"Don't beg," the Sheep says contemptuously. "It's unbecoming."

I ignore her and examine the sill at my feet. It is crammed with a row of dusty vials.

"Down here—are these secrets, too?" I ask.

She huffs. "Are you blind? That's no more a secret than you are a girl."

"I am a girl."

"No, you're not. You're a little goose."

A retort dies on my lips as I look down at myself.

What am I *wearing*?

I smooth my hands down my white apron and utilitarian blue dress. On my feet are scuffed Mary Janes. When I touch my head, my hand brushes against a piece of cloth. I'm wearing a headband.

When we were kids, Evie and I played dress-up in my mother's old clothing. In the first few months after Mom immigrated to the U.S., she worked as a maid. Years later, Evie found the uniforms in the garage and had the genius idea of using them in our games of pretend.

Back then, the two of us were practically swimming in the cloth. Now, the blue dress fits like it was made for me.

If I wasn't already certain that this was a dream, I am now.

On a whim, I pluck a vial from the sill. It contains a pale blue solution with flecks of gold that chase each other before settling to the bottom of the glass.

The Sheep peers at me over her spectacles. "Interesting choice of potion."

Normally I would demand to know what the strange note in her voice means, but if this is a dream, then what harm can come to me here? I can make impulsive decisions and not worry about the consequences. It doesn't matter if I don't think things through. It doesn't matter if I'm too cold, too logical, too strict, too...*safe*.

In real life, I don't take risks. But no one is supervising me now. No one is waiting to hold me accountable the instant I make a mistake.

"What is it?" I ask.

"I don't insult my wares by naming them," she scoffs. "Can you imagine if you knew what you were buying all the time?"

"Okay, then. What does it do?"

"It shows you the path."

I stare at the Sheep, waiting for her to elaborate. Her head is bent over her knitting once more. Her needles blur into a frenzy.

"The path to what?" I prompt.

"Your destination."

With heroic restraint, I do not snatch the needles from her grip. I fight to keep my voice level. "Which destination, exactly, does the path lead me to?"

"Your greatest desire," she says.

My gaze falls to the blue-tinted vial in my scarred palm.

The answer to her question is simple.

More than anything, I long for certainty. Up until now, my studies in physics have always given me that.

Physics brings order to a chaotic universe. Studying its laws and forces makes me feel small, yet powerful. Although I might be inconsequential in the grand scheme of things, I still dare to ask *why* and *how*.

But physics can't explain what happened to me…or to Evie.

I set the vial on the counter and push it toward the Sheep. "How much does this cost?" I ask.

She nudges it back at me. "Drink. Then pay."

I'm not sure whether to sigh or laugh. Everything is backward here.

"Shepherd's Landing cannot be held liable for side effects, including but not limited to: rapid growth or shrinking, invisibility, language-changing, shape-shifting, and hiccups," she recites.

"Death isn't a side effect?" I ask.

It can't hurt to make sure. I'd prefer not to die, even in a dream.

She throws back her head and bleats a laugh. "Don't be a little goose."

I decide to take that as a no.

A tremor runs through the walls of Shepherd's Landing. Or maybe it is just my hand shaking as I unstopper the vial and raise it to my mouth.

The potion glides down my throat. It tastes like cinnamon and orange. I lick my lips. Then the aftertaste hits me, sour as vinegar.

I swallow hard and barely keep the potion down.

With a shudder, I run the back of my hand over my mouth. I hope the potion has not spoiled. Who knows how long it's been sitting down here in the dream-world?

"What do I owe you?" I ask the Sheep, slipping the vial into my apron pocket.

She scoffs. "It's not me you have a debt to."

Maybe it is because I visited Evie's room today for the first time in months, or because I am wearing the same dress I used to play pretend in, but as I stand before the shabby counter, the memory of the last thing I said to Evie rears in the back of my head.

I slam that mental door shut. It doesn't stop the guilt from crashing over me in waves.

You didn't know she was going to die, I tell myself.

I don't know how to stop fearing that, at any moment, my life will shatter again. I want to put everything behind me. I want to be the unafraid, ambitious girl I used to be.

The thought comes to me unbidden: *I wish I could see my sister again.*

The potion warms uncomfortably in my gut.

My eyes lock on the Sheep. A torrent of words spills from my mouth. "I will journey through perilous lands and combat the creatures that arose from the poisoned mantle of this world. I will enter the Red Castle and conquer the monarchs who reside there, and avenge the Lost Queen. This I swear I will do."

My voice echoes through the dusty shop. The cuckoo on the clock shuts its beak. The shelves in the aisles rattle.

I touch my lips in disbelief. My ears ring. It felt like someone else was speaking through me. Like I was merely a vessel.

The Sheep *harrumphs*, breaking my trance. She waves a knitting needle at me. "Why are you still here, little goose? You have no time to waaaaste!"

An arrow of warmth settles behind my heart, its presence scattering my irritation and my fear and my doubt. It prompts me forward, its pull magnetic. I sway with its urgency.

What waits beyond is the destination I long for most: the future I'm meant to have.

The journey begins, a voice whispers in my head. *Walk.*

I balk. If I walk forward, I'll bump into the counter. I doubt that would make the Sheep happy.

You can surpass anything, the voice insists. *Pay no heed to earthly obstacles.*

My legs move me forward despite the rational part of my mind that screams, *What are you doing? You can't defy the laws of physics!*

I keep my gaze fixed on the opposite wall as I take a step. Then two. Then three, until I have passed the Sheep in her chair.

She continues to knit calmly, as if I did not walk through her counter.

I hold my hand in front of my face. It is corporeal. Yet when I wave it through the counter behind me, it passes straight through the wood. I inhale a shaky breath.

"Am I dead?" I murmur. "Am I a ghost?"

"No more than memories are," the Sheep answers. Her

needles click like a metronome. The rhythm steadies me somewhat.

"You're still loitering!" she scolds. "Go now. Pay the price."

Everything you want can be yours, I tell myself. *Stop being scared.*

The unknown can't hurt me in a place that doesn't truly exist. Right?

Taking a fortifying breath, I push through the wall. The wooden boards blur like long-fingered hands, pulling me forward.

Suddenly, the muffled sound of footsteps resounds through Shepherd's Landing.

Someone cries, "Alice, wait!"

Recognition strikes me. I try to turn around, to scrabble for purchase.

But I am already fading into nothing.

CHAPTER 5

MY SHOES SINK into loamy soil.

I am standing at the entrance of an otherworldly garden where the flowers tower hundreds of feet above me.

The sky is a watery blue. Clouds drift overhead in scattered formations, as fluffy as the circus-tent-like thing that the Sheep was knitting. The scene is picturesque—and familiar. Evie might have put it in one of her dreamy watercolor paintings.

But I can't focus on it at all. All I can think of is the voice that called my name as I vanished from Shepherd's Landing. It can only belong to one person.

"Mikayla!" I shout. My shoes kick up damp earth as I spin in a circle. "Where are you?"

No response.

Unease coils in my gut. It doesn't make sense that Mikayla would be in my dream. People from real life rarely show up in my dreams…except Evie.

A soft chiming noise catches my attention. At the entrance to the garden is a lovely array of vivid bluebell flowers. As I watch, it becomes apparent that they are emitting the music—like actual bells. It's the same melody I heard through the doorway.

As I wander forward in a daze, I startle a flock of cerulean butterflies. Each one is as large as a hang glider. They sweep into the sky in a V-shaped wave, the force of their flight making my hair flutter off my shoulders.

In another corner of the garden, massive daisies have petals the size of airplane wings. Next to them are long-stemmed red roses that could rival some water-towers. A few feet away from me is a lofty tiger-lily whose fiery orange petals are dusted with the barest blush of pink.

"If only you knew what I've gone through, and the day is hardly half over," I say, half to it and half to myself.

"Hello, visitor!"

I have enough presence of mind not to yelp. As it is, I let out a half-choked sound. I step back from the satellite-dish-sized flower, looking around. There's no one else here except me. Which means...

The Tiger-lily lists sideways. Its voice has a smooth alto timbre. "Will you say something? You're making me nervous, standing there like that."

I find my words with some difficulty. "You...can talk?"

"Well, of course we can!" a Black-eyed Susan pipes up in a shrill, breathy tone. It is modestly tall compared to the Tiger-lily, about the height of the flagpole outside Willow Creek High School.

"Mind you, you shouldn't yell so!" it continues. "You'll awaken the young'uns."

The Tiger-lily puffs its petals out, putting the other flower into shadow. "Hush! Respect the visitor. We rarely receive them anymore."

The Black-eyed Susan obediently shrinks back.

The Tiger-lily turns back to me. I push my glasses up the bridge of my nose and detect the suggestion of a mouth in its petals, which shifts as the flower says proudly, unfurling a browning leaf, "Welcome to the Living Garden. Most of our kin are slumbering now. It has been a while since we were all awake. The earth has not brought good omens recently."

I lean forward. "Like what?"

The Tiger-lily shudders. "Do not ask me to speak of the terrible things that invade Meer."

The Sheep implied that there were strange things roaming this place, too. I struggle to recall exactly what she said: *You're the first to come to Meer in a while. The usual travelers are hiding… They're scared to provoke the darkness.*

Who are the other people that come here? Is Mikayla one of them?

No, it can't be. This is a dream. I'm reading too much into it.

Then, a shadow engulfs me.

I stumble back, craning my neck to see the scarlet Rose looming overhead. Words dry up in my mouth. Chills sweep across my arms.

It is one of the flowers I hallucinated at Evie's funeral two months ago, magnified to the size of a Ferris wheel.

My head spins. Is this truly a dream? Or is this another hallucination?

"Tiger-lily, should you be talking to *her* kind?" the Rose asks in a reedy tone.

"I talk to whomever I want," the Tiger-lily retorts. "As I was saying, Alice…"

The shock of hearing my own name is delayed because she says it as if she's known me all my life.

"You know my name?" I ask.

It's a stupid question. Of course, this flower knows my name. It's a figment of my subconscious.

The Tiger-lily waggles a leaf. "Name, yes. Title, no. But perhaps the Lady of the Moon can help with the second."

My brain seems to be lagging one word behind. "Who?"

"You haven't grown much since we last saw you," the Rose interjects. "Your petals haven't changed either. Still dull and dark, like you're withering away. You should try a better fertilizer."

"Be considerate," a mellow voice reprimands. "Some can't help their nature."

A colossal tulip emerges between the Rose and the Tiger-lily. Its sleek jet-black petals, edged with violet, curve gently in the wind like parachutes.

The Rose furls its petals in derision. "Of course *you* would say that. You're not a true Black Tulip. The Lost Queen only made you that color because you begged her to."

The Lost Queen. The Sheep mentioned that name. I invoked it myself in Shepherd's Landing. Part of the price for my potion is that I will avenge her...whoever she is.

"Enough!" the Tiger-lily interrupts, thrusting out its sail-sized leaves. Wind buffets my apron. "Be civil! She is a visitor!"

"Is she really a visitor if she's been here before?" the Rose mutters.

I fold my arms. "I would remember if I'd dreamed about this garden."

"You can call this a dream, if you'd like," the Tiger-lily replies. "We've been growing as long as you have and then quite a bit."

If they remember me, then that means they've been growing for years. I would say that's impossible, except that this is a dream...

Then again, something about the fear in Mikayla's voice was far too real.

The sound of the bluebells is replaced by a raspy hiss.

A hulking shadow spills across the soil, between the sky-scraper-sized blades of grass.

"Has some creature trespassed into our territory?" the Rose demands, twisting toward the noise. "Beasts do not dwell here!"

The Black Tulip trembles. "It can't be. The sentries would have warned us of an intruder."

"The Violets are young and inexperienced," the Tiger-lily says grimly. "They've never needed to guard us before."

The Rose's barbed thorns gleam as it twists its head. "Violets! Answer me!"

Its shout echoes through the Living Garden. No reply comes.

The Black Tulip bends to the earth, brushing its leaves against the topsoil. "They slumber. They will not wake."

"Lazy things," the Rose growls. "I'll give them a good tongue-lashing later!"

Another hiss reverberates through the garden, and an acrid scent hits me. I wince. It smells like something burning.

The Tiger-lily swivels to its companions, petals quivering. "Do you feel that? He is here! He is killing us!"

"Who?" I ask, but I'm drowned out as the flowers erupt into a confused clamor.

My eyes catch on a flurry of movement heading towards me. The lush-emerald grass gives way to a sickly shade of yellow that sweeps from root to tip. The fibers crack, turning brittle, then disintegrating.

The dirt pulls at my Mary Janes when I step back.

"Your Majesty the White Queen!" the black Tulip calls,

weaving between the other flowers. "Hear us and come to our aid!"

"She is not coming," the Rose snarls. "She is lost. The others in her court have abandoned us too."

The White Queen...Is she different from the Lost Queen the Sheep mentioned in Shepherd's Landing? The White Queen must have ruled over this garden.

I wonder who the "others" are.

The Tiger-lily hovers over me, extending a petal as if to stroke my cheek. "Alice, you must go! It is not safe for you here."

"Why?" I ask.

I get an answer when the serpent bursts into the Living Garden.

His dull, mossy scales do not reflect the sunlight, making him seem more shadow than beast. As he slithers forward, he crushes smaller flowers under his colossal coils. His hiss drowns out their shrieks of pain.

A forked red tongue flickers between hooked fangs. Alabaster venom drips to the dirt, which sizzles and transforms into ashen, parched slabs. The smell of burning intensifies.

The yellow sickness that killed the grass afflicts some of the surviving flowers that huddle together. Their screams are high-pitched and agonized. They writhe and collapse, crumbling from towering blossoms into heaps of dust.

I swallow hard. Maybe if I stay still enough, the serpent will overlook me. I'm the smallest thing in this garden. I have a chance of going unnoticed.

That hope is dashed when his hypnotizing malachite-colored eyes fix on me. His maw gapes.

He lunges.

"NO!" the Tiger-lily shouts.

I can't dodge. I can't even scream.

Unexpectedly, the serpent sputters. He rears back on his coils, spitting dawn-orange petals from his maw. He lets loose a raspy shriek as he swings his head back and forth.

I stagger backwards, ears ringing, and reach for the stem of the Tiger-lily to balance myself.

But it's no longer there.

I process the next few moments at a delay. The shredded orange petals that drift from the serpent's mouth to the soil. The stem snapped in half in the withered dirt. The emptiness of the air that rushes to cool my face.

"Tiger-lily?" I whisper, staring at the remains of the flower that called me by name. "Tiger-lily, wait—"

I drop to my knees, scrabbling for the fragments of its petals. They crumble in my trembling fingers like sand. My breath comes in sharp, shallow pants.

This cannot be real. You're dreaming. You'll wake up soon.

The taste of copper fills my mouth. I'm biting my tongue. I'm struck by how *immediate* the pain is. Not at all like the sluggish haze of a dream.

The sound of crunching, collapsing grass reaches my ears. The serpent spits out an orange petal, which instantly withers into dust.

He hisses at me. The sound drills through my head. He rises so high that he blots out the sun. His fangs, twin scimitars, are silhouetted against the sky.

Even if I could shake off my paralysis, I have nowhere to run. I clench my jaw and close my eyes.

Then, a voice screams, "Hey!"

In unison, the serpent and I look for its source.

A red-haired girl steps out from behind a daisy. Her face is familiar: high cheekbones and a smattering of freckles across pale cheeks. She wears a white, frilly, long-sleeved blouse beneath a green pinafore dress that matches the flecks of emerald in her peacock earring.

She's breathing hard as she waves her arms at the reptile. The white bandana on her head has come slightly untied on one side. "Want a snack so badly? Then come and get me, you ugly heelbiter!"

Then I recognize her. She is the only one of Evie's friends in my grade.

"*Hailey*? What are you doing here?" I say more loudly than I meant to.

The serpent's attention swivels back to me.

She scowls. "I'm trying to distract it. Get to safety!"

"You're unarmed," I point out. "What are you going to do?"

"Just do what I say. Don't worry about me."

Without waiting for a reply, she faces the snake and taunts, "What's the matter? Too scared to come after easy prey? I could've escaped five times already!"

Hissing, the serpent rises to strike.

Hailey doesn't run. She doesn't even flinch. She curls her lip and stands her ground.

"What are you doing?" I scream. I run toward her, shoes sinking with every step. Perhaps I can push her out of the way. Deep down, I already know I'll be too late.

Then the serpent chokes.

He sways. He lets out a choked snarl. White venom spurts from his fangs. I barely manage to dodge the drops, which froth in the soil, turning it into dry clay.

Hailey cups her hands around her mouth and shouts, "You cut it a little close, Mikayla!"

Mikayla?

Shielding my eyes, I spot a dark-haired figure atop the serpent's head. I catch a flash of silver from her wrist as she waves at us. How did she get up there?

"Get Alice to safety!" Mikayla hollers.

The serpent's body stiffens. His coils buckle under his own weight.

I'm rooted to the spot, unable to process my sister's best friend defeating an oversized snake.

Hailey grabs my arm when his colossal shadow looms over us. "Come on!"

I dig my heels into the dirt. "We can't leave Mikayla!"

"She's fine. Khalil is with her."

Khalil? That raises another host of questions. They don't matter right now. Mikayla is in danger.

I wrench free of Hailey's grip. "She'll be killed!"

Then the serpent slams into the dirt.

I'm thrown off my feet.

When I regain my senses, I'm lying in a thick clump of dirt. Clouds of dust billow around me. Coughs shudder through my body. I sit up. By some miracle, nothing is broken, not even my glasses.

"Alice!" Hailey calls. She hurries into view. Her face and hair are smudged with clay. "There you are."

She offers me a hand. I let her help me up.

"Mikayla," I gasp. "Where is she?"

No person could survive a fall that high. Yet I cannot make myself believe that she is gone.

"She's fine. So is Khalil." She points above us.

I do a double take. Two figures drift to the ground, green tarps stretched over their heads like parachutes. No—not tarps, but massive leaves. Soon, they land before us.

Instead of her usual half-grunge, half-skater style, Mikayla wears slim gray trousers beneath a fawn-colored tunic-like garment. With the silver sheath at her hip—which complements the silver bracelet on her wrist—she looks like some kind of medieval adventurer. Her strange new ensemble is complete with a pair of beat-up leather boots.

Khalil wears a similar pair of boots, although his are less scuffed. Rather than his usual red varsity soccer jacket, he is dressed in an olive-green tweed vest and a collared short-sleeved shirt over black pants. He resembles a professor, except for the dust covering his unruly hair and the jagged slash through the hem of his pant leg.

Before I can say anything, Mikayla grabs my shoulders. She's breathing hard. Her choppy bangs are a tangled mess. Her usual black eyeliner is gone. Without it, her face is softer. More vulnerable, even.

"Alice, you shouldn't be here," she says.

"Tell me about it. I want to wake up."

"No, you don't get it. You're not *supposed* to be able to come to Meer."

"What are you talking about?" I glance between her and the others. Khalil's dark eyes, wide with worry, are fixed on me. Hailey is brushing the dirt off her green dress.

"How did you get here without Evie?" Khalil asks.

I frown at him. "I fell asleep. This is a dream…which you're invading, I might add."

"It's not a dream," Hailey says.

Khalil holds up his hand. "One thing at a time. Let's not overwhelm her." He shoots a look at Mikayla.

She blinks, as if registering how tightly she's been holding on to me. She lets go and steps back. "Sorry."

I rub my shoulder as Khalil asks, "Alice, how did your dream start?"

What an odd question.

"Dinah was acting erratic," I say. "She ran into Evie's room and made a mess. And then…she went through a mirror that looked like a doorway. I followed her."

I hear a sharp intake of breath from Hailey, and her hand goes to her mouth. Mikayla says nothing, but her eyes widen.

I frown at them. "What?"

Khalil speaks first. "That portal has been inactive since Evie died."

I narrow my eyes. "Are you implying that *more* portals lead into this place?"

"Well, of course. Mirrors are portals into Meer."

"By that logic, there must be hundreds of portals."

He taps a finger on his chin. "Maybe there are, but we only use the mirrors in our houses. It's simpler that way."

I stare at him. This is a dream. There is no other way to explain this except as a horrible joke.

"She doesn't believe you," Hailey says. She is assessing me like one of the stories she scribbles in her notebook during English.

"Obviously I don't," I snap. "You're figments of my dream!"

"This isn't a dream, Alice," Khalil interjects.

"Not a dream?" I sweep my arm at the withered flowers and the carcass of the serpent. "What about this is *real*? If it's not a dream, then what is it? A hallucination…?"

Oh.

Oh no.

"Alice?" Khalil says. "You look a bit pale. Do you need to sit down?"

I don't answer.

Today, a hallucination *spoke* to me for the first time—the

doll-like couple who set out a feast. They knew I was watching. They were setting that table for me.

You are our honored guest, they told me in eerie unison. *Just like your sister.*

Are Khalil, Hailey, and Mikayla the people I know, or are they part of the hallucinations that have haunted me since Evie's death? Perhaps I am no longer witnessing these hallucinations. Perhaps I am *living* them.

I am assaulted by too-real sensations. The smell of freshly upturned earth. The coarse apron clenched in my fists. The distant tinkling of bluebell flowers.

Frost crawls up my throat. Even if I could speak, all that would come out is, *No, no, no.*

I pinch myself. The pain is sharp and fleeting. I wait to break the surface of this dream.

Nothing happens.

Mikayla's mouth moves. Not one of her words registers. She reaches for me.

I bolt.

Startled cries follow me. I don't listen as I dart in between the flower stems. My breaths come cold and sharp. I pay no attention to where I'm going. I rip my skirt from cottage-sized brambles. Somewhere behind me, Mikayla calls my name.

My foot catches on a thick root. I go sprawling. Pain shoots into my hands as I break my fall.

In the time it takes me to get to my feet, the others catch up.

I let them. I can't outpace them; they must be as familiar with this place as I am unfamiliar with it. All I can hope for is to surprise them.

"Alice, what's wrong? It's me, Mik." Mikayla strides

forward. When I step out of her reach, confusion—and hurt—flashes across her face.

I swallow to thaw some of the frost in my throat. My words come out rough. "You can't fool me. You're part of the hallucination."

Khalil takes a cautious step toward me like I'm a skittish animal. "This isn't a hallucination, Alice. Why do you think that?"

My laugh is brittle. "Why shouldn't I? For the last two months, I've been seeing things that no one else sees. You saw me break the mirrors in Advanced Physics today. You don't know what I saw and heard. Maybe you wondered why Evie's little sister can't get a grip after her death." I motion to our surroundings. "Well, this is why!"

"Alice, this isn't like you." Mikayla's voice wavers. She's looking at me with a new furrow in her brow. "What's going on?"

Some fragile tether within me snaps. "For the last two months I've been having visions of things that don't exist. Red castles. Mazes. A man and woman who called me by name. And today, an eye was watching me in the side mirror of your car!"

In their stunned silence, I dig my nails into my palms. The scars from the night of *The Incident* sting.

My shoulders slump. My voice cracks. "You don't know what it's like to be lost to your own mind all the time."

"Actually," Mikayla says, "you're talking to the only people who understand that feeling. The three of us have been having visions like yours too."

My mouth falls open. No sound comes out.

"We've been seeing similar things since Evie died," Khalil

clarifies. "It must have been terrifying for you, since you didn't know about Meer."

Then, understanding unlocks a memory.

The Living Garden is familiar. Not only because I've seen it in Evie's paintings, but also because she used to tell me stories about a place where impossible things came true.

Once upon a time, she whispered to me, *I dreamed up Meer.*

"Meer is the world she pretended to visit as a child," I say slowly. "It had strange creatures and magic." A rueful laugh escapes me. "She was very creative when it came to make-believe."

The three of them exchange glances. Hailey shakes her head. "Don't look at me. I'm no good at explaining."

Khalil sighs. "Meer is not make-believe, Alice. Every part of it is real."

"That's impossible."

"It's not," Mikayla says. She meets my eyes. Her stance is rigid. "You need to know something, Alice. It's about your sister."

You don't always know the moment your life is about to change. I knew that when I told Evie hateful, hurtful things, our relationship would never be the same. I didn't know that it would be our last conversation before she died under circumstances I couldn't explain.

Now, however, I have no doubt that whatever Mikayla tells me is going to upend everything I thought I understood.

I want to tell her to stop. To leave me alone. But I can't make myself act. I am frozen as her voice cuts mercilessly through the air.

"Evie's death wasn't natural," she says.

All the sounds that I've taken for granted—the rustle of grass, even my own shallow breaths—fall away.

Frost creeps back into my throat. I squeeze my eyes shut and shove the howling, sharp-edged sensations of *The Incident* into the farthest recesses of my mind.

It's no use. What she told me is what I have suspected for two months.

How can anyone explain the abrupt death of an uninjured seventeen-year-old, or the missing memories of her fifteen-year-old sister?

How do I make sense of the hallucinations that have plagued me since *The Incident*?

I lift my head. Some of the coldness seeps from my limbs.

There are two possible explanations.

One: I have gone completely mad.

Two: Logic cannot explain what has been happening to me.

I do not prefer the first. I am terrified of the second, although it also compels me. If logic cannot explain this chain of events, then what can? I don't believe in magic, yet I do not believe in coincidences either. Perhaps it is no accident that I have found my way to the fantasy that served as Evie's refuge.

For two months, I have longed for answers without considering that they might be rooted in my hallucinations. If Mikayla, Hailey, and Khalil see the same things that I do, I may not be losing my mind. Or perhaps we are losing our minds together.

Right now, all I care about is that I'm not alone.

Mikayla watches me, her brow knitted. She twists her silver bracelet on her wrist, as she does when she's anxious or impatient.

In the last few weeks of her life, my sister blurred the line between fantasy and reality. I suspect that I now stand on that line.

I can think of only one word to say. It is burdened by reluctant acceptance, if not complete belief. "How?"

The three of them exchange glances again.

"It's a long story," Khalil says.

My tone brooks no room for argument. "I have time."

CHAPTER 6

"GIMME A SEC," Mikayla says. "I have to get my knife."

"Your...what?" I ask.

"How do you think I killed the snake?" She points to the silver pommel protruding from the serpent's head. I'd been so distracted by her and Khalil's arrival that I didn't register the blade sunk to the hilt in its skull.

She clambers up the serpent's massive coils, using his scales for leverage. She braces her foot against his head and yanks at the red-spattered blade.

"This might take a bit," she says.

Hailey grimaces. Her face is as green as her dress. Khalil puts a hand on her shoulder, turning her away from the serpent's carcass.

"Thanks," she says. Her words are a little muffled because she's clapped her palm over her mouth. "I can't stand the sight of blood."

There's a sound like a saw scraping pavement, and Mikayla jumps down next to the snake's head, weapon in hand.

"Look at these fangs," she remarks, tracing them with her

blade. "See all the venom? Like a firehose. Maybe I could put some on my knife."

"I wouldn't recommend that. It's similar to acid, considering the way it killed the plants," Khalil says, toeing the yellow, cracked earth with his boot. "Also, what if you accidentally hurt yourself? Or what if the venom corroded the blade?"

"Hmm. I guess. It's a shame to let it go to waste, though." Her voice is muffled as she peers inside the serpent's maw. Finally, she ducks away and returns to us.

I don't consider myself a squeamish person, but the sheen of blood on her blade is off-putting. She picks up an umbrella-sized leaf from the ground and wipes the knife clean. Instantly, the leaf hisses. Holes speckle its fibers.

"Be careful!" Khalil warns.

Mikayla tosses the leaf to the ground. It curls into a brown, desiccated husk, then crumbles.

"I can't believe you brought that snake down by yourself," I say. "Where did you learn to fight like that?"

Her mouth quirks. "I'm a girl of many talents. Khalil and Hailey helped a little, too," she adds as an afterthought.

"Helped a *little*?" Khalil echoes. "I provided parachutes so we didn't fall to our untimely deaths."

"And I distracted it from chomping on Alice!" Hailey says, putting her hands on her hips.

Mikayla shrugs. "True. I knew you'd annoy it the most."

Hailey swats her.

I suddenly have more respect for Hailey. She confronted a colossal serpent without knowing whether Mikayla or Khalil would intervene at the right time. And she did it for me—a person she hardly knows.

Some of the humor leaves Hailey's face. "It bothers me

that the snake died," she confesses, more quietly. She gives the corpse a sidelong glance. "I know it was a threat, but…"

"Someone had to kill it," Mikayla says.

"I get that. Still…" Hailey's shoulders slump. She bows her head. "The Living Garden was Evie's favorite place in Meer. Now look at it."

The four of us assess the snapped stems and the wilted petals littering the earth. When I shift my weight, the dirt crumbles under my heels.

A lump rises in my throat. If Meer is real…then what would have happened if the Tiger-lily had not sacrificed herself in my stead? If I "died" here, would I wake up on Earth?

Perhaps I do not want to learn the answer to that question.

"We shouldn't blame ourselves for the attack," Mikayla says. "We couldn't have known it would happen."

"We didn't know because we've never stayed away from Meer for so long," Hailey counters. "I told you we should have visited!"

"Yes," a wheezing voice says. "You should have."

The Rose emerges between wilted stalks of grass. Its once-proud stem has bent into the shape of a question mark. Its head of scarlet petals—now faded to a sickly pink—leers in our direction. Shriveled thorns bristle at the four of us.

"You abandoned us when you were supposed to protect us," the flower snarls. "The lot of you are cowards."

Khalil is the first to speak. His calm tone reminds me of the way Evie used to coax Dinah into the cat carrier for long car trips. "We wouldn't have left if it wasn't an emergency. The Queen died."

"She is now the Lost Queen," the Rose agrees. "Why do you not avenge her? I thought better of you, Bishop…and of you, King."

Why does the flower call them by these titles? Are they code names? Each one has a royal connotation…except the Bishop. I'm not sure what pattern it fits.

Mikayla's jaw tenses. She stabs her knife into its sheath with a little more force than necessary. "Was killing the snake not enough for you?"

The black Tulip peeks out from behind the Rose. "You allowed Meer to decay," it accuses. "Now it grows and over-grows and nobody knows where it ends."

Hailey clasps her hands together. Her voice is bright with desperation. "We can make things right. Please give us another chance."

"You have done enough!" the Rose shouts, brandishing its thorns. One shoots out faster than I can flinch, lodging in the dirt at Hailey's feet. She yelps and stumbles back, eyes wide.

"Let that be a warning," the flower says into the stunned silence. "Your court is no longer welcome here."

"You can't decide that for us!" Mikayla exclaims. Her fists clench at her sides. "Evie—the Queen—would be disap-pointed. As your King, I order you to let us stay!"

The flower twists toward us. "When you abandoned us, you renounced your reign. We are ruled by different monarchs now."

Mikayla staggers like someone punched her in the gut. Her mouth opens and closes before she manages to say, "Who? Why did you accept them?"

"We had no choice! You did not defend us."

"Rose, can you explain who these rulers are and where they came from?" Khalil asks, holding out his palms placat-ingly. "We need to understand this, to fix things."

The Tulip starts to speak until the Rose unfurls a leaf in warning. The black flower shrinks back.

The Rose faces us. "You will discover that soon. Too soon. Now, leave!"

The wind picks up, battering dead stalks and leaves around the Garden in small cyclones. Twigs as long as crane arms whirl past us. I uselessly brace my hand against the onslaught.

A chorus of voices—weeping, hissing—surrounds us.

"*Traitors. Liars. If we faced the danger without you, you can face it without us.*"

Then I sprawl into the dirt for the second time today.

My head spins as I push myself up. To my left, Hailey groans.

The Living Garden is gone. Gray sky stretches above our heads.

A wave of vertigo hits me as I realize that the grass is brushing my palms, rather than scraping the sky. We are no longer ant-sized. We have landed on a faintly curved plain that stretches for miles in every direction. The landscape is devoid of trees. No flowers are here either, although the air smells like crushed petals. Beneath the sweet scent is a darker note that might be soot.

"What happened?" I demand of Mikayla, who is combing her sweat-slicked bangs out of her eyes.

She scowls. "I think the Garden banished us."

"Banished?" Hailey echoes blankly. She pushes herself into a kneeling position. Her white bandana unravels, causing her red hair to half-obscure her peacock earring. "But we need to cross through the Garden to get Alice back to Earth."

I press my fingers to my temples. This conversation is already giving me a headache. "If Meer is separate from Earth, does that make it a planet?"

In unison, Khalil and Hailey look at Mikayla.

She lifts an eyebrow. "What? Just because I was there when

Evie created Meer doesn't mean I can explain it. It's another dimension, not part of our solar system."

"That's not possible," I say, although my words lack conviction.

"Trust me, it is," Khalil says. "All of us have been coming to Meer for years."

"Then why did the Flowers accuse you of abandoning them?" I ask.

"Long story," Mikayla says.

"No, it's not," Hailey snaps, drawing our attention to her. Her cheeks are as flushed as strawberries. Her fingers dig into the grass. "Evie trusted us to be the guardians of Meer, and we failed."

"It wasn't safe to come back!" Mikayla retorts. "You of all people know that, Hailey."

Hailey juts out her chin. Her hand drifts to her peacock earring as if she is drawing strength from it. Her voice holds a slight tremor as she says, "So, then, what? At the first sign of trouble, we run? We're better than that."

"You don't get it! I didn't want us to take chances after... what happened to Evie."

"If we hadn't gone after Alice, how much longer would we have stayed out of Meer? Weeks? Months?"

I clear my throat. "Excuse me. What are we talking about, exactly?"

The two girls fall quiet. Hailey stares into the gray-green grass. Mikayla glances at her, then says, "You were in the last vision I had, Alice, in my car mirror when I was driving home from school today. You were wearing the clothes you're wearing now. Wandering through the garden. A shadow was following you."

My hands bunch in the folds of my blue maid's dress. So

that's why Mikayla nearly crashed her truck today. The impact of the curb echoes through my bones.

She continues, "I can also sense when people come or go to Meer, because I was there when it was created. Maybe twenty minutes after I dropped you off at your house, I felt someone enter the world. It wasn't Khalil or Hailey. And, well, it didn't take a genius to figure out who it was."

"Mik called Code Thorn—an emergency," Khalil explains. "We went through our separate mirror portals and met in Shepherd's Landing."

My eyebrows shoot up. "Do you communicate through your mirrors?"

He laughs. "No, just through phones—like everyone else on Earth. We don't do telepathy."

"I wish we could," Hailey mutters. "Then maybe *someone* would have answered more quickly." She throws a meaningful glance at Khalil.

"Hey, Ma wanted me to do the dishes!" he says. "Besides, you delayed us, too. You were more interested in browsing Shepherd's Landing than finding Alice."

"Something caught my eye," Hailey retorts. Her hand drifts to her pocket. "It wasn't all my fault. The Sheep wouldn't give us a single straight answer about Alice."

Mikayla throws up her hands in exasperation. "Ugh, don't get me started on that ewe!" Her voice pitches high in an uncanny impression of the Sheep. "'She left. She left on a journey. A journey to her greatest desire.'"

"What happened, Alice?" Khalil asks. "It looked like you fell through the wall."

"Oh." I wince. "That wasn't the Sheep's fault. Not completely, at least."

I tell them about drinking the potion, and the price I'll

pay for it: fighting strange creatures, conquering the monarchs of the Red Castle, and avenging the Lost Queen.

When I'm done, Hailey whistles, long and sharp. "How did you mix yourself up in *that*?"

I train my gaze on the grass beneath my scuffed Mary Janes. "I don't know! I thought Meer was a dream. All I wanted was to find my cat."

Hailey waves her hand. "Oh, Dinah will be fine. She knows her way around Meer."

I gape at her. "Dinah has been to Meer?"

"Of course! She came with Evie all the time."

That raises a new host of questions. I force myself to focus. "How will we find Dinah? She could be anywhere—"

"She's a cat. The rules that apply to us in Meer don't apply to her," Hailey says like it's obvious. "She'll probably find us before we find her."

I hope so. If I return to Earth without Dinah, how do I explain it to Mom and Dad?

Hailey interrupts my thoughts. "So, why did you take the potion? Drinking a strange substance, even in a dream, doesn't seem like the best idea."

Easy for her to say. She has known about Meer's existence.

I can't stop the sarcasm from seeping into my voice. "Yes, because dreams famously make perfect sense all the time."

"Alice, you said the potion is supposed to lead you to your greatest desire," Mikayla cuts in. "What'd you want?"

I cast my mind back to Shepherd's Landing, standing before the moth-eaten counter, the soured taste of the potion lingering on my tongue.

"I don't know," I say slowly. "I still thought it was a dream. I thought about my career. My future. But I also thought about...Evie."

Surely the potion cannot lead me to my sister, though. She is dead. She cannot be in Meer.

"Do you feel any different, Alice?" Khalil asks. "Fever or chills? Any dehydration or dizziness?"

I arch an eyebrow. "What are you, a doctor?"

"Hey, this might be important in case she poisoned you."

My heartbeat quickens. "She would do that?"

"No," Mikayla says. "Probably not."

"That's comforting."

"The Sheep is unpredictable but not cruel," Khalil says. "She wouldn't try to hurt you."

"I'm not sick," I say. "All things considered, I feel normal…"

A strange warmth stirs in my gut, spreading to my chest. It is a probing pressure, like an arrow behind my heart. I angle my head toward the gray sky. It turns translucent, rippling like a curtain. My anxiety folds into its expanse.

Do not delay your journey, a voice in my head warns. *You are near the Labyrinth now. You must travel through its corridors.*

The arrow nudges me sideways. I shuffle to face the horizon, inhaling the soot-tinged air.

"Alice!" someone shouts.

Then Mikayla is in front of me, shaking my shoulders. Her eyes are wide with panic. "Alice, snap out of it!"

I wrench myself out of her grip and take a wary step back, adjusting my glasses before they slip down my nose. "What are you doing?"

"What are *you* doing?" she retorts. "You went quiet and then you walked away!"

For the first time, I realize that I am standing, not sprawled in the grass. Mikayla, Khalil and Hailey have jumped to their feet. When did that happen?

"We must keep going," I say, befuddled. "We can't waste any more time. The Labyrinth is close."

"How do you know that?" Khalil asks. "You've never been to Meer before."

"I…" I balk.

Fear buzzes in my ears. How *do* I know that? The dull grass stretches in all directions. Nothing resembling a maze is within sight. Yet I know without a doubt that the journey to the Labyrinth is a matter of minutes walking northward.

The voice in my head does not speak. I sense its sibilant presence in the back of my mind. Somehow, I know it is waiting for me to follow its instructions…as I did in Shepherd's Landing.

Under the gazes of the others—skeptical, confused, concerned—I struggle to come up with an answer.

"I think this is the potion's effect," I say at last. My hands curl in my apron. "This may sound crazy, but…there is a presence in my head. A voice. It says we have to travel through a labyrinth. I heard the same voice after I first drank the potion in Shepherd's Landing. It told me to walk through the wall… and I did."

"Hmm." Mikayla drums her fingers on her knife sheath. "Well, that explains some things. And if it's telling you where to go, that'd be helpful for the Labyrinth."

"I wouldn't get too excited yet," Khalil says. "It could be a trick. Things are rarely as they seem in Meer. Besides, we don't know the long-term effects of this potion."

He's right, of course.

I pace in the grass, shoving my hands into my apron pocket.

Thoughtless. That is the best word to describe the decision that landed me in this predicament. I am used to planning ten or even twenty steps ahead at any given time. Without structure—without discipline—my future means nothing.

Recklessness is a privilege I have never been able to afford. Why should I have forgotten that now?

The arrow in my chest pricks, clearly impatient. I brace myself against its magnetic pull.

"At the least, we may as well go somewhere," I say. "It doesn't have to be the Labyrinth."

"Well, maybe it does," Khalil muses. "The Labyrinth leads to the one place where we might find answers—about Evie, about our visions, and about the potion."

"What is that place?" I ask.

"The Moon!" Hailey says. Her face splits into a smile. "I should've thought of that! The Lady will know what to do."

Mikayla grimaces. "Ugh, not her. She never gives a straightforward answer."

"You're an artist, Mik. Don't you like analyzing meaning?"

"Not when it comes to words. That's your thing."

A headache throbs at the base of my skull. I hold up my hand. "Sorry, who is this 'Lady'? And why does she live on the 'Moon'?"

Khalil opens his mouth to speak, but Hailey beats him to it. "She's the one who gives us quests—she can send us anywhere. She sees and hears everything that happens in Meer: she's all-knowing." As she talks, she reties the white bandanna around her head so her peacock earring is showing again.

"And she's a nutcase," Mikayla mutters.

My brow furrows. "I thought there was a Man in the Moon."

Hailey snorts. "That's what people on Earth think. Meer's Moon is different."

I rub my eyes, trying to sort out the mess I've stepped

into: a talking sheep, sentient flowers, and a Woman in the Moon. It's the stuff of fairy tales—exactly what I would expect of Evie.

A pit opens in my stomach. After two months, my sister's death still lingers like a bruise. I'm afraid of the pain, but I must endure it if I want answers.

"You owe me an explanation about Evie," I tell them.

They trade weary looks. Hailey's hands drop to her sides. Mikayla thumbs the hilt of her knife. Khalil exhales, and for the first time, I notice the depth of the shadows beneath his eyes.

Have their hallucinations, like mine, been haunting them day and night, depriving them of rest? I understand why I wasn't aware of Khalil and Hailey's hallucinations. Mikayla, however, should have been easier to read.

Then again, I thought I was going insane. I doubt I would have believed Mik if she confessed to having hallucinations. In fact, it probably would have made me more paranoid.

Khalil is the first to break the silence. "It's easiest if we start from the beginning of the world."

CHAPTER 7

AS THE FOUR of us cross the plain, Khalil recounts the origins of Meer.

The world began as a daydream shared between Evie and Mikayla. It took on a life of its own the day they found the doorway in Evie's mirror.

They were both seven years old. Logic and caution were concepts they hadn't grasped yet. They walked through the doorway into a refuge of impossibility. A never-ending adventure. For years, it was a secret between the two of them, until they became friends with Khalil and Hailey.

That is as far as Khalil gets before I can't contain my questions anymore.

"So how do the mirror portals work?" I ask.

Hailey, who walks on my right, glances sideways at me. "Magic."

From her tone, I might as well have asked what two plus two is.

I direct my next question to Khalil, on my left. "So you're telling me that my sister was like a witch, or…"

"Oh, definitely not," he answers. "She was as human as we are."

"Then how did she make…" I wave my hand at the landscape. "All of this?"

The land is unnaturally empty. No animals are in sight, not even birds or insects. The only movement is our footfalls through the grass. The gray sky is cloudless. As we walk through the plain, I feel dull. Drained of color. If not for my compass-like intuition, I would not suspect that anything exists beyond this place.

Khalil and Hailey look at Mikayla, who is trailing a few steps behind, scanning our surroundings with a hand on her knife.

She frowns at us. "What? Just because I saw her create Meer doesn't mean I know how she did it. It's like she dreamed it into existence."

"That's impossible," I mutter, chewing the inside of my cheek.

Hailey smirks. "You'll learn to erase that word from your vocabulary once you've been in Meer long enough."

I don't want to stay in Meer. I want to go home.

Never mind that my house is empty and silent. At least it's familiar, unlike this uncanny, uncomfortable, *impossible* world.

"Think of it this way," Khalil says, splaying his hands apart. "On Earth, mirrors are like strings. Evie was able to tie those strings to Meer." He touches his palms together, interlocking his fingers. "That's how Earth and Meer are connected, and that's why we each have our own portal—including you."

I press my fingers to my temples. The more I hear, the less sense it makes. "So is Meer some kind of parallel or alternate universe? Even assuming that's true, cosmic inflation makes it highly improbable that Earth and Meer would ever interact."

"I don't know anything about the finances of the universe," Hailey says.

"*Cosmic* inflation," I correct. "Not the inflation of money. Cosmic inflation is the process before the Big Bang, when the universe exploded outward. Maybe if I knew more about the mechanics of Meer's universe…"

Hailey raises an eyebrow. "No offense, but I think you're overthinking this."

Khalil clears his throat before I can retort. "It doesn't matter how Evie created Meer," he says. "It only matters *why*."

"No," I insist. "There has to be more than that. Otherwise, it's—"

"Let me guess," Hailey says, crossing her arms. "Impossible?"

I ignore her. "This story has too many holes. Science has barely begun to *theorize* about parallel realities. Yet Evie somehow made one, or found one?"

"You're assuming that this is a parallel reality," Khalil notes.

"It isn't?"

He shrugs. Amusement gleams in his eyes. "Who knows?"

"Thanks. That's very helpful."

"Maybe a better way to phrase it is that Meer doesn't have to live up to any expectations. It is the expectation, and then some. Asking questions doesn't mean we'll get answers. Anyway, sometimes it's better for us not to know everything."

I trace the lattice of scars across my hands. I squeeze my eyes shut against the confused darkness of *The Incident*, which hovers at the edge of my consciousness.

You're wrong. It's not always better.

In the distance, a long line of shadow emerges. I can't make out its details, but my compass-sense hums in approval.

You will reach the Labyrinth soon, it says in my head. *Keep going.*

As we continue walking, Khalil tells me about the four

main lands of Meer: the Living Garden, the Labyrinth, the Moon, and the Nacre Coast. Shepherd's Landing is like the origin point of Meer: every time someone comes into Meer, they enter the shop first.

"Travel is inconsistent in Meer," Khalil explains. "Sometimes we end up in the same place by going a certain way. Sometimes we don't. We usually rely on the Lady of the Moon to send us to different places."

"That sounds inconvenient," I comment.

"It's not so bad. I suppose you could say that we have special privileges."

I recall how the Flowers addressed the three of them in the Garden: *Bishop, Knight, King*. Evie was the *Queen*...or rather, the *Lost Queen*.

"What are you, royalty?" I ask, half-joking.

"Close. Evie gave all of us titles that are inspired by chess. We make up a royal court."

A chess court. That makes more sense. To my knowledge, the Bishop is not considered a royal figure. But...

"Evie didn't play chess," I say. My words are oddly loud in the deserted landscape.

As kids, Mom and Dad often signed up me and Evie for activities—piano, tennis, chess, and so forth—without asking for our permission. They hoped we would discover natural gifts through those activities. Unfortunately for them, if Evie had any gift for chess, she did not nurture it. She flat-out refused to play. She could be as stubborn as Mikayla sometimes.

I was more receptive to the game. I was no chess prodigy, but I had enough talent to win some youth tournaments. A few years ago, I stopped playing it altogether. I preferred to focus on my piano lessons.

Khalil spreads his hands. "I think she found it a creative

idea. Something more interesting than your average royal court."

This revelation still does not sit right with me. I'm not sure why.

He continues, "I don't know if we officially introduced our Meer-titles, but I'm the Bishop. I'm like an advisor to the monarchs. Mikayla here—"

"I'm the King. Yes, even though I'm a girl." She bobs a sardonic bow in my direction. Her dark eyes dare me to challenge her.

I smile. "It suits you. After all, you're a tyrant on the roads."

She huffs. "Because nobody knows how to drive in Willow Creek!"

Khalil and I laugh.

"I'm the Knight," Hailey says. "And as you might've guessed, Evie was the Queen. Or, I suppose…Meer calls her the *Lost* Queen now."

We crest a gentle slope. The grass has grown to my waist, and the soot-tinged wind causes wavelike patterns to ripple toward the nearing Labyrinth.

"If Evie wanted a royal court, she could have made everyone Kings and Queens," I muse, half to myself.

Mikayla snorts. "Who ever heard of multiple Kings and Queens ruling at once?"

She has a point.

"She could have made room for a Prince and a Princess, at least," I amend.

"I don't mind being the Bishop," Khalil says. "I like being an advisor. Somebody has to stop Mik from being irresponsible."

Mikayla punches him in the shoulder.

"Ow! That was uncalled for." Mock hurt plays over his features.

He starts to say something more until Hailey interrupts, her words tumbling over each other. "There's nothing wrong with being the Knight! I'm not inferior to anyone. I'm the personal guard of the King and Queen. It's an *honor*." Her arms fold tightly across her chest.

I fall a step behind, startled by the vehemence in her tone. "I never said it wasn't," I say.

She doesn't respond, forging faster through the grass.

My eyebrows knit together. I didn't mean to upset her. All I did was make an observation.

As I'm considering how to respond, the Labyrinth looms into view. The gray sky grows darker over the hedge-wall corridors, which are roughly nine feet tall and crowned with serpentine vines of ivy.

I rub my bare arms. The air has plunged a few degrees, gaining a distinct metallic tinge that reminds me of ozone.

"I have another question," I say. "If you're royalty or royal-adjacent, then shouldn't you have robes and crowns, or something a little more dignified?"

"Meer chooses this clothing for us when we visit," Hailey answers. "It marks us as adventurers." She twists around to gesture at my outfit. "It chose your clothes, too."

I smooth the coarse fabric of my apron, wondering why Meer did not fit me with something like Khalil's pocketed vest or Hailey's pinafore dress. It could have given me a weapon like Mikayla's silver knife. Instead, it chose my mother's old maid uniform. Among the earth tones of the others' outfits, my blue dress makes me stand apart. Perhaps Meer is sending me a message: *You do not belong*.

It wouldn't be the first time I've been deemed an outsider.

"So…you're a Knight, and you don't have a sword and armor?" I ask her.

She scoffs. "Of course I do. I left them on our pirate ship the last time I came to Meer."

I laugh before glimpsing the thin line of her mouth. "Oh. You're serious."

"I wouldn't lie about Meer."

A pirate ship? That raises a new host of questions that I bite back. I doubt Hailey is in the mood to answer them.

"If you were able to come to Meer, Alice, you might have a chess title," Khalil interjects before the tension can grow too thick. "We just don't know what it is yet."

"Evie would've known," Mikayla mutters. She twists the silver bracelet on her wrist.

"She would have," he agrees. "But since she isn't here, the Lady of the Moon will have to tell us."

The ground slopes abruptly, leading us straight to the entrance of the maze.

The Labyrinth is guarded by a locked iron gate whose black spear points scrape the sky. The bars of the gate are wide enough for two people to comfortably walk through side by side. Beyond is a dizzying tessellation of hedges. If I attempt to focus on the distinct corridors of the Labyrinth, spots smear my vision, as if I've been staring too long at the sun.

I shiver. The maze, shifting and shadowed, is exactly as it appeared in my hallucinations.

"Welcome to the Labyrinth," Hailey announces. "Let's try not to get lost."

CHAPTER 8

THE LABYRINTH ENJOYS illusions.

As we near the gate, my shoe twists in the dirt. I stumble and quickly right myself. When I glance up, I do a double take.

Seconds ago, the bars of the gate appeared wide enough to walk through. Now, I can barely squeeze my wrist between the gaps. I step forward and give one of the cold iron bars an experimental tug. Of course, it does not budge.

I think about asking if the others noticed the abrupt change, but they look resigned. Perhaps the Labyrinth has played similar tricks on their eyes before.

Mikayla bumps my shoulder when she slips between me and Hailey. She cracks her knuckles. "Stand back, guys. I'll get us through in a minute."

She twists her knife in the rusted keyhole of the gate lock. When that proves unsuccessful, she jams the hilt into it. I wince at the screech of metal. About five minutes pass before she throws up her hands, muttering some colorful choice words.

Khalil sighs, shaking his head. "That's three dollars for the swear jar."

She bangs her fist against the gate for good measure,

then snaps her fingers at him. "You. Give Alice a boost. We're climbing over."

"Are you implying that I'm short?" I ask.

"You're five feet tall. You *are* short."

"You left off an inch," I grumble, but shuffle to Khalil's side. We take perhaps a minute and a half to scale the gate.

Once inside, I turn in a slow circle. Vines of ivy wind along the center of the walls like railings. Ahead of us, the path forks into branches to the left and to the right. A soft, wistful scent drifts through the leafy corridors, like honeysuckle, even though we must be miles from the Living Garden now.

You must hurry, the compass-voice insists. *Find the heart of the Labyrinth.*

A magnetic force pulls at me. My feet move of their own accord, shuffling through the rust-colored dirt. When I look down, the tips of my Mary Janes are pointing...

"According to my compass, we're supposed to go left at the fork," I tell them.

"Isn't that a corn-maze trick?" Mikayla says, swiping her black hair behind her ears. "Going left all the time?"

"I'm not sure," I admit. "That's just the first turn we have to take."

"Is it a good idea to follow Alice's directions?" Khalil asks. He shifts his weight from one foot to the other. "What if it makes us more vulnerable to the Labyrinth's tricks?"

Mikayla snorts. "You worry too much, Khal. Everything is a trick in Meer."

"Besides, our other option is to wander the Labyrinth and never come out," Hailey chimes in.

"All right," he concedes, gesturing toward the left passage. "We can try following Alice, but for the record, I still don't like this."

Mikayla flicks his shoulder. "Don't be a pessimist. It'll work out."

Khalil scrunches his nose. "I'm a realist, not a pessimist."

"True. Alice is the pessimist."

I cross my arms. "I wouldn't call myself that. I prefer to expect the worst so I'm surprised by the best."

Mikayla snickers. "Same difference."

We take the left fork and begin our journey through the Labyrinth.

The dirt path is embedded with colorful ceramic squares, as if someone broke a mosaic and tossed the pieces there haphazardly. They wink at us in shades of scarlet, tangerine, and emerald.

As I walk, I put my hand into my apron pocket. My fingers brush against something small and smooth. Pulling out the mysterious object, I open my palm to find the empty vial of potion I bought in Shepherd's Landing.

I hold it up for the others. "By the way—this is from the potion I drank. I don't know if it tells you anything…"

"Is there a label?" Khalil asks.

"No, the Sheep only described its purpose." I tilt the glass tube. Not a single drop of the potion remains. "If it has a name, she didn't give it to me."

Mikayla rolls her eyes. "Typical. Annoying us is her full-time job."

"Keep it," Khalil advises. "Maybe we can show it to the Lady of the Moon. She might be able to reverse the effects of the potion and return you to Earth."

I hope so. I slip the vial back into my pocket.

We reach a crossroads in the maze. The bristling shadows of the hedges lengthen as my compass-sense tugs at me.

"Turn left again," I announce.

It's strange to lead people who have been coming to Meer for years, but Khalil and Mikayla follow me without question. Hailey glances between the intersecting paths before she, too, falls into step with us. She surveys the walls of the new corridor, rubbing her peacock earring between her thumb and forefinger. Looking at her, a question occurs to me.

"Hailey, you told me earlier that Meer changes your clothing when you go into Meer," I say. "But if that's true, then why do you still have your earring, and Mikayla still has her bracelet?"

Hailey's hand immediately drops into her pinafore pocket. "It's my token," she says.

"Your what?"

"Anyone who travels between Earth and Meer has a token," Khalil explains. "A token is something that we keep from our lives on Earth. Meer doesn't change it."

He lifts his hand from his vest, slowing his pace a bit. A delicate chain spills from a bronze pocket watch. He snaps the watch open. On the clock face, black serif numerals surround an ivory interior.

He rubs his thumb on the bronze casing. "This is my token. When my father immigrated to the U.S. from Pakistan, his father gave him this watch. Then my father gave it to me.

My grandfather died when I was young, but I feel closer to him when I speak Urdu."

"Are you a heritage speaker of Urdu?" I ask.

"Yes, I picked it up as a kid," he confirms. "I still speak it with my parents and my older brother at home. I also use it with my relatives."

I press my lips together, envying the quiet assuredness with which he speaks about his heritage. I wish I had that confidence in my connection to my parents' culture. Unfortunately, I don't speak my parents' native language, Cantonese. I've never been to Hong Kong, either. In the past, I suggested to Mom and Dad that we visit my grandparents there. I stopped asking when I learned how quickly they shut down that topic.

I return my attention to the watch, noting the frozen minute and hour hands. "I think your watch is broken."

"No, it always stops when I come to Meer. When I leave, time starts again." He frowns and gives the timepiece a gentle shake. The burnished chain rattles. "Although it's been malfunctioning ever since our visions began."

"So, time passes differently in Meer than it does on Earth?" I ask him.

"Yes. Sometimes you lose a couple of seconds or minutes, but it's not too much of a difference."

Fascinating. That might explain why I never noticed Evie disappearing into Meer. Even if she were gone for hours, it would likely register as only a few minutes in Earth time.

"So, all of you have tokens?" I say.

"Yup," Hailey says, tilting her head. The multicolored gems of her peacock earring gleam in the pale light of the Labyrinth. "Evie gave mine to me as a birthday present. I haven't taken it off since."

I remember her wearing the earring at Evie's funeral. It

demanded attention amid the black-clad mourners. Yet perhaps it was not the act of disrespect that I assumed it to be. Perhaps, Hailey meant to honor my sister by wearing her gift.

Mikayla holds up her wrist, showing her bracelet. The band of silver gleams. "This is my token. Evie gave it to me."

"What was Evie's token?" I ask.

Mikayla takes a breath, but Hailey beats her to the punch. "She had a bracelet like Mikayla's. They were the same color. Even the same size."

Mikayla shoots her a slightly irritated look, like she wanted to tell me that information. "Yeah," she says. "That was Evie's token."

That's right: Mikayla and Evie have worn matching bracelets for years. I can't remember which one of them came up with the idea. Probably Mikayla. Evie preferred gold jewelry.

Hailey glances at me, lowering her voice. "Evie was buried with that bracelet, right?"

I don't know. My memory of the funeral is spotty at best. I was too focused on my sister to notice what jewelry she was wearing.

"I don't remember," Khalil says. "I assume she was."

Mikayla's face is expressionless. Her hand drifts to her wrist.

"No," she says, so quietly I strain to hear her. "She wasn't."

Hailey's head snaps up. "*What*?" she exclaims, her words carrying over the grassland. "Are you sure?"

Mikayla's tone is flat. "I'm positive."

"Maybe it was misplaced," Khalil suggests.

She gives a tight shake of her head. "No. She wouldn't have lost it."

Hailey doesn't say anything. Her eyebrows knit together, and she shoves her hands into the pockets of her dress.

"That's odd," Khalil murmurs. "But we can at least figure out what Alice's token is. Maybe it's similar to Evie's."

Mikayla scrutinizes me. "No, she isn't wearing jewelry. But...Oh!"

Her hand blurs in my periphery.

The world goes sideways. I almost stumble into the Labyrinth's thorny wall. Beside me, the others stop in their tracks.

"Hey!" I round on Mikayla. "Why did you poke my glasses?"

She smirks. "Just checking my theory."

I adjust my glasses. As soon as I touch them, a strange current pulses through my fingertips. It's not like the needling warmth of my internal compass. It is more of a hum, like the vibration of a violin string. I flinch, shaking my hand.

"What did you do?" I demand.

"I didn't do anything," Mikayla says. "Just confirmed my guess. Your glasses are your token. Your last connection to your other life."

I don't like how final that sounds...as if I might not make it back to that other life.

I cross my arms over my apron. "Did you have to ambush me to figure that out?"

"A token has a certain resonance that you can feel," Khalil says. He shoots a deadpan look at Mikayla. "You could have been more gentle."

She waves him off. "Relax! It's not like I broke anything."

"You're lucky you didn't. Then Alice could be in trouble."

My heartbeat quickens. "What do you mean?"

"Your token connects you to both Earth and Meer," Khalil says. "If it's missing or broken, that could interfere with... well, I'm not exactly sure, but I doubt it would be good."

"Probably not," Hailey says. "Then you might not be able to go back to Meer…"

She trails off, tilting her head. The corners of her lips turn down. The distance in her eyes reminds me of how Evie looked when she lost herself in a daydream.

I clear my throat. "Or, presumably, you might not be able to return to Earth," I prompt.

She jumps at my voice. "Oh, yeah," she says hurriedly. "I suppose that wouldn't be good, either."

I touch my glasses again, better prepared for the resonance that thrums through my fingers. Without Mikayla's interference, I would not have guessed that my glasses would be my token. I inherited my father's poor eyesight. After wearing glasses for so many years, I hardly give their weight a second thought. Yet now, they mark me as someone of two worlds.

As we navigate the Labyrinth, the air becomes heavier. The sky darkens. The multicolored tiles disappear from the dirt.

The next turn leads into a passageway so narrow that we need to traverse it in pairs. I long to hear more about the history of Meer from Khalil. Unfortunately, he is talking in a low voice with Mikayla, which means I walk on Hailey's left side in awkward silence.

Hailey's long red hair flutters in the wind, nearly catching on the spindly branches of the maze walls. Her head jerks at the smallest movements around us, from the pebbles ricocheting off our shoes to the ivy leaves quivering in the hedges. She fiddles with the pocket of her green pinafore dress.

"I can't believe that Evie was coming here for so many years, and I never knew," I say, more to myself than to her.

"Most people wouldn't believe in Meer," she replies. "They'd think it's pretend. Or they'd call us insane."

She says that far too casually for my liking.

"Why do you believe in Meer?" I ask.

She's silent for a moment. Her hand skates along the Labyrinth's wall. Ivy curls at her touch, then sinks back into the hedges.

"I've been longing for a place like this my entire life," she murmurs, lifting her gaze to the jagged tops of the gray-green hedges. Dimples mark her smile. "I love reading and writing stories with magic and adventures. But there's nothing quite like *living* in one of those stories."

"Earlier, you said our clothing marked us as adventurers," I recall.

"Exactly. Meer is my chance to be part of something larger than myself. I'm the Knight. I protect others." Her smile fades. "Well...I'm supposed to protect others, at least. For the last two months, I haven't been able to."

"What happened?" I ask.

She sneaks a glance behind us, where Mikayla and Khalil are still absorbed in conversation. She lowers her voice. "After Evie died, we stayed away from Meer. They thought it was too dangerous."

"Mikayla said that you of all people should know that," I say, thinking of their argument after the Living Garden banished us. "What was that about?"

I might be overstepping a line, but I can't help myself from asking.

She has the same grim, slightly nauseated expression as when she turned away from the serpent's carcass in the Living Garden.

"It's a long story," she says. "It has to do with our chess titles."

The Labyrinth's path veers right. The air grows thick with

fog that clings to our skin. The branches in the hedges resemble knobbled, lanky fingers that reach toward us.

Hailey draws in a breath. "You know that Evie gave chess-inspired titles to Mikayla, Khalil, and me. She made herself the Queen. Well, it turns out that she gave titles to the other creatures of Meer, too. We didn't know because she made them promise not to tell us. And even though she's gone now, they're still bound to secrecy."

I frown. "Why would she do that?"

Hailey laughs bitterly. "She didn't want us to find out about the game."

She spits the last word like a curse.

The game. The Sheep mentioned that back in her shop, though I didn't think anything of it at the time. Are Mikayla, Khalil, and Hailey part of this game? Am I?

"It's a chess game?" I guess.

She nods. "All these years, it's been going on behind our backs. We had no idea about it until last December."

The passageway splits, and my compass guides us left. The temperature plunges lower. I rub my hands over my bare arms. Somewhere behind us, Mikayla and Khalil's conversation has faded to a murmur.

I'm almost afraid to ask my next question. "If we are part of a game, then who is our opponent?"

Hailey's green eyes fade. "You know the visions that we've been having since Evie died? Some show places in Meer that we've never seen before. We call these places the shadowed lands. They're controlled by people who want to poison Meer. I'd bet my favorite writing notebook that those people sent the serpent to destroy the Living Garden."

I recall some of the places that I have glimpsed in my

visions: a dark hall lit by floating glass bottles and a spired castle the color of blood. I shiver.

"The Talking Flowers said that Meer is ruled by a new King and Queen," I say.

"Yes. They seem to have others on their side, too. I know that because I wandered into one of the shadowed lands. It happened by accident. I was exploring a cave on the Nacre Coast, and then..." She folds her arms tightly around her torso. "I was somewhere else."

"What happened there?" I ask.

"That's not important," she snaps.

From the bloodless slash of her mouth, I'm not sure that is true.

Instead of pushing her, I ask, "What did Evie say?"

"She refused to explain what happened to me. Mikayla didn't get the truth from her until before she died."

Her words fade alongside our muffled footsteps. The dull darkness of the leaves is broken by the occasional red or green glint of small mosaic tiles lodged in the dirt. The tiles are identical to the ones we encountered at the start of the Labyrinth.

The corridor diverges. We can either continue straight or turn right. My compass tells us to turn right.

Mikayla and Khalil have been quiet for a while. How much of our conversation did they hear?

I glance over my shoulder and stop in my tracks.

No one is behind us.

Fog pours in our wake, cloaking the walls of the Labyrinth. Above us, the sky has lost any semblance of light. Darkness presses in on us, pure and unflinching.

Any second, Mikayla will barge around the corner, Khalil in tow, and scold, *Why'd you let us out of your sight?*

Hailey inhales sharply.

"Alice," she says, her too-loud voice echoing against the hedges. "You need to see this."

Reluctantly, I follow her gaze.

A wrought-iron black gate looms ahead. Its hinges creak in the wind with a sound like laughter.

"It looks like the gate we climbed to enter the Labyrinth," I say.

"It is the same one!" Hailey marches forward and tugs on the unyielding bars. "We've come back to where we started."

That can't be true, I want to say. But it is, without question, the same gate. Even the multicolored mosaic tiles at my feet are the same. How is this possible?

Atop the gate's iron bars, a small shape moves.

A bright blue butterfly flutters overhead. A metallic sheen coats its azure wings. Wisping antennae twitch briefly in our direction.

The butterfly passes us, flying into the corridor we just walked through.

As I follow its retreating shape, my compass's voice whispers in my head: *It is going the wrong way, to a dead end. It will lose itself.*

Movement flashes beside me. Hailey runs headlong after the butterfly.

Urgency spurs me after her. If she gets separated from me now, we might never find our way out of the Labyrinth.

I come within inches of her. Close enough to hook my hand around her elbow. We stumble to a stop. Dust rises in large clouds from our heels.

She spins toward me, cheeks flushed. "What was that for?"

"What's going on with you?" I counter. "Did you fall under a spell?"

"No! I was following the butterfly." She yanks her hand from my grip to point into the maze.

No matter how much I scan the thick banks of fog, I cannot detect the blue flash of the butterfly's wings.

"You're under some kind of enchantment," I decide. "The Labyrinth must be trying to separate us."

"No, you don't understand! That butterfly is the key to getting out of here."

"How do you know?"

"I have a gut feeling," she insists. She turns toward the divergence in the maze. "It was going back the way we came. Maybe we can still find it."

"According to my compass, it is traveling the opposite way we are supposed to go," I argue.

She shakes her head. "I don't even know which way we're supposed to go. We've been heading in a circle this entire time!"

CHAPTER 9

"NO," I SAY as my stomach sinks. "I followed every direction perfectly."

I focus on my compass-sense, hoping it will reassure me that we are in the right place. But its telltale warmth slips through my fingers.

Hailey crosses her arms. "What if your magic *wants* us to get lost?"

It can't be.

My certainty wavers as I survey the towering walls of the Labyrinth. Everything is a trick here. Who's to say the Sheep didn't play one of her own when she sold me that potion? To her, I was a stranger, ignorant of the dimension I'd stepped into. It would have been so easy for her to entertain herself by sending me on a wild-goose chase.

Is it true that the butterfly could have led us out of here, as Hailey suspected?

No, I don't think so. If it intended to help us, it wouldn't have vanished so quickly.

"Maybe we can retrace our steps to find the others," I offer weakly.

She raises an eyebrow. "And get lost again?"

"We won't get lost."

"How can you be sure?"

My face burns. I turn away from her to avoid replying, *I can't.*

The idea that I can't trust myself is nothing new. The idea that other people cannot trust me is something else entirely.

I peer down the corridor, which is still blanketed with fog. Tendrils of gray encircle my arms.

I cup my hands around my mouth and raise my voice. "Mikayla! Khalil! Can you hear—"

Pressure squeezes my lungs. I'm cut off by a wheezing cough.

I clear my throat, then scream, "We're over here!"

The words wisp into nothing.

My breath seizes. I double over, black spots swarming in my vision. My knees half-buckle.

A pair of hands grab me before I can topple sideways.

"Are you okay?" Hailey asks. "What happened?"

I force myself to breathe in steady increments, no matter how starved of air I feel.

"Can you call their names?" I ask hoarsely.

"Sure," she says hesitantly. She lets go of me and shouts, "Khalil! Mikayla!"

She chokes on the words. Her body stiffens. She sways on the spot. Now, it's my turn to steady her.

My mind races. *Think, Lee.*

Some kind of magic must be working against us.

"Are their names cursed?" I whisper.

"I don't know," she says in the same tone. "It could be anything. Mikayla and Khalil…"

She cringes, maybe expecting her air to be cut off again. But her breaths fall evenly in the weighted silence. Rings of fog dissipate in front of our faces.

Odd.

"Has anything like this happened to you in the Labyrinth before?" I say.

"Nope," Hailey says, straightening. "But the Labyrinth doesn't like to recycle its tricks."

Her peacock earring glitters in the fog. Tiny specks of green, purple, and blue reflect onto her cheek. She chews her lip, deep in thought.

"I'm going to try something," she says.

"Like what?"

She holds up her hand, peering down the corridor. Her words are barely more than breath as she says, "Mikayla. Khalil. Can you hear us?"

Their names pierce the fog—literally. Emptiness ripples through the white like an arrow shot at a target. Her words resound off the Labyrinth's walls, echoing louder and louder. *Mikayla. Khalil. Can you hear us? Can you hear us? Can you hear us?*

As I watch in disbelief, the fog begins to clear. Is it my imagination, or does faint laughter carry on the breeze?

My mouth is hanging open. I clamp it shut.

"How did you know—" I start.

"I didn't." Her smile grows wider. "It was a guess."

I huff a breath, half-annoyed and half-impressed. "Well, we're lucky—"

"Hailey?" Mikayla calls. "Alice?"

She and Khalil run around the corner, almost tripping over each other.

"There you are!" Khalil exclaims. "We weren't sure when we lost you."

"We ran into some weird stairs that never stopped,"

Mikayla adds, panting for breath. She braces her hands on her knees. "No matter how many times we turned around…"

"It wouldn't let us off," Khalil finishes. "When we escaped, we heard your voices and followed them."

Hailey grimaces. "Yeah, so, we have some bad news." She points at the gate of the Labyrinth.

He blinks a few times. "Wait. Is that…"

"The front gate," Hailey supplies. "Yep."

"So we've been walking in a circle this whole time?"

"Yep."

He pinches the bridge of his nose. "That is not good."

"That's an understatement," I mutter.

"No way," Mikayla says. She pushes past Khalil. At the sight of the gate, she throws her hands up. "Are you kidding me?"

She stalks away, cursing under her breath.

"I heard that!" Khalil calls after her. "That's another dollar."

Hailey sighs. "Of course you remember the swear jar at a time like this."

My brow furrows. Mikayla isn't passive by any means, but outbursts like this from her are uncommon.

When I look at the crossroads again, my compass sense points resolutely to the left—the same direction we took when we first entered the Labyrinth. But that can't be right: it has only led us back to the beginning.

"How are we supposed to get out of here if we're walking in circles?" I say.

"Good question. I thought you were the compass," Hailey replies.

I bite back a sarcastic retort. "I don't know what went wrong. I followed every direction correctly—"

"We can't afford to wander the Labyrinth forever."

"I *know*. I don't want to try that path again in case it wastes our time. Doing the same thing twice and expecting a different result is madness." I take a breath, trying to gather my thoughts. "What do you all usually do when the Labyrinth manipulates you?"

"Eventually it gets bored and shows us the exit," Khalil says.

We don't have time for that.

I glance at Mikayla. Her back is to us. Her arms are crossed, and her head is bent toward the ground. I decide not to bother her.

"Maybe I can try to convince the Labyrinth to listen," Khalil muses. He places a hand against the hedge. His gaze travels to the sky, which is the same smoky color as his hair. "Labyrinth, can you help us reach your heart? It's urgent. The Queen's sister, Alice, needs help."

I understand vaguely that the Labyrinth is sentient, but I hadn't thought of it as something you could speak to and receive a reply from. If the Labyrinth is so intelligent, then that means it is actively confusing us and separating us. It could keep us here forever if it so wished.

Don't think about that, I scold myself.

We wait. I count the seconds. Fifteen pass before Khalil drops his hand with a defeated huff. "I can't sense anything."

Hailey puts a hand on his shoulder. "Let me try."

Her eyes flutter shut. She speaks haltingly. "Please don't be angry at us, Labyrinth. We're sorry for leaving you to the mercy of…whoever has taken over while we were gone. We've come back to make things right, but you're preventing us from doing that." Her breath shudders before she continues. "Evie—the Queen—would want you to help us."

A breeze rustles the branches of the hedges. It carries the scent of violets, even though no flowers are in sight.

Hailey's eyes snap open. "I didn't hear anything," she says, "but...I think it listened."

"Hey," a voice says.

Mikayla approaches the group, not meeting our eyes. "Sorry about storming off," she mutters. "I'm just frustrated."

"It's okay," Khalil says. "You came back."

Her mouth lifts in a half-smile.

Movement registers in my peripheral vision. When I turn, a brilliant blue butterfly perches atop the gate, its wings unfurling like royal banners. I know instantly it is the same one we saw earlier.

The butterfly catches Mikayla's eye. She points at it. "It's back! I was wondering where it went. Khalil and I followed it out of the stairs."

Hailey arches an eyebrow. "It led you out?"

"Yeah. After we climbed up and down the stairs about seven times, it appeared out of nowhere and flew into a gap in the hedge. We followed it and fell into this section of the Labyrinth."

"You left out the part where I cushioned your fall," Khalil says, rubbing his shoulder.

She punches him lightly. "That's what you get for going first."

"What happened after that?" I ask.

"We heard your voices and followed them," Khalil replies. "Did you two run into the infinite stairs too?"

"No, we went into a fog that silenced us," Hailey says matter-of-factly. "We saw the butterfly too, but we lost it. I think it's a sign from the Labyrinth. It helped you two, and it brought the four of us back together. I bet it will lead us to the heart of the maze."

We examine the butterfly, which is still perched on the gate. Its wings flutter in rapid bursts. Then it flaps over our heads, heading for the rightmost corridor.

Hailey is already striding after it. She waves an arm at us. "Come on!" she says. "I think it's showing us the way."

Mikayla and Khalil follow her, but I balk as warmth pricks in my chest.

That is the wrong way, my compass insists. *You must go left.*

"No!" I blurt out. "That's the wrong way."

The three of them stop and stare at me.

Beyond, the butterfly alights on a hedge. If I didn't know better, I'd swear it was watching me.

"We turned left at this fork before," Hailey says, putting her hands on her hips. "And we came back to where we started."

"Maybe if we follow my directions again, the Labyrinth won't fool us again," I say. My voice wavers. My compass feels so insistent, so *correct.* Yet I can't fault her skepticism.

She casts a glance back at the butterfly, which stretches its wings open. "Maybe. But I think your compass is being fooled by the Labyrinth."

"How?" I ask.

"Real compasses have magnets, and magnets have poles, right?" she says.

"North and south. What does that have to do with—"

"The Labyrinth could have thrown your poles off. Maybe your compass is right, but it's oriented the wrong way."

"That...is plausible," I admit, annoyed I didn't think of that sooner. I should have remembered that Meer does not play by Earth's rules. "So, then what?"

"We follow it," she says. "Even if I'm wrong."

As if on cue, the butterfly flutters from its perch, its wings shimmering as it flits farther down the corridor.

Hailey takes off after the butterfly, her footsteps crunching in the gravelly dirt.

Khalil glances at Mikayla, who shrugs. "We can't let her go alone," she says before jogging after Hailey.

The butterfly guides us through the tangled maze. Right, right, left, another left, right, left…I can barely keep track because at every fork in the Labyrinth, my compass wrenches me in the opposite direction. I grit my teeth and put my head down.

Wrong, wrong, wrong, the voice in my head chants. *Lost, lost, lost.*

Khalil gives me a funny look. "What was that?"

Oh, no. Did I say that aloud?

"Nothing," I say too quickly. "What were you and Mikayla talking about before we got separated by the Labyrinth?"

It's not the most graceful deflection, but then, I'm rattled.

He eyes me before answering, "We were comparing notes on our visions and what we might run into in Meer. I've been meaning to ask: did you have the same vision as me today, in Advanced Physics? I saw a couple in a dining room, setting out a feast."

A chill runs down my spine. The rasping laughter of the man and woman echoes in my head. *Join us,* they'd said. *You will never want to leave.*

They said I was their honored guest, like my sister.

My fists clench on the skirts of my dress. How do they know Evie? Did she meet them?

"I saw them," I confirm. "What did they tell you?"

His eyes crinkle in confusion. "They didn't say anything

to me. I never hear my visions. I only see them. That's true for Mikayla and Hailey too."

Panic closes a numb fist around my heart.

What does it mean that my hallucinations spoke to me but not to the others? What is wrong with me?

"Oh, of course." I fumble for something innocuous to say. "They looked a lot like dolls."

He shudders. "I don't like dolls. It's because of those horror flicks Mikayla picks on our movie nights."

A couple of steps in front of us, Mikayla scoffs. "Like *you* don't force us to watch every spy thriller in existence."

"Yes, but those aren't as gory or psychologically scarring."

"Oh, come on. That's the fun of horror."

Khalil rolls his eyes. "Are you scared of anything, Mik?"

She throws him a smirk over her shoulder. "That's for me to know and you to figure out."

"She's afraid of the police," I offer.

She whirls toward me. Her smirk slips, and her arms fold across her chest. "No, I'm not! I just didn't mean to get caught that time."

"What time?" Khalil says. "I didn't hear about this, Mik."

"Never mind!" She picks up her pace. "If everyone minded their own business, the world would go a lot faster."

"If the world went faster, we'd have shorter days and rising global sea levels," I say.

Khalil chuckles. "It's an expression, Alice."

"Well, obviously—"

I break off, noticing that the corridor around us has changed.

The hedges thin, branches showing like rib cages. Under our feet, the dirt gives way to a stone path. We approach a hedged arch heaped with vines of white heart-shaped flowers and ivy. Our shadows spill across the stones; above, the pure black sky gives way to the blinding light of Meer's Moon.

We have reached the heart of the Labyrinth.

CHAPTER 10

BEHIND THE ARCH, stones form a patterned spiral in a clearing. At the center of the spiral is a red-tinted pedestal. The butterfly skims over it before soaring over the tall hedges, out of sight.

"Well, I won't say I told you, but…" A smile creeps onto Hailey's face. "Actually, scratch that. I did tell you all."

"Yes, good work," I say testily. "Now what?"

After playing tug-of-war with my internal compass at every turn of the Labyrinth, I'm in no mood to hear her boast.

She sweeps an arm toward the pedestal. "This is how we get to the Moon."

I glance at it, then at her. "I'm sorry?"

"We climb to the Moon," Khalil clarifies. "On a—"

"Shhh!" Hailey scolds. "Don't spoil it!"

He pretends to lock his lips and throw away the key.

My stomach sinks. Climbing does not bode well with me. I am not fond of great heights, and I am less fond of falling from them.

"To get to the Moon, we have to unlock this pedestal,"

Hailey continues. "It's like a puzzle. You can't solve it if Evie didn't tell you the answer."

"Well, I have a mind for puzzles," I say. "I'm sure I could try this one."

She looks a little surprised. "Oh…are you sure?"

The skepticism in her tone, though not unreasonable, chafes at me.

Khalil coughs, drawing our attention. "We shouldn't delay too much. We need to see the Lady as soon as possible."

"Right," Hailey says, stepping into the clearing. "I'll unlock the pedestal, obviously—"

"No." My voice comes out a little louder than I mean it to. "I want to try. Give me a chance."

Khalil glances at Mikayla, who looks at Hailey. The red-headed girl shrugs.

"Sure," she says. "Why not?"

"Okay, Alice," he says. "Only if you're sure. If you take too long, we'll give you the answer."

There won't be any need for that. After my mistakes in the Labyrinth, I'm determined to get this right. I'm already moving ahead, my eyes fixed on the pedestal.

I step forward and brace my hands under the top square of the pedestal. Perhaps when lifted, it reveals something. When it does not give way, I turn my attention to the corners of the pedestal—maybe they twist or rotate. However, after that idea fails, I'm forced to admit that nothing about this pedestal is designed to move in that way.

I glance at the others. Immediately, Hailey averts her eyes. It's not hard to guess what she had been looking at. Where my hands rest on the pedestal, the slivered scars on my skin are fully visible.

By now, I'm used to the stares and the delayed double-takes

when someone notices the scars. People deliberate between pity, horror, or morbid fascination, but they all wonder the same thing: *How did it happen?*

I know how. I just don't know *why*.

Think, Lee, I remind myself. *You have a puzzle to solve.*

I run my hands over the surface of the russet-colored square and realize that the top of the pedestal is proportioned in sixty-four red-and-white boxes. As I survey the checkered pattern, a long-forgotten memory stirs in my head.

I spent ten minutes making sure each red and white chess piece was perfectly aligned on the board before I called my sister to the living room.

"Evie, look!" I dropped to my knees by the red side of the chessboard, beckoning her to sit with me. "Do you like it?"

When Evie smiled, the gap between her teeth showed. "It's nice, Al."

My big sister was ten years old, and she taught me everything she knew, which was a lot. She told me about the best and the worst teachers at Willow Creek Elementary School. She said I should get in the lunch line early on Fridays to buy pizza. If Mom packed us lunch on that day, then I could throw some of it out. No big deal. No one wanted to trade for Chinese food anyway.

She slouched on the white side of the chessboard. I didn't point out her bad posture, even though Mom would have. If I corrected her, she would get annoyed, and I couldn't risk chasing her away.

She wagged a finger at me. "Don't forget, I'm only playing this game because you said we'd play Kings and Queens after!"

"We have kings and queens in chess too." I pointed them out on both sides of the board. "The Queen moves as much as she wants in any direction. The King moves one square in one direction at a time."

She perked up. "Oh, so the Queen is more powerful than the King!"

"Sort of. But if she's captured, the game goes on. If the King is captured, then the other side wins."

She picked up the White Queen, rolling the piece over in her fingers. "That doesn't seem fair. She should be more powerful."

"It's just the way it is," I said. "Let's play! You're White, so that means you go first."

"Okay." Evie jumped the White Queen over the first row of Pawns.

I clicked my tongue. "You can't do that. The Queen doesn't move until the pieces around her move out of her way."

"That's a silly rule," she muttered, returning the Queen to her proper square. "Whoever invented chess had no imagination."

Her hand hovered over the board before settling on the Pawn in front of the Queen. She moved it forward one square and raised an eyebrow at me. "Is this allowed?"

"Yes," I said, already reaching forward for a Red Knight. "It's my turn now."

The top of the pedestal is stamped with sixty-four red-and-white boxes, exactly like the chessboard I painstakingly set up on the living room carpet eight years ago.

My knowledge of chess is rusty—these days, I have more important things to do than play games—but I recall that the most critical part of the board is the center. From there, it is much easier to launch attacks on your opponent.

Evie didn't think like me, plotting two or three steps ahead in every game. Instead, to my dismay, she preferred to make up her own rules in chess. I could never decide whether her defiance was more endearing or exasperating.

Right now, I'd give anything to hear her contradict me again.

My breath catches. It has been months since I last heard the soft and teasing lilt of her voice. I struggle to recall its exact cadence.

If I am already forgetting her voice, what else might I lose of her? Her smile? Her laugh?

No. I grit my teeth. I cannot let myself be distracted.

I focus on the white side of the chessboard. D1 is the square that the White Queen occupies—the first chess piece that Evie ever touched.

Praying I'm right, I press my fingers to the fourth box from the left. Still, nothing happens. I'm ready to admit defeat until the pedestal whirs softly. Something *clicks* into place. The chessboard square rotates and then folds inward like origami.

I release a quiet breath of relief, then turn to the others. "So, how long did that take?"

The three of them stare at me. Mikayla's mouth is agape.

Khalil recovers first. He smiles. "That can't have been more than two minutes. Impressive."

"Yeah," Hailey says. "How did you figure it out so fast?"

I can't hide a smile at the grudging respect in her voice.

"I know my sister," is all I say.

Mikayla beckons me. "Hey, by the way, you might want to step back for this next part."

"What part—?"

As if on cue, the ground rumbles.

I almost trip in my haste to reach the safety of the ivy-covered arch. I spin in time to see thick green strands explode from the pedestal.

They weave together like a braid, forming a gnarled column that surpasses the gray clouds within seconds. Filaments unfurl from the column, blossoming into broad-rimmed leaves.

Then the noise stops and the earth quiets.

Eventually, I remember how to form words. I drag a hand down my face.

"Please don't tell me that's a beanstalk," I say.

Khalil looks at Hailey. "Uh…"

"It's strong," Hailey says, pointing at the ludicrously large plant. "None of us have ever fallen while climbing to the Moon."

"We're *climbing* to—" My jaw drops. "We have no safety equipment!"

She walks forward, giving an affectionate pat to the pedestal. "It's how we've always reached the Moon."

I hardly hear her. I can only think of how easy it would be to lose my grip on those glossy leaves and tumble to my death.

"Alice, why don't you climb before me?" Mikayla suggests. "I can keep an eye on you. It's safer that way."

I manage a nod. I'm not sure if I've ever told her about my fear of heights, but she can probably read it on my face.

"Dibs on going first." Hailey braces her hands on the pedestal and pulls herself up. She climbs the beanstalk with an ease that could fool me into thinking she's done this her entire life. Soon, she's ten feet above the ground.

Before Khalil scales the pedestal, he pauses, glancing my way. "Are you okay, Alice?"

I set my jaw. He seems to have a sixth sense for pinpointing my moments of weakness.

"I'm fine." I nod at the beanstalk. "Let's get this over with."

After he follows Hailey, I'm left peering into the snarled spirals of green above.

I choke down a hysterical laugh. I cannot believe I'm about to climb a beanstalk to the Moon. This sounds like the opening to a bad joke, or perhaps a twisted fairy tale.

At my side, Mikayla says, "Ready?"

Pain courses through my hands. I've been digging my fingernails into the crescent-shaped scars of two months past. I force my fists to unclench.

"I suppose," I say.

In a softer tone, she adds, "I'm not going to let you fall. I promise."

I meet her eyes, so dark brown they are almost black, and I know she is telling the truth, because she never says things she doesn't mean. She has been present for me since Evie died. I can trust her better than nearly anyone.

Some of the tension in my shoulders dissolves. "I know."

I rest my hand on the first broad leaf that juts from the stem. It is silky to the touch. The scars on my hands pulse.

For Evie, I remind myself.

I climb.

CHAPTER 11

I TRY NOT to look down. It's easier said than done. So, I focus on finding one foothold at a time, testing each one before I trust it with my weight. Slowly, I find my rhythm.

The breeze carries the scent of candied violets. I inhale it. My shoulders relax a fraction.

"Alice!" Mikayla calls.

A couple of feet below, I spy her choppy black hair flapping in the wind. She waves at me, her silver bracelet gleaming on her wrist. She holds on to the beanstalk with one hand. I almost yell at her to be careful until I remember she has been climbing this beanstalk for years.

"Watch out for the clouds!" she continues, shielding her eyes with her free hand. "We're crossing into their territory."

Clouds? I must have misheard her.

"What?" I shout back.

"They won't hurt you, but don't get distracted!"

I start to ask her to repeat herself until the beanstalk lurches sharply.

My stomach dips. I dig my fingers into the stems of the

broad, glossy leaves as a menagerie of animals bursts into motion around me.

Three clouds shaped like otters twirl and zip in circles, chasing each other's tails. Wisps of vapor trail from their paws. An alabaster bird perches atop a storm cloud rhino's head, pecking at invisible insects. To my right, two bear cubs tussle, rolling over each other. Their growls sound like thunder.

One of the bear cubs rears onto its hind legs and snarls at the other. A sharp, pungent scent crackles through the air, followed by a blast of cold wind.

I pull myself closer to the beanstalk's stem and squeeze my eyes shut. My breaths come in shallow gulps.

Evie wasn't scared of heights. She held her twelfth-birthday party at an outdoor climbing course, much to my dismay. I remember gripping my harness and standing at one of the lower levels of the course as she careened down the zipline, wavy hair streaming behind her.

"If you close your eyes, it's not so bad," she claimed afterward, her cheeks flushed with exhilaration. But closing my eyes wouldn't help me forget how far I had to fall.

I shake myself into the present. I am not on a climbing course with safety harnesses and helmets. I am clinging precariously to a beanstalk.

Mikayla is right. Distraction is fatal.

Get a grip, I scold myself. *Keep going. Otherwise, you'll be left in the dust.*

I force my limbs out of their strangling paralysis. I reach for the next leaf. Then the next. I reestablish my rhythm—until something canters to a stop beside me. My blue dress ripples against my legs.

A cloud unicorn regards me. Its mane is made of white,

wispy curlicues. Puffs of vapor expel from its nostrils. A gasp catches in my throat.

"You can touch it," Mikayla calls below me. "The cloud animals don't bite."

"But—clouds are moisture!"

"Not ours. Try it!"

Curiosity wins out. I reach toward the unicorn.

Touching its mane is like sticking my hand out the window of a moving car. Wind tumbles over my fingers, cold and abrupt.

The unicorn rears back, hooves kicking a gale into my face.

I cry out in surprise. In the time it takes me to gain a stranglehold on the beanstalk, the unicorn is fading into the distance. Soon, it is nothing more than a dot on the horizon.

"Told you," Mikayla calls to me. "Keep going!"

I peer up past the tangle of vines and leaves. Above us, Khalil and Hailey are becoming mere silhouettes.

Don't fall behind. It becomes a mantra that I chant as I scale the beanstalk.

As we go higher, pinpricks of light replace the clouds.

A lump forms in my throat. Of course, Evie put stars in her fantasy world. She loved constellations.

Aren't they beautiful? she said to me once. *They're lonely, too. They're so far away. I visit them when I can.*

Stars are billions of light years away, I told her.

She scoffed. *Not to me.*

She often talked like that, in half-nonsense. I didn't think anything of it. Now I wonder if she was referring to the world tucked behind her mirror.

I played the standard games of make-believe with Evie when we were kids: pretending to be forest fairies in meadows or draping ourselves in blankets to become Queens. Not once did I accompany her to Meer.

My head throbs. Maybe this really is a dream, and I have gone well and truly insane.

"Alice!" Mikayla's voice snaps me out of my thoughts. "Are you okay? You're slowing down."

A numb chill spreads through my trembling arms. I squeeze my eyes shut. I won't help myself by pushing past my limits.

Though I wince at the idea of lagging further behind, I ask her, "Can we take a break? I need a few minutes."

I doubt she needs to rest—she isn't even out of breath—but she nods. "'Course."

We sit together on a hefty vine. I keep my arm wrapped around the stem of the beanstalk. Next to me, Mikayla swings her feet like a kid. Her dark hair flutters around her shoulders.

The horizon is speckled with yellow patches of light. They glow softly and pulse in gentle, radiating patterns. I did not notice them during the climb.

I point the lights out to Mikayla. "What are those?"

She follows my gaze. "Fireflies."

"Really? I didn't know they could survive at this elevation."

"Meer's fireflies are different," she says matter-of-factly. "Usually they don't stay so far away from us. Maybe they're nervous." She grimaces. "Or maybe they're mad at us, like the Talking Flowers."

"The fireflies remind me a bit of the lanterns we used to make for the Mid-Autumn Festival," I say. "Do you remember that?"

Her lips twitch. "Duh. That was where I first met you and Evie."

Since the Wongs moved into my neighborhood, they have

hosted the Mid-Autumn Festival for Willow Creek's tiny Asian population. There, Evie taught me how to make lanterns. Her hands covered mine, showing the folds until I could follow them from memory.

"I'm glad your family hosts the Festival," I tell her. "Maybe someday I'll experience it in Hong Kong."

"I've visited Hong Kong before," Mikayla says. "I wish I enjoyed it more."

"Why?"

She's silent for a moment, picking at the tan fabric of her tunic. "It's a beautiful city, don't get me wrong. But I don't speak Cantonese fluently—which is my fault. I didn't learn it as a kid because I thought it was one more thing that would set me apart from my classmates. So, when I finally visited Hong Kong, I couldn't keep up with all my relatives' conversations and activities. I was left out. I don't blame them, though. It just happened that way."

Her voice is taut with resignation, rather than anger. I study her with newfound curiosity. Of all the emotions I might attribute to Mikayla, shame isn't one of them. In fact, I've always envied her confidence. I wish I cared less about what others think of me.

"It's weird to go to the 'motherland.'" She puts the last word in air quotes. "I have a Hong Kong face, but everything else about me is American. My clothes, my speech, even the way I act. I'm an outsider. A tourist."

"I'm sorry," I murmur, unsure of what else to say.

"Don't be." She leans back against the beanstalk. The yellow light of the Moon washes over her angular chin. "You know, that's partly why I love Meer. You belong by *not* belonging. Evie did that on purpose. She knew how I felt."

Although my parents always shut down the subject of

traveling to Hong Kong, Evie and I agreed that we would visit together someday. My heart twinges. That won't happen now.

Mikayla swings her arm across the horizon. "Evie loved this view. She got inspired for a lot of her most popular paintings by sitting on the beanstalk."

"You mean the paintings she sold in her small business?" I ask.

She nods. "People loved her nature scenes. Meadows, sunsets, shorelines…things like that. Most of her pieces were inspired by Meer, actually."

I'd forgotten about Evie's business. She'd started it in her junior year of high school. Mom had hoped it would inspire Evie to learn more about entrepreneurship.

For a while, Evie was happy with the work. She spent hours on her paintings. She packaged every print with handwritten notes and homemade gift paper. Then she paused the business at the beginning of her senior year. She claimed she was in a creative rut.

That was one of the first signs that something was wrong. Art wasn't something Evie made time for. It was something she was bound to do. She couldn't stop creating any more than she could stop breathing. But surely, if she had been struggling, she would have told me.

"Most of her customers were family friends," I recall.

"Yeah. They compared me to her all the time. They were happier to support her than me."

Something in her tone makes me look sharply at her. "What do you mean?"

Mikayla unsheathes her knife and idly flips it in her hand. If I didn't know how good her hand-eye coordination is, I might worry she'd drop it into the Labyrinth below.

"I tried starting an art business last year. I shut it down after a few months. People aren't interested in my art because I take too many risks. Do you remember the piece of mine that was disqualified from the Willow Creek Art Fair two years ago?"

"I think so. Was it the sculpture that strung machine parts and human limbs in a web with the faces of five world leaders?"

"Yeah, that one. I spent about eight hours on it. The judges disqualified it because it was 'too political.'" She surrounds the last two words with air quotes, then scoffs. "People say they want to avoid controversy. Really, they're scared of having hard conversations."

"There's a time and a place for those conversations," I offer. "Maybe the judges thought that the Art Fair wasn't the best context."

"If we always waited for the best time and place, then we'd never talk about anything." She huffs. "At least Evie won that year."

I close my eyes, remembering my sister's acceptance speech for the Willow Creek Art Fair Award. When she focused on Mikayla, the rest of the auditorium might as well have been empty. Evie said, *I'd like to thank my partner in crime, Mikayla. No one understands me like you do. You're like a sister to me.*

My eyes fly open. My fingers dig into the stem of the beanstalk. I rise to my feet, causing the leaves around us to tremble.

"Come on," I say. "We should probably catch up to Khalil and Hailey."

"Right." She stretches languorously and stands. "Don't want them to think we've fallen to our deaths."

I wish she wouldn't say things like that so casually.

As we continue climbing, the harsh light of the Moon grows stronger. I squint against its glare. It's odd seeing it so close. Earth's Moon is thousands of kilometers across, whereas the diameter of Meer's Moon can't be more than a quarter of a mile, if that.

A figure waves at me through a chute in the rock.

"You're almost there, Alice!" Khalil calls. "Just a little farther."

The temperature plunges further the higher I go. Earlier, the scars on my hands throbbed. Since then, my fingers have turned blessedly numb. Beads of sweat cool on my forehead.

As I approach the Moon, Khalil extends his hand toward me. "I've got you, Alice."

"I can't believe…you three climb this every time…you come to Meer," I pant. "There should be an easier way to the Moon."

"Easier, maybe, but not as fun," Hailey says from somewhere behind Khalil.

"And you'll appreciate solid ground a lot more after this," Khalil offers.

Just a few more feet.

I roll my eyes, letting the conversation distract me from the insistent ache in my shoulders. "I already appreciated it, thanks."

"What took you guys so long?" Hailey asks, pushing Khalil aside to peer at me. "We've been waiting forever."

"I'm so sorry that I haven't climbed a beanstalk before—" I start to retort.

My shoe slips as I reach for Khalil's hand. My fingertips arc past his.

For a few precious seconds, I'm suspended in the air, one arm still outstretched.

My center of gravity shifts, and the rush of wind in my ears drowns out his cry of alarm.

I sink into the endless azure sky.

CHAPTER 12

PAIN, SWIFT AND hot, shoots up my arm.

My shoulder wrenches in its socket. A cry catches in my throat as my legs flail, shoes searching for any kind of purchase.

"I've got her!" Khalil shouts. "Hailey, help!"

I must black out.

The next thing I know, I'm sprawled on the crater-riddled surface of the Moon. My breaths come short and sharp. I dig my trembling hands into the rock, ignoring the sting of pain.

I wonder if Evie felt this kind of panic in her last moments, if she knew she was going to die.

I wish I didn't want to know.

Khalil's voice calls as if from a distance, "Alice, you're safe. You're okay."

Those last two words become a mantra in my head. *You're okay. You're okay.*

The ache in my shoulder ebbs as I catch my breath. The pain in my wrist does not.

I sprained it seven years ago, tumbling out of a tree that Evie convinced me to climb. Aside from some occasional stiffness, it healed fully—so I thought. Since *The Incident*, its mobility has not been the same.

Sharp-edged sensations lurk at the margins of my mind, close enough to taunt me but not close enough to touch.

"Alice," Mikayla says. She kneels in front of me, brown eyes filled with concern. "Are you okay?"

"I'm fine," I gasp, my heart still beating wildly in my chest. "Just…I need a minute."

She nods and steps back to give me space.

My eyes flutter shut. I tamp down the breathless terror of falling, locking it in the far corner of my mind. If I allow myself to dwell on what I just experienced, I will be paralyzed to act. Right now, I need to be functional.

Jagged silver rock encloses us on all sides. We are in a tunnel that arcs low above our heads. Khalil, the tallest of us, has to stoop a little. Torches of gossamer-like yellow fire line the walls. The light flickers over my companions' faces, giving their expressions an eerie cast like a Halloween mask.

I stifle a stab of disappointment. After everything I've heard about the Moon and the Lady who inhabits it, I expected something more…well, impressive.

I push myself to my feet. My mouth is as dry as sandpaper. I clear my throat. "Thanks for rescuing me."

Hailey bumps Khalil's shoulder. "It was a group effort. He stopped you from falling, and I stopped him from falling with you."

He coughs. "Yeah, sorry about that, Alice. But welcome to the Moon."

"It's not made of cheese, in case you were wondering," Hailey jumps in. "It's made of wishes."

I glance at the lunar rock encasing us on all sides. I must have misheard. "Excuse me?"

Hailey raises an eyebrow at Mikayla, as if saying, *You explain.*

Mikayla sighs but obliges. "You know how terrible the light pollution is in Willow Creek? When Evie and I were younger, we used to wish on Earth's Moon because we couldn't see the stars." She sweeps her arms around the tunnel, the sleeves of her tunic fluttering. "Over the years, those wishes sneaked into Meer and formed *this.*"

"Where are the wishes?" I ask.

She smirks. "They're all around us. Watch. Here's a wish I made."

She digs her fingers into the wall and pulls out a chunk of lunar rock. A wisp of silver shoots up from the rock, weaving into the image of a small house and a garden.

The door of the house opens. A girl emerges, carrying a sculpted jar to the garden, where another girl has set up an easel. The first girl hands the jar to the painter. The painter accepts it, and they stand together in silent harmony, surveying the wildflowers of the garden.

Neither of the girls have faces.

My attention goes to Mikayla. She isn't even looking at the scene—just somewhere past it. Her eyes glisten.

"Mik?" I say.

She jumps. The rock—no, the *wish*—drops from her hand. The scene of the two girls snuffs out.

Hailey lunges to catch the wish. She is too late.

The sound of it breaking is like the stifled peal of a bell. The wish dissolves into tendrils of silver mist that snake toward the ceiling.

I wince. "Sorry. I didn't mean to startle you."

Mikayla waves me off. She turns away. "I made that wish

a long time ago. I've forgotten what it was. Let's go find the Lady. We're wasting time. "

The edge in her tone warns me not to press. Yet I can't shake the suspicion that the vision had something to do with Evie.

After a few minutes of walking through the tunnel, we arrive at a large, arched door. The doorknob is peculiar because it rests at the center of the door, rather than to the side. It resembles a clock, with twelve spoke-like lines protruding from it.

My breath catches as my compass tugs at me with an insistence that thrums in every fiber of my body. Whatever waits behind that door is key to the next part of our journey.

"I wonder what kind of mood the Lady is in," Hailey muses. "Do you think she'll be mad at us for being gone for so long?"

Mikayla scoffs. She puts her hand on the door, ready to push it open. "She's always mad. Just not in that way—"

She's interrupted by the sound of a distant bell tolling. It is the same noise I heard when the wish broke into pieces on the ground.

Khalil, Mikayla, and Hailey barely have time to exchange concerned glances before the door dissolves into dust.

I throw up my hands instinctively to protect myself, but the debris whirls past us in thick clouds, down the corridors we came through.

We regard the empty space where the door was. Smoke curls from the edges of the frame, lending the air a bitter tang.

"That's never happened before," Khalil says at last.

I bite my tongue. I am completely out of my league among the figures of my sister's imagination. No matter how much I try to follow along, I'm constantly one step behind. I am always on the outside of her greatest secret.

Khalil runs his hand along the frame where the door used to be. "There are no hinges here. It's like there was never a door…"

Hailey grabs his arm. "The Lady! You don't think she's in danger, do you?"

"She's a goddess," Mikayla says. "I bet she can take care of—"

Hailey is already rushing past the entryway into the chamber beyond.

We follow her.

Unlike the tunnel we took to get here, the chamber is dark, lit only by the constellations that fleck the marbled indigo ceiling, rather like a planetarium. The floor is empty other than a few small tables piled with star charts and inkwells.

At the far side of the chamber stand two arched doorways similar to the one we came through. One of the doorways contains a blue-flecked vortex that makes my head feel fuzzy. The other stretches with a milky whiteness that gleams like a soap bubble.

Mikayla inches in front of me. "Be careful," she warns. Her voice sounds muffled, as if she's underwater. Her jaw clenches.

I don't know what she means until we approach the Lady of the Moon.

I haven't read the fairy tale of Snow White in years, but looking at the Lady, I understand her unsettling beauty. Skin as white as snow, indeed. With her tapered ears, she resembles an elven queen. Her ivory hair reaches her waist. Her pearl-colored dress cascades down her willowy figure. She towers above us at about nine feet tall.

Although we are in her field of vision, she does not acknowledge us. Her head twitches sporadically while her hands seize in empty air.

Khalil steps forward and bows. "Hello, my Lady. The four of us need your advice."

Hailey and Mikayla bow with him. After a brief hesitation, I follow suit.

The Lady of the Moon clutches at the folds of a shimmering cloak on her shoulders. Her eyes, which are a splintered shade of cobalt, fix somewhere to the left of Khalil's face.

"Four?" she asks. Her bright, airy tone reminds me of a flute. "And yet—it came to pass."

"This is not the Queen, Evie," he says gently. "This is her sister, Alice."

The Lady's eyes meet mine.

I am swallowed by a darkness as vast as it is cruel. I gasp, or I would if I could breathe, because the air is trapped in my lungs. I'm merely a consciousness untethered in ether. Nebulae clash. Stars burn into being. The universe undulates like cloth, rippling and tearing. It requires no explanation, only witnesses.

Suddenly, I'm back in my body, shivering. A dull ache thrums behind my eyes.

Mikayla's hand grips my shoulder. "You okay?" she whispers.

I manage a nod.

Khalil clears his throat. "Lady, Alice needs your help."

The Lady of the Moon lifts her chin. "Then tell me what you desire, Pawn."

Pawn. I exchange a startled glance with Khalil. Is that my title?

He inclines his head a fraction, looking as perplexed as I feel.

I am the most numerous and most disposable piece on the

chessboard. I shove down my disappointment. There are more important matters at hand.

"Yes. I want to stop having visions of this universe. I want to go back to Earth." My voice catches. "I want my life back."

"Then you wish to cut the string between yourself and Meer," the Lady muses. "The Lost Queen feared such a thing. Now, she is trapped in the world of her own making."

My attention snaps fully to the goddess. My nails dig into the scars on my palms. "Evie? What do you know about her?"

The Lady of the Moon lowers her head. Her white hair curtains her face. "She does not exist as she once did. How cruel it is, to never be home among so many places."

Is every conversation with the Lady of the Moon this confusing? I'd huff in frustration if I weren't worried she might detach me from reality again.

"Can you tell me how my sister died?" I persist. "I don't understand what happened. Did it have something to do with Meer?"

"Let me see..." The Lady plucks at the air as if searching for the strings of a harp. Silver glistens on her fingertips, then turns black, like she spilled ink on herself. Her cobalt eyes widen. She staggers backward, toward the arched doorways, clawing at the air.

"My Lady!" Hailey rushes forward. "What's wrong?"

She stops at the sight of the blackness on the Lady's fingertips. It bleeds down her wrists in rivulets.

The goddess bares her teeth. Her shadow envelops us as she draws herself to her full height. "The Lost Queen is not gone, but finding her is not your duty. For what you ask, Pawn, you must fulfill the consequences of the choice you made in Shepherd's Landing. You and your companions must travel to the end of Meer to conquer the Red King and Red Queen who have brought darkness upon all."

My stomach sinks as the full implication of her words settles in. Not for the first time, I curse myself for drinking the potion. Because of one foolish, reckless decision, I'm tasked with something that I can't begin to comprehend. I never wanted this. I wanted a *normal* life, without hallucinations and missing memories and worlds that shouldn't exist.

It occurs to me that I did not tell her about Shepherd's Landing. How did she know? Did she read my mind?

Beside me, Hailey's entire body goes rigid. Her mouth works uselessly for a few seconds before she manages to ask, "My Lady, what do you mean that Evie isn't gone?"

"You do not listen," the Lady of the Moon rebukes. "Your task does not lie with the Lost Queen. You must conquer the usurping monarchs. "

Hailey doesn't answer. She lowers her head, lips pressed together in deep thought. She puts her hands into the pockets of her dress, rocking back on her heels.

Khalil addresses the Lady. "I don't understand. How did someone gain power in our place? We are Meer's original Court."

"The Lost Queen kept secrets even from her Court," the Lady says. "If you do not defeat the Red King and Queen, you will never leave Meer. You will meet the same fate as the Lost Queen, with your dreaming and waking as one and the same."

Mikayla's eyes narrow. Her chin juts out. "How long have you known about these new rulers in Meer? Why didn't you tell us about them earlier?"

The Lady turns cold cobalt eyes on her. "What the Lost Queen did not wish for me to know, I did not know. I do not have dominion over Time; I merely listen to its frequencies.

I can only do so much to warn you in your limited Space. The places and beings that rise from the darkness are not as restricted as I am. To find the Red King and Queen, you must travel through the places that arose from the darkness. You must bridge the void that divides them."

Next to me, Hailey raises her head. Her half-shadowed face is still troubled. Her gaze flickers into the dark recesses of the chamber.

Her eyes widen as she collapses to her knees.

"Hailey!" Khalil exclaims, rushing toward her. "What's wrong?"

Mikayla starts to draw her knife, then stops. She scoffs. "Dramatic much, Hailey?"

Hailey kneels next to a table of inkwells and star charts. She leans forward, ruffling the fur of a tabby cat that nuzzles into her hands. The blue bow-shaped collar around the cat's neck reads, *Dinah*.

I whirl on the Lady. "How did you get my cat?" I demand.

"You can talk to *me*, you know. I make better conversation."

I do a double take. It sounds like the voice came from Dinah. But that's impossible—and probably for the better. If Dinah could talk in real life, she'd be insufferable. Well, *more* insufferable.

Dinah cocks her head. "Are you just going to stand there looking like a fish?"

Her mouth moves in time with her words. I must be seeing things.

"Give her some time," Khalil says. "I think the cat's got her tongue."

Mikayla rolls her eyes. Hailey groans loudly.

Dinah's nose scrunches. "What a gross expression."

I finally find my words. "Dinah, how did you get here?"

She huffs. "I've been going with Evie to Meer for as long as it's existed. I know it as well as anyone. I got here long before *you*. I thought you were never going to find the portal in Evie's room."

My head pounds. I press my fingers to my temples. "You can talk," I say.

Dinah circles me, her tail brushing my legs. "Are we stating facts now? Birds fly. Squirrels scamper. Mice scurry." She eyes my apron strings. "I like your dress. It's interesting in a peasant way."

"You mean *pleasant*?"

"No. I mean peasant."

"Animals are not commanded by the Laws of Time and Space like humans are," the Lady says, drawing our attention. She holds out her arms, examining the darkness that snakes through her veins. "They go where they wish in Meer."

"Are you able to see into different layers of Time? Different futures?" I say, recalling the wish-rocks that compose Meer's Moon. "Like an accumulation of probabilities?"

Her forehead wrinkles. "I would not say it like that."

I push my glasses up my nose. "Then how would you say it?"

"With a great deal fewer long words."

She starts to say something else, then hisses in pain. She opens her palms. The blackness on her fingertips bleeds up her arms and into her shoulders, curling like inky poison as it spreads toward her collarbone.

A tremor runs through the Moon, but the four of us maintain our balance. The stars overhead sputter out, one by one. Chips of rock rain down at our feet. The table of star charts near Hailey topples, and she scrambles backward as an inkwell smashes to bits at her feet. I flinch at the noise.

"See you later!" Dinah yowls. She twists sideways, pawing at the air. She is gone in the time it takes me to blink. I don't have time to question it.

On the far side of the chamber, the two doorways—one dark blue, one pearlescent white—swell rapidly, straining at the boundaries of their frames. Then they rupture.

The blast almost knocks me off my feet. I throw a hand up to shield my face.

The maelstrom of matter stings like snow and prickles like electricity. Glittering particles wheel past us, leaving streaked tails like a group of comets.

When the noise quiets, I glance at my forearms. They are singed with a white hue. The scars on my hands flicker—one moment there and one moment not. The air still crackles with the aftershock of the blast. Somehow, we are all still standing. Hailey clings to Khalil's arm. Ink puddles at her feet, staining her shoes, but she doesn't seem to notice.

The Lady of the Moon turns toward the now-empty archways.

"Enough," she snaps, though her thin voice quavers. "You four cannot linger in my home, nor can I. I will seek refuge elsewhere. You must travel to the Nacre Coast."

"But the portals are gone!" Mikayla points at the empty doorways.

"She can still send us there," Hailey says. "Right?"

The Lady's lips press tightly together. "I cannot. The darkness festers in my power and makes me weak." She extends a dark-veined hand toward me. "The Pawn will show you the way."

Everyone's eyes go to me. I shrink back.

"There must be a way that we can help you!" Hailey says to the Lady.

The goddess casts a withering look at the marbled indigo

ceiling. The stars have gone pale and fuzzy, resembling patterns of white mold.

"You cannot save the Moon," she says. "If you go now, perhaps you can still save something of Meer—"

She gasps, her words cut off as her cracked cobalt eyes widen. Her fingers curl into claws. Her expression warps into a sneer, then a smile, then an expression of outright horror. Her mouth works uselessly before she snarls, "Go. *Now!*"

Her command rings through the Moon in one pure, tolling note. It drills through my head. I stagger.

"Wait," I croak. My vision swims. I squeeze my eyes shut. "I need to know about Evie. I need to know how she died."

"She is Lost," she states simply. "She is Gone from your universe, but that does not mean all of her is Gone."

My thoughts have slowed to the pace of molasses. "What does that mean?"

Her hiss of impatience reminds me of Dinah. "Listen. You will gain the crown she possessed, though the price is steeped."

I wish I understood why everyone in Meer is allergic to answering direct questions.

"You mean, *steep*?" I ask.

"The price is steeped," she repeats, "in poison. Yet if you do not play the game, you will never leave Meer."

More questions form on my tongue. But when I open my eyes, she is gone.

The stars above us flicker, then go out, plunging us into total darkness. Mikayla curses. Hailey shouts in surprise.

"Everyone link arms!" Khalil yells on my left. His hand closes on mine, gritty with dust. I take some comfort in the warm pressure of his grip.

"Is everyone here?" Hailey asks. It sounds like she's on Khalil's other side.

Mikayla's reply brushes past my right ear. "Yup," she replies.

Her arm loops into mine. Her skin is cool and clammy. "Alice, how do we get out of here?" she asks.

The needle of my compass yanks at me.

Go left, it says. *Through the Moon. Bring your companions.*

"Go left," I echo, dazed.

"What?" Khalil says at the same time that Hailey shouts, "Nothing's there except the wall!"

High-pitched hysteria lines her voice.

I share her doubt. My compass led us astray in the Labyrinth. If it fails us here, too, the result could be fatal.

Warmth hums beneath my skin, strong and constant. My breathing steadies with its rhythm. I lift my chin.

Even if it does not work, we have to try.

"Trust me," I say with all the confidence I can muster. "Just walk."

Above us, the ceiling starts to crumble. Pieces of rock rain on us. Coolness gushes against my skin: the silver mist of a broken wish.

Mikayla curses again.

"Follow Alice!" Khalil shouts. "Don't let go!"

I walk forward, following my compass needle. The others shuffle awkwardly to keep up.

We pass through the wall. A sensation like a cold current washes over my skin. It reminds me of a wind system or an ocean tide. I didn't feel like this when I went through the wall in Shepherd's Landing, but I have no time to second-guess myself.

We cross into nothingness.

CHAPTER 13

EVIE WAS QUIET. Too quiet.

She traced a spot on the countertop, looking through the window by the sink. Even a daydreamer like her would have trouble conjuring vivid fantasies in a backyard enclosed by a chipped picket fence. I wondered what she was really thinking about. She had been in the kitchen today for about as long as I had been studying for calculus: two hours. I was finishing up a late breakfast at the dining table while poring through my color-coded notebook and binder.

I raised my head from the table. The clock over the sink read 11:11 a.m..

"You didn't make a wish," I noted.

Unlike me, the only time she liked numbers was when they lined up perfectly.

She was silent for so long, I did not think she had heard me until she glanced in my direction. Not at me, per se. I instantly gathered she was off in la-la-land. She should've broken herself of her daydreaming habit by now, but my parents seemed to think that there were worse problems to have.

They might have thought differently if they spent more time at home.

"I don't need to." There was an odd note in Evie's voice. She raised her hand, then lowered it to the counter. "I have a special place for every wish I've ever made. I visit it often."

I toyed with the edge of the file organizer in my blue binder, which I'd devoted to math. Evie insisted that math was represented by the color red, not blue. She couldn't comprehend how math could be represented by a calm color—or how it could be calming to me. Math held a comforting structure of rules, formulas, and theorems. I could find an answer without doubting whether it was the correct interpretation.

"Shouldn't you be studying for the SAT?" I asked.

"I will." The corners of her lips drifted down. "I wanted to study with Mikayla, but her parents won't let her come over. They don't want me distracting her, I guess. I'll start studying at nine o'clock."

I stared at my blue binder. "Evie," I said.

"What?"

"Have you seen the time?"

Her eyes darted to the clock. A full ten seconds—I counted them—passed before her face fell. She slumped against the counter. She raked a hand through her dark waves of hair. They had become frizzier and more unkempt lately.

"I must have lost track," she said.

I gestured to the chair next to mine. "Do you want to study with me?"

She waved me off. "No thanks. I don't want to distract you."

She said it like a joke, but we both knew that there was a kernel of truth in it. I needed complete quiet in order to concentrate. Evie relied on other people. Mom often told her she needed to be more self-sufficient.

"That must have been a really good daydream you were having," I said, hoping to break the tense silence.

She turned back to the kitchen window.
"It should have been," was all she said.

I'm not sure when our interlinked arms separate.

I stumble forward, half-hunched, through a solid darkness that surrounds me, until warmth presses against my eyelids.

I burst from a granite tunnel onto a dune of fine black sand.

Black-sand beaches exist on Earth, but I've never seen any with such an ocean like the one hundreds of feet below, with pure white waves rising and falling in a hypnotic pattern. White sunlight scatters over the water, reflecting an iridescence that reminds me of abalone shells. It's a bright contrast to the dark Labyrinth.

My blue dress flutters in the breeze. I inhale deeply, expecting to smell salt. Instead, a cloying sweetness settles on my lips.

Behind me comes a bout of cursing. Mikayla rubs her head as she crawls out of the granite outcropping.

"Are you okay?" I ask.

"I hit my head," she grumbles. "Stood up too fast."

Khalil follows her onto the sand. "How much do you owe the swear jar this month, Mik? I think it's something like ten dollars."

"Sounds about right."

I stare at them. How can they banter like we weren't seconds away from death? If we had delayed any longer on the Moon, it would have crumbled with us inside it. We would have plunged into the Labyrinth in a long, hard descent.

Hailey is the last to emerge from the tunnel. The wind

teases tendrils of red hair from under her bandana. She peers over the black dunes.

"Alice, thanks for getting us out of the Moon," Khalil says, drawing my attention. He rubs the back of his neck thoughtfully. "I'm not sure what I was expecting when we walked through the wall. It definitely wasn't that."

"Agreed," Mikayla comments, probing her head where she hit it in the tunnel. She winces.

"Are you okay?" Khalil asks. He reaches toward her, but she swats his hand away.

"It's just a bruise!" she protests.

He nods sagely. "Yes, you'll be fine. You've got a hard head."

"Oh, shut up. You—hey, wait, Hailey, where are you going?"

A few feet to my right, Hailey stops walking over the dunes. She glances over her shoulder, hair streaming down her back in coppery ribbons. Black sand flecks her shins. She carries her shoes at her side.

"That's what I'm trying to figure out!" she exclaims. Her voice carries to the beach below. "A snake invaded the Garden. The Moon is destroyed. We have a quest to defeat an enemy we know nothing about. What's next?"

A weighted silence descends on us. The only sound is the waves crashing onto the shore.

The mirth disappears from Khalil's face. It's strange to see him look so serious.

"The Red King and Queen must have staged a coup while we were gone," he says. "I don't understand why Evie didn't tell us about them. If we had enemies, we should have faced them together."

"Evie kept a lot of secrets," Mikayla says. Her choppy black bangs rustle over her forehead. She wraps her arms around herself as if she's cold. "Even from me. It was all I could do to find out which shadowed land Hailey found—"

"—when I was exploring the caves here," Hailey finishes. Her knuckles tighten on the folds of her dress. "You don't think…I have to go back to Conchae Maris, do you?"

Conchae Maris. That has to be the name of the place that Hailey discovered in a cave on the Nacre Coast. The dread in her words makes me wonder what happened to her there.

Khalil gestures to me. "We'll go wherever Alice leads us, to the end of Meer. The Lady of the Moon was clear about that."

He and I must have different definitions of "clear". Most of what the Lady said didn't make any sense. She was oddly insistent that Evie wasn't dead. *She is Gone from your universe, but that does not mean all of her is Gone.*

I'm sick of evasions and half-answers. Can't something make sense for a change?

"But Meer has no end," Hailey says uncertainly.

"That we know of," Mikayla mutters. "I bet the Lady could have told us. She's all-knowing. It'd be nice if she shared everything she knew for once."

I recall the Lady's distant gaze and the convulsions that gripped her limbs. She never seemed to focus completely on what—or who—was before her. Her movements were confined. Painful, even.

"At least we found out what Alice's title is," Khalil offers.

The Pawn. I doubt that's much of a consolation. If I knew other Pawns, I could exert more power in this game. On my own, I will not make much of a difference.

Perhaps the others have more powerful positions because they chose Meer, whereas I wandered in by chance. It doesn't matter. I'll make the best of it.

Mikayla grips the hilt of her knife. "The Lady didn't give

us much to go on. Follow Alice, sure. But how are we supposed to fight another King and Queen without knowing who
they are? It's not a fair fight. We don't have a Queen anymore."

Her voice catches on the last sentence.

For some reason, I think of the last things the Lady said to
me. Most of it sounded like nonsense. But she told me something about my sister—the Lost Queen.

*You will gain the crown she possessed, though the price is
steeped.*

Then it clicks. I almost laugh. I should have thought of
this sooner; it's so obvious.

"Well," I say, "that may not be true for long."

The three of them frown at me.

"What do you mean?" Mikayla asks. The sweet-scented
breeze blows pieces of her bangs into her eyes, and she brushes
them away.

I pace over the black sand, hands clasped behind my back.
"The Lady implied that I would inherit my sister's title. If a
Pawn reaches the opposite end of the chessboard, it becomes a
Queen. The move is called Queening."

A divot forms in Hailey's forehead. Her fingers drift to
her peacock earring. "So, you're going to be our new Queen?"
she says.

Is that curiosity in her voice? Incredulity?

"Maybe," I say. "It could give us an advantage on this
journey."

"*Quest*," Hailey corrects. "The Lady always assigns quests."

I blink. "Right…Anyway, the Queen is widely regarded as
the most powerful piece in chess. She can move in any direction she wants for any number of squares. If I went from a
Pawn to a Queen, I could help us win this game."

"So, when we reach the end of Meer, you'll become Queen?" Mikayla asks.

"I'm not sure," I admit. "I've seen a Red Castle in my hallucinations. We'll likely find the monarchs there. And then…I suppose we'll see what happens."

She shrugs. "Sounds good to me."

"We should keep going," Khalil interjects. "We can't afford to stay here too long."

"You're right," Hailey says. "Where do we go now?"

She addresses this question in my general direction. Her brow creases as she surveys the slanting dunes, then lowers her gaze toward the glittering waterline hundreds of feet below. Her shoulders are rigid.

My compass hums to life, skimming the surface of my ribs.

Go down to the shore, it murmurs. *Follow the coastline.*

I point. "That way."

On the way down, we pass a cone-shaped formation of rocks. Scattered across the black sand are fifty-foot-long skeletons. Some of them appear to be whales. A set of bones with a colossal, curved spine catches my eye. It must have once belonged to a snake-like beast, except the backbone has jutting spurs that I've never seen in any snake species.

Hailey frowns at the skeletons. "Something's off here."

Khalil follows her gaze. "There must have been some storms while we were gone. The bones are farther from the beach."

He keeps walking, but she stops in her tracks. Her pinafore dress flaps around her sand-streaked legs.

"No," she says. "The bones look exactly the same as when we left." Her eyes widen. "But the beach doesn't."

Without another word, she takes off through the sand, dress billowing behind her.

Not again. We're always chasing after her.

When we reach the waterline, I'm not prepared for the sight that greets me.

The pirate ship in the water could have sailed straight out of a history book. Colossal royal-blue sails hang from the mast alongside wiry black rigging. Golden-brown wood makes up the ship's sleek bow. What captures my attention most, however, is the figurehead of a wicked serpentine dragon. As I examine the ship more closely, I notice that its sides protrude slightly, as if in imitation of wings.

While I am staring at the ship, Mikayla and Khalil plunge into the water after Hailey. The redheaded girl has already advanced a couple of yards in the water.

I shake myself from my stupor, stuffing my shoes into my apron pocket before wading after them.

To my surprise, the ocean is warm. Ripples spread out from my waist, radiating iridescence.

I meet up with the others in the shallows next to the ship. Khalil, the tallest of us, isn't affected by the current. Neither is Mikayla. But Hailey and I, the shortest of the group, sway with every wave. I focus on keeping my feet anchored in the sand.

Countless boards are missing along the sides of the ship. Long gashes score the wood, as if the ship scraped against a coral reef or a rock formation.

Hailey points to the bow of the ship. "The *Minnowshark* went aground while we were gone."

"The sea level sank," I guess. "This is the pirate ship you mentioned earlier?"

She nods absently, bracing her hands against the side of the ship and peering at the mast. "She should have had enough magic to fix herself."

"Things haven't been the same since we left," Khalil says. "Maybe the enchantment was damaged when Evie passed away."

"One way to find out." Mikayla cups her hands around her mouth. Her shout carries across the water. "*Minnowshark*, prepare for flight!"

Flight? Surely I misheard her…

The ship lets loose an awful, echoing groan. The wooden wings of the boat creak and warp but do not extend from their folded position. The *Minnowshark* lists sideways, then slumps back, engulfing us in shadow once more.

Mikayla huffs and drops her arms to her sides. "Stupid block of wood."

But I can hear the worry beneath her words.

I clear my throat to get their attention. "Sorry, I have a question. Does this ship *fly*?"

"She's supposed to," Khalil replies. "She prefers the ocean, though."

I consider the ship as waves lap at my waist. Is the *Minnowshark* sentient like the Labyrinth, able to sense and interact with us? Does the vessel have a sense of identity, or even a soul?

Hailey bows her head against the wooden planks. "*Minnowshark*, fix your wounds. Come on. I know you can do it."

She's met with the reverberating groan of splintered, defeated wood.

My gaze rakes over the ship. Even damaged, its tattered sail and towering mast have a dignified air. On the far side of the boat, at the front, the dragon figurehead leans forward, as if poised to spit fire. I wouldn't be surprised if the dragon *did* breathe fire.

"Is the ship magical?" I ask.

Hailey pulls away from the ship. "Of course it's magical. What did you think it was, a common boat?"

I bristle at her sarcasm. "I was only curious—"

"Hey, calm down, you two," Khalil says, holding his palms up. "To answer your question, Alice, Evie enchanted this ship. We haven't taken it on an expedition since…" He trails off.

Since Evie died, I surmise.

"My armor," Hailey says abruptly. "It's below decks!"

"What about your sword?" Khalil asks.

"I don't know. I dropped it in the cave that led to Conchae Maris."

Mikayla raises an eyebrow. "You took your sword to go exploring in the caves?"

Hailey crosses her arms, her bottom lip jutting out. "I feel better when I have it with me."

Khalil clears his throat to get our attention. He points at a rope ladder dangling from the side of the ship. "How about we see what we can salvage?"

Standing at the railing of the ship, I shield my eyes. The horizon is faded, as if a large hand has smudged its line.

Khalil tells me that a handful of singing whales and at least one sea serpent live in the ocean. The animals tend to keep to themselves. "They're shy," he says, like that explains everything. He tells me about past adventures, such as diving for treasures: sand dollars, pearls, the teeth of beasts, and uncanny seashells that don't resemble any shells on Earth.

"How far does the ocean go?" I ask him.

He looks thoughtful. "We've never found where it ends. Meer might be a round world, but we don't know for sure."

"We once sailed miles out, trying to see where the ocean ended," Mikayla says. She tugs the helm, which doesn't budge. "We didn't find anything. We had to turn around eventually."

"We didn't want to be away from Earth for too long," Khalil clarifies. "Maybe we could have kept going since time passes differently in Meer. But we missed Earth."

"I wanted to try the voyage again and see if I could go farther." Mikayla gives the helm one final yank. It doesn't move. She huffs in disgust and stomps away. "Guess I'll never get the chance," she says over her shoulder.

"Is there a map of Meer?" I ask.

Hailey speaks for the first time since we boarded the ship. "We never needed one. Evie knew Meer like the back of her hand."

She leans against the mast, shrouded in its shadow. Her hands, as usual, are shoved inside the pockets of her dress. Over her head, the shredded rigging of the mast flaps in the sea breeze, as if a massive bird slashed talons through it.

A shadow falls over the ship, making me shiver. It passes as quickly as it came, making me wonder if I merely imagined it.

Khalil pushes away from the railing. His brown skin, usually a warm shade, has paled a few degrees. "Let's go below," he suggests.

We follow him.

The longer we traverse the ship, the more my senses prickle with warning. We encounter rotted stairs with gaping holes. Battered doorknobs make it easy for us to slip through what should be locked doors. Scrapes and scuffs mar the floorboards. Crates and cargo have been thrown aside carelessly, as if someone was rummaging through them.

Khalil's lips are pressed into a concerned line when we step off the stairs into knee-deep water. Hailey observes every new wound in the ship with a wince.

"It was in perfect condition when we left it," she says, trailing her hand along jagged tears in the walls. "This doesn't make any sense."

"It's been two months," Mikayla says matter-of-factly. "Probably more than enough time for the Red King and Queen to make themselves comfy in Meer."

"Do you think they sabotaged us?"

"I wouldn't put it past them." Mikayla aims a vicious kick at a broken porthole. The remaining glass clinging in the frame crumbles.

"Rulers usually leave dirty work to their followers," Khalil notes. "If the Red King and Queen sanctioned this destruction, I bet they sent their subjects."

"The other pieces on the chessboard," I muse. "But then why haven't they confronted us directly?"

"They likely want to figure out our strengths and weaknesses from a distance. They'll collect information on us before making a move." He pauses, then adds, "That's what I would do."

Mikayla raises an eyebrow at Khalil as we wade farther into the ship. "I didn't realize you knew so much about military strategy."

The ghost of a smile crosses his face. "I don't. I study politics, which is about power and the lengths people go to keep it."

The creak of a door punctuates his response.

"Found it," Hailey announces. "Welcome to the Treasure Room."

The damage below decks doesn't seem to have tainted the contents of the room. Uncut jewels, ivory instruments, gleaming armor, and other trinkets in battered wooden chests cast a luminous glow over the ship walls.

Unfortunately, Hailey's armor is not included among those treasures.

Her mouth falls open in dismay as she holds up a breastplate coated in rust. "Look at this! It's ruined."

"Are you sure there's nothing else?" Khalil asks. "Another sword, maybe?"

She drops the breastplate to the floor, where it joins the visor, gauntlets, and greaves. She points to a corroded sword hanging on the wall. Its guard is studded with white quartz. "Just this one, but it's in no condition to use. Besides, it's not my favorite sword." Her shoulders sink. "I should never have brought *Wayfarer* into the caves. I'll probably never find it again."

It's odd that Hailey left her armor here: the humidity of the environment would have obviously caused oxidation. She must have assumed she would come back for it soon.

"Did you name your sword?" I ask.

She scoffs. "Of course. Why wouldn't I?"

"Um—" I cough. I turn to Mikayla, who's poking through a box of uncut jewels in the corner. "Mik, does your knife have a name?"

She snorts. "Nope. Hailey just reads too many fantasy books."

"Oh, so when Tolkien names weapons, it's 'dignified and

meaningful', but when I do it, I'm 'taking things too seri-ously.'" Hailey uses air quotes.

Mikayla rolls her eyes. She lets the lid slam shut on the box of jewels. "Don't be so sensitive, Zimmerman. I never said that."

I intervene with a question. "What did you need armor for? Surely you didn't fight any wars."

"Sparring," Khalil answers. "Sometimes we held mock tournaments."

"What do you mean by *we*?" Hailey says. "All you and Evie did was sit and watch as Mikayla and I did all the work."

Khalil imitates her tone. "What do you mean by *all the work*? Being the swordplay referee was plenty hard! You two were always threatening to cut off my head."

"Good times," Mikayla says wistfully. "And me and Hailey took turns getting heckled by Evie."

Hailey jumps in with, "Evie was such a cheat. She harassed me more than you."

"That is so not true."

"Oh yeah? Do you remember that time I backed you against the cliff and she yelled…"

They bicker about their wins, losses and draws. I look away. The air below decks grows heavy.

Evie made Meer so she could find belonging, yet I am all too aware of how much I do *not* belong here. Every minute I spend in my sister's world reminds me of the secrets she kept.

Why didn't she trust me with them?

My compass needle snaps to attention, tugging at me.

Do not delay, it whispers. *You must continue your journey.*

I clear my throat. "Maybe we should leave. I don't think it's a good idea to linger."

"The ship's magic is unstable," Khalil agrees. "Let's not test our luck."

Hailey straightens. She surveys the room, her face tightening. "Yeah, but...I don't want to abandon the *Minnowshark*."

"We're not abandoning it," Mikayla says. She lifts her chin. Her eyes gleam with an intense light. "We're avenging it."

Hailey stares at Mikayla, then averts her gaze. "Yeah," she says quickly. "Of course."

She casts a last glance at the Treasure Room before turning her back on the gold and jewels. Her shoulders droop. The circles under her eyes are more prominent than ever when she sighs, "All right. Let's go."

CHAPTER 14

WE WADE BACK to the shore. According to Hailey—and my internal compass—our quest will take us to the network of caves beneath the Nacre Coast. However, Khalil argues we should rest.

"You all look like you're about to drop," he says. "We can wait a few hours."

"Why don't we camp on the ship?" Hailey suggests, glancing over her shoulder toward the *Minnowshark*.

Before I can suggest that's not the best idea, Mikayla huffs in disbelief. "Really?" she asks.

Hailey crosses her arms, tendrils of red hair whipping across her freckled cheeks. "What?"

Mikayla gestures toward the creaking ship. Her dark brows arch. "We just got off because its magic is broken, and now you want to go back on?"

"Hey, everyone, let's calm down," Khalil interrupts, voice slightly strained. He rubs his eyes. "How about a compromise? We can sit on the beach in sight of the ship."

"That works," I say quickly before the girls can keep arguing.

The weather is temperate despite the sun dipping below the horizon, and before long, my dress has dried. I help Khalil and Mikayla lay out blankets on the sand, which we salvaged from the ship. The four of us sit close together as the gray sky darkens. The *Minnowshark*'s dragon head prow looms in the water like a mythical guardian.

The only light comes from Khalil's pocket watch, which casts a faint bronze glow like a lantern. The night sky is noticeably devoid of the coin-shaped Moon.

I find myself wondering what happened to the wishes that made up the Moon. Were they lost, like the childhood wish that Mikayla showed us?

In her wish, two faceless girls reached for each other in a garden. They seemed at peace. Happy. Although Mikayla refused to explain what it meant, I'd bet my A in Advanced Physics that the girls were her and Evie.

I wish I could ask Mikayla more about it, but she's already curled up in a nest of blankets, snoring like a locomotive. In sleep, her face is more relaxed, almost childlike. I smile a little, wrapping my arms around my knees and gazing at the milky ocean.

On Earth, the Moon manages the tides. If it vanished, then the tides would drastically weaken. Perhaps the loss of Meer's Moon reduced the water levels of the Nacre Coast, causing the pirate ship to run aground. Yet that would have needed to happen in the short time that we traveled from the Moon to the Nacre Coast. Besides, the *Minnowshark*'s condition suggests that it was damaged long before the Moon crumbled. I'm not sure what to think.

I scan the sand dunes and the jutting rocks of the coastal caves, hoping for a glimpse of dark-smudged ears or a bow-shaped collar. Nothing stirs. As far as I can tell, we are the only living things on the beach right now.

Khalil follows my gaze. "Did you see something?"

I shake my head, then confess, "I'm searching for Dinah. I'm worried about her."

"She'll be fine." Hailey stretches her arms over her head. "She's probably off to terrorize somebody else. Maybe she wandered back to the Living Garden. I'm sure the Talking Flowers would forgive her more easily than us."

"We'll earn our way back into the garden," Khalil says. He draws his knees toward his chest.

"I hope so. I never thought we'd be exiles," Hailey says softly.

"It's not really an exile. It's temporary." His tone is half-hearted.

I lie back on my borrowed purple cloak, folding my hands behind my head.

For a while, I listen to the milk-white ocean waves crash onto the shore. Then, Hailey murmurs to Khalil, "The Lady of the Moon told us so much, but so little, at the same time. She said something about Evie being trapped. Does that mean she's not dead?"

"I don't know," he replies. "The Lady might have spoken figuratively. I mean…we went to Evie's funeral."

"That's true. But I think there's something more to this that involves Evie's token. Mikayla said that Evie didn't have her bracelet when she was buried. And before you say that's only a coincidence…I don't think it is."

"How can you possibly know that?" Khalil asks.

Cloth rustles. "I…"

"I remember Evie was wearing her bracelet the last time I talked to her," I say.

Hailey jumps at the sound of my voice. I glimpse her pallid face and strained smile. Her hand falls from her dress pocket onto her blanket. "Oh, hi, Alice. I thought you were asleep."

I adjust my hands behind my head. "No, I'm just resting."

"You're not tired?"

I should be after weeks of sleep deprivation. For some reason, lying on the black sand of the Nacre Coast, breathing in the sweet-scented air, I feel more alert than I have in months. The constant hum of my compass keeps my exhaustion at bay.

I shake my head. "No, I'm not."

"Are you sure?" she presses. "I can take the first watch with Khalil. It's no big deal."

"It's fine."

"If anyone needs to rest, it's you," Khalil tells her. "Don't think I didn't notice you swaying on your feet earlier."

"I'm not sleepy—" Her words are split by a huge yawn.

He raises an eyebrow. "You were saying?"

"You can sleep, Hailey. I'll help Khalil keep an eye on the camp," I say, pushing myself up to a sitting position.

After a pause, Hailey heaves a sigh. She rubs her eyes. "All right. If you say so." She pokes Khalil in the shoulder. "Wake me up if you notice anything."

"I will," he promises solemnly.

She flops down on her blanket. Within a few minutes, her breathing slows into a steady rhythm. I wonder what I interrupted between her and Khalil. Whatever it was, it involved something she didn't want me to hear...or see.

Or maybe I'm reading too much into things.

In the sand, I trace different Greek letters used in physics calculations.

"Don't worry," Khalil says.

I blink at him. My hand pauses midway through sketching the lambda letter. "What?"

"About Dinah," he clarifies. "She's more than a match for anything she comes across in Meer."

"I hope so." I complete the letter with a small flourish. "When I get back to Earth, I need her with me. Otherwise, my parents will have a fit."

"She'll find us again," he promises. "Are you sure you're not tired? It's been a long day for you."

"Has it been a full day in Meer?"

"Well, time is tricky. Relatively speaking, you've been through a lot in a short amount of time. How are you handling it?"

"I'm fine. I promise I'm not tired. Even if I were...I'm prone to bad dreams."

My nightmares began in earnest after *The Incident*. The one thing they all have in common is Evie. Sometimes she's screaming at me. Other times she's laughing. The worst times are when she's calling out for me, crying in pain, and I can't reach her.

Khalil says, "You don't have to worry about that. When you sleep in Meer, you don't dream. Also, you don't get tired as easily as you would on Earth."

I throw him a sideways glance. "Then why were you so insistent that we rest here?"

His smile falters. "Usually Meer sustains us. For example, we don't need to eat or drink when we're here. But the world's magic seems weaker...and if that's the case, I'm not anxious to push us past our limits."

"I feel fine," I note.

"That's because you've never been to Meer. You're not as

affected as the rest of us." He tips his head back, surveying the starless sky. "Still, that's not the only reason I wanted us to rest. If we continue like this—stressed, anxious, angry—we can't complete our quest. We need to have clear heads to work together."

Instinctively, I look at Hailey, curled up on her blanket. She shifts in her sleep, folding an arm across her torso.

I lower my voice when I tell Khalil, "By the way, I'm sorry for eavesdropping on you earlier. I didn't mean to. I thought you knew I was awake."

"Don't worry about it. We're all a bit on edge right now." He hesitates. "Evie's death hit us hard."

At the mention of my sister, I scrape my palm over the black sand, blotting out the Greek letters I drew.

The Lady of the Moon insisted that Evie wasn't gone. But I saw her buried.

I can still picture the reflection of the red roses in her casket. It reminds me of the Talking Flowers that towered over me like skyscrapers. It feels like a dream now, standing in the ruins of the Living Garden as Mikayla told me, "Evie's death wasn't natural."

How did she know?

I ask Khalil this.

He gazes at the shoreline. The wind ruffles his curly hair. "Mikayla has the ability to sense when someone leaves or visits Meer, remember? That's how she knew you wandered in. The night that Evie passed away, Mik said she felt cut off from Evie. Like a wall had been thrown up between them."

"Evie was perfectly healthy," I say quietly. "No allergies, no unknown medical conditions. Her heart just…stopped. The paramedics couldn't resuscitate her."

The words taste like ash in my mouth. My eyes sting.

"I'm sorry," Khalil murmurs.

I exhale, unable to escape the feeling that I'm plunging over the edge of a precipice. "I think I was with Evie when she died."

He twists toward me, eyes widening. "What?"

This is exactly why my family tried to hush up *The Incident*. If word got out, people would pry. I couldn't bear to have others dissect Evie's memory or examine me under a microscope.

I brace myself. What I am about to tell him, I have not told anyone else, except my parents. But I can't hold it back anymore. It has been steadily suffocating me for the last two months.

"My mother found me and Evie in the same room. Evie didn't have a mark on her, but I was injured and unconscious." I trace the scars along my hands. "I should know what happened that night. But I don't remember a single thing. It's like someone carved all the memories out of my mind."

He rubs his chin before responding, "That's strange."

"No," I say. "It's coincidental. And if there's one thing I don't believe in, it's coincidences."

The seed of an idea takes root in my mind. As much as I'd like to deny it, it refuses to be ignored.

"Khalil, I have a question. Has any creature from Meer ever escaped to Earth?"

"No. My friends and I are the only ones who travel between worlds. But our visions imply that the boundaries of Meer have weakened. You don't think…"

"That the Red King and Queen had a hand in her death?" I finish. "I'm not ruling it out."

He clutches his pocket watch to his chest. The bronze light peeks through his fingertips. "Do you think she was… murdered?"

Murder. My breath catches. That word has been hovering at the edges of the conversation. Spoken aloud, it has a razor-sharp heft.

My hands curl into fists in my lap. "I'm operating on the assumption that something—or someone—from Meer played a role in her death. It may not be murder."

I don't say I hope her death was not an accident.

Otherwise, everything I have endured will have been for nothing.

"I hope not," he murmurs. "I hardly recognize Meer anymore. Nothing is as I knew it."

I'm reminded of the history that the three of them have here. They've lived entire lives in a time and space tucked away from Earth. They've been warriors and rulers, pirates and pioneers. I cannot appreciate what it means to return to the world of their adventures and find a shadow of the place it was.

I study the clouded sky and consider what the Lady of the Moon told me about my sister. *You will gain the crown she possessed, though the price is steeped.*

If I am destined to become Queen, as the Lady of the Moon implied, stepping into my sister's role could help me understand what happened to her.

Or, a darker part of my mind whispers, *it could make you a target.*

At sunrise, the four of us bid the *Minnowshark* farewell. We pick our way along the coast, following my compass' instructions.

Throughout the hike, Hailey remains at Khalil's side. She

has been oddly quiet all morning. Whenever someone speaks to her, she startles, as if torn from a daydream.

I can't shake the suspicion that last night, Hailey was about to show Khalil something until I interjected. Does it have something to do with Evie's death? I want to ask her about it, but I suspect she won't give me any answers.

Eventually, my compass guides us to an almost invisible juncture in the rocks. A series of algae-covered stones leads inside the cave like a staircase. I climb down first, slowly so I don't slip.

My footfalls are softened by the abundant algae as I emerge into the cave. The air is warm and damp with a slightly metallic tang. It sticks my hair to my cheeks. The cave itself is made from some kind of sedimentary rock—limestone, maybe. It's impossible to tell in the near-total darkness.

I take a step forward and stifle a yelp as water soaks my sock. I've stepped into a puddle.

"This place is creepy," Mikayla says behind me. Tinny echoes of her words bounce off the walls. "And pitch-black. How are we supposed to see? Somebody go make a torch."

"We don't have to," Hailey says. "Look."

Suddenly, light bursts behind me. I whirl.

Blue-and-green shapes swim across Hailey's face, matching the colors of her peacock earring. The light illuminates her hand as it trails along the algae-covered walls, where shelves of uneven rock jut out at various angles. Bioluminescence flares in patterns that remind me of the serpentine ivy of the Labyrinth, reflecting in the puddles scattered underfoot.

Hailey pulls her hand away from the algae, which continues to pulse blue and green.

"It's activated by touch," she explains. "I found out when

I came here last time. Keep your hand on the wall, and you'll light your way."

Khalil cranes his neck to watch the bioluminescence spiderweb across the ceiling. "I didn't know that existed. To be fair, I've never been down in this cave."

"Me neither," Mikayla says. Spots of blue and green reflect in her brown irises. "Evie said it was unstable."

"I didn't plan to go far," Hailey says defensively. "You know, I think Evie warned us to stay away from this cave to keep us from discovering Conchae Maris." She scowls. "She should have been honest with us."

That's ironic of her to say, considering the secret she seems to be keeping. But I let it slide.

"How did you get to Conchae Maris from here?" I ask, stumbling over the unfamiliar name.

She shrugs. "I don't really remember. It's not that important. Your compass will take us there, right?"

"Yes." I instinctively seek its reassuring warmth in my chest. The needle points forward.

My gaze goes to Hailey again. "And...what happened in Conchae Maris?"

Shadows pool across her cheekbones and the dip of her throat, making her look skeletal.

"We should start walking," she says, her tone dull. "We can't stand here forever."

"How did you get out?" I persist.

She doesn't say anything. I suspect she's ignoring me until she replies, "The girl let me go." Her words are almost lost in the sound of trickling water.

The girl. I wonder if this girl has any position of importance compared to the Red King and Queen. While I'm reluctant to push Hailey on the matter, I have a sinking suspicion that I will learn more soon—firsthand.

I step through the newly lit cave, taking care to avoid the puddles. The others follow me. The next few minutes are filled with our panting breaths and footsteps. Whenever Mikayla slips, she curses. I can practically hear Khalil adding up the change for the swear jar.

I pour my focus into navigating the path, keeping my hand to the wall. If my mind is racing ahead, then my doubt can't catch up.

Khalil falls into step behind me. "Penny for your thoughts, Alice? You've been quiet."

"I think my thoughts are worth more than a penny," I counter, throwing him a glance over my shoulder.

He spreads his hands. "Name your price, then."

"You sound like the Sheep," I note.

A soft chuckle. "Yeah, I guess I do. I could make a deal with you."

I grimace. "I've had enough of deals, thanks."

I walk under a jutting shelf of rock, while he's forced to duck. We continue in silence for a few minutes until he says meditatively, "You remind me a bit of Evie."

I can't help but rise to the bait. "How so?"

The blue-green glow of the algae mottles his face, shifting when he says, "She often got lost in her head. She had trouble knowing when to come back to Earth sometimes."

I bite my lip before replying, maybe a little harsher than I mean to. "Yes, well, the difference is that I do."

"What do you mean by that?"

If it were anyone else, I would recognize that I've said too much. But something about Khalil invites openness.

"Evie didn't think about her future enough," I say

eventually. "It was like she assumed that she could be a kid her entire life."

He tilts his head. "What makes you say that?"

I recall the conversations with my parents that accompanied every report card. When final grades were released, I braced myself, knowing that Mom and Dad would identify every area in which I had underperformed. If the grade was below an A, it wasn't good enough. *I* wasn't good enough.

I learned that the hard way during one conversation about my sophomore year report card.

"We need you to do better," Dad told me.

"It's an A-minus!" I protested. "It's almost an A."

He scoffed. "Winners aren't winners because they were 'almost' the best."

"What about Evie?" I retorted. "You didn't say anything about the A-minuses on her report card."

"We push her, too," Dad said. "We expect the best from both of you."

I scowled and didn't reply.

Mom put her hand atop his. "All we ask for is your best. Can you give us that, Alice?"

"Of course I can."

"What about being better?" she persisted, her eyes boring into mine. "What about being the best?"

After that, I stopped complaining. I understood. Or at least, I wanted to.

I did not become irritated when my parents texted me in the middle of the school day to inquire about a test grade I hadn't even seen yet. I no longer acted sullen and distant during our report card sessions. And, unlike Evie, I did not cry.

Sometimes, when I worked late into the night, I heard

her muffled sobs across the hall. I imagined telling her, *It's not so bad. They want what's best for us. We'll get through it together.*

But we didn't. From my sophomore year into my junior year, Evie brushed me off. On the rare occasions that I engaged her in conversation, she'd turn toward me with a dazed expression and say, "I missed that. Can you repeat it?" If I spoke about school or our parents, she scoffed. *What are* you *worried about?* she implied. *You're doing everything they want.*

I hoped that she, of all people, would understand the pressure I was under. Instead, I felt as though I had to compensate for both of us.

Maybe I can't stop myself from getting lost in my head. But I can stop myself from losing my head about what I can't control.

When I finish explaining this to Khalil, he considers my words. The space between us is filled with the sound of water trickling through limestone.

"Alice," he says, "I'm not saying that you're wrong, but I think you might be looking at this the wrong way."

"I know my sister better than anyone," I say.

He raises his hands in surrender. "I'm not saying that you don't. But maybe Evie had her own reasons for being withdrawn. Did you ask her why she felt the way she did?"

"I…" I hesitate. "No. I thought…I assumed…"

"It's better to talk to someone on their terms. It's more honest."

My face flushes. "Of course," I say through gritted teeth.

I'm angry. Not necessarily at him, just at the truth of his words. Why didn't I think of that? It should have been obvious.

Evie pushed me away in the end, but I could have done more to prevent it. If only I had paid more attention…if only I had asked her…

Don't fall down that hole, I scold myself. *Hypotheticals will get you nowhere.*

My compass pulsates in my chest. I march forward.

One second, I am stepping over a threshold into a new cavern. The next—

I open my eyes to find a veil of gray as far as the eye can see. It presses against my mouth and nose.

Three shadowed forms emerge into the grayness beside me. I know without a doubt that they are Mikayla, Khalil, and Hailey. I try to turn toward them, then find that I can't move. I am an insect trapped in amber.

My heart pounds as the gray veil bears down on my body. Painful pressure pops in my ears.

I black out.

CHAPTER 15

SOMEONE IS WATCHING me.

I'm aware of this in the way I'm aware of my thudding heartbeat.

I'm lying on a cold, smooth surface. The air is stale and dry. Wherever I am, it's not the cavern below the Nacre Coast, nor the stagnant veil of gray that I passed through moments before.

Questions knot together in my head. *Where am I? Where are the others?*

Near me, something shifts. I stiffen.

I mentally slap myself. *Great job, Lee.* That movement was too unnatural. Whoever is there—if anyone is there—they will know that I am awake.

I take a shallow breath, bracing myself. Then I spring to my feet, hoping to catch the other person off-guard.

Instead, with a chill, I realize that I'm inside a *bottle*.

It is about ten feet high and closed with a cork. I have no hope of scaling the slippery walls—or breaking through them. The glass looks about a foot thick.

No one is around.

"Hello?" I venture. My voice is scratchy.

Hello, hello, hello.

I flinch at the echo of my words.

Dizziness swamps me. I place my hand on the wall for support.

Between my hand and the glass, fog curls. It spreads like a stain, enveloping the entire bottle.

"You have nothing to fear, unless you wish me ill," an airy voice—a child's voice—says. "Do you?"

Blood roars in my ears.

"Who's there?" I demand.

A girl with strawberry-blonde hair and a heart-shaped face materializes outside of the bottle. She can't be older than seven. I don't think I've seen her in any of my hallucinations.

She flounces closer to the glass, smoothing chubby hands down her frilly yellow dress. "Hello! I am Primera. You haven't met me, but I know you, Alice."

Cold engulfs me. "How?" I blurt out.

"Why, from your own sister, of course." Her lips curl into a gap-toothed grin. "She and I had an understanding. She gave me the most painful parts of herself. I preserved them."

Preserved. For some reason, the image of organs floating in formaldehyde jars flashes through my mind.

"I bargained with her on behalf of the Red Court," she continues. "She was young and scared and could not banish us. So she let us lay claim to our own parts of Meer, as long as we stayed hidden. She agreed to share her secrets with me. How foolish to keep all her secrets in one place! For years, we grew strong on the morsels she gave us."

My head is already spinning. I focus on the part that seems the most pressing. "You're in the Red Court. The other side of this chess game?"

Her eyes twinkle. She flicks her fingers against the wall of the bottle. "Yes, I am a Red Pawn. Not quite as fresh-faced as you, though."

"How do you know I'm a Pawn? Have you been spying on me?"

Her grin widens. "I don't need to. Many things roam the surface of Meer. Their deeds make impressions. With them come thoughts. Emotions. All of it trickles down to Conchae Maris in the end."

"You don't speak like a little girl," I note. It's a stupid thing to say, but I'm trying to shake off my lethargy.

"Who said I was a little girl?"

"You're the enemy," I accuse.

"Only because you won't recognize the pieces of yourself you've come to fear." She cocks her head. "Evie forbade us from searching for her friends. She said nothing about her friends coming to *us*. Thank you for finding me. With your secrets, the Red Court will rise further from the shadows."

"I won't give you any secrets, and neither will the others."

She giggles. "I'm afraid you have no choice in the matter. Evie herself gave me dominion over Conchae Maris. While you are here, you will pay my price. Your Knight is not exempt. Just because she gave me one secret doesn't mean I can't extract another."

Extract. The word is so ugly. Violent.

My thoughts scatter. She knows our titles. How much more does she know about us?

"Don't hurt her," I say. "Don't hurt any of them—"

"Shhh." Primera leans closer, putting a finger to her lips. Her blue eyes dance. "Answer me this. Why is a butter knife like a secret?"

"If I give you the correct answer, will you let me go?"

Her bottom lip sticks out in a pout. "What price will you pay?"

She vanishes without another word. I reel back.

Why is a butter knife like a secret? That's utter nonsense.

Then something slams sideways into my mind.

I gasp, stunned at the vicious hand that flicks through my recent memories.

Dropping mirrors in the physics lab. Making up the tests I missed when Evie died. Seeing roses in her casket that weren't really there.

You can't have her! I might be screaming it aloud. I don't know.

I kneel on the cold glass floor of the bottle, gripping the sides of my head. I do not remember falling. Silver rivulets run down the sides of the bottle like tears.

"Then what can I take?" Primera replies. I can't see her, but her words echo like she's right in front of me. "You must decide quickly if you wish to escape."

"You can't have anything." I hurl the words at her.

She sighs. "I must."

Right after Evie's first All-State Lacrosse Championship, she ditched her teammates to spend time with me. Our parents indulged us on the condition that we find a ride to get home.

"It's getting late, and your mother and I need to wake up early tomorrow," Dad said. He patted Evie on the shoulder and left.

My sister and I went straight to Yuzu Deli, the only boba shop in Willow Creek. We arrived twenty minutes before closing time. Mr. Wei, the owner, greeted us cheerfully and waited for us to skim the boba menu.

I nudged Evie. "Hurry up. I know what I want."

She playfully shoved my shoulder. "Of course you do. You always pick strawberry."

"And you never commit to a flavor!"

"It's called being adventurous, Alice." A spark entered her eyes. "Hey, I have an idea. Since I helped Willow Creek win, how about I get to pick your tea flavor?"

I could not argue with that. As a sophomore, she was unmistakably the best goalie the team had ever had. She could conceivably play at the collegiate level.

"You'd better choose something good," I threatened.

Evie placed a hand on her chest. "I have great taste! Tell you what, I'll get strawberry. Is that fair?"

"Only if you let me pay for both. It's your reward for winning," I added when she started to protest.

When we received our drinks, I tried mine—and almost spit it out.

She laughed. "You don't like pineapple? That's not normal."

We ended up swapping.

"No," Primera muses. She ruthlessly peruses the weeks and months of my life. "I need something with more luster."

On the day of my first high school math competition, in my sophomore year, I didn't have high hopes that my parents would show up.

They had warned me beforehand that my competition clashed with Evie's lacrosse game. "It's not certain if we will both get work off," Dad told me. "If we do, we will try to make whatever we can."

The competition took place in Willow Creek's dilapidated gym, at white folding tables. The first round was easy. My team of four finished a group exam well under the 90-minute time limit.

While we waited for the other teams to finish, movement on the bleachers caught my eye. I glanced up and saw my parents crossing quietly to sit on the bottom row of benches, closest to the gymnasium floor.

I barely looked at them throughout the next two hours. After all, they had taught me to focus on my work and nothing else. Yet in my peripheral vision, I noticed how they leaned forward, watching me more intently than they had watched any of Evie's lacrosse games.

During the second round, a written exam, I was the first student to finish: I waited nearly fifteen minutes for everyone else. I memorized Mom's subtle nod of approval.

10 a.m. came and passed. By now, Evie's lacrosse game must have started. I thought my parents would soon leave to watch her. Instead, they remained in the bleachers.

I did not allow myself to wonder why. Distraction would derail all the hours I'd put into preparing for this competition.

Round 3 was speed-based. Teams worked against each other to provide timed answers, Jeopardy-style. If the person who buzzed in first provided the wrong answer, then the next team to buzz in could answer the same question.

Willow Creek inched ahead of the other teams. Our confidence grew with our accuracy. By the end of the third round, we had outpaced everyone.

Another hour passed during which the judges made their final scores and remarks.

At 12 p.m., the winner was announced: Willow Creek.

My team accepted the trophy on behalf of the high school. My peers nominated me to hold it. Its heft felt like my future, like something worth working for, if only I could see the pride in my parents' eyes again. The school photographer corralled my team for a picture, and for once, instead of giving a closed-lip smile, I grinned with all my teeth.

"I'm proud of you, Alice," Mom told me after the competition. "It's nice to see them recognize your merit. Too bad that schools hand out more athletic prizes than academic prizes."

My smile slipped. The mention of athletic prizes reminded me of something. "Wait, wasn't Evie's lacrosse game today?"

Dad sighed. "Unfortunately, we didn't have time to go. It was delayed because of rain. But I found the score online, and Willow Creek won." He put his arm around my shoulder. "You deserve to be celebrated for your wins as much as Evie does."

I basked in their praise on the car ride home. After they dropped me off, they left on a joint errand. Evie returned home a few minutes later.

She dumped her lacrosse bag on the floor by the door, a habit that Mom always scolded her for. She wore a troubled expression as she untangled her frizzy braid.

"How was your tournament?" I asked.

"Huh?" She focused on me. "Oh, we won, of course."

"I heard the game almost got rained out."

"No, the storm stopped after fifteen minutes. Did Mom and Dad make it to your competition?"

I hesitated. If the weather had improved, then why didn't Mom and Dad see Evie play? They would have had plenty of time to attend her tournament, especially since part of my competition was taken up by judging.

I shook off my unease. Either Evie or my parents must have misremembered the weather. I could not believe that Mom and Dad would favor me over her.

"Yes, but they weren't there for the whole thing," I responded. "I met with them at the end."

It was the truth, though not the whole truth.

I didn't want Evie to feel hurt, or to argue with Mom and Dad. She might even get angry at me, although I hadn't influenced our parents.

She shrugged. "Huh. I must have missed them."

"You must have," I echoed.

I only wanted to keep the peace. What else could I do?

The walls of the bottle sway before me.

"Let me go," I mutter thickly. "You can give up on getting anything from me."

"Ah, but I don't want just any secret," Primera says. "I want your pearl."

"My...pearl?"

I must have misheard her.

From a middle school science class, I recall that pearls are formed when an irritant, like sand or a parasite, sneaks into a mollusk. To defend its fragile body, the mollusk surrounds the intruder with a hard shell that eventually becomes a gemstone.

"Yes." Primera sounds amused. "I want the secret you have trapped inside yourself with your own lies until you have almost succeeded in not believing it. If you do not choose it, then I will."

Every breath I pull into my lungs takes more effort. I've never been afraid of tight spaces, but my soul shivers at the thought of spending much more time in this place.

I search my apron pocket, hoping against hope that I can find something to help me break out of this bottle. All I come up with is the empty vial of the potion I drank in Shepherd's Landing. Useless.

I pound my fists against the unyielding glass, to no avail. The scars on my hands sear with pain, and I scrabble backward. My lungs burn. Tears blur my vision.

I raise trembling fingers toward the glass with the unsteady sensation that I have done this before. In a different place. In a different time.

When I think of secrets, I think of Evie. I think of what we both held back from each other until it was too late, of the words we exchanged that could not be taken back.

"Fine," I gasp. "I have a secret. It's not long."

"Sometimes strength matters more than length," Primera murmurs.

"The last thing I remember telling my sister..." A dry sob catches in my chest. "The last thing I remember telling her was that I hated her."

I had said it calmly as she and I stood in the hallway connecting our rooms, as if it were an undeniable law of nature: *Every action has an equal and opposite reaction. An object in motion will stay at rest or stay in motion until an external force acts upon it.*

Perhaps I wasn't being fair. Perhaps I had provoked her first. But that did not excuse what she had said to me, either. It did not excuse all the times she had ignored me, all the times she had escaped, leaving me to salvage her mess...

"That's more than I might have asked for, Pawn." Primera sounds grudging.

Her presence withdraws from my mind.

The pressure in my head eases. Coolness presses against my cheek.

The scars on my hands waver through the tears that slip down my face. I hardly notice when the bottle melts away around me.

Why is a butter knife like a secret? Primera had asked.

"If you take it the wrong way, it's too slippery to hold on to," I whisper.

"Alice!"

Khalil hurries to my side. He helps me to my feet.

"Thanks." I struggle to focus on him and Hailey. He looks about as haggard as I feel. Dark circles ring his eyes. His curly hair is tangled over his forehead. Hailey's face is pale, and the skin on her bottom lip is torn, like she was biting it hard enough to draw blood.

"What happened?" I ask. "Are you both okay?"

"Primera happened," Hailey says bitterly. "She's a little demon."

"Shhh!" Khalil's head swivels. "She's still here, somewhere."

"I don't care. I gave up a secret the last time I was here, and it wasn't enough! She goes against everything Meer is supposed to be. She's *unnatural*."

I wholeheartedly agree.

"Where's Mikayla?" I ask.

Hailey points behind me. "Still trying to break out of her illusion."

Illusion?

I turn around.

Mikayla kneels on the ground not far away from us, her palms braced on the ground. Her black hair half-obscures her face.

"Mik!" I run towards her, only to collide with something solid. I stagger back, searching wildly for my attacker, but no one is in front of me—just empty air.

Khalil catches me by the shoulders, steadying me. "We already tried that," he says.

I stare at Mikayla. Why can't I reach her? I extend my hand and brush against the invisible barrier again.

"You can't hear or see anything past the illusion," Hailey

says. "And no one outside it can interfere. We've been waiting for a while now."

How was the bottle an illusion? My burning lungs and the impenetrable glass felt so real. My senses couldn't have been fooled so easily.

The enormous hall we are standing in resembles a tortoise shell, with a spine that curves from one end to the other. The ceiling contains rows of mottled gray-green hexagons... and rows and rows of glass bottles floating in space, revolving gently. My breath hitches. I have seen those bottles before, in a vision. I cannot glimpse what is inside them from this distance.

I inhale a shaky breath. The air carries a hint of brine and something more sulfuric, completely unlike the cloying scent of the Nacre Coast.

Something small digs into my palm.

I open my hand and find the empty vial I took from Shepherd's Landing—except it's not empty anymore. Inside is a translucent, shimmering liquid. I tilt it back and forth.

Hailey's eyes snag on the newly filled vial. "When did you get that?" she asks.

"I didn't—"

"Get out of my head!" Mikayla shouts so loudly that the three of us jump. Her fingers rake through her hair. "You can't have her! Nobody can."

Primera must be speaking in her mind, but we bystanders can't hear it. Whatever Mikayla is experiencing, she is experiencing within her own senses.

She slams her fist into thin air. I wince even though her knuckles don't come away weeping with red.

She bares her teeth. "You can try," she says to no one.

Then she doubles over. Her struggle does not last much

longer. When her shoulders sink, I know who has won, and it isn't her.

The illusion fades from her eyes. I can tell it from the way she rises on unsteady feet and looks at us. Her knife hangs uselessly at her side.

"What," she says, "was *that*?"

Even though I explain it twice, Mikayla refuses to comprehend that Evie allowed the Red Court's existence in Meer.

"No," she snaps. "Evie wouldn't help *them*."

She clutches her tunic tightly around herself. She has not stopped shivering since she was released from the illusion.

"Mik, it could be true," Khalil says gently. "There's a lot we don't know."

"You're going to believe that—*thing*—over Evie? No. It's not possible."

They all focus on me.

"I'm repeating what Primera told me," I protest. "Evie struck a deal with the Red Court."

Mikayla continues to shake her head. "Evie wouldn't put us in danger."

"She already has," Hailey says heavily. "Alice, you said that the Red Court has existed in Meer for *years*?"

"I think so," I say. "Primera said that Evie was young when she chose to give away her secrets."

Mikayla throws up her hands. "But why would she keep this from me—I mean, us—for so long?"

"You should be honored to be a part of her game," a child's voice says.

Primera materializes in front of us, barefoot upon the stone floor. Her frilly yellow dress billows as she sweeps a curtsy to us. When she straightens, I spy a leather cord around her neck.

She grins, revealing a gap-toothed grin. "Welcome to Conchae Maris."

Mikayla draws her knife, which makes a metallic rasp.

"Put that down, White King." Primera wags her finger at Mikayla. "You can't hurt me here. I'm the mistress of this place."

Mikayla sucks in a startled breath at the sound of her title. Her eyes narrow. "Says the kid who should be in daycare. Who even are you?"

"Some would call me a ghost. I think of myself as a sentry. I guard your pearls. You can thank me for that. I don't mind."

No one says anything.

"Ah, well." Primera gives a flippant shrug. "It has been so long since I've had visitors. The Lost Queen gave me many pearls. Such perfect specimens."

She points at the glass bottles revolving gently on the tortoiseshell ceiling. There must be forty in total. Each one glows with a perfectly spherical ball of white light. If Primera is correct, each one represents one of Evie's secrets.

"Not only her secrets," Primera says.

I flinch. "Did you read my mind?"

"I don't need to. Pearls are more than secrets. They are memories. Regrets. Wounds. Evie gave them to me willingly, to rid herself of them." The girl giggles. "She betrayed you with her own fear and pain. What she didn't know is that all this time, she was the one poisoning Meer."

I spin, craning my neck to get a better view of the bottles above us. Their brilliant lights mock me.

If what Primera says is true…then each of those pearls represents Evie's suffering.

"It can't be true," I say.

But I know in my bones that it is.

In my peripheral vision, I see Mikayla's arm blur.

Primera stiffens. She throws her hand up. Red light bursts with a sound like a firecracker.

It takes precious seconds for the spots to clear from my eyes. Primera's figure wavers in front of me. Something skitters across the floor: Mikayla's knife.

"Naughty, naughty," the girl chides. "I told you, White King. You cannot harm me here."

Mikayla wipes away the tears streaming from her eyes. "Worth a try."

Khalil's mouth falls open. He takes a step toward her. "Mik! You were going to pull a knife on a child?"

"She's the enemy," Hailey mutters.

He rakes his hands through his hair, dark curls gripped between his fingers. "Not you, too! I can't believe that either of you would stoop that low."

Hailey lowers her head, shoulders sinking, while Mikayla juts out her chin. "I wasn't going to actually hurt her, just scare her," she says.

"It doesn't matter," Khalil insists, his voice rising. "It's not right!"

I gape at him. This is the closest I have seen him come to yelling. His words echo through the hall.

Despite what Primera has done to us, the thought of wielding a weapon against her—even with no intention to harm—unnerves me. I couldn't be as ruthless as Mikayla.

"Listen to him," Primera says. "You seek to reclaim Meer. Yet what makes you think you have any right to rule it anymore?"

She steps toward Mikayla. "You are unfit to be King and

you know it. You are not interested in who you protect, but rather in what you can gain. And still, it is not enough. You are still haunted by what—or perhaps I should say *who*—you do not have."

Mikayla's jaw tenses, and her hand flexes at her side. She glances toward her knife a few paces away.

"I wouldn't reach for that if I were you," Primera cautions. "And I wouldn't try anything either, Knight."

Her gaze lands on Hailey. Her mouth twists in a sneer. "You cannot imagine a life without Meer, but it can go on without you—just as your chosen family can go on without you. The Lost Queen was correct to make you a Knight. You did not merit a more noble title."

All the fight goes out of Hailey. She shrinks back as if she's been slapped. Her eyes are wide and wounded.

"Leave her alone." Khalil draws himself up to his full height, looking down on Primera. "We've paid your price. Now, release us."

Primera winks at him. "You have a noble heart, Bishop, and you squander it on those who do not deserve your time. That makes you idealistic...or perhaps naïve. You cannot change people out of sheer want. When the time comes for you to choose a side, who will you give up on first?"

He stiffens, his eyes devoid of the warmth I've come to expect in them. "I will not have to choose," he says, his voice flat. "I won't lose any of them."

"If you say so."

Primera turns to me. Instinctively, I take a step back.

"Don't be scared, Pawn," she croons. "You have a long path ahead of you if you seek to be Queen. It is another contest where you cast yourself as the victor. You are no one if not your parents' prodigy. A crowning achievement indeed."

I wipe all emotion from my face. I will not give her the satisfaction of provoking me. Even so, her words hit home.

Have I really thought of myself as better than other people? As better than *Evie*?

Evie and I were like distant planets: inhabiting the same solar system, but not in adjacent orbits. We had different talents in different areas. For that reason, I did not compare myself to her.

But others did. Among my parents and their family friends, comparison is inevitable. The adults disguise their bragging about their children as praise: "So-and-so got the highest test score in her class" or "So-and-so got into the most prestigious university in this state." I eavesdropped on every conversation for mentions of my name. I did not consider that when my name occurred in conjunction with Evie's, hers was illuminated in a lesser light. All I cared about was hoarding every compliment that anyone paid me.

How could I have been so blind?

Primera tilts her head, the picture of wide-eyed innocence. "From one Pawn to another, since you offered your pearl willingly, I present you with a gift."

"I don't want it," I say on instinct.

"Oh, but you have already accepted it." She grins. "Teardrops are valuable things. I captured yours. They will cure any ailment you may encounter on your journey. Use them wisely, as they can be used once, and only on yourself."

My fist clenches on the vial. I'd forgotten I was still holding it. Repressing the temptation to smash it on the floor, I drop it into my apron pocket. I vow to myself to never drink the contents.

Primera flicks her wrist. Four luminous pearls appear out

of nowhere, threading onto the leather cord around her neck. "I'll be taking these for safekeeping. They are safer with me."

Mikayla glares at Primera. "Are you done?" she spits.

"For now." The girl's face flickers, though her smile remains constant. Her form thins into wisps of fog. "Time will tell if we meet again."

The four of us are left standing alone in the colossal hall, staring at the place where she vanished. The silence is deafening.

Mikayla breaks it first. "Let's get out of here."

She scoops up her knife and stabs it into its sheath with more force than is strictly necessary. "Which way do we go, Alice?"

My compass leads us to the exit of Conchae Maris. The fissure at the far end of the tortoise shell is almost imperceptible. It must have once led to the tortoise's head. It descends below the shell like a staircase. I take the lead.

When I twist my head to make sure everyone is following me, my foot slips.

Suddenly, I'm tumbling into a smothering gray veil.

It is the same void that we passed through from the Nacre Coast to Conchae Maris. Gray envelops my limbs, scattering my sense of being. I sink further and further into its grip, dimly aware of the shapes of the others around me.

The compass in my chest burns painfully.

Vision blurring, I think uselessly, *Let us through*.

Shadows shift in the space between me and the void. My hand catches against something that might be solid.

I wish I could open my mouth to scream.

CHAPTER 16

MY EYELIDS FLUTTER open.

Above me, what seems to be miles away, is a narrow ceiling of roughly hewn wood.

My first thought is that I'm dreaming. Then I remember it is impossible to dream in Meer.

I push myself up with trembling limbs. Black dots swarm my vision. I adjust my glasses, and a current of resonance passes through my fingertips. The sensation of my token grounds me. I am no longer in the void where time meant nothing and identity meant even less.

I am sitting on a narrow stretch of cedar wood that is as long as an airstrip. To my left is a long, dark wall that rises to the miles-high ceiling. To my right is a massive sheet of what might be glass, though the sheer number of nicks and gouges makes it impossible to see through.

"You're up," someone remarks.

I jerk toward the familiar voice. Hailey sits cross-legged a few feet away from me. The wood in front of her bears black markings from the piece of charcoal clutched in her hand.

She raises a pale eyebrow. "How do you feel?"

"I've been better," I groan.

"Same. I'm not sure how much longer we'll have to wait for them." She points to the two forms on the floor.

Mikayla is curled in the fetal position. Her black hair has slipped from behind her ear, hiding half her face. Khalil slumps on his side with his head tucked inside his arm.

I spring to my feet, heart thudding until I register their chests are moving in even, audible breaths.

Hailey watches me curiously. I force myself to walk a few paces away and resist the impulse to confirm that Mikayla and Khalil are breathing. It's obvious that they are.

"How much time has already passed? Why didn't you wake us earlier?" I demand.

"I tried!" she protests. "I shook you, yelled in your ears, and sang the greatest hits of Queen. Nothing worked."

I press my fingertips to my temples. My head is spinning. "Fine. How long has it been since then?"

"Long enough to get my voice back after attempting 'Bohemian Rhapsody.'"

I shudder despite myself.

"Yeah," she agrees. "It wasn't pretty. Neither is this place—wherever it is. I've never seen it in any of my visions of Meer. Have you?"

"No." My eyes are drawn to the charcoal markings that she made on the cedar floor. No, they're not mere markings. They're letters.

I peer closer. She has written three sentences, and the third is unfinished.

"What are you writing?"

Her cheeks flush pink behind her tan freckles. "It's nothing. Just a story."

"Looks pretty short for a story," I say, tilting my head.

She tucks her copper-colored hair behind her ears. "I didn't get far before you woke up."

"What kind of stories do you usually write?"

"Any story that's not set on Earth," she replies. "Then I can escape my own mind. I've struggled with anxiety a lot in my life. Disassociation was how I dealt with it, until I found Meer. Coming here is the closest I've come to feeling safe…or free."

I pick at my apron, unsure how to respond. I wish I could relate to her. Meer has only made me less certain of my own sanity.

"I'm sure you've had some great adventures in Meer," I say.

She half-shrugs. "Mikayla says I take my role too seriously, but I believe Meer has a soul, like we do. Or maybe it's part of Evie's soul. Either way, it's more than a way to escape. It reflects another version of yourself."

"Being the Knight must be rewarding, then."

Her mouth puckers. She shoves the charcoal into her pinafore pocket. "It is…mostly. But I don't want to completely define myself as the Knight, whatever Mikayla thinks. It's easy for her to take pride in her title. She's the King."

I try to parse her tone. Is it defiant? Defensive?

For some reason, I think of Primera's words to Hailey in *Conchae Maris*: *The Lost Queen was correct to make you a Knight. You did not merit a more noble title.*

More questions whirl in my head. I don't have time to ask them.

Khalil stirs beside us. He rubs his eyes. His curly hair is rumpled on one side of his head. "What's going on?" he asks, his voice groggy.

"Khail!" Hailey exclaims, rushing to his side. "How do you feel?"

He winces, pushing himself up. "Like my brain has been microwaved."

She huffs a laugh. "Welcome to the club."

"Traveling to this place must have taken a lot out of us," I say. "It seemed harder than going to Conchae Maris."

Hailey's expression sours as soon as I mention Primera's realm. I don't blame her.

I hate you, whispers a distant memory of months past. I shove it down.

I cannot think about what I sacrificed in Conchae Maris. If I do, I will not have the strength to continue on our quest. The vial of tears that Primera gave me weighs down my apron pocket.

I close my eyes, remembering the indifferent emptiness we passed through. Some of its chill remains in my bones.

"We passed through some kind of void," I say. "What is it exactly?"

Khalil frowns a little. "I'm not sure. I think the Lady of the Moon mentioned it, but I don't remember her exact words."

"Maybe it's a side effect of traveling between the shadowed lands," Hailey suggests. "The Red Court might be using some kind of dark magic against us."

Something about that hypothesis doesn't sit right with me. Whatever that void was, it was not opposed to us. It was merely indifferent, which is almost worse.

Before I can say so, Mikayla bolts upright.

Her eyes are wide, and her bangs are a disheveled mess. Her knife sheath is lopsided on her hip. "What—?" she mutters, her head swinging back and forth between us.

"Welcome back, Sleeping Beauty," Hailey says. "How are you doing?"

Mikayla burrows her head in her arms. Her reply is muffled. "Don't talk so loud. It makes my head hurt."

"If she's grumpy, that's a good sign," Khalil notes. He twists his head, taking in the strange, narrow place we are in. "Where are we?"

"Question of the year," Hailey mutters. "Alice, what does your compass say?"

I reach for my compass-sense. *Which way do we go from here?* I ask.

Its arrow swivels toward the dark wall to my left. Energy sparks in my veins, and I take a few steps toward the wall, extending my hand.

Before I can touch it, a thunderous sound rattles our surroundings. The wall splits in two with an awful screech. I stumble back. The others are on their feet in an instant.

It takes me a few moments to comprehend that the wall is not a wall.

It is actually a massive curtain that only the giant before us would be able to part.

His face is planet-sized and red, with crater-like pustules dotting his cheeks. His nostrils could fit several jets inside. He breathes through his mouth, exhaling a noxious cloud that tugs at the skirt of my dress. I gag at the stench. It reminds me of the bathrooms at Willow Creek High School.

He wears a coarse linen shirt and tan suspenders, which are paired with a bright blue necktie. His clothing bears several rips and scorch marks. Clearly he doesn't know how to mend. Maybe his massive hands, which could easily rival some stadiums, can't handle the delicate task of a needle and thread.

The giant hasn't noticed us. Of course not. We're like insects to him: easily swatted and easily killed.

Khalil whispers through gritted teeth, "On my mark, move *slowly* toward the left side of the windowsill."

I look to my left. Fortunately, the edge of the windowsill is a short sprint away.

"One," he begins. "Two…"

The giant opens his mouth, revealing cracked, craggy teeth.

His yawn holds the force of a plane taking off. A foul stench slams into me, lifting my hair off my shoulders. My eyes water uncontrollably, and it's all I can do not to fall over.

I'm not sure which one of us screams—probably Hailey, who's clutching her stomach—but the giant squints at us. To my horror, I recognize the swamp-green shade of his irises.

He recently watched me in the side mirror of Mikayla's truck.

"You!" I gasp.

He lowers his face until it's hovering mere yards from us. The four of us link arms to avoid getting sucked into his nostrils. Still squinting, he produces a pair of antique-looking glasses with cracked lenses and holds them over his face.

"Much better," he muses in a voice like tectonic plates shifting. "I can't see you little gnats all the way up here."

I glance at Mikayla, hoping that she'll have a cunning retort. She gapes at the giant, arms hanging at her sides.

"Which one of you addressed me?" he demands, swinging the glasses back and forth. "I heard it! Someone said, 'You.' Or maybe it was 'Who.' Or 'polly-doodle.'"

My sense of responsibility overpowers my sense of self-preservation. I begrudgingly raise my hand. "I did."

His bushy eyebrow lifts. "You know me? Perhaps we've met in a dream. I see many things. Some of them are even real. Are you real?"

Khalil catches my eye. He mouths something. I can't read his lips...*Let's act? Smack him? This cat is?*

What? I mouth back, too late. He retreats toward the left side of the windowsill, Hailey in tow.

"That depends," I say, forcing my attention back to the giant. "What is the difference between something real and unreal?"

The giant drums his fingers on the windowsill. Each tap sounds like an army marching to war.

"Well," he says with a thoughtful frown, "usually I start by introducing myself and seeing if they introduce themselves back. Most dream-creatures don't talk to me. It's quite rude."

"You don't have to worry about that from us," I mutter.

He grins. I wish he wouldn't. Any dentist would cringe at the state of his teeth. "I'm sure I don't! I am Hamwishbone, Rook of the Red Court, at your service." He sweeps a leather cap off a head with a few greasy strands of brown hair.

Rook of the Red Court. I appraise him, wondering what kind of powers or abilities he has. Unlike Primera, he does not appear to have identified our Court. Perhaps someone of his stature can't imagine us being a threat.

"Alice Lee, at yours," I reply instinctively.

"Nice to meet you! Welcome to my humble hut. I've never seen any creature like you. You're like me, but smaller."

"Yes, well...we're humans. This is Mikayla. She's my friend."

Mikayla scowls at the prospect of being introduced to a giant.

The giant frowns. "Why does she have one name, while you have two?"

"She has a second name, too. All of us have at least two names."

"You must be greedy creatures if you have so many names! Well, Alice Lee—"

I wince at the sound of my full name. "I'd prefer you call me Alice, actually."

"How wishy-washy. Very well, Alice."

He puts his hands in his pockets and rocks back on his heels, revealing more of the room.

The hut's walls are made of cracked, weather-beaten logs: each is roughly as thick as an oil tanker. I wonder how many forests died to make this place. In the far right corner of the hut is a pile of rags that I assume is a bed. In the left corner, a fireplace contains a heap of smoldering coals. The middle of this place has a reddish wood table with a matching, brittle chair. Judging from the splinters in the furniture, he carved it himself.

His booming voice brings me back to the present. "What is the second name for, if you don't use it?"

"Lee is a surname. Most humans have them."

Mikayla's elbow catches me in the ribs. She gives me a glare that says, *Are you really going to teach this giant about human naming conventions?*

I force a smile. "Yes, anyway, we're definitely real. We're not part of a dream."

"Hmm. I can check that." Hamwishbone scratches his bristled chin. The gesture is strangely familiar, but I'm not sure why.

I still don't know what Khalil was trying to tell me. I surreptitiously glance to my left. While I have been entertaining the giant, Khalil and Hailey have crept farther along the windowsill.

"How so?" I ask.

A shadow engulfs me.

Then a pair of hands shoves my shoulder.

I hit the ground. Hard.

A spike of white-hot pain shoots up my right wrist. My breathing goes jagged. I squeeze my eyes shut as nameless voices murmur at the edges of my mind. The vial of tears in my apron digs into my torso. Somehow, it didn't break in my fall.

"Come on!" Mikayla yells in my face. She seizes my elbow and drags me to my feet. "He's trying to kill us!"

I risk a glance over my shoulder and wish I hadn't. Hamwishbone's enormous hand is descending over our heads.

Mikayla dives forward. I follow not a second too soon.

The edge of Hamwishbone's palm comes down behind us. The force sends us flying forward.

I land, dazed, at the end of the windowsill. Beside me, Mikayla shakes her head like a dog, trying to get her bearings.

"What…" I mumble.

"No time!" She pulls me up. We're standing on the edge of the windowsill. "Just trust me."

Below, I make out the shapes of Khalil and Hailey climbing down the edge of the ragged curtain. Well, *climbing* is a generous term. What they are doing is more akin to sliding down a fire pole, at an astonishing speed. They are soon out of sight.

I peer over the lip of the windowsill. How far is it to the floor?

Too far.

Cold sweat slicks my face. My stomach turns. I sway on the spot.

Mikayla's grip on my hand tightens. "Alice, look at me."

I do. Her eyes spark with steely determination.

"It's not a long way down," she says. "I promise. Close your eyes and it will be over in no time."

"Okay." My voice is small.

The giant laughs thunderously behind us.

"Interesting!" Hamwishbone bellows. His shadow envelops us once again. His mossy teeth show. Spittle flecks the corner of his mouth. "I haven't decided if you are real or not yet. All the creatures run. Only the dream-creatures live."

Nothing motivates you quite like a bloodthirsty giant.

Mikayla gives me a fierce nod. Then she lets go, leaping onto the curtain and sliding out of sight.

I squeeze my eyes shut and follow her.

Sulfurous air rushes past my face. My hands burn against the rough fabric of the curtain. The throb in my wrist doesn't help.

Then my feet collide with solid ground. My knees fold. Fortunately, I've landed on a swath of white cloth. No—a napkin.

Mikayla hauls me to my feet for the umpteenth time.

"Told you you'd be fine," she says.

I'm too out of breath to retort. We stumble toward Khalil and Hailey.

Khalil gives me a thumbs-up. "Good job on distracting him."

I tilt my head, recalling the words he mouthed to me on the windowsill. "Oh, is that what you wanted me to do earlier?"

His brow furrows. "Yes...?"

The giant interrupts us, "Run, run, if you can! I'll catch you. You can't escape punishment."

I shudder. He sounds like an admonishing teacher.

Something about his words nags at me. Have I heard them somewhere before?

"Catch up later," Mikayla interjects. "Avoid death first."

We take off, weaving through the unfathomably large legs of the giant's chair and table. The heat of the nearby fireplace tugs at my skin. It is guarded by a corroded metal gate. A long iron rod—a poker—rests against it.

The dirt-covered floor quivers as Hamwishbone stomps toward us. Vertigo threatens to overwhelm me at the sight of his ragged shoes, cobbled together of leather and cloth and the pelts of unidentifiable beasts.

"Are you real or not?" His cackle echoes through the house. "If you know the answer, why don't you just say it?"

Recognition strikes me. I nearly trip.

He is familiar, but not because I have seen him in a vision. It's because I know someone like him in real life.

"There!" Khalil shouts. He points to a crack in the wall that is barely large enough for us to squeeze through.

We pile inside the dim, musty mousehole. There's a little light to see by, thanks to the cracks in the weather-beaten logs that make up the hut's walls. The ceiling of the tunnel narrows, forcing Khalil and Mikayla to duck their heads. Gravel crunches under our feet.

I'm not sure how far we run. Far enough that eventually, the clamor of the giant fades.

"I can't go any farther," Hailey groans, flopping against the wall. "Let's stop."

"Okay," Khalil agrees. His breathing is barely labored. That seems unfair when the rest of us are half-wheezing.

I do not pay attention when he and Hailey start to banter. I focus on Hamwishbone's identity. Where I have seen him, or rather, someone like him, before.

"—Right, Alice?" Khalil turns toward me. The teasing edge in his voice crumbles. "Alice? Is something wrong?"

"I recognize Hamwishbone," I say.

Mikayla chimes in, "Yeah, I think I saw him in a hallucination."

"Not like that." I press my fingers to my temples. "I don't…He's similar to a person back on Earth. I thought it was a coincidence at first, until the last thing he said."

"What does that have to do with anything?" Hailey asks.

"A lot, depending on whether you had Mr. Hammond as your middle school math teacher."

Mikayla's mouth falls open. I knew she would understand. After all, she and Evie shared his pre-algebra class.

"'If you know the answer, why don't you just say it?'" she repeats. "He said that when he cold-called students."

The students at Willow Creek Middle School despised him. Not only did he call on everyone in the class, he made a special point of targeting those who were struggling.

"He should've been a prison warden," Evie remarked once. "He enjoys punishing people more than he likes it when they behave."

She would know, since she was one of his favorite targets. He made a habit of asking her to explain a problem, then mocking her mistakes. Normally a social butterfly, she became withdrawn and distant. Her smiles grew rarer.

Although the students hated Mr. Hammond, the parents did not. He pretended to have a sympathetic ear. He encouraged my parents to get Evie tested for ADHD, saying with false concern, "I don't think she's learned a single thing this year."

Our parents disagreed. "There's nothing wrong with her. She's just distracted," Dad stated.

If anything, after that, Mr. Hammond treated Evie worse.

I hated him on Evie's behalf. He knew I was her sister. Every so often when I passed him in the halls, I swear he sneered at me. Now, I can admit that I probably imagined that. But I didn't imagine his cruelty to Evie.

In high school, her math grades were straight C's. I can't count how many times I suggested to my parents that I tutor her. She refused to accept help. "I'm bad at math," she said. "That's it."

I underestimated how deeply Mr. Hammond's words had cut. He made her believe she was stupid. He made her believe it was better not to try at all.

Hailey tilts her head. "I think I remember him. He had bad breath, right?"

"You could smell it from the back row," Mikayla confirms.

"Do you really think that the giant is Mr. Hammond?" Khalil asks, keeping us on topic.

"It is not him," I correct. "It is more like a representation of him. A caricature. This may be consistent with what Primera told us."

Mikayla shifts her weight from one foot to the other. Her bracelet—her token—catches a thread of light from a crack in the wall and glows silver. "What do you mean?" she asks.

"Primera told us that the Red Court grew strong on Evie's fears and pain. My sister's experience with Mr. Hammond affected her for years. Maybe Primera took that memory from her, and it manifested in Meer as the giant."

"If what you say is true...then do you think Primera is a representation of someone in Evie's life?" Khalil asks.

"It's possible," I say. "I'm not sure who it would be, though."

"You could ask the giant," Hailey teases.

"I'd rather not," I say, grimacing.

Khalil thumbs the thin bronze chain of his pocket watch. In the dark, the token has a faint glow. "Regardless of whether your theory is true, memories definitely hold power in Meer. And Primera has some of our worst ones."

"She's holding them hostage," Mikayla speculates. "She'll probably use them against us."

"Blackmail?" Khalil wonders.

"Maybe. But if our memories are so powerful, I bet she's got other plans for them."

My stomach sinks. If the others learn about the things I said to Evie…they may view me with suspicion, even though I didn't have any part in my sister's death.

I take a lungful of the tunnel's musty air. "We'll stop her. She's only a Pawn."

"But so are you," Hailey says.

"I won't be one for long."

Hailey glares at the floor. "Oh, right. Then you'll be our Queen. Above everyone and anyone."

I startle at the hard edge in her voice. There isn't enough light in the tunnel to read her expression. All I can make out is her rigid silhouette and her clenched hands.

I'm not sure what kind of conclusions she has jumped to. Maybe she assumes I am trying to replace Evie. I'm not. All I want is to end this game and go back to my normal life. That's what she should want, too.

Khalil clears his throat. "If Primera knows that you intend to become Queen, Alice, then maybe the Red King and Queen know too. What if this is what they want? What if we're playing into their trap?"

"The Lady of the Moon said I'd gain my sister's crown," I say with more certainty than I feel. "I believe her."

Hailey pushes away from the wall. "How will you become Queen? Do you have a plan?"

My lips tighten. It's difficult to plan ahead when I'm encountering one near-death escape after another. The skepticism in her questions doesn't help.

"My plan is to escape before the giant plugs up this mousehole and traps us here forever," I say, tone clipped.

Hailey sweeps an arm at me. "All right. Then lead the way, *Compass.*"

What is her problem with me?

"Don't call her that!" Mikayla interjects.

"It's fine," I say. "It's still better than A-Plus Alice."

There follows an infinitely more awkward pause.

"People call you that?" Khalil asks, eventually.

I turn away from them even though they can't see my face burning in the dark.

In middle school, I was shunned after I skipped a grade. My new classmates called me a "try-hard" and a "know-it-all". They ignored me during class discussions. Whenever there were group projects, I prayed that the teacher would choose our partners. Otherwise, no one would choose me.

My thoughts are interrupted by the sound of something dragging across the floor behind me.

I whirl, heart pounding in my chest. A scream catches in my throat as a mouse the size of a rhino lumbers into our section of the tunnel. Its whiskers snuffle in our direction. It wears a jockey cap and...fingerless gloves? The shadows must be playing tricks on my eyes.

Hailey inhales sharply, as if she's going to scream. Mikayla claps a hand over her mouth.

The mouse trudges past. Its long yellow nails scratch the

dirt, shredding my already frayed nerves. A thick rope of a tail slithers in its wake.

As soon as the mouse is out of sight, Mikayla drops her palm from Hailey's face. "I can't believe you licked my hand!" she complains.

Hailey puts her hands on her hips. "You held me against my will!"

"Hey, it could've been worse," Khalil says, nodding at the trail the mouse left in the dirt. "It could have been a tarantula."

We collectively shudder.

Hailey smacks her palm against her forehead. "Great, now you've jinxed us."

"Let's hope not," I reply. "I don't plan to stick around long enough to find out what else lives here."

My compass leads us further through the mousehole. Fortunately, we encounter no more huge creatures—mice or otherwise. The crunch of gravel under our shoes sounds disproportionately loud. I hope the giant cannot hear it.

Finally, a thin line of light appears ahead—stronger than the weak beams that have crept through the cracked walls.

I hold out my arm, warning the others to stay back. I creep toward the mousehole's exit. Holding my breath, I peek out.

Heat skims my face. Twenty yards away, small flames sputter behind the gate of the fireplace. The giant must have stirred the embers in our absence.

Hamwishbone sits at the table in the middle of the cabin. With a knife the size of an aircraft carrier, he whittles a piece of wood into an object resembling a comb. He breaks off a splinter and uses it as a toothpick. His swamp-green eyes are fixed on the mousehole where we escaped, by the window on the opposite side of the hut.

I cast my senses out like a net. My compass tells me where to go.

No. That can't be right.

But as I continue to scan our escape routes, I can't deny where the arrow of my compass leads.

I return to my companions. "We have to go into the fireplace," I whisper.

Hailey's eyes widen, then she huffs a laugh. "You're joking."

"I know it sounds strange—"

"Strange?" she hisses. "We're going to burn to a crisp!"

I hold up a hand. "Look, you'll have to trust me. We weren't hurt when we walked through the wall of the Moon. I'm sure we won't be hurt by the flames, either, as long as everyone stays close to me."

"I've faced worse odds," Mikayla says, rolling her neck from side to side. Her brown eyes have a steely glint. "Let's go"

"How are we going to do this?" Khalil says softly.

I match his tone. "Run—on my mark."

I peer into the enormous room. The giant flings his toothpick to the floor and releases a belch. Even from the safety of the mousehole, my eyes water at the stench. He picks up his knife and whittles his comb.

It's a given that Hamwishbone is going to see us. The real question is whether we can escape before he catches up.

"Whatever you do," I say, "don't stop. *Now.*"

We sprint toward the fireplace.

Our footsteps arouse Hamwishbone's attention. He rises with a gleeful bellow, kicking back his chair. It topples to the floor, the impact rattling my teeth. My vision swims, or maybe it's the heated haze of the fireplace.

I put on a spurt of speed. Twenty yards turns into ten. Then five.

The others are close on my heels. I don't stop to look at them as I scramble through the fireplace's metal gate. Heat sears my skin.

Hailey cries out. She trips on the gate and goes down hard into a heap of ash. A flash of silver tumbles from her pocket.

"Hailey!" Khalil shouts. He starts toward her.

A missile of iron smashes into the cinders beside me, sending up a volcanic blast. Hot waves of black billow into my face. I choke.

We scatter as the giant stabs the fireplace poker at us.

Flames erupt, sweeping over the exposed skin on my legs and arms. I brace myself for the blistering pain of a burn but it doesn't come. Instead, the fire curls over my skin as if I'm not there at all.

Hamwishbone cackles. He raises the poker. "Come back! I still haven't proved if you're real!"

"Shut up," Mikayla growls. She steps out of the smoke, reaching for my hand. Soot stains her forehead. At the same time, Khalil stumbles to my side.

"Where's Hailey?" he asks, his dark eyes wide with panic. Smoke curls from the sleeves of his once-white shirt. "I lost her!"

Mikayla points. "There!"

About twelve feet away from us, Hailey kneels amidst the embers. I barely make out the green-blue sheen of her peacock earring. She sifts through the ashes, scrabbling against the bottom of the fireplace.

"What are you doing?" Mikayla screams. "Come on!"

"I lost something!" Hailey shouts back.

"Leave it!"

"I can't—Oh!"

Her lips stretch in a triumphant grin. She clutches her left fist to her chest. Silver flashes. "Got it!"

I grab Khalil's hand. My gut tugs with the presence of my compass.

"Hurry!" I call to her.

She lurches to her feet and runs toward us.

I don't know if she makes it to us in time. Everything turns sideways and fades into the same color as the smoke.

The gray void descends on us with a crushing embrace. The silhouettes of my companions look as though they're sinking through water. Khalil's and Mikayla's eyes are closed. Their chests are unmoving.

Panic tears through me. *Let us through!*

When I reach out, something reaches back.

CHAPTER 17

THE WORST ARGUMENT between Evie and my parents started with my name.

At least, that's what I first overheard.

Although Mom and Dad had closed Evie's bedroom door behind them, my sister's voice, clear and stubborn, filtered through the wood.

"Alice doesn't need my example. She's doing well enough on her own. You've made sure of that."

Dad released a loud sigh. The floorboards creaked. I pictured him pacing back and forth by the wall like he did when he was frustrated. "You imagine so many things. Why not consider what you could be like if you applied yourself more?"

"I know what that means. I'm not like Alice, so don't try to make me like her."

"We know you have different strengths. You're unique in your own way—"

Evie groaned. "Not this again!"

"Genevieve," Dad said. Her full name was a warning that she obeyed in sullen silence.

"You need to ensure your future," Mom said. "You need to try harder in school."

"All I do is try!" There was a loud thump followed by a clatter, as if she'd smacked her desk and knocked over a jar of paintbrushes. "I'm not as smart as Alice. But I can figure out my future for myself."

Mom's words sounded strained. "You have to plan. You can't barge blindly into things. It's foolish."

Evie's voice rose. "Oh, so I'm stupid now?"

"Enough!" Dad shouted.

I flinched. I'd never heard Evie accuse our parents of such things. And I had never heard either of my parents raise their voices like that at us.

Dad's tone softened. "Your mother and I want the best for you, Evie. You can attend a good college if you improve your grades."

"Schools don't judge you based only on grades nowadays," Evie argued. "They also look at clubs, creative projects, personality…"

"Imagine going to a school because you have a good personality," Dad scoffed. "Merit predicts success better than anything. Grades are important."

Mom cut in, "She can put her painting business on her college applications. I've been telling her all the time that she should advertise herself more."

"I don't want my art to become a bullet-point on my resume," Evie objected.

"Then why are you doing it?"

"It's not about the money. It's about the art, and sharing it with people."

"Hmm." Mom sounded less than convinced. "Well, start

thinking about where you want to apply for college. Mrs. Wei's son goes to Brown University. I can ask her—"

"No," my sister said. "I'm not going there."

"All we're asking you to do is explore," Dad said. "You're running out of time."

"It's already too late. No Ivy League university is going to accept me, and you know it—"

"You can get into any school if you are motivated enough," he interrupted. His syllables became choppy, slipping out of the usual smooth cadence of his English. "Don't be stubborn. We understand what you are capable of."

"If you're so set on me going to college, can't we compromise? I'll go to community college."

A long pause.

"Community college?" Mom said. The two words held a world of derision.

Evie stumbled over her words. "I…it's more cost-effective. It helps me figure out what I want to do, long-term. And…"

The pitch of Mom's vowels turned flat, as it did when she was upset. "Anyone can get into community college. You want to be another face in the crowd?"

"I can do two years at a community college, then transfer," Evie suggested half-heartedly.

"It's not enough!" A strange note rang in Dad's tone. It took me a second to figure out it was.

Fear.

Mom drew in a breath. Her voice was slightly more measured when she said, "Evie, you are confused about what you want and what you need. You must listen to us. We left our families and our lives in Hong Kong. Why?"

"So you could find your American Dream," Evie said.

I wished I could elbow her and tell her to have some

respect. *We are the daughters of immigrants. So much hope rests on us. And we are lucky to have more choices than our parents—because our parents worked hard to give us those choices.*

I held my breath, waiting for Mom to continue. She and Dad never discussed our relatives, especially our grandparents.

"We chose to leave because we dreamed of something better—not just for ourselves, but also for you and Alice," Mom said.

"I have dreams, too," Evie replied. "But they're different from yours…"

Mom spoke over her. "A dream isn't as easy as wanting something. A dream changes the people you won't grow old to know."

"Okay, I get it. I'm disappointing you."

"Don't put words in our mouths," Dad said.

Something thudded against the wall. "You're talking *at* me, not with me. Listen, okay? I don't want to be an accountant or a doctor or an engineer. That would never make me happy. I need a career that I look forward to, even if it's not 'stable.' I want to do what I love for a living."

"That's a privilege that not many have," Mom warned. "You can't afford to gamble everything on it."

"I know. That's why I'll make it happen."

Dad sighed. I pictured him removing his glasses and pinching the bridge of his nose. "Genevieve, we only want the best for you."

"That's funny, because I'm not sure you do."

"Don't be so difficult." Mom's voice turned sulky. "You're behaving like Mikayla. That girl is a bad influence on you."

"I'm done with this conversation," Evie said. "Get out."

"Evie—" Dad began.

"Now!" she shouted.

A chair's legs scraped against the floor.

"We will continue this talk later. Then, you may see things differently," my father said.

It sounded like a threat.

The door creaked open. Footsteps entered the hallway.

From the safety of my room, I released my breath, glad that they had stopped raising their voices. The argument was bad, but it could have been worse.

"She has so much potential," Mom murmured to Dad outside my bedroom.

"If only she…" he replied.

The rest of their exchange was lost as they left.

CHAPTER 18

EVIE IS GRIPPING my hand as she leads me into my room.

I feel a stab of wrongness, though I can't fathom why. She looks the same as always. Her long black hair falls in a braid over her shoulder. She wears a loose yellow tank top over paint-stained denim shorts. I examine her hand in mine. She wears multiple pieces of jewelry, of Mikayla's making and her own: pastel clay rings, gold beaded rings, friendship bracelets…

Strange. The silver bracelet that Mikayla gave her is missing. I've never seen her take it off.

Evie releases my palm and perches on the blue throw blanket folded at the corner of my bed. Her posture is iron-rod straight. Something nags at the back of my mind as I remain standing in front of her.

My sister never merely sits. She sprawls in increasingly ridiculous positions that cause Mom to close her eyes and shake her head. Slouching is one of the few childhood habits that Evie didn't break, along with daydreaming and nail-biting.

"Is something wrong?" I ask.

"Funny you should say that," she says with a smile. But her lips stretch too wide, and her teeth don't show.

I frown at her. "Why are you here?"

"I'm not here…not really. Neither are you. Actually, you're in the Elsewhere: in-between. That means I can talk to you."

Shadows gather in the corners of my room. The image of my sister sways like a mirage. "I…I have no idea what you're talking about," I manage to say.

Her eyes sharpen. "This is not a dream. You can't dream in Meer."

Meer. That one word evokes all my memories of labyrinthine corridors and the shadowed spaces that exist as nightmares. Cold clarity rushes back to me.

I stare at my sister. Her living flesh. Her warmth.

It can't be her. She's dead. I saw her casket lowered into the ground.

But I can't dream in Meer, either. How do I know what to believe?

It doesn't matter. At least I have a chance to loosen the knot of grief that has been in my heart these past two months.

"Evie," I say, my voice fraying. "I'm so sorry."

Her mouth quivers. She doesn't meet my gaze.

I lean forward, awaiting her response.

Finally, she throws back her head and laughs. I flinch. The sound is high-pitched. Jeering. She laughs so hard, tears shine in her eyes.

"Do you actually expect three measly words will fix everything?" she says. "Don't say things you don't mean. You haven't earned that right."

My lips part. No reply comes to mind.

It occurs to me that, all the times I apologized to Evie in my thoughts or my dreams…I never imagined what she would say in response. I did not anticipate that she would meet me with anything except gentle understanding.

This Evie—bitter and cruel—is not the kind, dreamy sister I remember.

She wipes a tear from her cheek. A mask of cold scorn replaces her amusement. "I brought you here because you screwed everything up."

"I don't know what you mean," I whisper. "I only ever did my best."

"Maybe your best isn't good enough." She tips her head. "Remember that? I do."

Defiance overwhelms my shock. Is this really Evie? Could this be some shadow creation of Meer, trying to ensnare me by wearing her likeness?

I can think of one way to determine whether this is true.

"What happened the night you died?" I ask softly. "What *really* happened?"

She stills, then averts her gaze to her lap. "You were there, Alice. You know."

"But I don't remember!" My hands form fists, my nails digging into my scars.

"I never left Meer."

"Then—" I can't quite grasp what she is saying. "You're here?"

"I went from being a Queen to being a ghost. Because of *her*," she spits.

Her. The one person I can think of is…

"Did the Red Queen cause your death?" I ask.

"She—" Evie gulps, her eyes widening. Her mouth works uselessly. She cradles her head in her hands.

"I can't betray her," she pants. "I can't say."

"Can you tell me if she killed you?" I press.

"She promised she wouldn't leave me. She lied, like all the others. She made my paradise into a prison." Evie's close-lipped smile turns into a warped, toothy grin. Her eyes glow with a feverish sheen. "Come on, Alice. I thought you were supposed to be the smart one."

Despite myself, I reply, "And I thought you were supposed to be the understanding one."

She raises her hands. "You know more about games than I do. You're so good at playing them. But you forgot the most important rule of chess."

"What's that?"

"Only strategy breaks a stalemate."

I resist the urge to scoff. If a chess game ends in a stalemate, it's a draw. She's talking nonsense.

A hint of her real smile returns to her face: the one that lifts slightly off-center so that it resembles a smirk. It falls just as quickly.

Her shoulders slump. She reaches for me. "I wish it didn't have to be like this, Alice."

I regard her outstretched hand warily.

Her dark eyes are beseeching. "I'm sorry for what I said. I really am. Please…come here. For me."

In spite of my misgivings, I do.

I don't mean to hug her, and yet my arms twist around her torso. She strokes my back as I bury my neck in the crook of her shoulder. Her voice brushes past my ear.

"The murdered comforting the murderer," she muses. "How ironic."

Murderer?

"What?" I rear back. Cold air rushes into the space between us.

"I felt dead a while before I died," she says. All of the light left in her eyes has vanished. "You trapped me, too, you know. So did *she*. So did everyone else."

"Then let me fix things," I say, my words blurring into each other. "I can find you and free you, wherever you are. I can…"

"Do what? Save me?" Her expression hardens. "Here's some advice. Don't."

"But—you're imprisoned. You don't want to be freed?"

"I chose this prison. I'll stay here forever and then longer." She cocks her head. "I can't hold you in-between much longer. It's time for you to go. The Elsewhere will take you back."

Around me, the room fades. That should not be surprising, seeing that we were never there at all.

The gray veil between the shadowed lands, the home of echoes and ghosts, descends to tear me away from my sister.

"Wait!" I cry. My words are muffled, as if I am underwater. "I don't want to leave yet!"

There is still so much I do not know. There is still so much I want to say.

Evie replies, "Oh, I think you do. Otherwise you'll end up like me…and you've never wanted to be like me, have you?"

The edges of her face blur. Gray rivulets cascade around me like tears.

My lips barely manage to form the last question on my mind. "Evie—where's the bracelet Mikayla gave you?"

Her words chase me into the Elsewhere.

"I've had many things taken from me. That's just another."

CHAPTER 19

MY SHOES SINK into soft, damp dirt. My left hand curls around something slender and brittle.

Gradually, my eyes adjust to the low light. I'm holding onto a sapling with ash-colored bark and dark foliage. The trees surrounding me are identical to it. The branches interweave, blocking out any sun that might be present. The forest I'm in stretches as far as the eye can see.

How did I get here?

My companions and I escaped Hamwishbone's hut. We emerged into the unending gray veil. Then something pulled me away.

No, not something. Someone.

This is not a dream. The sentence echoes in my mind, accompanied by the memory of Evie's face.

Her smile. It was wrong. Why was it wrong?

She was missing her silver bracelet. I'm not sure why that detail, of all things, sticks out to me.

Bits and pieces of conversation spiral through my skull. My legs waver. I'm glad I'm gripping the tree.

She told me about her death—or rather, her imprisonment

in Meer. She didn't want to be freed. What hits me the hardest, though, is that she didn't want me to find her.

My gut churns as I remember her sneer at my attempted apology. I want to be angry, but part of me wonders if I deserved her reaction.

I step away from the tree. My shoe crunches on a twig. I wince. The sound is as loud as a gunshot.

It's too quiet here. Where are the others? Were we separated in the gray veil between the shadowed lands?

"Mikayla?" I call. "Khalil? Hailey?"

My words are deadened, as if the trees are absorbing all noise. I can't help but recall the Labyrinth's similar suppression of my voice.

My compass pricks to life in my chest, pointing me forward. *You must continue*, it tells me. *Leave the forest.*

Wherever the others are, I will not find them here.

I walk through the dense woods and call their names at intervals. I am careful not to raise my voice too loudly. So far, nothing living has shown its face, but that doesn't mean I won't attract unwanted attention. Heavy, humid air sticks my hair to my forehead and neck, its almost sweet tang reminding me of the Nacre Coast.

Gazing at the trees, I think of *Peter Pan* and how the Lost Boys built a house for Wendy in the woods.

I haven't thought about that novel in years. My parents used to read it to Evie and me before bedtime, to practice their English and spend time with us.

Peter Pan was Evie's favorite story. No matter how many times she heard it, she had the same curious gleam in her eye and the same dreamy smile on her face—until the ending. Whenever Mom or Dad narrated Wendy's choice to grow up, a pout rose on my sister's face.

"I don't like that ending," she said once. "It's too sad. It's not true."

"Of course it's true," Dad said gravely, patting the slim green hardcover. "It's in the book."

She crossed her arms. "I don't believe Wendy would become a grownup. She loved Neverland and Peter too much."

"Her daughter goes to Neverland, and her daughter's daughter goes to Neverland too," I said. "They all get adventures with Peter."

"But Wendy never gets another adventure! It's not fair."

Mom smoothed her hair. "Many things aren't fair, Evie."

"The author is wrong," Evie insisted. "Wendy didn't need to leave Neverland because she had a family there."

"What about her real family?" I asked. "Her mom and dad missed her."

She cocked her head. Uncertainty flickered in her eyes. "Oh. Well…"

"It was time for Wendy and her brothers to go back," Dad said. "That's all."

Evie nodded, a troubled expression on her face.

I wonder how much Evie identified with Wendy. She had her own Neverland, of sorts.

Evie told me in the in-between—the *Elsewhere*, she called it—that she never left Meer. She called herself a ghost. I don't believe in ghosts, but the desolation of these woods tempts me to think otherwise. I scan the trees, half-expecting a mirage to appear.

As if on cue, the brambles of a nearby scarlet hawthorn bush crack. Something scuffles inside.

On instinct, I duck into a crouch. My arm shoots out, finding a knobbly tree branch. I grip it with trembling hands.

The branches of the hawthorn bend and sway. Twigs break.

A brown-streaked, furry head pops out from the bush and regards me with narrow eyes.

"Took you long enough to find me," Dinah says. She shakes herself, rattling her bow-shaped collar.

I relax. "Dinah! What are you doing here?"

She swaggers out from the thicket. Her fur is matted with dirt and thorns, though it doesn't seem to bother her. "I couldn't leave you by yourself. You're useless without me."

"Nice to see you too."

"Did you worry about me? You shouldn't have. I didn't worry about *you*."

"Thanks," I say dryly.

"Don't be so sensitive." She casts a sideways glance at me. "What's the sword for?"

"I don't have a—" I cut off as I realize I am in fact holding a sword.

Its ivory hilt is embedded with diamonds. I remove the sheath, and the freshly polished blade flashes in my face. The weight is awkward in my hands—far too heavy. A bolt of pain shoots through my wrist, nearly making me drop the sword. I hastily sheathe the blade.

"I think this is the *least* strange thing that has happened to me since I came to Meer," I muse.

Dinah licks her paw, indifferent. "Where are we going?"

"I'm not sure. My compass is leading me out of the forest, I think."

She flattens her ears against her head, pawing at the grass. "I don't like the smell of this place. Let's go."

I'm all too happy to comply with her command.

Time is difficult in Meer. I have a good mind for estimates, but without sunlight, I can't tell how long we walk for. Perhaps an hour or so.

I keep a careful eye on our surroundings. Though I can't shake the feeling that I'm walking in circles, we never encounter the same landmark twice: a carving of twin hearts pierced with an arrow in a rotting tree, a multicolored mushroom twice as tall as I am, and a series of stepping stones that lead the two of us up a grass-lined slope.

Dinah is stubbornly tight-lipped when I ask her where she has been.

"Places," she answers.

I suppress a sigh. "Were you in the shadowed lands?"

"Of course not. That's for you four to deal with."

"Wow, thanks."

"What? It's your quest, not mine." She pauses at the top of the slope, lowering her nose to the ground.

I wait for her. "Do you know what happened to the Lady of the Moon?"

"No. You ask too many questions."

"I'm trying to gather information..."

I trail off as I realize she's sniffing at a broken shard of pottery. Where did that come from?

A chill sweeps down my spine. I raise my gaze. The slope we are standing on opens into a clearing. I do not know what to make of the sight that awaits.

A makeshift table made from weathered planks is aligned over a fallen, scorched tree. Around the table stand crooked tree stumps that act as chairs.

My lips move silently as I count the stumps. *Fifteen, sixteen, seventeen.*

The table is a mess. Porcelain cups are either placed in haphazard stacks or tipped over. A blue china teapot lies cracked on its side. Brown liquid has dried at the spout, staining the crumpled lace tablecloth. The chipped plates are covered with foul-smelling crumbs and stiff curds that look disturbingly like human finger bones. Tarnished forks and knives are scattered across the stumps and the ground. Many are bent at odd angles.

It's the oddest tea party I've ever seen.

Shadows pool in the forest canopy. Light flashes in my peripheral vision. When I turn, nothing's there. My eyes must be playing tricks on me.

We can't delay here anymore. We need to find the others.

"Come on," I tell Dinah. "Let's keep going."

Then something hisses near my head.

I jerk away, heart pounding in my throat. I search the branches of the tree I was standing under. They are completely still.

Dinah's ears flatten against her head, and she hides behind my leg. "Did you hear that?"

"Hear what?" I start to say until the noise reaches me: panting and repetitive. It sounds a little like…well, laughter.

"It's only the wind," I say, trying to sound confident.

Something cold and smooth brushes the side of my neck. I swat at the sensation absently. My fingers come away with a thin line of red.

I stare at it, uncomprehending. A branch must have scratched me when I wasn't paying attention.

But I'm not standing near the tree anymore.

"*Do not run…It will make things easier.*"

The voice by my ear has the rasp of an ignited match.

I don't think. I react.

My feet fly over the uneven terrain. Branches scrape at my elbows. I ignore them. I must run while I still can. I must live to tell the tale.

I trip on the sprawling roots of a gnarled tree.

The impact knocks the breath out of me. I pick myself up, heart racing. The hem of my dress is caked in mud. A sword clangs to the ground beside me. That's curious. I'd forgotten I carried it.

I unsheathe it and point it at the shadowed trees.

Dinah circles my feet. Her tail is coiled tightly. "What happened?" she asks.

"I don't…I'm not sure." I keep my gaze focused for any signs of movement in the forest. The blade quivers in my hand. "Someone is here."

"I don't smell any humans. Except you, obviously."

A terrible thought occurs to me. Evie said that she was a ghost. Is it possible that she's haunting this forest right now?

I cannot bring myself to believe it. She was angry with me, but she wouldn't toy with me like this. At least, I hope she wouldn't.

My cat sits on her haunches. "We're lost, aren't we?"

I barely keep the impatience out of my words. "No, we're not. I'm leading us. I have a compass."

"You do?" Dinah's head tilts.

I don't disguise a sigh as I roll my eyes. "Yes. I told you that a few minutes ago."

"Hmm." She licks her paw. "Where's our next stop?"

I search for the guidance of my compass, but its warmth slips out of my reach. *Strange.* My fingers curl into fists. "I don't know yet. Hush. I'm trying to focus."

Dinah twitches her tail. "So we are lost."

"I just said we weren't!"

One of her ears pricks. "Did you?"

Something is wrong, my brain insists. *You should leave.*

My sword wavers as I peer into the endless swathe of trees. Vertigo upends my perspective. The forest's shadows encroach on where I stand. The tree branches resemble long-fingered hands, reaching for me.

"Evie," I murmur. "Are you there?"

No reply comes, although I don't expect one.

"Who is Evie?" Dinah asks.

I stare at her. Surely she is playing with me. She can't be serious.

But as the seconds drag on and her bright eyes don't veer from my face, I realize she is. My stomach sinks.

"'Who is Evie?'" I repeat. "You've known her longer than you've known me. My family adopted you when you were three years old."

"You're her sister?"

A disbelieving huff escapes me. "Yes! I take care of you more than she did!"

"Oh." She cocks her head. "What's your name?"

"What do you mean you don't remember my name?" I turn on her. "It's—"

Blood roars in my ears. My lips part. I can recall the shape of my name on my tongue. So why can't I form it?

I close my eyes, reaching for the letters. They slip out of my hands, except—

"L," I say at last. "I think my name starts with an L."

My voice curls up at the end, making it sound more like a question.

She licks her paw, smoothing it over her head. "Well, are we lost?"

I glare at her and open my mouth.

Until I realize I cannot find the space that her name occupies.

I balk. How is that possible? I was about to say it.

"I…what's your name?" I ask weakly. "I'll recognize it when I hear it."

"How funny. I don't know, either! Look at us, a bunch of know-nothings."

I fold my arms. "I still know plenty of things. Names are the least of them."

"Like what?" the cat challenges.

I need something simple to remember. Maybe a song, or a nursery rhyme. I clear my throat and recite,

> *"Falling up the rabbit hole or flying underland—*
> *'Twas once is now but never was*
> *And shows a winning hand.*
>
> *Hist'ry knows that castles crumble into pretty dust—*
> *That cats and cabbages and kings*
> *And all the rest are rust.*
>
> *Want some change? Well, here's the cents, we know it's*
> *quite a lot*
> *For we don't haggle here—you leave*
> *With nonsense or with naught."*

The cat's tail swishes. "I like the part about cats. Did you know that a cat may look at a king? That's in a book, so you *know* it's true."

I'm too busy trying to figure out why my words are different. Twisted. I meant to say something else, but for the life of me, I can't remember what it was.

Movement flickers in my peripheral vision.

The brambles of the forest press towards me, thorns

bristling. Branches grasp for my dress. One catches on my hair. I yank away, searching for a way out. I'm backed up against a tree.

While I'm distracted, the distorted limbs move with impossible speed, weaving into the bars of a living cage.

The cat yowls in terror. She squeezes between the twisting sticks and vines in a flash of brown-and-white fur. Pale hairs snag in the thorns.

Heart in my throat, I stagger back. My hand tightens on my sword. I prepare to swing the blade at the advancing brambles.

The gnarled hilt digs into the scars on my palm. The sword suddenly seems heavier. My arm bows under its weight.

I glance down. I'm holding a knobbly tree branch, its rough bark scraping against my skin.

A frustrated cry tears from my throat. I hurl the bough to the ground and thrust my hands out, as if I can fend off the brambles through sheer willpower alone. Offshoots of thorns rip my dress, my hair, and the exposed skin on my arms.

Black spots swim through my vision. My knees give way, and I sink to the base of the tree.

Perhaps I will lie here long enough to grow into the earth of this forest. Until anyone who knows me forgets my deeds.

Did I do anything worth memorializing?

My cheek rests against the damp, sticky roots. I close my eyes. It will be nice to rest for a change.

I have nothing more to do. I have served a purpose that I no longer recall.

Cold hands encircle mine.

The rasping voice follows me into unconsciousness.

"Welcome, Alice. We have been waiting for you."

CHAPTER 20

WHEN I OPEN my eyes, I half-expect to find myself in the Elsewhere again.

Instead of gray, I'm met with pure, overwhelming white light. The ceiling, the walls, and even the bed I am lying in threaten to blind me. I close my eyes against a wave of dizziness. My breath catches.

I remember waking up in a similar room months ago... though nowhere near as calmly.

Where's Evie? Where are you keeping her? I screamed when I came to in the hospital, struggling against the doctors who restrained me.

They didn't want my parents to intervene. Mom spoke anyway. She stood in the corner, leaning on my father.

Evie is dead, she said.

And it had to be true, because I had never seen my mother cry like that, her entire body shuddering until she couldn't stand up straight.

I swallow the lump in my throat and sit up among the plush pillows. The room has a faint, sickly sweet odor, like musty perfume—not the sterile smell of the hospital. I draw it deep into my lungs.

My bed is the one piece of furniture in the space. There are no windows. The bright light comes from a single daisy-patterned floor lamp in the corner. It looks a little like the lamp in Evie's room at home…but that must be a coincidence.

Where am I? Where are the others?

I hope I did not lose them in the Elsewhere. I remember trekking through a dark forest…I met my cat for the first time since the Moon. She disappeared again. I can't quite recall why, nor can I recall how I ended up here.

Beyond the door, I catch scraps of voices, distant and sibilant. My pulse races. Are those my friends? Perhaps they found me and brought me to this place.

I slip out of bed, wincing at the mud that smears from my dress onto the pure-white blanket and sheets. Pulling on my grimy shoes, I open the door of the room. It gives way with a terrible creak. I start forward, then grip the doorframe, overcome by vertigo.

When my vision settles, I creep into the hall. The floor has a checkered red-and-white pattern: each square is roughly the length of my foot. For some reason, I adjust my stride so that each step lands inside the squares. I feel like a superstitious child trying to avoid cracks in the sidewalk.

The wallpaper is the same as in my house: a shade of robin's egg blue paired with cream trim. Scattered over the walls are picture frames identical to the ones in the living room of my own home. The only difference is that these frames are missing photos.

I would accept it as a coincidence, except I don't believe in coincidences.

I approach the grand golden frame at the center of the

arrangement. In my house, this frame would hold the most recent Lee family photo, which was taken last November. Though it's absent now, I can picture the four of us smiling at the camera. My mother's hand is on my shoulder. My father's is on Evie's. In that photo, I always notice the distance in Evie's eyes. The stiffness of my mother's posture. The strained edge to my father's smile.

Unconsciously, my hand drifts toward the empty golden frame.

That's a mistake.

When I touch it, a vision assaults me.

Shadows shifted on the porch swing of the house.

The paint job was probably once white but had since acquired a sickly yellow hue. A riot of laughter and light overflowed inside the house. Outside, the smell of smoke was rivaled by the stench of the swamp beyond. No frogs sang from the wetland, though that was expected on an autumn evening like this one.

One of the shadows muttered, "I don't know what you want me to say."

The voice belonged to Evie.

"Talk to me," the other one pleaded. That was Mikayla.

"After you march me out here and start accusing me of things?" Evie said.

"I just want to know what's going on. Why have you been acting off lately?"

"Why don't you tell me? You're the one who's fishing for an answer."

"All right, then." Mikayla's voice hardened. "What are you on?"

"What are you talking about?"

"I need to know if you've been...using. I can't help you if you don't tell me."

"What does..." Evie choked on a laugh. "Wait. You think I'm doing drugs?"

The waver in Mikayla's words became all the more obvious when she asked, "You're not?"

"Of course not! I don't need pills or crazy ground-up powder to see things. People who use that see a fraction of what I see, anyway. They sense the colors, the textures, the sounds. But I live in another world. And I can do it without anything or anyone!"

When her shout stopped echoing into the swamp, Mikayla spoke.

"Evie...why did you ask me to come to this party with you?"

Evie laughed again, low and harsh. "I didn't come here to do drugs. I just want to get away. You, of all people, should understand." She sagged. Her voice broke. "I want to go home."

"My car is out front."

"No! I don't want to go back to my house. I want to go home. To Meer."

"And then what?" Mikayla asked. "When will you come back to Earth?"

"I don't know!" Evie snapped. She cradled her head. Her breath came in rapid pants. "I don't know," she repeated more quietly.

"Each time you go to Meer, you stay longer and longer. Don't think I haven't noticed."

"Does it matter? Time barely passes."

"Of course it matters. Evie, you can't leave Earth every time something bad happens. It doesn't fix things."

"It's enough." Evie rose from the swing. "I can't do this anymore."

Mikayla's reply was interrupted by the sound of tires. It came from the gravel driveway on the other side of the house.

Red and blue lights punctured the night.

The vision recedes as sharply as it came.

I recoil from the empty golden frame. My breathing is harsh in my ears. My head swivels around the hallway, but no one is in sight.

I retreat from the frame until my back presses against the opposite wall.

Though I did not witness that scene in real life, I know when it happened. That night was the source of the tension in our family photo: the hairline cracks in Evie's relationship with my parents.

Last year, Mikayla and Evie went to a Halloween party that was broken up when a neighbor called the police with a noise complaint. The two panicked and fled the scene when sirens appeared. It didn't take long for the officers to intercept them.

Two hours past her 10 p.m. curfew, Evie came home. She missed nine calls and dozens of text messages. My parents begged her, and then yelled at her, to explain herself. She remained quiet. She gazed at them with a blank expression. Then she locked herself in her room.

Evie never talked about what exactly had happened at the party. Neither did Mikayla. Yet the vision showed me the scene as if I had been there with them.

Mikayla suspected Evie of using drugs. The thought is ludicrous. Evie and I both knew to leave drugs alone. Even a rumor of them could disgrace our careers—academic or athletic.

Evie wasn't addicted. Not in the sense of drugs, at least.

Her words echo in my mind. *I live in another* world.

An ache forms between my brows. I knead my forehead, thinking of what signs Mikayla might have misinterpreted. Perhaps it was Evie's listlessness during activities she once loved, like lacrosse. Maybe it was the constant circles under her eyes and the way she stopped putting effort into her appearance. Or maybe it was the distance that she allowed to fester between the people close to her.

I'm not sure I would have come to the same conclusion as Mikayla. Evie's behavior was more symptomatic of mental illness.

In my family, the term 'mental illness' exists only as an abstract concept. We are practical, grounded people. We are *normal.* Any other feeling indicates a personal fault.

I'm not sure how much I believe that anymore.

I thought I was losing my mind in the two months after Evie's death. When my hallucinations didn't stop, I blamed myself. But maybe all this time, the madness was as natural as a reflex, and I couldn't have stopped it any more than I could have stopped the tides from rising and falling.

Deep down, I still wonder if it was my fault—my weakness—because it is so much easier to pin blame on anything and anyone except yourself.

I've been paralyzed in the hallway for too long. With a shuddering breath, I turn my back on the picture frames and continue down the corridor.

It opens into a round dining room that has the same red-and-white checkered floor as the hallway. Painted red flowers and vines wind along the legs of a round cherrywood table. Two individuals occupy the chairs surrounding the table. One is hunched over the table. The other stares out the bay window.

It takes a moment for me to form words. "Mikayla? Khalil?"

Khalil swivels toward me, his eyes widening. "Alice!"

My lips form my name unconsciously. *Alice.* The syllables are so familiar, yet so foreign.

Next to him, Mikayla bursts from her chair. "You made it!"

She tackles me in a hug. I stiffen, unsure of how to respond, until she pulls back and punches my shoulder. "It's about time you showed up."

I study her. Tension melts from my shoulders. She looks none the worse for wear from our escape from Hamwishbone's fireplace, other than a few scratches on her collarbone. Her clothes are singed but are otherwise intact. Her silver token gleams on her wrist. Curiously, her knife is missing from its sheath.

"It's good to see you too," I say. "What happened to your knife?"

Her face sours. "Long story. I—"

"Alice!" Khalil hurries over. His shirt sleeves are charred, and soot smudges his jaw. The bronze chain of his pocket watch peeks out from a flap in his olive-colored vest.

"Thank goodness you're here," he says. "When we first got to the forest, we couldn't find you. The keepers of this inn brought you here not too long ago, but they wouldn't tell us anything."

"And they locked all the doors, so we couldn't search for you," Mikayla grumbles.

I mull over this new information. We are in an inn—not a house. With any luck, our stay won't be long. "Who are the innkeepers? And where's Hailey?"

Khalil's face falls. "You mean she's not with you?"

"No. I did run into Dinah, but then she vanished again." I try not to be bitter that my cat abandoned me at the first sign of danger…although I can't remember what that danger was.

"Hailey was falling behind in Hamwishbone's hut," Mikayla says. She twists the silver bracelet on her wrist. "Did she manage to get to us before we teleported?"

"I thought she did," Khalil says slowly. "I guess not, though."

I sit down heavily in the chair that he occupied. "Hailey could be anywhere right now. We have no way of locating her or helping her."

"Don't say that. We'll find her eventually."

I wish I could trust the optimism in Khalil's tone.

"For all we know, she's still in Hamwishbone's hut, or perhaps she's stuck in the Elsewhere," I reply.

"The Elsewhere?"

"It's the name of the void we travel through," I explain. "Evie told me."

He turns toward me, mouth parting in shock. "*Evie?*"

Behind him, Mikayla stiffens.

"I'll tell you everything," I promise. "After you tell me about the people who own this inn."

Mikayla grimaces. "I don't think you can call them *people*, really."

"Why do you say that?"

"Well—"

"Dinner is served!"

My blood freezes at the sound of two raspy voices merged into one.

I know those voices. I heard them in a physics lab just before glass shattered at my feet.

A short, plump man with a black mustache and a

thinning hairline enters the room, carrying a red-and-white checkered tablecloth on one arm and a set of dishware in the other. A woman follows him, her pleated golden skirts swishing beneath a red blouse. Her rosy cheeks appear painted on, like her smile.

The man and the woman are smiling from ear to ear. I realize with a shiver that their eyes are black. Not dark brown, but pure black—a darkness that invades the entire eye socket. No mote of light escapes or enters those irises.

I back away from the table. I don't recall standing. My shoulders collide with the blue-papered wall.

"Welcome to the Pins & Needles Inn," the man and woman say. "We are Mr. and Mrs. Knightley. We have been waiting for you! Let us serve you!"

My throat closes up. I clutch the chair for support.

"Alice, what's wrong?" Khalil whispers. "You look like you're going to faint."

I can only shake my head.

The three of us give the Knightleys a wide berth as they prepare dinner.

The couple follows the same choreographed routine as they did in my hallucination, laying the table in perfect unison. A blizzard of silverware and food crowds the cherry-wood surface until it is set for three.

The Knightleys back away from the table, arm-in-arm. They separate to whirl and bow to each other. A number of spins and promenades follow. The metronome in my head automatically switches on, even in the absence of music: *one, two, three, four, five, six, seven, eight.*

Mikayla's eyes are as round as the plates on the table. "Are they...square dancing?"

Khalil watches them closely. "Yup, they're doing a do-si-do. I had to learn it in middle school."

"Seems like cruel and unusual punishment."

I can't focus on their banter. I'm rooted to the spot as the Knightleys walk away from the table, their dance complete.

They face me. I meet their gazes, willing myself to remain calm even though my heart is threatening to drum its way out of my chest.

"Welcome!" they say. "We have waited so long, oh, so long, for new guests. We are happy to have you."

"Yes, thank you for saving us from the evil forest," Mikayla interrupts. "Can you perhaps point us to the Red King and Queen?"

The Knightleys' bodies swivel to her in unison. "What?"

"I apologize for my friend here," Khalil interjects, a note of warning in his tone. "She sometimes speaks without thinking."

They don't stop smiling. Maybe it is their permanent expression. Their voices echo loudly. "Of course! We hope you enjoy your stay! Please, sit, sit."

They push each of us into a chair with deceptive strength.

Mikayla tries to pull away from Mrs. Knightley, but the woman has an iron grip.

"Tell us if you would like more," they say in bright unison when we are seated.

Khalil gives them a polite smile. "I think we have plenty here, but thank you."

The table is heaped with more food than three people could possibly eat. Platters of finger sandwiches accompany a white-and-red teapot with diamonds and hearts patterning the spout. Ripe bananas, plums, and apples occupy two large crystal bowls. Oysters are artfully arranged across two platters. There's also a soup that I can't identify. It smells of brine, which reminds me unpleasantly of Conchae Maris. Dessert is a dark pudding embedded with pieces of strange fruit.

The Knightleys retreat to the edge of the room and clasp their hands over their stomachs.

Reluctantly, I pick up my spoon.

It clatters into my soup bowl.

A shriek catches in my throat. I feel like a hand is gripping my lungs.

Khalil's head whips toward me. "What's wrong?"

Mikayla is quicker on the uptake. She plucks the spoon from my bowl. Except for a slow exhale, she doesn't show her shock. She tilts it so that Khalil can see the words engraved in the silverware.

LET'S PRETEND.

I can't count how many times Evie said that phrase when we were children. It was her signal that we were starting a new game of pretend. I have not heard it in years.

"Do you need another spoon?" the Knightleys ask.

"No, it's fine," Mikayla answers for me. "She's just disoriented from waking up here, you know."

They nod. "Of course. The Nameless Forest can be unkind. How fortunate that we were there before it drained you completely."

"The Nameless Forest?" I ask, startled out of my stupor.

They regard me with those pitch-black eyes. Their mouths curl in too-large smiles. "It is a long and weary journey through the woods. We take in many visitors who need to rest. They enjoy their stay so much, they do not wish to leave."

"We're the only guests right now," Khalil notes.

"Yes. We have been waiting for you." They emit a series of harsh clicks that could be considered laughter. "How nice of you to come at last."

Even Khalil can't manage a smile at that.

As I stir my soup, I probe at my internal compass. *Which way do we go from here?* I ask.

I wait a few seconds, then a few minutes. Its warm, reassuring presence does not manifest. Unease curdles in my gut.

It could be nothing. Or I'm too thrown off by this place to concentrate...

Mikayla slides her plate to me. "Can you put some sandwiches on this? I can't reach them from over here."

This time, the message is engraved along the rim of the plate: DON'T SLOUCH. I can practically hear my mother saying it in my head. I automatically straighten. With trembling fingers, I scrape some sandwiches onto her plate and hand it back to her.

While the three of us maintain the appearance of eating, fears crowd my head. What if they have poisoned the meal? Or what if consuming the food enchants us to do their bidding?

Maybe at least the drinks are safe. I reach for a pitcher of lemonade until I read the message on the handle: LISTEN TO ME. My heart pounds. Abandoning the lemonade, I dry my clammy hands on an embroidered napkin, only to find the phrase, YOU'RE TOO OLD TO CRY, in its lacy spirals.

The Knightleys watch us in smiling silence. They do not seem to realize that we are pushing the food around on our plates and sipping from empty cups. Even if I'd been tempted by any of the dishes, I've lost my appetite ten times over. Now, I understand perfectly how the Pins & Needles Inn received its name.

"We're done here," Mikayla announces. Her chair legs scrape against the floor.

Khalil raises his head. He's been tying his napkin into knots. Its edge flashes out at me: DON'T BE UNGRATEFUL.

"Mik…" He assumes a calm, easy manner. "…is right. Thank you for your hospitality, but we are feeling a bit unwell. We need some time to ourselves, I think."

"Oh, no worries! None at all!" the Knightleys chirp.

They clear the table with the same efficiency as earlier, topping off their dance routine with a flourish.

"You may have the parlor!" they announce. Their lips, still stretched in eerie grins, barely move. "Second door on the left. If you need anything at all, please hesitate to ask."

Their simultaneous style of speaking still unsettles me.

"You mean, *don't* hesitate to ask," I correct as they dart out of sight.

The Knightleys' cackling fades with their reply: "We mean what we say."

I move toward the hallway when Mikayla puts a hand on my arm. Her dark eyes, crinkled in confusion, halt me in my tracks.

"Alice, who were you talking to?" she asks.

"The Knightleys. They said we could have the parlor."

"No, they didn't."

I stare at her. "You didn't hear them?"

Khalil's expression is concerned. "They didn't say anything. They just left us."

My hands crumple the blue skirt of my dress. I think back to the first time I encountered the Knightleys, in the mirrors in the physics lab. Khalil told me they did not speak to him. Only I heard their voices. Only I am tormented by them.

I am not sure if I want to know why.

CHAPTER 21

THE PARLOR IS stately and small.

The robin's egg shade of blue wallpaper is the same as the rest of the house. It doesn't match the warm red tone of the four Victorian-style chairs arranged in a circle around a cherry-wood coffee table. Nor does it complement the ornate crimson rug that my shoes sink into.

Like the bedroom I woke up in before our tense dinner, the parlor has no windows. The sole source of light is the brick fireplace at the far end of the room. A large rectangular mirror hangs above the fireplace. As I step further into the parlor, I make startled eye contact with my reflection.

Khalil follows me inside, then Mikayla. She throws her shoulder against the door, which rattles shut.

She faces us. Her disheveled bangs frame her wide eyes and slightly wild expression.

"Okay," she says. "Where should we start?"

"Tell me how you got here," I offer.

Mikayla and Khalil take turns telling the story—or rather, Khalil does most of the telling while Mikayla interrupts him.

After the two of them emerged into the Nameless Forest,

they searched for me and Hailey until an unseen pursuer knocked them unconscious. They awoke in the Pins & Needles Inn a few hours before I arrived.

Mikayla is especially irate because her knife is missing. "One of the Knightleys took it while I was unconscious," she grumbles. "I'll get it back if it's the last thing I do."

"It's kind of blurry, how the Knightleys found us." Khalil touches his temple. "It was like I fell under a spell."

Mikayla digs the toe of her boot into the rug. "Same. I remember hearing things that weren't there, like the voices of people I know."

I recall the tree branch that turned into a sword and the brambles that closed in on me. Were those hallucinations or were they real? I glance at my arms, which were scratched bloody by the thorns.

Or so I thought. My skin is dirty and bruised, but not broken.

My head spins. How much of my experience is real or false? Can I trust my senses or my memory anymore?

"Your turn now," Mikayla says, crossing her arms. "Where have you been? And what did you say about Evie earlier?"

I summarize my journey through the Nameless Forest. Then, I backtrack to my meeting with Evie in the Elsewhere. I leave out her implication about my role in her death. *The murdered comforting the murderer*, she'd said.

The mere thought of harming her makes me feel sick. How could she ever believe me capable of that?

Still…the way she spoke, she seemed to know something I didn't.

Khalil wears a troubled look. "Are you sure that was Evie you saw? It might have been a trick."

"It was her. I know it was." I close my eyes. "But she wasn't acting like herself. Something about the conversation was... off."

Mikayla paces beside the Victorian chairs, dragging her hand over the plush velvet backs. Her token flashes silver on her wrist.

"Evie said that she's a ghost, right?" she says. "Is she haunting Meer?"

"It's possible."

I don't know whether I want to believe it or not. On one hand, if my sister is not completely gone, then I may still be able to find her and bring her some peace. On the other hand... Evie is clearly not herself. What if she is being corrupted along with her fantasy world?

She may no longer be a piece in this game, but her presence still shadows every move.

Mikayla's head snaps up. Her eyes gleam with hope. "Maybe we can find Evie! We can free her from wherever she's trapped. We can make things right."

I purse my lips. "I'm not sure. The Elsewhere isn't exactly a place that you can explore. We're powerless there."

"Besides, we lost Hailey," Khalil adds. "We need to find her before we defeat the Red King and Queen."

For some reason, I find myself thinking about what Primera said to Hailey in Conchae Maris. She claimed that Meer could go on without Hailey—and that her 'chosen family,' which must refer to Mikayla and Khalil, could go on without her too.

Primera predicted our separation. Maybe she even caused it.

I look at Khalil and force myself to return to the topic at hand. "I agree. The Lady of the Moon also said that searching for Evie wasn't our duty."

Mikayla stops pacing. "You're going to let that stop you?"

I bristle at the reproach in her tone. "Evie herself said that she doesn't want to be found."

I don't understand why, though. If she has a chance of being rescued from a shadowed existence in Meer, then why won't she take it?

"She's probably not thinking straight if she's been imprisoned here for two months," Mikayla argues.

"Unfortunately, I think Alice is right," Khalil says. He rubs his forehead. "We have so many other things to do. If we can help Evie, we should. But we don't even know where to begin."

Mikayla turns her back on us, gazing at the flickering fireplace. My heart twinges with regret.

"I'm sorry," I say. "Believe me, I want to find her more than anything. But it can't happen right now."

"I get it," she mutters. "It's okay. It's not your fault."

Khalil changes the subject before silence can descend between us. "Alice, was there anything else?"

I nod reluctantly. "Evie implied that someone from Meer had a hand in her death."

I tell Mikayla about the gaps in my memory and Evie's inexplicable death before describing how Evie withheld the identity of her potential killer.

"Killer?" Mikayla asks. "You think she was murdered?"

The blatant disbelief in her voice makes me defensive. "I'm not sure. The circumstances are suspicious, that's all."

Her face is pale and drawn. She studies her silver bracelet.

"If someone killed her, they're going to pay," she spits.

The scars on my hands burn in agreement.

If someone murdered Evie, and if they were from Meer, then I can't guess at their motive. They may have killed her and left me alive as a taunt or a threat. Perhaps they assumed that I wouldn't find out, and that even if I did, I wouldn't track them down in another world.

Unfortunately for them, I've never been able to leave well enough alone.

"Maybe the location of Evie's death matters as much as the cause," Khalil comments, breaking me out of my thoughts.

I shoot him a quizzical look. "Why?"

He laces his hands together. "Her body was found on Earth. But did she die on Earth, or did she die in Meer?"

The three of us fall silent. I had not considered that before.

"We have no way of knowing," I say at last. I meet Mikayla's eyes. I need to discuss some things with her before I do anything else.

"Khalil, can I ask you a favor?" I say.

"Of course."

"Can you step out for a bit? I want to talk with Mikayla alone. It won't take long."

Khalil inclines his head. "Of course."

He walks to the parlor door and shuts it quietly behind him. I wait for his footsteps to recede before I tell Mikayla about the vision that Pins & Needles triggered in the hallway.

"I need you to tell me what really happened at that party," I finish.

Her shoulders sink. The shadows under her eyes are more apparent than usual. "Evie and I were in the wrong place at the wrong time. It's my fault the police held us. I ran first. She followed me."

"That's not what I meant. I want to know why you thought my sister was on drugs."

"I didn't believe she was. Not really." She sighs. "Really, I was too scared to think of the alternative. At that point, Evie depended on Meer to get through the day. She barely slept. Her grades fell, and she almost quit the lacrosse team. She was slipping away from me. I wanted to blame something else. I *hoped* it was something else."

"Why didn't you tell me?" My voice comes out more accusatory than I mean it to.

"If I told you the truth about Meer, you wouldn't have believed me. Besides, I didn't know how to help her."

"My parents didn't understand why she went to that party," I say. "She missed the midnight deadlines for three college applications."

"You remember the college applications, of all things?" Mikayla snorts. "Priorities."

She doesn't understand. Those were the only three schools that Mom and Dad convinced Evie to explore. My parents were angry that she'd wasted her time.

Mikayla folds her arms around herself like she's cold. Her gaze darts around the parlor, and her breathing quickens. "This place is too much like your house. Even the wallpaper is the same. And the messages in the dining room…I see now what Primera meant about Evie's memories leaching into Meer."

"What do you mean?"

"How we feel inside this inn is how she felt in her house. Trapped. Scared."

I stare at her, dumbfounded.

"No," I manage. "That can't be right. I know she had a hard time, but surely it couldn't have been that bad—"

"Evie tiptoed on eggshells even around you because she knew you'd side with your parents. You were so obviously the favorite child. She felt like she couldn't talk to anyone in her own house. She was so *lonely*."

"She stopped talking to me first." My words are so soft, Mikayla doesn't seem to hear them.

She barrels on. "I get it now. The parts of Meer we experienced were the parts of her we knew. The shadowed lands were the secrets she didn't trust us with."

I automatically shake my head. "She was struggling, yes, but she was getting better. Two weeks before she died, she told me she wanted to go skydiving."

"That's your proof?" Mikayla's hands clench into fists at her sides. "Do you know how messed up you have to be to prefer fantasy to reality?"

I flinch. I've never heard Mikayla raise her voice like that at me before.

Then, her anger deflates. Her body shrinks.

"I couldn't help her," she says, her tone brittle. "But God, I tried."

Evie would have rather lived among the figments of her imagination than with her own family. Does that say more about her or about us?

All this time, I haven't realized the scope of Evie's mental health.

My stomach turns. No. I can't avoid the ugly truth, which is that I did suspect what was going on. I just ignored it.

And the worst part of it is, I'm still tempted to shut out Mikayla's words. I can't shake the grudge that follows me like a shadow. It makes me want to shake my sister and ask, *Why did you shut me out when I needed you?*

Evie should have been the one asking me that.

"Forget it," Mikayla says. Do I imagine the shimmer of tears on her face? "It's not all your fault, Alice. You can't fix it now, anyway."

She raises her head. Her eyes snag on something behind me, and she stumbles backward, almost tripping over the Victorian chair.

I whirl around, heart pounding. I half-expect the Knightleys to be there.

Instead, spidery words bleed red ink onto the blue wallpaper.

SOON, IT'LL ALL BE OVER.

Although the fireplace in the corner crackles merrily, I have never felt colder.

"That's how Evie felt in your house," Mikayla says, her voice splintering. "Like she was the problem. Like nothing she did was right, or good enough."

"Mikayla," I whisper. "I'm sorry."

Her expression softens a fraction. "I'm not the one who needs that apology."

She storms out of the parlor.

I don't have a chance to reconvene with Khalil and Mikayla.

When I finally emerge from the parlor, the Knightleys claim that they have gone to bed. I'm not sure how much I believe the couple, but I let them guide me back to my room, too unnerved by their grinning silence to resist.

My bed has been newly made. The sheets are once again pristine white. The muddy prints I left on the floor earlier have been scrubbed away.

I sit on my bed and try to calm my breathing. I reach for my compass-sense. Its presence still does not manifest.

I'm not sure how long I sit there, staring at my lap, until a chill creeps down my spine. I can't escape the feeling that someone is watching me.

A droplet of red—like blood—splashes onto the milky white blanket beside my hand.

Slowly, I lift my head, every hair on my neck rising.

There is no logic to the scrawl of the dripping words on the ceiling: IT'S ONLY A DREAM.

I jump to my feet and fling open my door. My eyes sting. My nails clench into my palms hard enough to leave new scars.

I have to find the others. We need to get out. Get out, get out, get out—

I hurry past the empty portrait frames hanging in the hallway. I try the knob of a random door. My hands are shaking so badly, it takes a few tries for me to register it is locked.

I start to move away until the door eases open.

"Alice." Khalil moves the door an inch wider. His dark curls are mussed on one side of his head. "Is everything okay?"

My mouth is dry with panic. Stars pinwheel in the corners of my vision. How can I make him understand?

"Evie is haunting me," I gasp. "She won't leave me alone."

A second later, the pressure of his hand is at my elbow. He guides me into the windowless room, which is identical to mine except for a small ivory settee on the opposite wall. A daisy-patterned lamp partially illuminates the space. The same lamp rests in my room in this inn…and in Evie's bedroom at home.

I squeeze my eyes shut, but the bright flowers dance on my eyelids, taunting me.

"Alice, sit down," Khalil says. "Just breathe."

I half-collapse onto the carpeted white floor. I rest my head between my knees as my chest constricts. I'm dimly aware of him settling against the wall beside me, instructing, "Breathe, Alice. In for five and out for five."

For once, the numbers slip from my grasp. Fresh tears well in my eyes. I inhale shakily. "I can't—"

"I'll count for you. One, two, three, four, five." He counts over and over, settling into a rhythm.

Slowly, my lungs obey my brain again. I'm not sure how much time passes. Enough that the world stops spinning.

I push myself up, spine straight and elbows in. I wipe my forearm across my face.

"How do you feel?" Khalil asks.

"Better."

I'm glad that it's dark so that he can't see the shame burning my cheeks. What does he think now that he's seen me crying and trembling like a girl half her age? My breath wobbles again.

"Hey," he says. "It'll be okay."

Carefully, he places his hand on my back. When I don't object, he keeps it there. I'm not usually one for close contact, but the weight of his presence is reassuring, like an anchor.

"Evie felt trapped in her own home, like we do here," I say. My voice is scratchy. "My parents found fault with her. I didn't defend her."

No wonder she escaped to Meer so often. It allowed her to exist without strings attached.

"You didn't know everything Evie was going through," Khalil replies gently.

I cradle my head in my hands. "Please don't make excuses for me. I've made enough for myself already. I could have helped Evie, and I failed."

"'Failed' is a strong word. You made some mistakes, but you obviously regret them."

I dig the heels of my palms into my eyes. "Evie wouldn't accept my apology when I met her in the Elsewhere. I was angry. But if I were in her place, I would have done the same thing."

Khalil exhales. He shifts his weight, and the pressure of his palm on my back deepens. "Has anyone told you that you're too hard on yourself, Alice?"

I'm startled enough to lift my gaze to his. "What does that have to do with anything?"

He smiles wryly. "Just listen. You can't change what happened in the past, so maybe you should focus on the future instead. About what you can do better."

"How? She's..." I hesitate on the word *dead*. Technically, she still exists in Meer. I settle on, "Gone."

"Think about what she would want you to do. What mattered most to her?"

My instinct is to say *Art*. Instead, looking around the shadowed room, I say, "Meer."

He nods. "All right. She would want you to save Meer."

"That's what we're doing," I point out. "We need to defeat the Red King and Queen."

"That settles it then, right?" he asks.

"I suppose." I rest my head against the wall.

I am hinging my hopes on the fact that I will be a Queen by the time we reach their territory. If something goes wrong...

It won't. It can't.

"If I become Queen, I'll make her proud," I vow. "I'll finish what she started. I'm sorry you and the others had to be dragged into this."

Khalil's eyes crinkle in confusion. "What do you mean?"

I speak the truth that has been haunting me since I left the Sheep's shop. "If I hadn't drunk the potion in Shepherd's Landing, none of this would have happened."

His hand falls from my back as he turns to face me fully. "And then you wouldn't be where you are now. You were meant to find Meer when you did, just like we were meant to come with you on this quest."

I let his words sink in. He's right. It probably would have been worse if I had not ventured into Meer when I did. Then I wouldn't understand the reasons behind my hallucinations. Worse…I wouldn't have any hope of learning what happened to Evie.

He continues, "I'm Muslim. I believe that Allah does not make mistakes. Everything has a reason, but sometimes humans can't understand those reasons. Or they are not meant to know those reasons. Sometimes, that's hard for me to accept. When Primera confronted me in Conchae Maris about giving up on others…that struck a nerve. I try to believe the best of people. I think everyone is capable of change. To believe otherwise feels hopeless."

I stay quiet, as I suspect he has more to say.

His shoulders slump. "My older brother hasn't spoken to my parents in almost a year. He dropped out of college in California. Then he came out as gay. My family didn't take it well. They fought. He went back to California and hasn't come home since. My parents want to make amends. They may not understand him, but they love him. That has to count for something."

"I think it counts for everything," I say softly.

"He insists he needs distance, but it's obvious he misses them, too. I wish they would talk to each other. I'm trying to be a bridge between them…I don't know what I'm doing wrong."

His words bring to mind the uneasy relationship between my parents and my grandparents. Since my grandparents stopped visiting us, my parents seemed content to keep an ocean between us. For the first time, I wonder if I could have asked more questions—if I could have done more to bridge that distance. Maybe I was too comfortable with the way things were to imagine what things could be.

Despite the seriousness of our conversation, a slight smile tugs at my lips. "Has anyone told you that you're too hard on yourself?" I ask.

He raises an eyebrow. "Are you using my line against me?"

"It's a good one. And it's true. You can't blame yourself. You're only doing your best."

"I hope so. I refuse to give up on any of them, no matter how naïve that makes me."

I gnaw on my lower lip before murmuring, "I don't think that makes you naïve. I think it makes you a good person."

Once, I would not have believed that. After everything I've learned about Evie, however, I cannot bring myself to be so cynical.

"Thank you. That means a lot." He fiddles with the chain of his pocket watch. "My family is one of the most important things in my life. My parents work so hard to provide for me and my brother. They want the best for us. They want the best *from* us, too. I make my goals with them in mind."

As much as I have adventured with Khalil in Meer, I know startlingly little about him as a person. I don't know what his hopes or dreams are, or what he plans to do once we escape this world.

So I ask, "What kind of goals?"

"I'm studying international relations at university next year. I'd like to be an ambassador or a diplomat."

I twist toward him. "You want to be a politician? Why?"

"You sound skeptical," he notes.

"Well, you seem too nice for politics."

That gets a laugh out of him. "Possibly. Or maybe too many politicians are narrow-minded." He sobers. "Too often, they turn a blind eye to suffering, like war or famine, because it doesn't affect them personally. But I think all of us have a duty to help others."

I marvel at the conviction lining his every syllable.

He slips his pocket watch into his hand, snapping it open and shut in a nervous tic. His head lowers. "Still...sometimes, the world is too heavy. Too hopeless. Meer offered me a place to escape for a little while."

"Then it must be hard to see how much it has changed," I say. At least, that's what I mean to say. A yawn splits my mouth, cutting me off.

"You're tired," Khalil observes. He nudges my shoulder. "You should rest. You've been through a lot today."

"Yes," I agree. "Can I ask if...no, never mind."

He raises an eyebrow. "What were you going to say?"

"Nothing. Just a question."

"Are you sure?"

Under his inquisitive gaze, I admit, "I'd rather not be alone right now. I was going to ask if I could stay here tonight, but I don't want to inconvenience you—"

"You won't!" he says, cutting me off before I can start rambling. "Of course you can stay. On one condition."

I blink at him. I wasn't expecting him to give in so easily. "Oh. What is it?"

He gestures to his white-blanketed bed. "You take the bed. I'll sleep on the settee."

"I can't do that!" I protest.

Khalil rises to his feet and offers me a hand. I take it.

"But you will," he says. "My mother taught me better than to mistreat a guest."

While he gathers blankets for a makeshift nest, he shoos away my objections. To my surprise, I find myself smiling. Our conversation has left me with a soft, stirring emotion. I almost don't recognize it for what it is: hope.

Eventually, we settle in for the night. I slip between the white, sterile sheets of the bed. The white ceiling is devoid of cryptic messages. Even so, a lump rises in my throat as my breathing struggles to find an even rhythm.

Across the room, Khalil remarks, "I'd say 'sweet dreams,' but you can't dream in Meer."

"Maybe Meer itself is the dream," I say.

"I can see that. It draws so much from Evie's love of art." He pauses, then says in a fainter tone, "She was determined to have art in her future, one way or another."

"Making a living from art is—" I nearly say *impossible*. "—difficult. It would have been better to keep art as a hobby while she found a stable job."

"That wasn't an option for her. She dreamed of it meaning more."

I rub my thumb over the broken-glass scars that crosshatch my skin. "Sometimes, dreaming can distract you—if it's not realistic. A real dream is wanting something greater for yourself or wanting something greater than yourself."

Khalil shifts. The settee creaks. "You can't define a dream for other people, Alice."

"That's how my parents thought. They wanted the best for me and Evie."

"Yes, but they may not have always done the best thing."

A retort dies on my tongue. As much as I'd like to, I can't argue with that.

"If dreaming isn't the problem, then what is?" I ask.

For a long time, he doesn't answer. I assume he's asleep until he replies, quietly, "That we live in a world so hostile to imagination."

CHAPTER 22

TWO WEEKS BEFORE she died, Evie barged into my room and declared, "We should go skydiving together."

My instinctive reaction was irritation. Mom and Dad generally insisted on an open-door policy, though they allowed me to close mine so I could concentrate on homework. They rarely granted Evie the same privilege. "We need to make sure you stay on task," they often chided her. My sister knew not to disturb me when my door was closed—except now, it seemed.

Someone, probably Hailey, had braided Evie's hair into a crown. My sister would've looked like a princess except for her paint-splattered yellow tank top and cutoff shorts. Judging from the colorful stains, she'd been working with acrylics, not her favorite watercolors.

Placing my freshly sharpened pencil in my SAT workbook, I asked, "What gave you that idea?"

She winked at me. I noticed a smudge of blue paint on her cheekbone as she said, "I came up with it myself."

"Very funny."

Secretly, I was glad that she'd marched in here to make a ridiculous proclamation. That felt more like the recklessly creative sister I knew and less like the reclusive girl who'd recently taken her place. Maybe she was finally getting back to normal after months of brooding.

"Oh, I interrupted you." Evie hovered over my shoulder, squinting at the workbook. "What are you working on?"

"Literature. It's my only weakness on the SAT. I wish the questions were more objective. I can narrow the answer down to two options, but then I choose the wrong one." I sighed, picking my pencil back up from the bulky study guide.

"I'm pretty good at that section. The rest of the test, though…" Her mouth pinched. She wandered to the wall and leaned against it.

"Can you move a little?" I asked, pointing my pencil at her. "You're blocking my to-do list."

"Oh, sorry." She inched away from the long slip of paper on my bulletin board. "Did you know Mom and Dad want me to take the SAT *again*? This is the third time." She imitated Mom's high-pitched voice. "'So you can qualify for better scholarships.'"

"I'm sure it'll work out," I said. "At least you're confident with literature. That's probably because you're an artist. You know how to interpret things the right way."

She snorted. "I interpret things the way they want us to. That doesn't mean I like it. Art has more to it than a multiple-choice answer."

I glanced at my workbook. "Yeah…I think I'll pick C for this one."

"Where did our picture go?"

I paused midway through shading the answer bubble. "What?"

Evie studied my bulletin board, a pensive expression on her face. I followed her gaze.

Unlike the bulletin board Evie kept in her room, mine had more notes than photos. The few pictures stood out. My eyes were drawn to one of my parents in the top right corner. Standing shoulder to shoulder, they gave the camera close-lipped smiles.

Evie lifted my to-do list, peering underneath it. "Where is the Polaroid of us at Anna's party?"

I didn't like that picture. At a graduation party a few years ago, a family friend ambushed us with a camera. I looked like I was nervous to ask a question in class: wide-eyed, my shoulder half-raised. Evie, meanwhile, flashed her dimples in a grin while slinging her arm around me. I'd put that photo on my bulletin board because she insisted.

"I'm not sure," I said. "Why?"

She stepped away from the board. "That was my favorite photo."

"I can put it back up," I offered, though I had no idea where it had gone. I didn't categorize my photos the way I categorized my cheat sheets.

"How long has it been gone?"

"I have no idea." I examined the board. Come to think of it…with that photo gone, there were no more pictures of us together. I wasn't conscious of that change until she pointed it out.

Evie's eyes clouded. That meant she was retreating into her mind again.

No. I couldn't let that happen.

"You came here to invite me to skydive," I prompted. "Even though you know I'm afraid of heights." My stomach churned at the thought of plummeting through the air while the wind stripped the screams from my lungs.

She stirred, twisting the silver bracelet on her wrist. "We'd do it with professionals. It's safe."

"I'm sure that's been said before many accidents."

"It's not a crime to go out and have fun. The world won't stop if you take a break, Al."

I pressed my pencil against the workbook. The pointed lead ground down on the paper, promising to leave an unerasable mark. "I can't."

"Why not?" Evie pressed.

The lead snapped, and I tossed the pencil down. My voice rose slightly. "I might fall into bad habits! I can't be complacent."

She crossed her arms, jutting out her chin the way Mikayla often did. "That's not the point. You'll burn yourself out if you keep going at this rate."

"I know my limits."

My sister arched an eyebrow. "Mm-hmm."

She didn't understand. I wasn't stressed because I was busy. In fact, nothing brought me more satisfaction than keeping busy. Having my life laid out in bullet-points, color-coded down to the minute, comforted me. Productivity was the fulcrum around which my life pivoted.

What I feared was the absence of an objective: a goal worth striving for. I couldn't imagine what was like to not be working toward something. Who was I without a focal point?

I lifted my chin. "If I convinced myself I didn't need to try, then I'd be giving up on everyone."

"And by everyone, you mean Mom and Dad." Her words had an uncharacteristically bitter edge.

I stared at her. What was she trying to say?

Yes, Mom and Dad's input mattered to me. That was natural. They had sacrificed so much for me and my sister. They taught me to never settle for anything less than my best effort. But my life didn't completely exist in their shadow.

It just happened that what I wanted—my education, my research, and my career—was also what they wanted.

I didn't know how to reply to Evie. Fortunately, I didn't have to.

Her posture relaxed. She gave me a rueful smile. "Sorry, Alice. I didn't mean to stress you out…or interrupt. I should've known that you were busy."

"It's fine. Thanks for visiting me."

Her eyes were already clouding over. She blinked. "Sorry, what did you say?"

"Evie…" I paused, realizing I didn't know what to do. "Is everything all right?"

"Mm-hmm. Fine." Her tone was distracted. Distant.

I didn't bother to stifle my sigh. She wouldn't hear it, not when she was slipping away from me again, retreating into her daydreams.

Who knew when she would emerge?

"Is there anything else you want to tell me?" I asked.

"No," she murmured. She drifted toward the door. "That was it."

CHAPTER 23

THE NEXT MORNING, I wake up with the weight of a familiar warmth curling in my chest.

My compass-sense has returned.

I sit up in bed. Across the room, the ivory-colored settee is vacant. The blankets neatly folded over its cushions mean that Khalil must be awake. The door is ajar, which confirms my suspicion.

I place a hand on my chest, savoring the warmth of my compass. I did not realize how much I relied on it until I lost it. Why did it vanish in the first place? Maybe the Nameless Forest confused me. Or I may have been rattled by the Knightleys.

Whatever the reason, I'm glad to have it back.

The voice in my head is an urgent whisper. *The way to the next land is near.*

I don't question it and allow myself to be pulled from the room. Treading softly through the unlit hall, I pass two, then four doors. Finally, I stop at the second-to-last door on the right: the same door that Mikayla slammed shut behind us yesterday.

That's curious. My compass is indicating that the exit to this inn is in the parlor. *Please don't be in the fireplace*, I plead silently. I don't want a repeat of the events in the giant's hut.

I twist the ornate doorknob.

Locked. I should have expected that.

I flatten my palm on the door, wondering if I can walk through it, the way I did in Shepherd's Landing and the Moon. But the wood does not yield to my touch.

I turn away, trying to ignore my sinking stomach. Maybe Mikayla and Khalil can help me figure out a way to enter the parlor. We need to leave. Soon.

Although it is morning, no sunlight pours in through the bay window in the dining room. Yesterday, there was little light too. The Nameless Forest seems to keep the Pins & Needles Inn in a perpetual twilight state.

Mikayla and Khalil are standing around the cherrywood table, deep in conversation. The table is empty except for a blue china vase filled with white-stemmed flowers.

My blood goes cold. That same vase rests on the kitchen island in *my* house. Yet the flowers are different—not the lilies that Mom prefers.

One blossom falls onto the table. It is not a flower, but rather a folded-up playing card. The red, regal face of a woman sneers at me: the Queen of Hearts.

Khalil swings toward the sound of my footsteps. "Good morning, Alice. How are you?"

"Better," I answer. "Thank you again, Khalil…for what you did for me last night."

He smiles. "Of course. I'm always here."

Mikayla shifts on her feet, but says nothing.

I raise an eyebrow at Khalil. "Although I have a question. Did you let me oversleep?"

"Not that long!" he hedges. "You probably needed the rest."

"She probably did," Mikayla agrees. "She gets, like, four hours of sleep, and that's on a good night."

"You're one to talk," I say.

She puts a hand to the empty knife sheath at her hip, then scowls, probably remembering that the Knightleys confiscated it.

"Alice, by the way—I'm sorry for what I said to you yesterday. It was pretty harsh. I was stressed. And scared."

"It's all right," I say, and I mean it. Her words loosen the knot of grief that has ached in my chest since my sister died.

"It's just that…" She twists the silver bracelet on her wrist. "All of us come to Meer to escape something. To forget about what goes on in our real lives. When we got to Pins & Needles, I guess it hit me that there *is* no total escape. Maybe there never was."

I remain quiet, unsure what to say.

"The inn bothers me because it's so familiar." She locks eyes with me. Her face is pale. Her voice is the smallest I have ever heard it. "Evie isn't the only one who feels invisible in her house."

Shame washes through me. I should have considered that Mikayla had her own reasons for acting the way she did. Instead, I have been thinking of myself.

"Oh, Mik," I say. "I'm sorry. I didn't know."

She gazes at the fallen playing-card flower on the table. "No reason you would. I mainly talked to Evie about it."

"If you need to, you can talk to us, too," Khalil says gently.

"I know." She inhales, setting her shoulders back. "Well, as long as we're all here, how about we talk about how to leave this godforsaken place?"

"Well, it might be easier than you think," I say. "I consulted my compass. It led me to—"

"Are you pleased with our hospitality?"

The twin voices of the Knightleys make me jump.

They have materialized at the edge of the dining room. Their smiles, as usual, are unnaturally wide. Their pitch-black eyes bore into us. How much of our conversation did they overhear?

Khalil recovers the quickest. "Of course," he says. "We are wondering if we can skip breakfast? We're pretty busy making plans right now."

"We're leaving soon," Mikayla says bluntly.

"NO!"

Their raspy shriek whistles in my skull like a teakettle. Mikayla's face twists in a half-grimace, half-snarl. I grab the back of a chair for support. Khalil stumbles into the table, causing the vase to wobble.

My ears ring in the abrupt silence.

The Knightleys' smiling faces are unchanged. They haven't moved an inch from their places.

"Why, you can't leave yet!" they say. "That would be extraordinarily rude. It would never do. It would never do."

"We don't want to burden you," I say. "I'm afraid that we may cause you trouble."

Their heads swivel towards me.

"Burden us?" Mr. Knightley says.

"Cause us trouble?" Mrs. Knightley says.

"Why," they say simultaneously, "we are happy to be inconvenienced! Let us bring you breakfast. Let us serve you. We have been waiting so long."

Before we can say anything else, they dart from the room.

I barely have time to exchange an uneasy glance with

Khalil and Mikayla before the Knightleys return, bearing dishes piled high with food: strawberry tarts, buttered toast, jam, and tea-cakes.

The couple dances around each other, whirling arm-in-arm. One by one, they fling the dishes onto the table, weaving in and out of my pulled-out chair. Mr. Knightley provides the teapot, which skids all the way to the edge of the table, steam rising from its spout.

Mrs. Knightley takes me by the arm. I fight the urge to yank away. The waxy skin of her face stretches in a grin.

"Sit, sit!" she croons. "Come partake of your meal."

Reluctantly, I let her push me into a chair.

"Come partake of your meal!" Mr. Knightley echoes. He takes Mikayla and Khalil by the elbows and deposits them in adjacent chairs. When Mr. Knightley lets Mikayla go, she rubs her arm, glaring at him.

"I have a question," Khalil says, drawing everyone's attention. He addresses the Knightleys. "Is it easy for you to travel through the Nameless Forest? How do you usually leave the inn?"

Their heads tilt in unison. "Leave it?"

"You have to go get food and other things, right?"

"Why would we need to leave?" Black eyes blink. "We provide everything at Pins & Needles."

Khalil's brow furrows. "Oh…okay."

"Isn't the forest dangerous?" I ask. "You had to rescue us from it."

Although I'm not sure I would call it a *rescue* when our current situation is captivity.

"Oh no," the Knightleys say, "it is only greedy. It takes the bones and leaves none of the brains. Better that we take you, yes, take you into our arms…"

My blood goes cold. I choke, "Excuse me? What did you say?"

Their pitch-black eyes fix on me. Their mouths stretch in ear-to-ear grins. There's a beat of silence until Khalil clears his throat.

He casts a nervous look at the Knightleys. "Alice...they didn't say anything."

Mikayla agrees with a shallow nod.

My thoughts unravel. My nails press into the scars on my palms.

Why is it that I can hear the Knightleys, but my friends can't?

The Knightleys knew who I was when I first glimpsed them in the mirrors. They called me by name. They have been waiting for me for who knows how long.

They must know who we are.

I pull my arms from the table, accidentally knocking over a jar of blackberry jam. The lid clatters off, spilling sticky preserves onto the table.

"Oh," the Knightleys gasp. "How clumsy. Here, take a napkin."

"No!" I snap. An ache pulses behind my eyes. "I...I'll clean it up myself. Please, just leave us alone. We have important things to do."

They laugh in small, hoarse shrieks. "Very well. Enjoy your breakfast. We will be back."

With that, they sweep out of the room, heels clicking in a staccato pattern.

"What did you hear?" Mikayla whispers to me.

"I don't know what it means." I cradle my head in my hands. "But I don't think anyone actually ever leaves this place."

Now that I've spoken it aloud, it feels more real.

"If we try to escape through the Nameless Forest, they'll probably hunt us down," Mikayla says, her eyes narrowing. "They caught us easily the first time."

"The way out is not through the forest," I say, raising my head. "It's in the parlor. That's what I was about to tell you before the Knightleys interrupted us. The door is locked. I tried it earlier."

Mikayla gets up from the table, cracking her knuckles. "It won't stay locked for long when it meets Mikayla Wong."

Khalil snorts. "How long did it take you to come up with that catchphrase?"

"The last ten seconds. So, are we going or not?"

"Yes," I say. "First, let me clean up the jam—"

I stop short.

The spilled blackberry jam spells out two words on the russet surface of the table.

RUN NOW.

I jump to my feet, knocking my chair aside. I can't think of anything. My logic short-circuits, leaving me with the desperate need to run as fast and far as I can—

Khalil puts a hand on my shoulder, forcing me to meet his warm brown eyes. "Alice, you're okay. It's okay."

No. It's not.

My gaze drifts back to the message. My thoughts slow down enough for me to recognize something different about it. Like some of the other messages that have taunted us, it is a command. Yet this one appeared as we talked about leaving.

It is a warning.

Last night, I said that Evie was haunting me. I meant it figuratively, but perhaps there is more truth to that than I realize…unless Meer is simply playing another trick on us.

Instinct tells me to close my eyes. My breathing slows.

Cold pricks at my arms. A distant humming sound reaches my ears. It dances at the edge of my senses. I hone in on the sound wave, trying to detect its frequency.

"Do you want to help us?" I murmur.

Khalil's hand falls from my shoulder. "What?" he asks, bewildered.

My eyes snap open, a feeling of foolishness flooding me. I am not sure what I expected. Certainly not for a ghost to manifest. I don't even believe in ghosts.

"Nothing," I say. "I think..."

A scraping noise issues from the dining table.

Mikayla flinches. She backs up against the blue-papered wall. Her voice is thin. "Guys, look."

She points at the butter knife on her plate. It has swiveled in a half-circle. The decorative whorls on the silver handle twist into letters: YES. LISTEN TO ME.

My breath hitches.

Khalil eyes the message warily. "That's new. What's going on?"

"I guess Alice found a new kind of Ouija board?" Mikayla quips, but her face is pale. She recoils from the message as if it's going to leap up and attack her.

I approach the table, hands clenched into fists. I reach again for that distant buzzing frequency.

"What are you?" I ask. "Why should we trust you?"

A teacup tips onto its side, staining the white tablecloth. With shaking fingers, I right the cup.

The dregs at the bottom of the cup spell out a new message: THEY KNOW.

"The Knightleys? What do they know?" I demand.

By my hand, a napkin's lacy spirals morph into spidery words: THEY COME FOR YOUR BODIES.

"That's all I need to hear," Mikayla says. She shoulders past Khalil. "Let's go. Now."

"What about Hailey?" Khalil protests. "We can't go on without her. She might still be in the Nameless Forest!"

"I doubt it," I say. "The Knightleys wouldn't miss out on the chance to have more victims—er, guests."

"We'll find her," Mikayla promises. "But we can't do that if we're being held hostage."

They stare at each other for a long moment. His lips tighten. He gives a grudging nod. "All right."

A cracking sound breaks the silence. On the tablecloth, a playing-card flower—the Queen of Diamonds—flutters free of the bouquet in the blue china vase. It unfurls to display a message along its red border.

THEY ARE HUNGRY. THE HOUSE WILL TRAP YOU.

Mikayla inhales sharply. "Are they going to *eat* us?"

"Why are you helping us?" I ask, ignoring the frost creeping through my veins.

My only answer is the tremor that passes through the floor. Cracks split the blue wallpaper, resembling the branches of trees. From the ceiling comes a hissing sound like a water leak.

Mikayla's eyes dart around like those of cornered prey. "We need to leave now."

Khalil follows her. I should, too, but one last question bursts from my mouth. "Are you Evie?"

I have no time to wait for a reply.

The frenzied shrieks of the Knightleys tear through the inn.

CHAPTER 24

THE THREE OF us race from the dining room into the dim hallway.

The empty portraits on the walls dislodge and fall to the tiled red-and-white floor. Metal shatters too close to my feet for comfort.

The scars on my hands blaze with phantom pain. My pace falters. I can't draw enough air into my lungs.

A hand yanks me forward roughly. "Don't stop!" Mikayla shouts in my face.

That's hard when the Pins & Needles Inn is doing its best to trap us. Along the hall, doors open and slam like eyelids. The floor bucks under our shoes like a spooked horse. Mikayla trips, but Khalil steadies her.

"You can't leave!" the Knightleys screech. "We need you, you need us, we need you!"

Their voices come from everywhere: the ceiling, the floors, the walls. The words magnify a thousandfold in my skull. My head threatens to split open.

"Shut *up!*" I scream. "Leave me alone!"

"Snap out of it, Alice!" Mikayla exclaims, gripping my arm.

Her nails dig into my wrist. "Don't listen to them. Don't let them win."

With a shuddering breath, I shove down the emotions that threaten to consume me. She's right.

We stumble to the parlor door. Mikayla cracks her knuckles, shifting her weight onto her heels.

Then, at our feet, the floor peels open. Mr. Knightley's face peeks through a hole in the tiles.

The three of us stumble back. I'm too surprised to shriek.

The innkeeper's black eyes fix on us. He licks his grinning lips. "You can't leave! The Red King and Queen will pay handsomely for your demise!"

My heart drops. The Knightleys knew who we were all along, luring us into a false sense of security with their hospitality.

"Leave us alone!" Khalil charges forward, and his shoe connects with Mr. Knightley's head.

The smiling man disappears. Far below the floor, something crunches and splinters.

For a moment, Pins & Needles turns calm. The tiles settle under our feet. The doors of the hallway flap weakly. I gape at the hole in the floor where Mr. Knightley vanished.

Khalil winces, flexing his ankle. "Ow. What's he made of—steel?"

"Are you okay?" I ask.

He waves me off. "I'm fine. Mikayla, do your thing."

"Right." She takes a fortifying breath, juts out her shoulder, and charges toward the door. She slams into it one, two, three times. On the second, the wood dents. On the third, the door shudders open.

We leap over the deep gap in the tiles and run into the parlor.

Instantly, the plush ruby rug coils like a snake beneath our shoes. While we try to keep our balance, the furniture creaks. The antique Victorian chairs and cherrywood coffee table totter from their usual positions toward us. They draw close, starting to hem us against the door.

"Help!" I shout, hoping that whatever entity haunts this house will hear us. If it warned us, perhaps it will come to our aid.

That hope is dashed when, above the fireplace, someone laughs.

"You can't get away. It's not so easy, no," Mrs. Knightley wails from inside the mirror on the fireplace mantel. She dances like a puppet. Her crazed smile taunts me. "You can't escape!"

"Oh, shut up," Mikayla growls. She slams one of the chairs to the ground, snapping its leg. She assumes a boxer's stance as another chair approaches her.

"Alice, go!" Khalil shouts, kicking away the coffee table. "Find the exit!"

They're buying me time. I need to make the most of it.

I block out the noise, drawing all my attention to my compass. Its needle snaps to attention.

And just like that, I know where to go next.

Mikayla and Khalil fight back the furniture enough so that I have a straight path to the rest of the parlor. I sprint towards the fireplace.

As I approach it, the flames roar up. I flinch.

Mrs. Knightley's face forms in the coals: a writhing mass of red and black. On instinct, I snatch up the poker leaning against the bricks.

For the first time, the woman lowers her voice. The gap between her front teeth sizzles with smoke as she croons, "It is easier to yield, Alice. We know what is best for you; we understand you want to do the right thing. You did everything you could. You bear heavy burdens, but you do not need to once you join us."

The heat of the fire sears my face and arms. The poker weighs down my hand.

I'm tired of running. It's so much easier to believe that I had no part in my sister's decline…that I'm utterly innocent.

"Yes," Mrs. Knightley hisses. "Come, come…we want guests. We have been waiting for you."

A desperate idea occurs to me.

"If I stay, will you let Mikayla and Khalil go?" I ask.

Across the room, Mikayla calls, "Alice, no!"

I glance in the mirror above the fireplace. My friends are still by the door. Pieces of mahogany wood, red upholstery, and glass litter the floor. They have dispatched all the furniture except a Victorian chair that hangs back, hesitant to attack on its own.

"We will take good care of you," Mrs. Knightley croons. Her black tongue darts between her teeth. "You lead a most heartbreakingly delicious life. All this time, we have waited for *you*, not them. We will let them go gladly."

"Don't do this, Alice," Khalil warns, pushing his sweat-slicked curls from his forehead. "Please."

I meet his gaze in the mirror and murmur, "I'm sorry."

Slowly, I kneel. The coals of Mrs. Knightley's face seethe with joy. My mouth unconsciously curves to match her smile.

I stab her with the poker.

She screeches as I rake her into a mess of cinders, brushing away the sparks that land on my arms.

"You ill-mannered, ungrateful brat!" she screams through molten, misshapen lips. "After all we did for you, you reject us!"

I shovel the firewood until a mass of smoke pours into my face and into my throat. Soot smothers my apron. No matter how many times I disperse her, her screams are a drill bit running through my brain.

I slam my eyes shut.

When I open them again, I almost scream, because Mrs. Knightley is standing in front of me.

Somehow, her dress is free of soot and smoke, unlike mine. All that has changed about her appearance is the gnarled expression of fury on her face.

Instead of confronting me, however, she faces Mikayla and muses, "Every piece is disposable to you, White King…not simply the Pawns. I admire that ruthlessness. Perhaps you can win, after all."

Mikayla's eyes narrow. She makes a vulgar gesture toward the innkeeper.

Mrs. Knightley hisses. She plunges a hand into the folds of her skirt. Silver flashes in her hand.

On instinct, I swing the poker up.

Clang. A knife clatters to the carpet, deflected from a trajectory toward its true owner—Mikayla.

Mrs. Knightley bends for the weapon. I kick it away and jab the poker at her, cornering her against the fireplace. My thoughts race. How do I lure her farther away?

Behind me, Mikayla curses as the final Victorian chair charges at her and Khalil. They grapple with it.

Mrs. Knightley's hand shoots forward, forming a claw on my shoulder. My arm goes nerveless from the pressure. I cry out, barely managing to keep my grip on the poker.

"Stop this," she rasps, wagging her finger at me like I'm a petulant child. "You cannot win. You are only a Pawn. Easily used. Easily discarded."

"You're part of the Red Court," I gasp.

Behind me, Mikayla and Khalil are still shouting and struggling.

Mrs. Knightley smirks. "Of course I am, White Pawn. My husband and I were knighted to protect the Red King and Queen. They knew the value of our service. They trusted us to guard the land before the Red Castle."

My hope flares. Does that mean we are getting closer to the Red King and Red Queen?

"I won't be a Pawn for long," I say defiantly.

Her laughter shrieks through the parlor. "Surely you do not entertain delusions of becoming Queen? It will never happen."

Ash chokes the air. I cough.

Doubt creeps in. What if she is right? What if my entire journey has been a fool's quest? I cannot hope to bypass all the horrors of Evie's life. They are reminders of how I have failed—of how I have continued to fail.

Mrs. Knightley finally releases my shoulder. She opens her arms, her voice turning gentle. "Come to me. I will ensure that you never feel pain again."

Her hand skims mine, and my mind becomes a glorious expanse of snow. Cold. Desolate. Undisturbed by grief.

Evie would view it as a wasteland.

I inhale a slow breath. Then, swinging the poker down to my side, I step forward.

I hug Mrs. Knightley like I hugged Evie in the Elsewhere.

She is my mother's height. My neck fits perfectly in the crook of her shoulder.

Distantly, I hear the voices of Mikayla and Khalil. Footsteps thud against the carpet. I shut out the clamor.

Mrs. Knightley's hands rest against my spine. The soot on my dress smears her forearms.

"It was always you, Alice," she whispers in my ear. "You understand. It is better to be used than shunned."

My hand tightens on the poker, adjusting my grip. I guide the point to the center of her back. Before she realizes what I'm doing, I thrust the iron rod as hard as I can.

It takes her an eternity to slump to the ground. She unfolds in a peculiar fashion: arm draped over her head, torso half-facing the ceiling. She is still smiling as her golden skirts pool like blood around her.

The poker protrudes from her spine. That's when I see a word on the handle that was not there before.

REMEMBER.

The inn falls into a glassy stillness. I hate it with all my being.

I stumble away from Mrs. Knightley's body and retch. Not much comes up except bitter bile.

Head spinning, I straighten. I wipe the back of my hand against my mouth.

Khalil and Mikayla rush to my side.

"Alice, are you—" Khalil begins.

I cut him off with a tight shake of my head. Later, I can process what I've done. If I stop moving now, I won't be able to start again.

I pick up Mikayla's knife and give it to her. She sheaths it without a word.

I lead them to the fireplace. The mirror glistens above the mantel. One by one, we climb onto it.

I touch the mirror's surface. A silvery fog emanates from it. My compass urges me forward.

We walk through the glass.

CHAPTER 25

I SINK INTO the Elsewhere.

My lungs strain. Gray rushes past my body. I grit my teeth, willing the burning warmth of my compass to guide us through the void. It sputters weakly.

Evie. Help us. I'm not sure where the thought comes from.

The Elsewhere churns around us in indiscernible currents. Some of the pressure on my limbs seems to lighten, though it may be my imagination.

My eyes drift shut.

No. I force my chin up. *Just a little further. Let us through.*

The gray stretches on and on until—

Red seeps into my vision.

Gasping, I break the surface of the Elsewhere. My knees collide with carmine-colored tiles. The impact shudders through my spine. Twin *thuds* on my left and right suggest that my friends have also landed.

We are inside some kind of foyer. Behind me is a burnished, heart-shaped door about ten feet high. On either side of us are soaring pillars of scarlet quartz carved in the shape of beasts with the heads and wings of eagles and the bodies of lions—gryphons. The ceiling is an intricate network of vaulted arches adorned with rubies. At my feet, a crimson carpet streams far beyond my sight, presumably to the other side of the colossal room.

If I had any lingering doubt about where we are, it dissipates when my compass whispers, *You have arrived at the Red Castle. Remember your vow. Avenge the Lost Queen and bring down the usurpers.*

Its warmth fades from my body.

I grasp at empty air, as if that will make it stay. *Wait!* I think. *Don't go yet.*

You have reached the end of Meer, it whispers. *You have no more need of guidance.*

Before I can muse on that, hollowness coils inside my chest.

I slump forward. My hands press against the polished, cherry-hued tiles of the floor as if to pry them apart. An ache pulses behind my eyes.

My glasses slide down my nose. I adjust them. A low resonant thrum passes through my token, steadying me slightly.

Beside me, Mikayla grabs a bloodred quartz pillar and pulls herself to her feet. Khalil follows suit and offers me a hand, which I take.

When I get to my feet, a trumpet blasts through the Red Castle. The three of us flinch.

A white rabbit hops between the pillars, slinging the trumpet over his shoulder. He is dressed in a red waistcoat, miniature trousers, and a white frilly ruff. Spectacles perch on his snuffling nose. The image is so absurd, I'm not all that surprised when he opens his mouth and says in perfect English, "Begging your pardon—the Red King and Queen have a proposition for you."

To his credit, he only quails a little under Mikayla's death glare.

"Who are *you*?" she asks. "A doorkeeper?"

His whiskers tremble. "I have announced your arrival to the rightful monarchs of Meer—"

Her scoff echoes through the columns of the Red Castle.

"—And before the proceedings, you may have your Knight returned to you," he continues doggedly.

The Knight. My heart leaps at the mention of Hailey. She's safe after all...or, at least, she's accounted for.

"Hailey is here? Where?" Khalil asks.

Mikayla jumps in. "Give her back to us!"

"Wait," I say. "How did she get here?"

This feels wrong. Too easy.

The White Rabbit shifts from one foot to the other. His round, pink eyes flit to me. "She came not long ago, by herself, and became a prisoner of the Red Court. She awaits the trial."

"What trial?" I say at the same time that Khalil asks, "What is she being tried for?"

"It is not *her* trial." The Rabbit darts a glance over his shoulder. "Their Majesties will not wait for long," he confides in a hushed tone. "If you want to receive your Knight, one of you must take her place as a prisoner."

"What? Why?" I protest.

"Why, you cannot have something for nothing! We must be assured that you will remain peaceful during the trial."

Mikayla's face darkens. "By using her against us?"

"I don't expect you to understand the wisdom of the *true* King and Queen of Meer," he sniffs.

Her jaw clenches. Her fingers twitch like she's fantasizing about twisting his trumpet into a pretzel.

"Can we visit Hailey first?" Khalil asks, shooting her a

look of warning. "It would be ideal if we could talk to her before coming to a conclusion."

The White Rabbit's eyes widen. "Oh, no. That is quite impossible. Your Majesties require a decision very soon." He mutters, "Otherwise, *she* will have my head, and that will simply not do."

I hope I heard that last sentence incorrectly.

Khalil forces a smile. "Excuse us, please. We need to discuss…in private."

"Be quick about it," the Rabbit says, pivoting.

The three of us form a tight-knit circle.

"This doesn't make any sense," I complain in a low voice. "In chess, if a piece is captured, it remains captured. You can't get it back."

"Well, this isn't a normal chess game," Khalil replies, matching my tone. "Either way, we're in enemy territory. That means we're at their mercy. Assuming they are telling the truth…I think our duty is to help Hailey."

"What are you suggesting?" I ask.

"That I take her place."

There's a heartbeat of stunned silence before Mikayla snaps, "No, you won't!"

I wince at how her words ricochet off the gryphon-shaped columns of the Red Castle.

Khalil lifts his chin. "If Hailey has intel on the Red Court, then we could gain an advantage."

"Or the Red Court is manipulating us," I counter.

"It's a risk," he admits, "that I think is worth taking. Hailey may have been captive since Hamwishbone's hut. If she's suffering, we need to rescue her."

Mikayla throws up her hands. "You'd be turning yourself over to the same fate! How is that any better?"

He fixes her with a resolute expression. "Sometimes, playing into the enemy's trap is the best way to beat them."

"You're not thinking straight, Khal."

Khalil says evenly, "You can't take Hailey's place, Mikayla. You're the King. Without you, we'll lose the game. Then, since Alice will be our new Queen, you both are too important to trade."

"And you're not?" Mikayla challenges.

His chest hitches, and his next words come out a little stilted. "I'm only a Bishop. I'm a supporting piece, not the most powerful. This makes me the logical sacrifice."

"Not when I'm still a Pawn!" I protest. "If anyone should take Hailey's place, it is me. She saved me when I first came to Meer. I owe her."

Khalil shakes his head vehemently. His eyes lock on mine. Light filters through the quartz columns of the castle, giving his warm brown skin a reddish glow. "No, Alice. You still have a role to play in this game, and it won't be as a Pawn."

"We've reached the end of Meer, which should be the end of the 'chessboard,'" I hurl back at him. "If a Queening happened anywhere, it would be here. But I'm still powerless, and my compass is gone!"

I don't mean to lash out at him, but I can't stop the frustration from brimming in my words. I didn't come all this way just to remain a Pawn. Our quest has to mean something more.

Mikayla's hand falls from her knife. "What do you mean, your compass is *gone*?"

"It happened as soon as we entered the Castle." I wave at the russet heart-shaped door behind us. "My compass said I had 'no more need of guidance.' I can't feel it anymore."

Khalil releases a heavy breath. "That's unfortunate, but at

least it brought us here. You will figure out how to become Queen, Alice. If anyone can, it's you."

I lower my head. I am not sure what I have done to earn his certainty.

"What if the Rabbit is lying to us?" Mikayla protests. She paces back and forth, boots clicking on the carmine tiles of the foyer. "This could be a trick. Maybe we can find Hailey and break her out and then get out of Meer—"

"It's not that easy," Khalil says. "We don't know our way around this castle. Besides, the Lady of the Moon told us to defeat the Red King and Queen."

"I don't care what she said!" Mikayla shouts.

The words echo so loudly in the foyer that Khalil and I both step back.

She's breathing hard. Her cheeks are flushed. Her hands knot into fists at her sides as she looks between us. "Meer isn't safe. Nothing is the same here. We can't trust anyone or anything except ourselves."

I've known her long enough to detect the undercurrent of fear in her outburst.

Khalil maintains his composure. He tilts his head. Dark curls tumble over his forehead. "If you miss a chance to help Hailey, can you live with that?"

His response is quiet, but judging from the way that Mikayla goes still, it stings.

"This is my choice to make," Khalil says. "It's the best choice."

I wish I felt more convinced that his answer is the right one. However, given the circumstances…it is the most logical.

People often assume that logic is unthinking and manipulative. They consider it too cold. Too rational. Too pessimistic. These are all adjectives I have borne, too.

I have always understood logic as a balanced equation. Like physics, it lends harmony to a world of disorder. And it is the path that I have always taken to get ahead.

Right then, I vow to myself that I will become Queen, no matter the cost. Khalil's sacrifice—his trust in me—cannot mean nothing.

"I trust you," I tell Khalil. "So long as you know we'll come back for you."

His mouth quirks in a crooked smile. "Of course I do."

"None of this is fair!" Mikayla objects.

Khalil's smile grows a little more lopsided. "My father says only fools believe in fairness. The rest of us make do with the hand we're dealt."

Mikayla's shoulders sag. She leans against a quartz column, crossing her arms. She glares at the floor.

"Fine," she mutters. She jabs a finger at him. "If you're determined to go over to the dark side, then we'll find you and free you later. Got it?"

He gives her a mock salute. Then glancing at me, he nods and squares his shoulders. "I'll see you again soon."

"Of course," I manage to reply.

As he approaches the White Rabbit, I can't shake the nagging suspicion that this is a mistake.

Khalil squares his shoulders and announces, "I will take the Knight's place."

The White Rabbit hops up. "Then the exchange is accepted!"

He blows two long blasts on his trumpet.

Khalil's eyes widen as his body blurs like muddied watercolors.

Then, someone else is standing in his place.

Hailey's coppery hair hangs lankly on her shoulders. Her

green pinafore dress is as starched and stiff as a playing card, while her peacock earring is as dull as her skin.

Her lashes crack open, revealing dazed green eyes. When she speaks, her voice is threadbare. "Alice? Mikayla?"

"Hailey!" Mikayla exclaims, rushing to her. "Are you okay? Did they hurt you?"

"No." Hailey focuses on us with some difficulty. "Where did you come from?"

"The Pins & Needles Inn," I reply. "Where have you been?"

Her breath shudders. "I came straight from Hamwishbone's hut to the Red Castle. I didn't stand a chance. They trapped me like a bug in a jar." Her hands clench on the folds of her dress. "You don't know who you're dealing with."

Foreboding sweeps through me.

Before I can say anything, the White Rabbit squeaks, "Their Majesties summon you for the trial!"

His trumpet sounds again.

The world blurs.

I lift my hand. It smears like paint, superimposing multiple images of my fingers. Red seeps from the castle into my skin and clothes. The pillars stretch like saltwater taffy, the gryphons carved in the red quartz giving us distorted grins.

I can't move. I can't speak. Even if I could, no sound reaches me in this vacuum. My mouth tastes like paper and mist.

The impact of falling to my knees jars me back to the present.

My teeth snap on the inside of my cheek. A coppery taste covers my tongue. I feel like I left my stomach at the Red Castle's foyer, now approximately fifty feet behind us.

Bang.

At the sound of a scepter smashing into stone, I flinch.

I look up and am met with the reflection of my pale, startled face.

The dais that I kneel before bears a narrow, horizontal mirror at just the right height to reflect supplicants. Atop the dais are two ornate red thrones.

My gaze drags to the first throne.

The Red Queen's figure reminds me of a game token: small and narrow at the top, tapering wide at the bottom. She wears a richly hued scarlet dress that, as she crosses one leg over the other, billows like a hearth flame. The color emphasizes the pallor of her ivory skin.

Her ruby-encrusted crown slips sideways on her head. She pushes it into place with a furious jerk. Her manicured hand, adorned with a signet ring, tightens on her scepter.

A perfect red heart is painted on her lips, which curl to reveal a set of large front teeth. Her heavy-lidded eyes, enclosed by suspicious black brows, are bright and hungry.

"Finally!" the Red Queen cries. "We shall punish those who are responsible for the end of the world!"

CHAPTER 26

"MY DEAREST," THE man on the throne next to her murmurs, "shouldn't we let the accused speak in their defense first?"

The Red King is a round man who shares the same pale skin and dark hair as the Queen. Unlike her, his ruby crown boasts jagged, gilded spires. He reclines on his royal seat, his fur-lined cape tucked over him like a blanket. I squint. Is he... sucking on his thumb? I must be seeing things.

At the interjection of her husband, the Queen slouches.

"But I love to put the verdict before the trial!" she whines.

The King doesn't reply. His head droops against the back of his throne.

A tremor passes through the floor, making my teeth rattle. It's gone before I can figure out if I imagined it or not.

I expect the Queen to resist her husband. Perhaps she will whack him with her scepter. Instead, she settles back without so much as a grimace.

"Very well," she says. "Prepare the jury for the trial!"

She addresses this to the White Rabbit, who blows two ringing notes on his trumpet.

All of a sudden, Mikayla, Hailey, and I are no longer kneeling on the floor before the monarchs. Instead, we are seated in chairs in a paneled wooden box to the right of the Red Queen. My gut churns at the abrupt relocation.

To my left side, Mikayla groans, "Somebody destroy that trumpet before I do."

On my right, Hailey mumbles an agreement.

When my head stops spinning enough to sit upright, I survey the throne room.

Generally, the members of a jury are supposed to sit together. However, the seats on this jury are divided in half. One box flanks the Queen and one box flanks the King. A ring of guards, barely visible, borders the sides of the throne room.

A metronomic clicking sound captures my attention.

In the bottom row of my box, the ewe from Shepherd's Landing knits a shapeless mass of blue-and-white yarn that curls over the tiles of the throne room. Her spectacles are perched precariously on her nose, like the last time I saw her. She does not glance in my direction, though I suspect she knows I am watching her.

I jump when the Red Queen barks an order at the White Rabbit. He flinches and makes a hasty bow. He scurries to stand at attention beside my jury box, his trumpet bouncing against his back. Mikayla zeroes in on him. She scowls and leans over the side of the box like a tiger poised to pounce.

As I consider whether to stop her from threatening the White Rabbit, someone says, "So you made it to the Red Castle, after all!"

Next to the Sheep, a little girl twists in her seat to stare at me.

Primera tosses her strawberry-blonde locks over one shoulder. Her heart-shaped face is flushed with excitement.

She looks exactly like she did when she stole my last memory of Evie in Conchae Maris, smoothing her chubby hands down her frilly yellow dress.

"Hello, White Pawn!" she croons. "I was wondering when I'd see you again."

Memories of floating bottles, glowing pearls, and brine-slick stone flash through my head. I grit my teeth.

"How are you here?" I ask. "*Why* are you here?"

"For the trial, of course!"

"What trial? What's going on?"

Her blue eyes dance with mischief. "Why, none of us could miss it! The Red King and Queen summoned us to witness which Court will win Meer."

"Have we been summoned to witness the trial, or summoned to be a witness in the trial?"

"Either. Both. I am prepared. I have evidence to offer." She thumbs the pearls threaded on the cord around her neck. *Our* pearls. They glow with an otherworldly luster.

Then it hits me. "You're going to show our pearls to the Red King and Queen."

"If they order it."

I say through gritted teeth, "Don't. Please."

It was bad enough to admit to Primera that my last words to Evie were hateful. Reliving it would be so much worse.

She taps a finger against her chin. "Hmm. What will you pay for me to withhold your pearl?"

"I've paid enough!"

It's all I can do to not raise my voice.

She tilts her head. A knowing smile plays on her lips. The gap in her teeth flashes.

"Don't despair," she says. "Do you still have the gift I gave you?"

The change in subject catches me off-guard. Against my will, my hand goes to my apron pocket, where a tiny vial rests. I remember the cool press of it to my face, collecting my tears, in Conchae Maris. I should have smashed it when I had the chance.

"Good," she says, even though I haven't answered her question. She winks at me. "Never waste a gift."

She flounces forward in her seat, ending the conversation.

I glare at the back of her blonde head before turning to my left. Mikayla is still muttering to the White Rabbit. His trumpet is intact, though judging from his quivering expression, that isn't any consolation. I sympathize with him until I remember how Khalil vanished on the spot. I hope that wherever Khalil is now, he remains unharmed.

I sneak a look at Hailey on my right. She stares blankly at the other jury box. I follow her gaze and find a familiar figure sitting in the box's top row. My heart leaps when I recognize the Lady of the Moon.

The silvery aura surrounding her flickers like a candle about to go out. Her eyes are closed. Her white hair is tucked behind her elfin ears. She clasps her hands in her lap, and her back is ramrod straight.

Beside her is Dinah, who is treating the wooden seat as her personal scratching post. Where has she gone since the Nameless Forest? I almost call out to my cat until I see who occupies the seat next to her.

The side of Mr. Knightley's plump face is scuffed with black marks from his tumble through the tiles of the Pins & Needles Inn. His clothes are none the worse for wear besides a torn sleeve. He turns his liquid midnight eyes onto me and smiles with broken, jagged teeth.

Although we are separated by what has to be at least fifty feet, his raspy voice echoes in my head.

Justice comes to those who run.

I tighten my grip on my chair to avoid clawing at my ears. Mikayla, Khalil, and I left Pins & Needles before Mr. Knightley did. How did he enter the Castle without passing us?

Primera said that the Red King and Queen summoned the Red Court. Maybe she meant that more literally than I thought.

The trumpet blasts once. I flinch, but I remain rooted in my seat. The Sheep doesn't so much as glance up from her knitting at the noise.

"Silence in the court!" the White Rabbit cries. "I bring forth the first piece of evidence!"

He slips white gloves over his paws and scurries before the Red King and Queen, holding a tray with a silver band. No, a silver bracelet—which is identical to the one on Mikayla's wrist.

Beside me, Mikayla stiffens. "Is that…"

"It looks like Evie's bracelet," I say.

"Her token," she agrees. "But it can't be the same. Right?"

"Behold, a relic of the Lost Queen," the White Rabbit announces. He makes a twitchy bow toward Hailey. "It was confiscated from the Knight of the White Court, Personal Guard of the Lost Queen and former prisoner of the Red Court. She carried it on her person."

Mikayla and I turn to Hailey in unison.

"What is he talking about?" Mikayla asks in a harsh whisper.

Hailey keeps her head down and twists her hands in her lap. "It's a long story. I—I didn't know they would take it."

"Wait, is that really Evie's token?" I ask, craning my neck to get a better view of the bracelet.

A flush enters Hailey's cheeks. "Yes," she says so quietly, I can barely hear her.

Mikayla draws back as if stung. "How did you get it?" she asks.

Hailey's face is pale, yet resolute. "I found it in Shepherd's Landing on a shelf. We were in a hurry to get to Alice, so I didn't have time to mention it to you and Khalil."

I recall the night the four of us camped on the Nacre Coast, when Hailey would have shared a secret with Khalil if I hadn't interrupted. Then I think back to Hamwishbone's hut, when she dropped something in the ashes of the giant's fireplace.

All this time, Hailey has been carrying my sister's token.

What I don't understand is why she would have shared that secret with Khalil, but not with me or Mikayla.

Mik's mouth opens and closes before she snaps, "You could have told us that at any time!"

"No, I couldn't."

"Why?"

A slamming noise interrupts us.

"Silence in the Court or I'll have the lot of you executed!" the Red Queen hollers, raising her scepter.

I wonder why I'm shivering, then I realize that I'm not. Pulsations rock through the floor as if the castle itself has a heartbeat, crashing and ebbing like ocean waves. Then they stop.

"No," the Red King mumbles into the dead silence. "Trial first. Execution last."

"Trial *third*," the Queen argues. "Verdict first!"

"Refreshments second," he counters. "And execution last of all."

The Queen considers this. "Very well."

She waves her manicured hand. A cart bearing golden goblets clatters from behind the White Rabbit. I hadn't noticed it before. There's a series of *clinks* as the goblets zip through the air, performing acrobatic loops before hovering at the hands of the monarchs and the jury-members.

Hailey reaches for the same goblet as I do. Our hands knock together.

"Oh, sorry," she says, quickly sitting back.

I take the goblet, swirling the burgundy liquid. White froth forms on the surface. The acrid scent burns in my nose. I have the uncanny feeling that I have smelled it before. I can't imagine where.

"This is wine, I think," Mikayla says, sniffing her goblet. She takes a gulp and nods. "Yup."

"It could be spiked with poison," I say.

"I doubt it. Why bring us all the way here only to kill us quietly?" Her eyes narrow at the Red Queen. "If I had to guess, she'll want a spectacle." She spits the last sentence like venom.

I examine the goblet. Curiosity overcomes me, and I take a sip.

It is tart and acidic, leaving an unpleasant throbbing burn in my throat no matter how hard I swallow. I cough and put my hand over my mouth to muffle the sound. Mikayla shoots me a concerned glance.

I try to place the goblet on the floor of the box, but it insists on hovering at my elbow.

Hailey raises her hand. "Objection! Can I have water?"

"We proceed with the inspection of the Lost Queen's token!" the White Rabbit calls. "Silence in the Court, please!"

The Red Queen strokes her chin. "The Lost Queen, you say? Yes, the make of it is not of Meer. Does it have any special powers?"

"Er…" He goes cross-eyed, peering at it. "Well, it must be handled with care. Touching it brings an inexplicable sensation upon the bearer."

"What is he talking about?" Mikayla asks Hailey.

The other girl hesitates, fiddling with the skirt of her green dress. "It's hard to explain. When I took the token from Shepherd's Landing, I had a vision of Evie's life."

Mikayla leans toward her. "From what part of her life?"

Haily presses her parched lips together before responding, "I think…it's from just before her death."

Mikayla's hand clenches on the hilt of her knife. "*What*? What was the vision?"

"I'm not sure. It was more of a memory than a vision—"

"Why didn't you tell us earlier?" she presses.

Hailey meets her gaze steadily, her pale face set in a firm expression. "Time for me to ask a question, Mik. Where were you when Evie died?"

I freeze. So does Mikayla.

Her dark eyes are chips of obsidian. She says in a dangerously low voice, "What are you trying to say, Hailey?"

Hailey's eyes widen. She shrinks in her seat. "I—"

"Silence in the Court!" the White Rabbit bawls. A blast from his trumpet shuts us up, though Mikayla doesn't take her eyes away from Hailey.

Below, the cross-examination continues.

"The token has no extraordinary powers?" the Red Queen asks, her high-pitched tone echoing through the space.

"None whatsoever," the White Rabbit answers, his ears twitching anxiously.

She wrinkles her nose. "How disappointing. I expected more from Meer's creator. Take it away at once. What is next? Call forth the next witness."

"Yes, your Majesty!" The White Rabbit nearly drops the tray in his hurry to pass it to a guard. Puffing, he scurries back to the monarchs and blows his trumpet.

"Come forth, Primera, the Red Pawn!" he cries.

CHAPTER 27

THE BAREFOOT GIRL flounces from the jury box.

She has barely reached the monarchs before the Red Queen commands, "Give us your evidence."

"I shan't." Her words resound like a bell.

The jurors shift in their seats.

The Queen narrows her eyes. "I beg your pardon?"

"I shan't," Primera repeats. She sticks out her bottom lip. "I don't want to give *this* back to you."

She raises her hand, showing off a signet ring. Recognition sparks in me. Minutes ago, that same ring was on the Red Queen's finger. How on earth did Primera take it? She didn't even get close to the Queen.

The ring looks familiar, though I can't place where or when I have seen it before. I try to make out more details, but my vision blurs at the edges. I blink hard.

The Queen's face turns crimson. "You little thief!" she sputters. "Guards, take her away to be executed!"

Ruby-armored soldiers stir at the edge of the throne room. They have been so quiet and still, I forgot their presence. They draw halberds and swords, advancing on Primera in an arrow-shaped formation.

Primera gives the Queen a gap-toothed grin. "Oh, but you won't. Because then you'll never get my other evidence."

She flips her hand, revealing four luminous pearls in her palm. She takes one and dashes it to the floor, crushing it under her foot. I wince at the dust that sprays across the smooth carmine tiles. Was that my memory, or did it belong to one of my companions?

"Stop her!" the Queen orders.

As the guards advance, Primera takes two more pearls and pulverizes them under her heel in quick succession. On my right side, Hailey flinches.

"One left!" Primera calls in a clear, childish voice. She holds the gleaming sphere aloft. "Shall I destroy this one, too? Then what will become of your precious trial?"

The Queen holds up her hand. The guards retreat to the edges of the room.

"Get on with your testimony," she growls. "But do not think I will forget this insult."

Primera grins. "I knew you would see reason."

She whispers something to the pearl. Silver mist rises from its lustrous surface. Then, a vision weaves in the air.

"Evie…what have you done?"

The two girls stood inside the chamber of the Lady of the Moon. Stars and meteors flecked the ceiling above their heads. The Lady herself was nowhere in sight.

Dark circles crowded Evie's eyes. Her wavy hair was unkempt and frizzy. "So, you found them," she said.

"You're putting us all in danger by letting those shadowed lands corrupt Meer."

Evie's laugh was bitter. "It's been corrupted for a long time."

"How long?"

"Too long." Evie's eyes lost focus. She opened her hand. A miniature nebula winked between her fingers and snuffed out. "I hoped that you, of all people, would understand."

"Maybe I would have found out sooner if you didn't shut me out so much."

"I think you were just scared."

"Scared," Mikayla countered, "for you."

"You were," Evie admitted. "For a while."

"What is that supposed to mean?"

"You're afraid that what you've built here will break. You're afraid that it's my fault. Well, so am I." She took a shaky breath. Her eyes were glossy with tears. "I'm making my choice, with or without you, but I'd rather have you with me."

"What choice?"

"The choice that will free us from our lives on Earth, of course. All you have to do is trust me. I'll show you what's beyond."

"Beyond where?"

"Beyond Earth…and even Meer. To a grand new adventure. You'll love it if you stay with me until the end."

"Of course I will."

"Promise me." Evie grabbed her hand. Mikayla winced at the strength of her grip. "Please, Mik. I'll never ask anything else of you."

"I promise."

Evie's shoulders slumped with relief. A dreamy smile graced her lips.

"Just you wait." She held her wrist next to Mikayla's. Their silver bracelets mirrored each other. "In the place beyond, there's no such thing as sadness."

The vision ends there.

The pearl crumbles. Mist curls from Primera's palm.

Mikayla's face is chalk white. She glares at the little girl.

I want to reach over to her, to offer her some measure of comfort, but I know she won't accept it. Her pearl—her most painful memory—was displayed for everyone in this room. It must be from just before Evie died: Mikayla was confronting her about the shadowed places of Meer.

The Red Queen addresses Mikayla. "What did the Lost Queen mean about finding a place beyond Meer?"

The White Rabbit coughs. "Your Majesty, you must call her as a witness. She can't give her testimony from the jury. It is the law—"

The Queen leaps to her feet. Her scepter clatters against the dais. Her voice is diamond-hard. "Listen to me now. I am your ruler. I *am* the law. And I order you to change that ridiculous rule at once, or else I shall cut your paws off and wear them as jewelry."

The Rabbit cowers. He clutches his trumpet close to his vest. "Yes, Your Majesty. Forgive me, Your Majesty."

"The Lost Queen wanted to escape Meer!" Mikayla screams.

Everyone falls silent, even the Red Queen.

Mikayla is on her feet, shaking with fury. She stabs a finger at the monarchs. "You twisted her mind. You ruined Meer."

"*She* ruined Meer," the Red Queen corrects. "We are part of her. She could not remove us without destroying herself."

"She was corrupted, then she corrupted others—not the other way round," the Red King murmurs.

"If not for you, she would still be here!" Mikayla shouts, her voice breaking.

I stare at her, startled. She sounds like she has a personal grudge against the Red King and Queen. Yet she has never encountered them before. None of us has.

"Treason!" the Red Queen declares. "My dear, I believe execution for the lot of them is well-advised."

"There is more to hear," the King objects.

I can't make out his face well because it's half-shadowed. He slouches worse than Evie ever did, which is saying something: his chin nearly touches his chest. Everything he says is so quiet, I strain to hear him.

The Queen sits without another word. Her face is still flushed with anger.

I wonder why the Red Queen obeys her husband. Her vicious authority should overcome his meek resistance. Perhaps he compels her through magic.

"Next witness!" the White Rabbit cries. "Jurors may be seated!"

Slowly, Mikayla lowers herself to her chair again. Her gaze is stormy. Her jaw clenches so hard, I worry she'll grind her teeth to stubs.

I had assumed that her pearl contained her regret about Evie's addiction to escapism. After her reaction, though, I wonder if there is something more to it.

My thoughts are interrupted when the Red Queen attempts to interrogate the Sheep. The Queen's escalating threats and the White Rabbit's visible agitation only seem to amuse the aged ewe, whose knitting needles never pause. She replies to their accusations and threats with, "Silly geese. They should have migrated already."

I question if she is trying to send a message to me—she called me a goose when I first met her—but her eyes remain fixed on her blue-and-white knitting, which has grown two or three times longer since the beginning of the trial.

The next witness is Mr. Knightley. His progress to the front of the thrones is hindered by his unsteady gait. One of his legs is bent the wrong way at the knee. I look away, swallowing a rush of nausea.

Mr. Knightley curls a gnarled finger at me and Mikayla like he's beckoning a dog. "These ones rejected my hospitality and vandalized my property!"

Mikayla doesn't miss a beat. "You were trying to hold us hostage!" she shouts at him.

"Nonsense!" Mr. Knightley stamps his good leg. "My wife and I saved these ungrateful brats from the Nameless Forest, and they repaid us by ruining our inn!"

"*Saved* us?" Mikayla laughs incredulously. "You tried to kill us!"

"If one more juror interrupts the trial," the Queen yells, "then it's OFF with her HEAD!"

I bite down on my tongue and taste blood. No one breathes for the next few seconds.

"That's better." Her smile is saccharine. "Continue, Sir Knightley. What did these children do?"

"My wife, my darling beloved, was murdered by *her*!" Mr. Knightley wails.

Every pair of eyes in the Court follows his trembling finger to me. I shrink under the attention. I would speak, but my throat still burns from the wine. My head is fuzzy.

"It was self-defense!" Mikayla cuts in.

"How was she murdered?" the Red Queen demands of Mr. Knightley.

His fingernails rake red grooves into his cheeks. "She used a fireplace poker, and...I can't even speak of it!"

"So inelegant." She grimaces. "The ax, on the other hand—now *that* is a beautiful instrument. It is exact. It commands respect."

"That is precisely what I think!"

"Hmm." The Queen strokes her chin. "It is unfortunate what happened to your wife. Off with you. Next!"

The White Rabbit's whiskers quiver as he blows another blast on his trumpet. "Come forth, Alice, the White Court's lowly Pawn!"

CHAPTER 28

I LEAP TO my feet.

Hailey cries, "Watch out!" a split second too late.

My elbow jabs into the golden goblet floating by my seat. Red liquid soaks my dress and apron. When I grab my skirt, my hands come away covered in crimson. I suck in a breath. My head spins.

It's wine, I tell myself. *Nothing else.*

Though I lift trembling fingers to my nose and confirm it is only wine, a coppery tang still coats the back of my throat.

"Next witness! The White Pawn!" The White Rabbit's bawl pierces my thoughts. He inhales deeply and blows his trumpet, the loud noise making me wince.

I approach the royal dais, my dress dripping with each step and staining the tiled floor.

"I should have you executed for defiling royal grounds," the Red Queen mutters. She taps her heels against the tiles. The guards lining the room advance a few steps forward.

Come on, Lee. Think! If I cannot stop this trial from happening, perhaps I can stall long enough to give Mikayla or Hailey a chance to come up with a plan.

Mikayla leans forward in her chair, as if she is ready to jump down and defend me. Hailey, however, is not observing the trial at all. She peers at the bottom of the jury box, then surveys the room. It's difficult to make out her expression.

I have to clear my aching throat three times before I can form words. Even then, my voice is as raspy as Mr. Knightley's.

"What have I been a witness to, exactly?" I ask the Queen. "That was never made clear. In fact, many things about this trial confuse me. Is my Court the defendant?"

Her nostrils flare. "I am asking the questions, not you, you insolent brat! What do you know about this business?"

My best line of defense is denial. That is not difficult, since I have no idea what is going on.

"Nothing," I say, then wince. My vocal cords feel blistered.

"Nothing whatsoever?" she presses, her words pitching higher.

"Nothing whatsoever," I confirm.

"How curious." The Red Queen raps her fingers on her scepter. "My dear, what do you think? Should we imprison the White Pawn for lying about her crimes against Meer?"

Beside her, the King stirs. "Meer is failing," he mutters. "It has been failing. I am now too close to awakening...too close."

My teeth rattle at the tremor that passes through the floor. It subsides as quickly as it came.

I study the King more closely. His grizzled beard obscures much of his face, but I can make out his eyes, which appear to be closed.

He must be using the word "awakening" in the figurative sense. He cannot actually be asleep when he is answering his wife or making offhand remarks toward the witnesses.

The Queen studies her husband, her black brows knit together.

I take advantage of her distraction to ask the first question on my mind, which has been haunting me since it formed. "What hand did you have in the Lost Queen's death?"

The Red Queen's attention snaps to me. "Are you accusing *me* of murder? You, a lowly Pawn?"

"I'm not accusing you of anything. But if you're going to hold me hostage in your Castle and interrogate me, I have a right to ask some questions, too!"

As soon as the words leave my mouth, I realize I'm yelling, no longer caring how much it hurts to raise my voice.

"Impossible!" the Red Queen declares. She stamps her scepter so hard, I'm surprised the mirror on the dais doesn't break. "The Lost Queen *aided* us. We had no reason to hurt her."

That was Primera's story too, when we met her in Conchae Maris. I still find it hard to believe. Evie would not have willingly let the Red Court ruin Meer...unless she didn't know how powerful they had become. Perhaps she underestimated what they would do to climb to power.

An ache coils at the base of my skull. I grit my teeth and spit, "You're lying."

"You miserable brat," the Red Queen snarls. "How dare you insinuate such treasonous things! Why, I never—"

"The Lost Queen begged us to live in Meer."

The King's words are quiet but forceful. The Queen gapes at him, startled out of her rage.

I collect myself first. "Why?" I ask, my pulse racing.

His eyelids flutter. "She stood where you stand now, and she pleaded to stay forever. I decreed..."

The Queen shifts toward him. "Do not indulge her," she says sharply. "Leave the questioning to me."

Sweat sheens on the King's forehead. His head lolls from

side to side. Words rush out of him in a torrent. "I decreed that she created us, but she was not of us. She had to leave. This was no longer her world. This was no place for her—she created us but she was not of us—SHE WAS NOT US—"

His murmur rises to a roar. With each word, his body contorts like a puppet's. The pain in my head amplifies, and I clutch my temples. My throat burns.

The Queen clutches his arm. "Enough! Stop this!"

I'm surprised to hear what sounds like genuine fear in her plea. Before I can wonder why, the room ripples like water.

Blue washes over my vision, and I am swept into the current. I will never be found again. I am a girl doomed to lose herself. To lose her way.

Suddenly, I am surrounded by minnows, their scales edged with gold and iridescence. I should safeguard the colors for my sister. I should do something more than sway with the current.

Evie's voice echoes in my head. *I won't let you fall. I promise.*

Do you? I ask.

"Whom do you address?" The Queen's face looms from her throne, causing the fish to scatter. "Answer me!"

"She's talking to thin air. She's mad. We can't trust her testimony." This comes from the Rabbit. I can't see him anymore. I can't see any of them anymore.

Then the water is no longer there. I am caged in the embrace of a tree that has sprouted from the tiled floor. Antique pocket watches dangle from the branches. The gears whir in hypnotic spirals. One clock glows with a golden light. It darts away as soon as I stretch out my hand.

Come back! I cry.

The entire flock of pocket watches flees when I lunge forward. I'm left peering up into the great castle ceiling, except it's no longer a ceiling but a hole into the night sky.

You will answer for what you did, the stars sing.

"Control yourself!" the Queen bellows to someone—not to me.

"This is not my doing." The Lady of the Moon's reply is barely audible in the chaos. "Even if it were, I cannot stop it. You cannot either. The Pawn comes into her own power."

The Queen continues screeching. I tune her out.

The whole of outer space swirls above me, and I throw my head back to welcome it. My mind disintegrates like the galaxies that melt together. My skin crawls with the heat of being made and unmade.

"Silence in the Court! Silence in the Court!" the White Rabbit puffs from a distance.

"Hey!" Mikayla yells. "Let go of Hailey! What are you doing?"

What is happening?

I forget everything when the first star enters my fingertips. It ignites me from the inside out. Fire licks at my ribs. I want to scream, but I'm pinned to the spot.

"The jurors may consider their verdict," the King says.

"No, no!" the Queen interjects. "Sentence first and deliberation afterwards."

Nonsense. Having the sentence first…it's all nonsense.

Then, a gasp rattles the universe. My sanity fractures.

I no longer remember who I am or what I want. It does not seem to matter anymore.

Twin glowing nebulae meet my gaze.

"So," the Red King says, with a grudging edge of respect in his voice. "You seek the Lost Queen's crown."

I can't reply.

A black hole opens in the floor and swallows me whole.

CHAPTER 29

TWO MONTHS AGO, while my family ate dinner, my father asked me, "Have you been studying for the SAT?"

The question was innocent enough, but I noticed his chopsticks pause on the edge of his bowl. He was waiting for my answer, which meant it mattered.

I didn't understand why Dad asked that question. He and Mom had suggested my study regime in the first place. Every single day, I analyzed and attacked my mistakes, marking up countless practice tests. I didn't allow myself to eat or take breaks until I had improved my score. Every hour of work would pay off. I knew it, and so did my parents. Still, I answered my father, "You know I have—since August."

Dad nodded slowly. "Of course. That's good; you will be more prepared. I'm glad that you take initiative."

Across from me, Evie picked at her food. The bruise-tinted shadows under her eyes were more pronounced than usual. Her hair was rough and tangled around her shoulders. She wore a faded T-shirt and sweatpants.

She was unkempt compared to the rest of us. I wore a royal-blue sweater and black pants. My mother hadn't changed out of her work outfit, a mauve skirt and blouse. My father wore a white button-down that was spotless despite the messy soy sauce served with our dumplings. His steady surgeon's hand meant that he never spilled anything on himself.

Now that I thought about it, I couldn't remember the last time we had eaten dinner as a family. Dad's schedule at Willow Creek General Hospital made it difficult, if not impossible, to have the four of us together for a meal. I wished Evie could bring herself to be more sociable. Who knew when our schedules would align like this again?

"Yes," Mom agreed. "Evie, how do you think you did on your SAT retake?"

My sister barely raised her head. "I don't know. Fine."

"Better than the last time, I hope." Mom gave her a critical once-over. "Take more food. You're looking far too thin lately."

Dad tapped his chopsticks against his bowl, which issued a faint chime. "What was your SAT score last fall, Evie?"

"I don't know," she repeated. "I don't care, either. The test doesn't matter after high school."

My parents exchanged a look.

"It may be just a test, but the skills you learn from it are useful even after the test is done," Mom said. "And getting higher SAT scores means you qualify for better college scholarships."

Evie hunched over her plate. "Most colleges don't even ask for SAT scores now," she muttered.

"What was that, Genevieve?" Mom asked.

My sister's eyes usually flashed at the use of her full name. This time, her face remained blank. "Nothing," she said.

Mom clicked her tongue. "Sit straight. If you don't have

good posture when you're young, you'll slouch for the rest of your life."

Evie propped her elbows on the table. She began folding her napkin into nonsensical shapes.

Dad coughed. "Well, it's good that you've studied hard for so long now, Alice. How is your progress?"

I blinked, recalibrating to the change in subject. "At the rate I'm going, if I increase my score by ten more points, I'll be in the ninety-eighth percentile."

Evie had returned to ignoring us. She stabbed a dumpling until the pork spilled out.

"Good, good. You can study with tutors like your sister," Dad suggested.

The tutors he mentioned were family friends. Mom and Dad had helped them find their jobs, so they felt indebted to us. Although they helped Evie during her first two SAT retakes, I refused their assistance. I didn't need anyone to tell me how to think or practice. I'd come this far by myself, after all.

"I don't need a tutor," I said. "I'm doing well on my own."

"It's good that you are independent, Alice."

I ducked my head, a slight smile rising to my lips. It was hard to win praise from my parents on the best of occasions.

"You can never be too sure, though," he continued. "I will call the tutors tomorrow and ask them to come over."

My smile slipped. "Thanks for thinking of me, but I'm fine."

"Hmm." Dad glanced at Evie. "Evie, perhaps you can retake the SAT around the same time Alice takes it. But it might be too late. If you want to get the score that she plans to, you need over two hundred more points."

I saw the exact moment that something in Evie's face broke.

Her chopsticks *clanged* in her bowl. I jumped.

Pushing back her chair, she sprang to her feet. "It's always *if, if, if,* when it comes to me. You talk about me like I'm already a lost cause!"

Dad shot her a look. "Don't be dramatic, Evie. We don't think that about you."

She didn't appear to hear him. Her chest heaved as she raised her voice. "I'm sick of this comparison game! I'm doing the best I can even though I'm not a natural genius like Alice—"

"I'm not a natural genius," I interrupted.

Evie rolled her eyes. "Sure. And I'm going to be a doctor and spend the rest of my life working myself to death."

"Don't use that tone of voice with us," Mom warned. "If you want to have a serious conversation, you need to be serious."

Evie threw up her hands. "Oh, come on! All this over a test?"

My mother pressed her lips together while I shrank back in my seat, uneasy at the turn the conversation was taking.

Dad answered, "The test teaches you how to problem-solve and adapt. That knowledge makes a huge difference in your future. You need to take this to heart, Evie. Be more diligent."

Evie scoffed, "Oh, yeah, so now it's *my* fault."

He laid down his chopsticks by his bowl. "I didn't say any-thing like that. Your mother and I only want you to study hard and receive the higher education that you deserve."

"I'm not going to any of the colleges you want me to," my sister said immediately. "All of them so far have rejected me.

I'm sure the rest will, too. I told you community college was the better option."

My mother took a heavy breath before she said, "If you don't take your education seriously, you'll be another poor worker, struggling to get by. I know because that was me. My parents did not trust me to climb the ladder in America. I succeeded, but it was difficult. It took many years because I was not prepared. My children will not make my mistakes."

She did not meet our eyes.

I was startled to hear her mention my grandparents. Mom didn't like to talk about them or her life in Hong Kong. She also refused to talk about the early days of living in America, though I knew she had briefly worked as a maid.

"Things have changed since you came to America," Evie said. "They're better now."

"Things haven't changed that much." I glanced down at my bowl as soon as I said it.

Three pairs of eyes lingered on me.

Evie spoke first. "You're siding with them now, Al?"

The disbelief in her voice stung.

"I'm not—" I paused, trying to think of the right words to say. I hated improvising. I wished I had more time to formulate a response. "I mean, you still need good grades and test scores to attend the college you want."

She slashed her hand through the air. "That's not my dream. It's yours. I'm doing something different."

"Like what?" Mom challenged.

Evie lifted her chin. "I'm returning to my art business."

Mom considered her oldest daughter. Her mouth twitched. Then she broke into a peal of laughter.

Red mottled Evie's cheeks. "What?"

Mom wiped her eyes, modulating her tone. "Your art

business is not enough to earn a living. We indulged your hobby for a while—"

"But you encouraged me to do it!" my sister interrupted. "You said it was a good idea!"

"I said it was a good starting point," Mom corrected. "That was until you couldn't keep up with the work. If you motivated yourself more…"

Evie's words tumbled over each other. "You don't trust me, or listen to me. As soon as I start talking, you want to hear something else, and you want me to be someone else."

Dad pinched the bridge of his nose. "All we want, Evie, is for you to have some realistic career goals…like Alice."

Don't bring me into this.

Evie's eyes slid sideways to me. "You mean you want me to *be* Alice," she corrected. "Too bad you had the bad luck of being stuck with me."

I flinched. Did she really think that Mom and Dad did not value her the way she was?

"That is not true, Genevieve," Dad said.

She shook her head. "You want me to be your American Dream, but I can't take it anymore. I'm sorry."

"You're putting words into our mouths," Mom said.

"Am I?" She took a shaky breath. "Fine, then. Answer one question for me. Just one. Then I promise I'll never mention this again."

Mom watched her. At last, she nodded. "We'll hold you to that," she said quietly.

Evie was a rigid silhouette in the dining room lights. Her hands clenched at her sides. "Even though I know—and *you* know—that I'm not good enough for you, why do you insist on pretending that I can be? Are you in denial or stupid?"

The legs of Dad's chair screeched.

He shook a finger at Evie, his face turning red. "That is enough! Genevieve, you can either apologize or go to your room to think about what you said."

"You can't ground me," Evie said incredulously. "I'm almost an adult!"

"Our roof, our rules," Mom said. "We did not raise you to behave like this."

She glared at her oldest daughter. The resemblance between the soft shapes of their faces struck me. The only difference was their expressions. Evie's mouth was half-open in dismay and anger. Mom's lips flattened into a quivering line.

Evie shoved her chair to the table and stalked away. My mother stared at her half-eaten dinner in a daze. I thought I saw wetness gleaming in her eyes.

I instinctively rose to follow my sister.

"Alice," my father said. The dining room lights caught on his glasses as he rested his palm on the table. "Dinner isn't over yet."

I couldn't make myself meet his gaze.

"I'll be right back," I said. "I promise."

The hallway was dark, but it was not difficult for me to make out Evie stomping toward her room. I caught up to her.

"Evie," I said.

She rounded on me. The circles under her eyes matched the blue wallpaper of the shadowed hallway. "What do you want?" she snapped.

"I—um—" I faltered. She had never spoken to me like that before. "Do you want to talk about it?"

"Talk about what? I think all that needs to be said has been said."

"You don't mean what you said back there," I said. "Right?"

"Every word and more. I've made up my mind on what I want my future to be, and it isn't what Mom and Dad want."

I didn't want to give up on her yet. Why couldn't she see what the rest of us could? Her plans would completely backfire on her. It would be like Mom had said.

"If you do better in school, you'll have more opportunities," I said carefully.

Evie laughed. "School? The education in this town is a joke. They tell us what to think and how to think. The universities that our parents love aren't any better."

"But you'd have the opportunity to do greater things there."

"I'd be miserable," she said flatly. "I'm not like you, Alice. I shrivel under pressure. And I'd rather do something that makes me happy."

My head tilted. "You want your future to rely on art?"

She leaned against the doorframe of her room, running her fingers through her snarled hair. "I thought you'd get it, Alice. I'm tired of being talked about like I'm not here...of having these discussions over and over, the same thing all the time, because none of you listen."

"I am listening," I protested.

She fixed me with a pitying look. Somehow, that was worse than her anger. "Sorry, Alice. I don't think you are."

How could she talk like that? *She* was the one who wasn't listening. My nails bit into my palms.

"Who are you to say what I'm doing or not doing?" I retorted. "It's not like you cared anyway."

Evie's face screwed up in confusion. "What is that supposed to mean?"

I took a deep breath. *Great going, Lee.* I was supposed to be the logical one. I'd learned from being a female student in

STEM that I couldn't lash out when I was frustrated. Then I would be accused of being too emotional, and even unintelligent. It was easier to say nothing at all.

Yet I'd broken that one rule.

"Never mind," I said. "It's nothing."

"It's not nothing, and I'm sure you know it."

My anger hissed like oil in a pan. I met her gaze. "Mom and Dad put all their hopes and dreams on me because you didn't try to achieve them. I wanted someone to understand what I was going through. You were too wrapped up in your own head. Every time I tried to talk to you, you were off in la-la-land."

"I was in Meer," Evie corrected. "You used to go there too. Until—don't you remember?—you left me."

I searched her face to see if she was joking, but her lips were pressed into a grim line.

How could she talk about games of pretend at a time like this?

"You need to grow up, Evie," I said. "You might almost be an adult, but you still act like a kid."

"What makes you any better?" Her tone hardened. "You think you're so mature, so smart, always playing by Mom and Dad's rules. News flash: it's better to make yourself happy. Once you taste validation, you'll spend the rest of your life chasing it. Better to stop before you get addicted. I learned that the hard way."

We both stood there, breathing hard. I wanted to weep and scream at the same time. Evie and I had never spoken like this to each other before, never.

The rational side of my mind screamed at me to take it all back before it couldn't be taken back. But we had already hurt each other. What was a little more pain?

"So I suppose that when you realized that, you shouldered your responsibilities on me?" I said.

"I'm sorry." Evie swallowed. I could tell that backing down cost her. "But you wouldn't understand why."

I crossed my arms. "Try me."

"I can't. You won't believe me."

My stomach sank. "Don't tell me it has something to do with Meer."

When she hesitated, I knew it did.

So we came back to this: dancing around the truth, going in circles until we were no further than where we had started.

"I don't want to deal with this anymore," I said. "You're hopeless."

"You, too?" Evie's voice rose. "You're no better than our parents!"

I winced at the way the words echoed off the walls. *No better...no better...no better...*

Hot shame flowed through my chest. I shoved it down.

"If I'm no better than Mom and Dad, then neither are you," I spat. "All of you turned your backs on me at one time or another. If you actually tried—"

"I've told you before, I'm trying my best!"

"Maybe your best isn't good enough!"

The words spilled out before I could think about them. Evie recoiled like I'd dealt a physical blow.

Once an object is in motion, I remembered from Newton's First Law, *it stays in motion unless acted upon by an external force.*

I had set all of this in motion. I couldn't stop it now.

Evie's face was an empty mask. "Don't expect sympathy from me when you fall from Mom and Dad's grace," she said.

"Because eventually, even you won't be able to keep up with their dreams. And you'll have no one to blame but yourself."

"I hate you," I breathed.

An ugly silence hung in the air: a raw, seeping wound.

I didn't mean it. Not really. I just wanted to hurt her as badly as she'd hurt me.

I should have been the better person...should have searched for a way to salvage the situation.

I didn't.

Evie slammed her door in my face.

CHAPTER 30

I AM INSIDE the Pins & Needles Inn.

Angry scorch marks mar the carpet in front of the fireplace, which is littered with the upholstery of splintered Victorian chairs. Dust motes and smoke mingle in the air, shrouding everything in gray.

This cannot be real. The last place I remember being was the throne room of the Red Castle, where I...I...

That's odd. I can't quite recall what happened.

Movement flickers in my peripheral vision. I whirl around.

Evie leans against the fireplace mantel. She wears a yellow blouse and cuffed denim shorts. Her black hair is braided down the side of her shoulder. She holds the iron poker casually in her left hand; the word *REMEMBER* is still engraved on the handle.

She lifts her head to meet my gaze. Her brown eyes are stormy. In a flat tone, she says, "Welcome back to the Elsewhere."

I remain standing. The sight of my sister unleashes a torrent of emotions. I can't decide if I want to hug her or shout at her. I open my mouth, but all that comes out is, "Why did you take me away from the Red Castle?"

"I didn't." Her chin dips. "Your Queening will happen soon. You made it to the last square on the game board when you stood before the Red King and Queen and spoke against them."

Hope stirs in me. "I'm going to become Queen?"

It's about time. I've spent what seems like an eternity on this quest, and it still feels no closer to the end.

She twirls the poker. "Becoming a Queen doesn't necessarily make things easier."

I'm annoyed to admit that there's some truth to that. For instance, what would be the point of becoming Queen just to be instantly captured by the Red Court?

"You have to let me go back!" I say. "I need to defend myself against the Red Court."

"Don't worry. No one is in your way. They can't stop you from becoming the White Court's new Queen. The first Queen to be crowned by Meer itself."

There is a strange edge to her words.

"Don't you want me to be Queen?" I look at her disbelievingly. "I'm trying to help Meer. I want to help *you*."

"It's not that."

"Then what's the issue?"

Her lips tremble, and she studies the poker in her hands. "You shouldn't *want* to be Queen. Having more power makes things worse, not better. You should stay a Pawn."

The Lady of the Moon implied that on this quest, I would become a Queen. I don't understand why Evie is so adamantly against the idea.

"If becoming a Queen stops this game, then I think it's worth it," I argue.

My sister's head snaps up. The poker clatters amid the ruins of the furniture. "No! You can't end this game."

"Why?" I demand. "It's the only way we can escape Meer."

She shakes her head, her face pale and drawn. "When it ends, Meer ends. And what's left of me will be lost."

I go completely still. We stare at each other.

I cannot think of anything to say. Unspoken words burn my throat. The idea of losing Evie a second time is more horrible than I could have ever imagined.

She walks in my direction, stretching her hand toward me. "Alice, please. Don't take the crown. You will win nothing from it."

"Can our side still win if I don't become Queen?" I ask.

"I don't know," she admits. "Your odds might be better if you did, but…Hey! Don't look like that."

My shoulders tense. "Like what?"

"Like you've already made up your mind."

If this game does not end in our favor, Khalil will remain imprisoned in Meer…or all of us will. If I don't return to Earth, then my parents will have lost two daughters. I can't subject them to another loss.

But if what Evie says is true, then winning the game would mean losing her forever.

I lift my eyes to her. "Why did you involve us in this game in the first place? Why did it take so long for the others to find out about it?"

She lets out a brittle laugh. "I didn't mean to. It happened because Meer formed from my mind. When I learned we were in a game, I kept it from them. I protected them."

"I'm trying to protect them, too," I say.

Maybe I *have* already made up my mind.

My chest grows painfully hot. It is like the weight of my

compass, but sharper. Deeper. It drags me past Evie, to the fireplace, where my hand wrenches around an object on the mantel.

I blink to clear the spots from my vision. Even then, I hardly register the sight of what is in my hands.

I run my thumb over the spires of the crown. It feels less like metal and more like water, flowing under my touch. It is inlaid with pearls and diamonds that glimmer in the smoky parlor.

Evie's braid swings over her shoulder as she rushes toward me.

"Alice, please," she begs, stretching out her hand. "Don't accept the crown. Do the right thing."

The crown pulls at me like an anchor.

I have always tried to do the right thing, even if I am the only one who thinks it is right.

She continues, "Is it because of what I said when we met in the Elsewhere last time? I didn't mean it. I was just so angry and so hurt and so *tired*."

Lightning-fast, she grabs for the crown.

I dodge out of her reach.

"Al," she pleads. "Don't do this."

I almost stop in my tracks at the rawness of her voice.

But I can't forget the way she treated me the last time we met like this. She laughed in my face when I tried to apologize for my words. She called me a murderer.

I don't know what version of Evie I am facing now. I know only what I must do for all our sakes.

"I'm sorry," I murmur. "I'm sorry that I couldn't save you, even though I don't remember what happened. I'm sorry for this, too."

I place the crown on my head.

It settles there so perfectly, I wonder if it was made for me. Its weight is cool and reassuring. My resolve is a royal mantle that gives me the courage to meet my sister's gaze.

"I'll make things right," I vow. "I'll repay the Red Queen for what she did to you."

Evie's face crumples as the room blurs into the gray of the Elsewhere. Her words echo in my mind like stones thrown down a well.

You are wrong.

CHAPTER 31

WHITE. RED.

Those are the only colors I can picture: the only colors that mean anything.

The waters of my consciousness are too dark to break, so I stay beneath the surface, dimly aware of my vocal cords vibrating. Am I speaking? Screaming? My body is blistering from the inside out. My heartbeat pulses sluggishly in my ears.

I surface long enough to hear the Red Queen's voice.

"You bargain for more time, White Queen. Measure it carefully. I will not be kept waiting. Your sentence will come soon enough."

Then I'm pulled under again. Until I'm not.

My eyelids crack open. The scarlet floor rises to meet me.

"Alice! What's wrong?" Mikayla's cry reaches my ears as if from a distance. Hands grip my shoulders, supporting me.

Something smooth and cylindrical digs into my palm. The vial that Primera used to bottle my tears in Conchae Maris. The girl's words blur in my head.

Teardrops are valuable things... They will cure any ailment you may encounter on your journey.

My mouth burns too much to talk. I open my hand weakly, hoping Mikayla will understand. The world spins in and out of focus.

A second later, coldness trickles onto my tongue. I swallow.

Instantly, my vision steadies. Coughs rack my chest. I wipe my mouth with the back of my hand.

Mikayla's arm slings around my shoulders, keeping me upright. "Alice! Are you okay? Can you hear me?"

Her voice drills into my skull. I wince.

"Yes," I say. My voice is dry and scratchy.

"Oh, thank God." Her grip on me tightens. "You should sit down. Rest."

"How long was I out? Where are we?" The words come out slurred.

We are not in the throne room anymore. The ceiling tapers low above our heads in the narrow hallway we are in. Sconces burn along walls carved from red quartz. Richly woven tapestries cover the walls. In one of the tapestries, I glimpse the woven images depicting the phases of the Moon.

Mikayla's brow furrows. "You don't remember what happened?"

I shake my head.

"I'll give you the rundown. But first, let's get a little farther away, in case the Red Queen decides to take back her promise."

She made me a promise? I want to ask more about it, but Mikayla's tone verges on panic.

I peer over her shoulder. The two of us are alone, and the silence presses on my ears.

"Where's Hailey? Where is everyone else?" I ask.

She sucks in a heavy breath before her shoulders cave in. She won't meet my eyes. "I'll explain in a bit."

My stomach drops. Something bad must have happened to Hailey. I'm too afraid to ask again.

I lean on her, and we shuffle forward. My shoes sink into the plush crimson carpet. White swaths unfold at my feet.

I reach for the wine-stained scrap of fabric that is my apron. But it is not there.

Instead, I am wearing a white empire-waisted dress with white seed pearls sewn into the bodice.

I stare at myself in wonder. My hand goes to my head.

The spires of a pearl-and-diamond encrusted crown pass beneath my fingertips.

My shoes—no longer Mary Janes but now white flats—catch on the carpet. I stumble.

Mikayla's grip on me tightens. "Keep going. Just a little longer."

After a few minutes, we stop inside a new passageway. The ceiling narrows to a point over our heads. The quartz walls are a lurid maroon. Rose petals cover the tiled floor. The flowers' sickly sweet perfume is made more cloying by the torches that light the hall.

"Can you stand by yourself?" Mikayla asks.

"I think so." I move away from her, leaning gingerly against the wall. I momentarily close my eyes against a rush of dizziness. "Tell me what happened in the throne room. I have to know."

When I look at her again, her eyes dart to my face, then away. She moistens her lips and examines the rose petals on the ground. "Long story short, you bought us some more time."

I frown. "What? How?"

Mikayla folds her arms. "You became a Queen. How did you do that?"

Her voice is equal parts awed and incredulous.

"I'll get to that," I say. "Just...please, tell me more about what happened in the throne room."

She obliges. I listen, spellbound, through her account of the trial.

Halfway through my testimony, I began raving and reaching for things that weren't there. Everyone thought I was mad until the throne room began to fall apart. The walls peeled open. The floor cracked into floating pieces. Beneath was only blackness. I shudder at the way she describes it.

"There was one casualty. Mr. Knightley fell into the abyss," Mikayla says.

"He's dead?"

She nods. "I heard the screams. He's gone. For real this time."

I search for relief, or shock. All I can muster is numbness.

Mikayla lowers her gaze, fiddling with her bracelet. "Before anyone else could die, the Lady of the Moon sacrificed herself to seal the tear in Meer. She used all her power. So she's gone, too."

Her words are flat. Her eyes are dull. She must be compartmentalizing, as I so often do.

My head thuds back against the wall. I can't fathom how all that happened while I was senseless to myself. One of our most powerful allies is gone. A pang of grief hits my heart.

"What happened after that?" I ask, fearing the answer.

"A beam of white light shot up around you. Suddenly, you were wearing a crown and a dress." She gestures at my outfit. "You also sounded...different. Like someone else was speaking through you. You told the Red King and Queen that both Courts needed more time to plan their next moves. They agreed. Then the trial ended. I followed you out of the throne room, and you collapsed."

I wish I could remember any of this. I feel unmoored all over again, drifting in a blue haze of delirium.

"It's a good thing I still had Primera's gift from Conchae Maris," I say. "It saved me."

I'm still not sure why she gave me that vial. Maybe she wanted me to be indebted to her.

Mikayla's face goes stony. "Primera is the enemy."

"I know that," I snap, then soften my tone. "It's strange. I wonder if she foresaw the trial."

"Maybe," she mutters. "Well, I couldn't have predicted that Hailey might have a role in this."

"What do you mean?"

Mikayla lowers her gaze. She twists the silver bracelet on her wrist. "She might have put something in your wine. That's why you hallucinated."

The words are so quiet, I hardly hear them. My stomach drops.

"What? How do you know?" I blurt out.

It can't be true. Maybe I'm not Hailey's friend, but I'm certainly not her enemy. We worked together on this quest.

The memory flashes in my mind of our hands knocking together when we reached for the same goblet.

"When you went down for your testimony, a vial broke at her feet," Mikayla says. "She wouldn't tell me what it was. All I know is that it looked like something the Sheep sells at her store."

My fingers dig into the unsmoothed edges of the quartz wall. The pain helps me refocus.

"Hailey wouldn't poison me," I argue.

"I don't think so, either." Mikayla sighs. "But she never told us exactly what happened to her in the Red Castle. Maybe they threatened her into helping them."

I rub my forehead. I can't reconcile this betrayal. It is so *wrong*.

I ask the only question left to ask. "Where is she now?"

Mikayla's hands curl into fists as she studies the rose petals scattered across the hallway. "The Red Queen had her arrested."

"What? Why?"

"She charged her with littering in the Court."

I put my head in my hands, trying to remember how to pull enough air into my lungs. The flowers' sickly sweet smell makes me woozy.

Hailey's capture means Khalil's sacrifice was for nothing. Now we've lost two friends.

I force myself to concentrate. "If she were truly on their side—if she'd agreed to poison me—then they wouldn't have arrested her, right?"

"Who knows? Nothing makes sense with the Red Court. That entire trial didn't make any sense."

"Fair enough."

I don't want to think about what the Red Court might do now that they have both Hailey and Khalil in their hands. It's up to us to get to them first.

"Where is the rest of our Court? Where is the Red Court?" I ask.

"No idea. Everyone scattered after the trial."

I knead my forehead, wondering how I can possibly salvage this situation. Every new piece of bad news weighs heavily on my shoulders.

Mikayla tries to smile. "Hey, at least you're a Queen now. Tell me more about how that happened."

I tell her about my hallucinations during the trial. Then I

summarize my encounter with Evie in the Elsewhere. Mikayla's eyes never leave my face as I talk.

When I finish, she says incredulously, "She didn't *want* you to be Queen?"

"No. But it's too late for that now, obviously."

She picks at her bracelet. "For what it's worth...I think you made the right decision. We have to end this game, even if it means losing her again. There's no other way." Her voice catches, and she clears her throat. "She deserves peace."

"It's strange that she visits no one besides me," I say. "Not you, or the others."

"Maybe it's all she can do, in whatever state she's in."

"That's possible," I muse. "Then what's next?"

"We avenge her," Mikayla says bluntly. "We pay back the Red Court for what they've done to Meer, a thousand times over. We'll tear their Castle down brick by brick. For her."

The Red Court is responsible for all of this. They corrupted the world that served as Evie's refuge. They have tormented all of us, and still they deny any role in my sister's death. I have made so many mistakes when it comes to my sister, but I am determined that her death will not mean nothing.

I promised her I would make things right with my power as Queen. I will make good on that promise if it is the last thing I do.

Evie's words nag at the back of my mind: *You are wrong.*

I push it away.

"For her," I say.

We stand in silence until a rhythmic clicking sound makes us jump.

Mikayla shoves a finger against her lips as she reaches for her knife. She creeps down the hallway, pursuing the sound. Reluctantly, I follow her.

We turn a corner. The sound grows louder, almost metronomic. It is too light and too precise to be footsteps.

Something slithers across the floor. I yelp.

"Little goose," a familiar voice scoffs. "You shouldn't sneak around so."

A train of blue-and-white yarn rustles into view.

The Sheep perches inside an alcove. Extra knitting needles stick out from the tufts of wool on her head, giving her a porcupine-like appearance. Her rectangular pupils observe me behind oversized spectacles. She *harrumphs*. It sounds a little self-satisfied. "I thought you'd be crowned."

Mikayla skirts in front of me. She does not re-sheath her knife. "How did you get here?" she asks.

"I went Diagonally," the Sheep says. "And then a little Sideways."

I frown. "That doesn't match any chess piece's movement, unless you're a King or Queen, and I'm sure you're not. What *are* you?"

"Baaaah!" she bleats, rocking forward in her alcove. Her hooves dangle over the floor. "You pay too much heed to rules. I trust that my potion guided you here?"

The change in subject catches me off-guard.

"Yes, until it wore off," I mutter. On instinct, I reach for the warm presence of my compass. Of course, it is no longer there.

"It fulfilled its purpose," she replies flatly.

The Sheep turns her attention back to her knitting. I look at Mikayla, whose arched eyebrows ask, *Can we go now?*

"Wait a minute," I tell her, then I address the Sheep. "Hailey was arrested for littering during the trial. Mikayla said that the vial she dropped might have come from your shop. Do you know anything about that?"

The Sheep doesn't lift her head. "A great deal of objects in Meer come from my shop."

"So this vial didn't?"

"It did."

I'd forgotten how frustrating it is to converse with the Sheep. I try to modulate my tone. "So, then—"

"Whatever was inside it was not of my maaaaking," she bleats.

"Then what was it?"

The pace of her needles slows, and she regards me with her eerie rectangular pupils. "I cannot say."

"Cannot or will not?" I counter.

"Sheep," Mikayla cuts in. "Is it true that you had Evie's token in your shop? Hailey said she found it there."

"A great deal of objects in my shop come from Meer," the aged ewe retorts.

I can't suppress a huff. "That's the same as what you said earlier."

Her black nose quivers in what might be a snort. "It's not the same thing at all, little goose. You still haven't learned the difference between what you say and what you mean."

"But how did it get there?" Mikayla demands. She takes a step toward the Sheep. With a jolt, I realize she still hasn't sheathed her knife.

"Mik…" I say uneasily.

She ignores me. Her dark eyes pierce the Sheep. "Well?" she says, voice rising. "Tell me! How did you find it?"

"Lost things have a funny habit of finding where they are meant to go," the Sheep says. I can't shake the feeling that although she is replying to Mikayla, she is really speaking to me.

The Sheep continues to knit. The rhythm of her needles puts my teeth on edge. It's too rigid.

"Why don't you give a straight answer for once?" Mikayla snaps, throwing up her hands. Her knife cuts through the air. I wince, giving it a wide berth.

My friend turns her back on the Sheep and stalks down the scarlet hall. At some point during our conversation—I'm not sure when—most of the torches burned out, suffusing the air with a heavy haze. Mikayla's features warp when she looks over her shoulder and says, "Alice, let's go."

I balk. "What? Where?"

"To find the others," she says, like it's the most obvious thing in the world. "This Castle must be huge. We need to start searching now."

I glance at the Sheep, who carries on knitting her mass of blue-and-white yarn. "I don't know," I say. "I need to ask the Sheep some things."

Mikayla slashes her hand through the air. "She's not going to help you, or anyone. Come on."

"I am always helpful," the Sheep sniffs. "You simply don't listen when I tell you things, like if you want to reach the dungeon, you take a right and two lefts in the next passageways, and go down the stairs. There you will find your Knight and Bishop. Mind you—don't take two rights and a left. That leads you back up to the throne room."

The ewe says this all in one breath. Her needles don't pause for a moment.

Mikayla and I wear twin expressions of disbelief.

"How do you know that?" I ask.

"I listen," is all the Sheep says.

Mikayla crosses her arms. "If you know where our friends are, then why don't you help us free them?"

"I cannot undertake your quest," the Sheep says. "If you wish to leave, White King, then go. If you wish to stay, White Queen, then staaaay."

When she draws out the last vowel, a nameless instinct sparks in the back of my mind. Perhaps it is a coincidence. But I have long since learned not to trust coincidences.

I turn to Mikayla, who is waiting a few yards away. "I can't leave without asking my questions," I admit. "It's important."

Mikayla grimaces. "We shouldn't separate."

I don't deny it.

"I need to do this," I say simply. "If you're determined to leave, you can. Don't go too far."

Mikayla hesitates, then nods. "Yeah, I am. Do you remember the directions to the dungeon?"

"I already memorized them."

"Follow me when you're done with her. I'll meet you there." She fingers the lip of her knife. For a moment, it blends in with her silver bracelet. Her dark eyes, the shade of bitter coffee, lock on mine. "Stay safe, Alice."

"Same for you," I reply. "Don't get captured."

She dips into a brief bow. A little of her usual smirk returns to her face. "Yes, your Majesty. See you soon."

"See you soon," I echo.

She takes off down the hall, the thud of her boots muffled against the petal-carpeted floor.

Unease gnaws at me as I watch her go. It feels wrong to separate from her in the enemy's Castle. I know she can manage on her own, but if something happens to her while I'm not around, the game will be lost.

I tighten my jaw. I have to make the most of my time with the Sheep.

"Did you know that I was going to become Queen?" I ask her.

"Unknowing and knowing is a tricky business," the Sheep says matter-of-factly.

I wait for her to elaborate. Of course, she does not. Talking with her is like playing tennis with an opponent who walks away every time you hit the ball. Perhaps the solution is to not maintain a single thread of conversation.

With that hypothesis in mind, I switch the subject. "Not many people must visit you in Shepherd's Landing."

"They don't come to visit *me*. They visit the shop."

I consider my next move. She enjoys frustrating people. Maybe if I return the favor, I'll provoke her into revealing something. "Hmmm. I bet the Red King and Queen would never embarrass themselves by showing their faces there."

She bleats derisively. "What do *you* know about it? I've commissioned products worth a King's ransom. I've always satisfied my customers' demands. Except one…"

"Who?"

She snaps her mouth shut.

My eyebrows lift. That was more than I thought I'd get out of her. I try a different topic. "Do you sell potions for remembering things?"

"I used to. I made them every two lunar eclipses."

"The Moon is gone now."

"Yes," she agrees. "It will never be in stock again."

My heart sinks along with my odds of remembering the night that Evie died.

"Fine," I say. "Can you give me information about the Lost Queen?"

"You are her sister. There is little I can tell you that you do not know."

I'm not certain about that. Just by adventuring through Meer, I have learned so much about my sister's fears and dreams.

"Can you give me information about her death?" I ask.

At that, the Sheep's needles pause. The silence presses in on my ears. She gazes somewhere over the top of my head.

"The Lost Queen was not killed," she says at last. "She sought a place Beyond. She exists there now."

Beyond. That word came up in the vision of Mikayla's pearl during the trial.

"What does that mean?" I ask.

"Your quest is not to find her," the Sheep says, so sharply that I jump. "Do not forget your payment for the potion. You must bring down the Red Court. Go find the White King, now. And take this with you. You may need it."

She extends her hoof. It takes me a moment to realize she is holding out the signet ring Primera stole from the Red Queen during the trial.

"How did you get that?" I say, eyeing the ring warily.

"We spoke and listened. We agreed it is better for you to have it. You must be aware."

"Of what?"

"You have the power to decide Meer's fate. She alone of the Red Court understands they do not belong in Meer. She is willing to aid you in this one way."

"It's a trick," I say immediately. "She's lying."

I'm not sure why the Sheep has any contact with Primera. She should know better. Primera is the enemy.

She clicks her tongue. "It is too bad that being a Queen doesn't make you any less of a goose. Help comes from strange places, but traitors come from stranger places. Take the ring. Remember."

The command is as heavy as my crown.

I take the ring.

It is the size of an acorn, a cool weight in my palm. When I close my hand, the metal band presses into the scars on my palm.

"I don't understand," I say.

"You will. Now, hurry. Free your captured Knight and Bishop before it is too late. I hear they are in handsome cells."

CHAPTER 32

I FOLLOW THE Sheep's directions.

I traverse a series of dim passageways and descend a spiraling granite staircase. The dungeon is damp and dark, and reeks of mildew. It opens into a T-shaped corridor where prison cells line both ends. Torches sputter in sconces, casting sinister shadows against the walls. The russet shade of the stone floor reminds me of dried blood.

Perhaps I should not have come here. I didn't need to obey the Sheep. In a way, she was the one who caused all of this to happen. If not for her, I might have remained in my old, logical life.

Though if I hadn't bought her potion, I would not have discovered the truth behind my hallucinations.

There you go again with the hypotheticals, I scold myself.

It doesn't matter anymore if I could have avoided this quest. All I can do is complete it.

A scraping noise reaches my ears.

Two red-armored guards march toward me, halberds and swords at the ready.

I look between them, my heart pounding. Where is

Mikayla? It's only been a few minutes since she went on without me. She should have been here, waiting.

Unless she was caught.

The soldiers advance. Their hands tighten on their weapons. Their faces are as hard-edged as marble and devoid of expression.

Slowly, I back away. I cannot outrun them up the spiral staircase. I do not carry any weapons. All I have is my Queen's crown and the Red Queen's signet ring. The ring is cold on the fourth finger of my right hand.

I ask myself a question I never imagined asking: *What would the Red Queen do?*

She wields her power through force and fear. She would not run.

A dark laugh escapes my mouth. It doesn't sound like me.

"You cannot touch me," I say. "I am a *Queen*. You are unworthy of my presence. Move aside before I make you."

Do I detect a flicker of hesitation in the guards' faces? If so, it's gone in an instant. The two march toward me, hemming me against the dungeon steps.

"Get back!" I command, thrusting my hands out.

White light engulfs us. I shut my eyes against the blast. A scream is trapped in my throat.

Seconds pass. I don't feel any different.

Cautiously, I open my eyes.

The white light is gone, and the guards are staggering to their knees on the stone. Their weapons clatter to the floor as they paw at their faces. Their pupils have turned milky-white.

Was that explosion of light *my* doing? I stare at my scarred palms in wonder until one of the guards gropes for his sword at my feet. I kick it out of reach.

"Which one of you has the keys to this dungeon?" I ask.

They cringe at my tone. The second guard fumbles with his pocket. Metal glints in his hand, but he draws his arm backward as if to toss them away from me.

I stamp on top of his wrist, pinning it to the ground. Bones crunch. He writhes in silent agony. Part of me cringes. A darker part of me finds grim satisfaction in prying the keys from his trembling fingers.

"Do not test my mercy. If you insist on defying me, there are fates worse than death." The words pour out of me, similar to the declaration I made in Shepherd's Landing after drinking the potion, as if someone else spoke with my voice.

Who am I becoming?

I can't dwell on it. My movements are mechanical as I throw the halberd and sword inside the nearest cell. The guards crawl toward it and pound on the bars as I run into the left wing of the dungeons. Rusted metal blurs past.

"Mikayla? Are you here?" I call.

"Alice?" someone says.

I stop short in my tracks at the person sitting cross-legged inside the last cell.

Hailey grips the bars of her prison. Her mouth forms a round *O* as she takes me in. No bruises or cuts mottle her skin, though one sleeve on her green dress is torn in half. Her hand goes to her peacock earring.

"What's going on?" she asks, dragging herself to a standing position. "And why were you saying Mikayla's name?"

My stomach drops. "She came down to the dungeon before me. You didn't see her?"

"No. The only people here are me, Khalil, and the guards. How'd you get past the guards? With a grenade? I saw the light."

I force myself to stop sorting through the possibilities of

what might have happened to Mikayla. I sort through the keys instead. There are sixteen in total. Each is made of copper and studded with a ruby. I begin trying the keys in the lock of Hailey's cell. My hands shake.

"I'm a Queen now," I whisper. "Which, I suppose, means I have…certain powers. I'm here to break you and Khalil out. Where is he?"

"On the other side of the dungeon."

I swear under my breath. That gives the guards more time to regroup and attack us. I'll have to be quick. I'm down to twelve keys now.

The question comes out before I can stop it: "Did someone spike my wine during the trial?"

Hailey's brow furrows. "No. I didn't see anything like that."

"Are you sure? Because Mikayla thinks you had something to do with it."

Her eyes widen. Her hands drop from the bars, hanging at her sides. "*What?*" she blurts out.

"Shhh!" I hiss, throwing a glance over my shoulder. Fortunately, the guards are not in sight. In rapid, hushed words, I share Mikayla's account of the trial, including the strange vial that fell in front of Hailey's seat in the juror box.

"That wasn't mine!" she protests. "It came flying out of the air."

I can't stop a disbelieving huff. "What?"

"It's true!" she insists. "When the White Rabbit blew his trumpet, an object burst out and landed at my feet."

"What was it?"

"I don't know! I'd never seen it before. After that, a lot happened at the same time. You started yelling at things that weren't there. The Red Queen accused me of littering. Mikayla tried to help, but they arrested me anyway." She tilts her head, then adds, "I remember that Mikayla yelled something kind of odd."

I shuffle through the keys. Five left. "Like what?"

"She said, 'It's not supposed to be her.'"

The next key yields in the lock with a *click*. The door screeches open, and the two of us stand face-to-face. Her green eyes are earnest. Wounded.

I wish I could believe that she is lying. Then I would not have to wonder what secrets Mikayla has been keeping from me.

"Do you really think I'd try to hurt you?" Hailey asks.

"No," I reply, a beat too late.

She lowers her head. "I'm sorry for how I've acted toward you in Meer. It wasn't because of you—not really. It was more about Evie and her game."

"What do you mean?"

Bitterness seeps into her tone. "I am the Knight. It's a great honor—until I'm inferior to my friends. Evie knew how much I loved Meer, and she still chose to give me a lesser title. Then, when you came along, you were a Pawn. But you could be more than that."

"I could be a Queen," I say quietly, tracing the spires of my new crown.

She nods. Her voice is taut. "When you said Primera was 'only a Pawn', it was like you already wanted to look down on others. But I got mad at you because I couldn't get angry at Evie for choosing Mikayla over everyone else."

The keys hang limply in my fingers as I mull over her words.

It makes sense that as its creator, Evie crowned herself Queen of Meer. It is logical that she made her best friend,

Mikayla, the King. Yet I had not considered that Khalil or Hailey might harbor resentment about being delegated to lesser roles.

Evie should not have allowed such inequality within her own friend circle. It troubles me to think of her being so indifferent—selfish, even. Maybe that is why we cannot dream in Meer: because there is room only for her.

"I'm sorry for taking Evie's bracelet," Hailey says, speaking faster. She steps over the threshold of the dark cell. "I should have told you, but I wasn't even sure if it was Evie's token until Mikayla confirmed it had gone missing. And then…I didn't know what to make of the memory it showed me."

"Why's that?"

"Because it'd mean that Mikayla was there when Evie—"

Her eyes dart behind me. A gasp catches in her throat. She surges from the cell—too late.

A blunt force drives into my legs. The keys fly out of my fingers and I hit the ground. A spike of white-hot pain hammers through my wrist. Panting, I raise my head, nose-to-nose with the stones of the dungeon floor. The stench of copper fills my nose.

Gauntleted fists wrench my arms behind me, deftly tying my hands with a length of thick rope. I struggle until a booted foot stomps on my back, expelling the air from my lungs.

I'm dragged unceremoniously to my feet by a scarlet-armored guard. His face is as blank as a puppet's, milky-white eyes staring somewhere past my head.

Stupid, stupid, stupid. The guards were blinded, but they could easily track noise. They must know this dungeon—no, this entire Castle—by sound and touch, not just sight. I was too caught up in Hailey's story to pay attention to them.

My white dress is streaked with dirt. Somehow, my crown

remains on my head, though it's been knocked askew to my left ear. My captor does not seem inclined to adjust it. I strain against the knots of my bonds. All I do is chafe the skin of my wrists. The Red Queen's signet ring digs into the knuckle of my index finger.

Hailey resists a little longer than me, but eventually she, too, is detained. Even with her hands tied behind her back, she's defiant. When her captor pushes her forward, she kicks his crimson gauntlets, copper hair flying around her shoulders. He doesn't appear to notice.

"Retrieve the White Bishop," the guard holding me says. "The Red King and Queen request an audience with them."

I jump at the sound of his gravelly, deep voice. This is the first time I have heard any of the Red Castle's guards speak.

"What's happening?" I demand. "I have a right to know!"

"I'm not going anywhere!" Hailey shouts. She flails in her captor's grip, letting loose a string of swear words that Mikayla would be proud of.

Where is Mikayla? Have the guards already apprehended her for a different kind of torment?

The guards do not acknowledge either of us. They march us to the opposite end of the dungeons, where a new guard awaits. He takes the keys from my captor, unlocks a cell, and steps inside. Moments later, he hauls out a bleary-eyed Khalil.

Khalil blinks rapidly when he sees us. I'm relieved to see that he looks none the worse for wear, besides a thin layer of grime on his forearms.

"Hailey? Alice?" he says. His eyes widen when he notices my crown and dress. "You're a Queen now!"

"For all the good it's doing me," I mutter.

"What's going on?" he asks.

"I was trying to break you two out. I didn't succeed, obviously."

He stumbles as the guard leads him forward. "Where's Mikayla?"

"I don't know," I say more sharply than I intend to. "But she'd better be safe."

My captor raps my wrists. "Silence," he says coldly. "Do not delay us."

I can't believe things went so wrong so quickly. I should have made a better plan. Or maybe I should have tried to find Mikayla first.

Mistakes upon mistakes. It only takes one to prove fatal.

CHAPTER 33

WHEN THE GUARDS parade us into the throne room, Mikayla is standing before the Red King and Queen.

Unlike the three of us, she is not a captive. Her posture is rigid, and her arms are folded across her torso. She appears unharmed.

My relief mingles with fear and frustration. I want to yell at her and ask her where she has been. But the sight of the Red King and Queen makes me pause.

The monarchs lounge on their ruby-studded thrones. The Red Queen licks her lips when she sees the three of us enter. She raps her knuckles on her scepter, eyeing us with undisguised glee. The Red King does not acknowledge our presence. The crown on his head is lopsided. His head droops onto his chest and his eyes are heavy-lidded. Though his posture is peaceful, a shiver of unease runs through my body.

The guards march us through the Red Castle's towering gryphon-shaped pillars. Ruby glints through the quartz, creating the illusion that the beasts are snarling at us.

The Red Queen speaks first. She curls a manicured hand in our direction. "Look, White King. I bring your subjects to you as a show of good faith, despite your new Queen's treachery." She assesses my tattered white dress. Condescension drips from her tone. "She is not so threatening now."

"Mikayla! Help us!" Hailey shouts—or tries to. Her captor drives a fist into her gut. She doubles over, wheezing.

"Hailey!" Khalil cries. He jerks against the grip of his guard, to no avail. His dark curls fall over his forehead as he struggles. The cold fury of his bared teeth is a startling contrast to his usual smile.

Mikayla's breath hitches. Her hand darts to the knife sheathed at her hip. "You said you wouldn't hurt them!"

"I have not hurt them," the Red Queen retorts. "My soldiers merely restrain your weak Knight."

Hailey lifts her head, glaring daggers at the Red Queen.

Mikayla talks as though she has made some kind of arrangement with the monarchs. How? And why? She was supposed to be with *me*. I try to catch her eye, but she isn't looking in my direction.

Mikayla swallows. Her voice is higher-pitched when she speaks again. "What about the cat?"

Dinah. Guilt rushes through me. I'd forgotten about my pet in the chaos of everything. I can't lose track of her again.

The Red Queen huffs. "Oh, no one could find the animal. I am certain it is avoiding my servants."

Mikayla chews her lip. "Fine. What about the Lost Queen's token?"

The Red Queen snaps her fingers. The White Rabbit comes forward bearing the silver bracelet on a tray. He sets it at Mikayla's feet, then scurries back to the edge of the room, but remains within shouting distance.

Mikayla picks up the bracelet with her sleeve and drops it gingerly into her tunic pocket. Before I have time to wonder how she bargained for it—or how she suddenly wields such authority with the monarchs—she tells the Red Queen, "Dismiss your subjects. That includes your guards. Tell them to seal the doors. I want this audience to be *private*."

Her tone is brisk, though it trembles a little on the final word.

It sounds like she is trying to negotiate with the Red Court, but that can't be right. If I know her, she wouldn't resort to that.

The Red Queen glowers. "I am not sending away my guards."

Mikayla folds her arms. "Then I will not discuss my terms of surrender."

The word *surrender* jolts me.

"Mik, what's going on?" I blurt.

I catch the barest shake of her head that seems to say, *Not right now.*

She and the Red Queen have a stare-down. I swear I can hear electricity sizzling in the air.

At last, the Red Queen relents. "Very well. But I will not forget this, White King." She addresses her guards. "All of you, leave. Seal the doors. Do not let anyone in or out of this room, no matter what you hear."

The soldiers salute and step away from us, retreating in an orderly fashion. My heartbeat flutters in my chest. Trapping us in here isn't the plan I expected from Mikayla. She freed us, but at what cost?

When the tall doors heave shut, Mikayla turns toward the three of us.

"Give me a moment with them," she says. She's dashing toward us before the Red Queen can reply.

She flings her arms around me. I stiffen inside her hug,

unsure how to react until her knife presses at my bonds. The rope loosens.

"If you pull, it'll come undone," she hisses in my ear. "But not yet."

"What's going on?" I whisper back.

"I'll explain. Just trust me."

It's not enough. I want to demand more, but she has already moved on to Hailey and Khalil, muttering the same thing in their ears. She steps backward, eyes lingering on each of us in turn. Her knife returns to its sheath.

Wait, she mouths.

"Are you quite finished?" the Red Queen says. "Mightn't I order the execution now?"

My heart goes cold. *Execution?*

Beside me, Hailey inhales sharply.

Mikayla's body tenses like a bowstring. She spins on her heel. "*No.* There will be no execution."

The Red Queen pouts. "Fine. Then give us what you promised."

"Your weapon and your surrender," the Red King murmurs. I'd forgotten he was here, he's so silent.

Slowly, Mikayla unclasps the sheath from her hip. She takes deliberate strides toward the monarchs, removing the silver knife from its casing. Crimson light refracts off the blade.

"This knife is one of a kind," she says. "You won't find another like it. It was forged from the wishes of Meer's Moon. The Lost Queen gifted it to me. It always aims true."

She bows her head as she advances the last few steps toward the mirrored dais. Her black hair curtains her face.

Then, silver arcs from her hand.

The Red Queen's body seizes.

Hailey makes a strangled gasp. Khalil's jaw drops. My eyes are slow to track the trajectory of the knife.

The weapon is buried in the Queen's throat.

By the time the monarch's head thuds against her throne, her gaze has gone glassy. Her scepter clatters to the floor as the wound gushes.

But it's not blood that pours out. It's sand—as if she were an hourglass. Hundreds of grains weep from the chasm in her throat, cascading over the folds of her elaborate scarlet dress onto the ruby tiles.

In the silence, the King's head lolls. His eyelids flutter.

"Admit defeat," Mikayla says. "Say the White Court has won. You're surrounded. If you won't go quietly, then I'll rid Meer of you, like I did with your Queen."

He chuckles. The quiet sound grates on my nerves. "You are a greater fool than I thought, White King. You do not understand the power you have provoked. You seal your friends' fates and your own."

Mikayla draws back, her forehead wrinkling in confusion...and maybe fear. She lifts her chin. "None of this would have happened if you'd let Evie live in Meer."

"She could not. She was not one of us."

"She created you!" she screams. Her eyes are dark and glittering. "And you repaid her by driving her out of her only safe place."

"We did nothing. It was she who did not belong. And now, foolish King, you do not bring about the end of the game. Instead, you hasten the destruction of Meer."

Mikayla draws herself up.

"Good!" she spits.

That one word sets me off-balance. I barely register the

rope falling from my wrists, or Khalil and Hailey moving forward. All I can focus on is the venom in Mikayla's voice.

It makes no sense that she would want Meer destroyed. Maybe she's playing a role for the Red King.

Deep down, though, I know she isn't.

In a daze, I follow Khalil and Hailey.

Khail calls, "Mikayla! What are you doing?"

She turns toward us, and some of her defiance fades. "I did the best I could with what I knew. Alice, I left you because I was trying to get to the Red King and Queen. I was going to fake our surrender, but I didn't think you'd go down to the dungeons so soon."

"I don't understand," I whisper. "Why would you go behind my back like this? Why would you put us in danger?"

Her face hardens. "I did it for all your sakes. We need to win the game to get out of this world alive. Nothing else matters."

"But we have to save Meer!" Hailey protests.

Mikayla laughs darkly. "The Lady of the Moon said we had to defeat the Red King and Queen. She said nothing about saving Meer…not that there's anything left to save. *They* ruined everything." The last sentence comes out as a growl.

Khalil speaks in a low, calm tone. "Mik, think about what you just did. You assassinated the Red Queen."

"Alice killed Mrs. Knightley!" she throws back at him. "How is that any different?"

My jaw locks as everyone's heads swivel to me.

The image of the rag-doll woman on the carpet of the Pins & Needles Inn wavers in my vision like heat vapor. I dig my nails into my palms, which itch with the memory of guiding the poker into her back. My traitorous mind conjures the too-wide grin that Mrs. Knightley wore to her death.

Khalil hesitates. "Alice had to—"

"Exactly," Mikayla interrupts. "I also had to. There's no more time for thinking, only action."

While I hate to admit that she has a point, I never envisioned precisely *how* I was going to defeat the Red King and Queen. I didn't want to face the reality that Mikayla has now forced us into.

"Don't you care if Meer is destroyed?" is all I can bring myself to ask.

Her lips press together. She takes a step back from us, averting her gaze. "It's already dying. All we can do is put it out of its misery."

"No," Hailey insists. "You're wrong. I don't believe that."

Khalil chimes in, "Mik, Evie wouldn't want this. If you leave Meer to die, you're letting her dreams die, too."

Mikayla's laugh is borderline hysterical. "Evie made me think my dreams were worth something. Now I know it's all useless! I'm sick of loving what I can't live. Meer is a lie. A beautiful one, but still a lie."

The floor might as well be crumbling into sand beneath me.

Mikayla was my sister's best friend. She understood Evie better than any of us. Why would she betray her memory so grievously?

Until now, I didn't understand what my sister meant when she begged me to stay a Pawn. But there is no glory in a crown that is only for show.

Upon his throne, the Red King stirs. He wheezes, "I awaken...You have forced my hand."

He grips the armrests of his royal seat. His body seizes, limbs spasming as if they are being manipulated by some unseen puppet master. Shock waves pulsate through the marbled floor of the Castle like a massive heartbeat, and I struggle to stay on my feet.

The Red King's eyes fly open. Scarlet pupils flare.

In the air, sharp and glistening filaments pull taut and *snap*.

A black vortex opens between the thrones. Spikes of red-and-white energy crackle from it. Tendrils of darkness seep from the hole, sinking into the walls and floor like the roots of an invasive plant. The air turns searing hot. The heat reminds me of my hallucination during the trial, when stars burned my skin. Chunks of quartz crumble from the pillars holding up the soaring ceilings of the Red Castle.

I dodge—not fast enough. A crystalline wedge scores my forearm with a stinging slash of pain. Quartz accumulates around us in piles, littering the lush crimson carpet. Dust and debris choke the air. I wipe furiously at my eyes.

"Ah!" Khalil clutches his shoulder. Blood trickles between his fingers.

"Watch out!" Hailey cries. She drags him backward. A slab of quartz the size of a bookshelf shatters inches from their feet.

My stomach twists. If they had reacted a millisecond slower…no, I don't even want to make that calculation.

Mikayla is a few steps in front of me, staring numbly at the vortex between the thrones. It expands with each passing second, obscuring the Red Queen's body, rippling in concave circles. The shape reminds me of a snake's yawning maw.

I realize what is happening too late.

"Get back!" I scream at Khalil and Hailey. My throat tears.

Mikayla does not move. If not for her hair fluttering around her shoulders, I might think she was a statue.

I dash to her and grab her arm. She flinches.

"We have to go," I call over the sound of the throne room breaking apart. "Or we'll be sucked inside!"

I point at the vortex. Finally, her eyes flicker with realization. Our legs blur into the same rhythm as we run away.

I already know it is not enough. I do not have to turn around to sense the magic that festers, stronger and stronger, in our wake.

Our shoes skid against the floor. A force tugs at our clothes, and then our limbs. In vain, we scrabble for an anchor as scarlet tendrils ensnare us.

The vortex swallows us whole.

CHAPTER 34

PRESSURE BEARS DOWN on my ears as if I'm miles under-water, throbbing with every beat of my heart. Gray rushes in waves past me. Stars implode across my vision. Then—

My hand drags against something rough. I stumble to a halt.

I am on the Moon—or rather, somewhere that resembles it, because the Moon no longer exists.

Craters and pieces of glass litter the floor. Tendrils of silver mist hang in the air. No constellations or comets adorn the ceiling. This place feels...temporary. Ethereal. Like if I turn around, it will disappear.

That must mean that we are in the Elsewhere.

Only one person could have brought me here.

I lift my head. "Evie?" I call.

No one answers.

My ragged breathing is far too loud in my ears. I feel like a musician cut off from the rest of the orchestra, bumbling through a symphony without a conductor's hand.

The air beside me ripples. Mikayla staggers out of the jagged opening and into the Elsewhere. She turns around as if to lunge back through the rift, but it has already sealed behind her with a loud *crack*. My ears ring.

Mikayla blinks in disbelief, then faces me, swaying on the spot.

"Where are we?" she asks, glancing around.

I wet my lips. "I think...we're in the Elsewhere. This can't be the Moon."

"Great." She takes a few cautious steps forward, surveying the vacant chamber. Glass crunches under her boots. "So how do we get out?"

I stare at her. All I can think about is her empty expression when she assassinated the Red Queen. Like it was merely an unpleasant chore to watch the sand pour from her throat.

Mikayla frowns. "Hello?" she says, waving a hand in front of my face.

An incredulous laugh escaped me. "Are you not going to explain what you did back there?"

Her eyebrows knit together. "I have."

"No, Mik. You owe me more than that." My voice rises until I'm nearly yelling. "What did you plan with the Red King and Queen? Why didn't you tell me about it?"

She matches my tone. "I couldn't explain because I had to improvise! The situation was changing too fast. The trial in particular messed everything up. The White Rabbit mixed up the goblets."

I consider this new piece of information. I didn't expect the Rabbit to have any part in this. He's such a loyal subject to the monarchs.

"Wait a minute. Did the White Rabbit spike my wine?" I ask. "Hailey said she had nothing to do with it."

Mikayla's shoulders curve. "She didn't. That was my

mistake. I should have tried to do more. But I panicked. I let them blame her."

A current of cold sweeps through me. "Then who poisoned me?"

Her hands curl into fists. "Alice—"

I interrupt, "Mikayla, what aren't you telling me?"

Her expression contorts before her gaze falls to her boots. At last, she murmurs, "It wasn't supposed to be your goblet."

The quiet confession hits me squarely in the chest. I can't breathe. My back knocks against the wall of the chamber.

I face the girl I've considered a friend since Evie died.

"What does that mean?" My words are barely a whisper.

"A long time ago, I bought a potion from Shepherd's Landing," she begins, her voice trembling. "I kept the empty bottle. In it, I collected some venom from the snake that attacked the Living Garden. Then, before the trial, I threatened the White Rabbit into spiking the Queen's goblet. I never thought you would be in any danger."

I press my fingers to my temples. My breathing is shallow.

"You almost killed me," I say in bewilderment. "And you said that Hailey did it."

"I'm sorry! Like I said, I panicked. You have no idea how much I regret what I did. Alice, please understand. I didn't mean for things to turn out so wrong." She reaches toward me, her eyes beseeching.

I step away. My shock crystallizes.

"What other secrets have you neglected to tell me?" I spit. "Is Evie's death the reason you want to destroy Meer?"

Mikayla snatches her hand back. Her laugh makes me wince. The only way to describe it is fractured.

"Everything is about Evie!" she cries. "Her life, her art. All of Meer was her dream, and it couldn't save her. *I* couldn't save her. The last time I came to Meer with Evie, one of us didn't come out." Her face crumples. "I couldn't save her, but I can still save you. I'll make things right."

A tremor passes through my heart. The last time I met Evie in the Elsewhere, I said something similar.

In the dungeon, before Hailey and I were taken captive, Hailey started to tell me about the memory that Evie's bracelet showed her. A memory that involved Mikayla.

"Hailey said that my sister's token showed her a memory," I say. "You were in that memory. Does it have something to do with Evie's death?"

She squeezes her eyes shut. "Alice—"

"Tell me!" My words reverberate in the desolate chamber. "I deserve to know!"

Slowly, she reaches into her tunic pocket and withdraws Evie's token. Her entire body is shaking.

"It's easier," she says, voice fraying, "to show you."

She drops the bracelet into my hand.

The past grips me in its jaws.

CHAPTER 35

"DO YOU REALLY think I'm so stupid that I wouldn't figure out what you did to Alice?" Evie said, her words guttural.

"I didn't hurt her!" Mikayla protested.

My sister's voice hitched. "You let me think for all those years that she chose to leave Meer...and me."

"She's always been too logical for her own good. She grew out of Meer."

"No, she didn't, because you took that choice from her!"

"I wouldn't do anything to Alice! She's your sister."

"I might not be able to tell when you're keeping secrets, but I can tell when you're lying. So tell me, Mik. What did you do?"

Mikayla paused for a beat before she answered, "I'll tell you... if you come back to Earth with me."

"You promised you'd be with me until the end!" Evie cried.

Mikayla's voice pitched higher than normal. "Yes, but I didn't think you meant this!"

"Just admit it. You're scared!"

A scoff sounded harsh in the air. "Scared that you're delusional, maybe."

"You're not listening, Mik. When we go Beyond, everything

will be as it should be. We'll never age or grow sick. We'll run away from reality and live out our wildest dreams."

"Living in a dream doesn't make it real. Come back, Evie. Please. For me."

Evie's tone hardened. "I think I've done enough for you. It's time I went on alone."

They are but older children whose fantasies have given way to fear. They are two girls who stood together as if in truce.

But like the world they ruled over, the truce was only an illusion.

A scream split the air—a heart-rending sound that stopped Time in its tracks.

Waves of disorientation and dismay rippled through Meer.

The Talking Flowers hid their faces from the waning sun, huddling together, too afraid to guess what would come next. On the milk-white oceans of the Nacre Coast, the Minnowshark lost course and crumpled into the nearest reef, grieving its captain. Above the others, the Lady of the Moon locked herself into her chamber and wept. She had foreseen this fate long ago, at the dawn of Meer's creation, though it made the sorrow no easier to bear.

When Meer's Queen was Lost, the Red Court rose to power.

The pearls of Conchae Maris glowed like beacons for the invaders. Hamwishbone's hut grew like a tumor from the earth. The Knightleys prepared the Pins & Needles Inn for new guests as the Nameless Forest expanded in greedy swathes around it. Far away, within the Red Castle, the Red King and Queen no longer sensed the presence of Meer's Queen: the Queen who had now lost herself and lost her way.

Not all of the Lost Queen's creations grieved her. But all knew the sound of a story cutting off before it was meant to end.

And it was that sound, of all things, that pierced the boundary between dreaming and waking.

CHAPTER 36

JANUARY, TWO MONTHS AGO

AT FIRST, I thought I imagined Evie's scream.

But as I lifted my head from my Advanced Physics homework at my desk, the scream came again. My blood went cold. Although my brain devised a half-dozen plausible explanations, my body reacted without considering a single one.

I rushed across the hall to my sister's room, but didn't expect her door to be unlocked. My momentum caused it to bang against the wall. I winced. Our parents hated the sound of doors slamming. Mom was in her home office—she'd probably come to scold me soon.

It didn't matter. My sister was in trouble.

"Evie!" I called, peering inside her room. "What's wrong?"

Everything in her bedroom was exactly as she'd left it: painting supplies strewn over her desk, and a rumpled bed still unmade from the morning. Her laundry was piling up in the hamper, and the trash can was overflowing. I wrinkled my nose.

She wasn't here.

Yet she had screamed seconds ago, and I would have heard her leave.

I had no idea what possessed me to turn around, but if I hadn't, I wouldn't have looked at the mirror on the wall…

And seen my sister trapped behind the glass.

Evie was haloed in fog, a half-ghost, half-girl, her dark hair fluttering like she was underwater.

When she saw me, she beat her fists against the glass. It rattled. I flinched, but the mirror didn't suffer a single crack.

I spun away, pinching my arm as tight as I could. My mind tore at the seams, trying to reconcile the sight of my sister on the opposite side of a looking-glass.

This isn't real. It's only a dream. You're breaking down from stress. You're imagining things that aren't there.

The window was thrown halfway open, letting in the freezing January wind. Hadn't it been latched when I entered the room? My sweater did nothing to stop the chill, and I stepped toward the door in a daze.

As soon as I reached to open it, it slammed shut.

I twisted the knob with all my might. It didn't budge. I grabbed the overflowing wastebasket and battered it. Smudged sheets of paper tumbled onto the floor. Still, the doorknob refused to give way. The fairy lights in the corners of the room flickered, burning as brightly as supernovas one instant and plunging me into darkness the next.

Evie's shrill voice assaulted my skull. *ALICE! Help me!*

I dropped the damaged basket and clutched at my head.

"This is a dream!" I shouted. "This isn't real! Let me go!"

I tried again to open the door, but to no avail. The winter wind howled through the window, tipping over jars and drawers. Paint and water splashed across Evie's white rug in colorful arcs. Pens and paintbrushes clattered to the floor, and the lampshade on her nightstand toppled over, cracking in three places.

It was never a dream. Evie's words came thick and furious. *You left me in Meer all those years ago. You left me then, and you're leaving me now.*

"This will be over soon," I whispered.

She smiled grimly in the mirror. *That's what I used to say, too.*

I leaped back in time to avoid being hit by her bulletin board, which crashed at my feet. The wind ripped photos through the window into the winter. The fairy lights blinked before stranding me in the helpless dark once more.

HELP ME! Evie screamed.

Something inside my head made a sickening *crack*. My entire vision went white. I fell to my knees. I wasn't a girl but a being of pain, loose and floating.

I crawled to the mirror.

For a few seconds, the chaos stilled. We gazed at each other. Sister and sister.

Evie's face crumpled. She leaned against the pane of glass. *You can break me out. I know you can. I need you. I've always needed you, Alice.*

I splayed my palm over hers. "Me too."

Then I reared back and drove my fist into the mirror.

For a second, all I could hear was the blood rushing in my ears.

I dispassionately examined the damage to my hand. Shards of glass pierced and splintered my skin. Red dripped from my knuckles and trickled down my wrist. My hand felt like a stranger's: disconnected and foreign. If not for the fact that my fingers twitched when I thought about moving them, I wouldn't have guessed that they belonged to me.

Be brave, Evie said. *You can free me.*

My fists curled.

"Let her go!" I screamed at the mirror.

The sound of cracking glass sounded like a song. I listened to it again, this time with both fists.

Again.

Again.

By the time I stopped, sharp fragments littered the floor. I forced myself to tilt my head up, away from the blood. If I didn't see it, perhaps I wouldn't feel the pain. It seemed to be working.

"Has it let you go yet?" I muttered. Lightning crackled through my vision.

Evie wept. The sound was distorted, as if it was traveling through television static. I glimpsed her hair, her cheek, her eye in the twisted shards of the mirror.

Her voice flickered like a candle flame. *This wasn't how it was supposed to end.*

I shivered in the empty vastness with nothing to protect me.

I used to think that when people talked about *seeing stars*, they were imagining it—until nebulae flashed in my irises, each brighter than the last.

No one had ever told me that stars had eyes. They clearly hadn't seen the ones that glared at me now, blinding me with fractal noise. Medically, that probably wasn't a good sign. But I was beyond caring.

"Stars," I slurred. "You like them, right, Evie? You made up your own constellations in your fantasy world. You said that Earth had only tragedies. You wanted a happily ever after…"

I said a lot of things I thought were true. I'm so sorry that I loved you and still abandoned you…

"Why?"

No answer came.

My hand brushed against something smooth and cold.

Evie lay on the floor beside me, her limbs splayed at odd angles. Her eyes were lidded, and her mouth was half-ajar.

Relief swamped me. Everything that had just happened was a dream—or a hallucination. It didn't matter. My sister was here, with me. Not trapped inside a mirror.

I shook her shoulder. "Evie! Wake up!"

She didn't stir.

Logic reinstated itself in my mind. Even if that had been a dream, Evie was unresponsive.

I pressed my fingers against her neck, searching for her carotid artery. At first, I thought I couldn't find it, disoriented as I was. Then I realized the truth. She didn't have a heartbeat.

I hovered my palm over her lips, counting the seconds. A minute passed. Then another. No warmth met my hand. Her chest stayed still.

The truth slammed into me: *My sister is dead.*

Evie's room became a vacuum: dark and cold, with no sound reaching me in all the nothingness. My skin crawled with frost. My bones turned to brittle ice. Any second, I would shatter to pieces with the mirror.

You can't, I told myself. *You still have to get up. Call for help...*

Softness pressed against my cheek. I was lying on the carpet. I had no memory of falling. But then, I didn't remember a lot of things...like what I thought I needed to do.

The darkness overbalanced the light.

I knew nothing more.

CHAPTER 37

I SURFACE FROM the past with a gasp.

Pain lances through my palm. I'm clutching Evie's bracelet so hard that new crimson lines crosshatch with the scars of two months ago.

The scars that I received trying to break my sister out of her own mirror.

The vision captured in Evie's token unlocked my missing memory of the night she died. Her screams echo in my skull.

I wish I had gone on forgetting.

A sound that is half-sob, half-whine, escapes my mouth. I stagger away from Mikayla. My breath comes in sharp, shallow pants, like a cornered animal. The glass shards on the ground of the enclosure splinter under my shoes. I clap my hands over my ears to block out the noise.

"Alice?" Mikayla asks. "Are you okay?"

Her voice sounds oddly loud in the desolate chamber. Wisps of white mist halo the silver bracelet on her wrist.

I flinch. I can't even look at her.

"You were there when Evie died, weren't you?" I say. "Tell me what really happened."

She recoils as if I've slapped her. Her eyes flare, but dull again in the next moment. "Last November, Evie made me promise to explore a place that wasn't part of Earth or Meer. She called it the *Beyond*."

Beyond. That word came up in Mikayla's pearl during the trial, and then later, in my conversation with the Sheep.

Mikayla continues, "It separates Meer from Earth. It's a gray area, not connected to either world."

"Like the Elsewhere," I say.

Her breath shudders on an exhale. "Yes. In December, Hailey found Conchae Maris. Evie wouldn't tell us about the Red Court. For a long time, none of us returned to Meer because we were afraid. Until January. One night, I sensed Evie going into Meer. I followed her. She brought me to the Elsewhere—I didn't know what it was called at the time. She told me that the Red King and Queen refused to let her live in Meer. So she had a plan to go somewhere else."

My heart sinks.

"She wanted to live Beyond," I guess.

Mikayla confirms with a miserable nod. "I didn't realize she was serious. I thought she was just making threats. Until she opened some kind of strange portal that led into darkness. She said it went Beyond."

"But...you didn't go into it?"

"Of course not! She wasn't in her right mind. I had a bad feeling about it."

I stare at her incredulously. "So you let her go by herself?"

She throws up her hands. "I tried to talk her out of her plan! But she wouldn't listen or answer any of my questions about the Red Court. She'd already made up her mind. And then, as if that wasn't enough, she started accusing me of all kinds of things."

In the vision, Evie asked Mikayla, *Do you really think I'm so stupid that I wouldn't figure out what you did to Alice?*

I blink back the sting of tears. "She said you did something to me."

Mikayla's shoulders sag. Her arms hang at her sides. "That *was* my fault," she admits. "When we were kids, Evie originally created Meer for herself and me. You were the first person besides us to come to Meer. You were six years old."

I shake my head. "I don't remember ever visiting Meer."

"That's because you thought it was pretend."

My sister's bracelet still glints in my hands. I slip it onto my wrist, flexing my fingers.

I recall entering the Living Garden, where the Talking Flowers knew me by name, though I had no recollection of ever meeting them.

"Did I?" I ask. The words come out as a harsh whisper.

She winces. "You did after I bought a potion for forgetting from the Sheep. After you drank it, you didn't believe in Meer anymore."

Is it true that once, I had walked in Meer with Evie, that I had been on the inside of her greatest secret and her greatest dream?

Then Mikayla stole my belief, and I had never known the difference.

Maybe one day, I would have outgrown Meer regardless. I might have refused to accept that I had ever roamed inside a fantasy as rich as this one. It is likely that I would have desecrated it with logic in the end.

But these are merely hypotheticals. I do not have the luxury of knowing what would have happened.

I manage one word. "Why?"

She hangs her head. "I should've known better. I was

jealous and thought of Evie as my sister. When she brought you to Meer, I was scared that she'd leave me behind. I know how dumb that sounds, but it's how I felt. I wish I hadn't done what I did. Evie was never really the same afterward. It took her years to trust anyone else enough to bring them in."

"Khalil and Hailey," I guess.

She slumps against the chamber's smooth, dark wall. "I let them stay because I didn't want to hurt Evie again. Sometimes I thought I'd tell her what I did to you. Instead, she learned the truth from the Sheep."

"How?"

"She didn't mean to. She tried to bargain with the Sheep to let her live in Meer. The Sheep refused, but let something slip about the price of the forgetting potion I bought years ago." She makes a lackluster shrug. "Evie guessed the rest."

The hairs on my forearms prickle. "What price?" I ask slowly.

"The Sheep warned me that because I'd controlled your actions, I'd one day lose control over mine. I forgot about it until January, when Evie tried to take me to the Beyond. I told her she wouldn't do it. She took that as a dare. She ran. I tried to restrain her. I couldn't move." Her mouth trembles. "She stepped into that portal, and she didn't come out. I'll never forget her scream."

I'd heard it for myself. It captured the agony of realizing, far too late, that the fate she had chosen was false.

Tears shine in Mikayla's eyes. She scrubs her sleeve over her face. "The next thing I remember was coming back through my mirror. I tried calling Evie, then you. Neither of you picked up. Your mother called 911 before I could."

I am uncovering secret after secret, and yet I feel only a crushing exhaustion.

"Why didn't you tell me any of this?" I ask, my voice barely above a murmur.

"If I had, you would've hated me, even though it was an accident. I should've known that you wouldn't be satisfied with leaving it alone."

I scoff. "You say that like it's a bad thing."

"Sometimes it is," she mumbles.

"Don't make this about me!" I retort. "This entire time, you knew how Evie died, and you said nothing. Were you ever going to tell me?"

"I wanted to! I was just—" She pauses, biting her lower lip.

"Scared," I say coldly. "A coward."

"I tried to be brave. That's why I killed the Red Queen. I'll do whatever is necessary to escape Meer and return our lives to normal."

"At what cost?"

"Any cost is worth it. Don't you get it?" Mikayla's voice rises. "You might have gone from being a Pawn to a Queen, but you're still a piece in this game, like me. The real Meer died with Evie. And I'll put whatever is left of it out of its misery."

"No!" I blurt out. I lunge forward, snagging her wrist. My fingers brush against her bracelet.

Waiting for a phone call that will never be returned.

Sweeping vases off shelves until they shatter.

Screaming at the full, mocking moon outside her bedroom window.

I reel backward, stunned at the ferocity of Mikayla's memories.

Her bracelet, the mirror image of mine, glistens. It is a reminder that all along, Evie's death was an accident. She was in the wrong place at the wrong time.

Mikayla knew this, and she still withheld the truth.

My grief and rage collapse inward. My emotions become a void, cold and still. Empty. I feel nothing at all, and…

It is freeing.

Mikayla eyes me warily. "Why are you looking at me like that?"

I shrug. "No reason."

"Alice, you're a terrible liar. Tell me the truth."

How ironic for her to insist on the truth, when it's more than she's ever given me.

Still, I say, "If you really wanted to end the game, you would have assassinated the Red King instead of the Red Queen. So why didn't you?"

"She seemed to be the bigger threat. I had no idea the Red King was hiding such powerful magic." Her voice quivers.

"You're still scared," I say. "Aren't you?"

Shadows pool along the crux of her throat as she swallows. "Of course I am," she says. "But when we make it out of the Elsewhere, I'll fix my mistake."

"How?" I demand. "By killing the Red King?"

When she doesn't meet my gaze, I know I'm right.

Mikayla thinks she's given up too much to face defeat. But chess isn't necessarily about the number of pieces you lose. It's about which ones you lose…or which ones you keep.

I won't find the answers I need in the Red Castle. Nor will I find them here.

I lift my face to the grayness of the Elsewhere. Letting the corners of my mind blur, I reach for the trancelike state that allowed me to communicate with the ghost of Pins & Needles. My thoughts scatter.

Take me where Evie went, I think. *I need to go Beyond.*

The air hums, then warps. I am folded inside endless currents of gray.

Mikayla cries out. Her eyes widen. She lunges for me, too late.

I fade into nothing.

CHAPTER 38

I STAND AT the bottom of a white hill.

Instead of gray, golden light floods my surroundings. A strange sense of warmth envelops me. The air carries a distant scent of wildflowers and freshly baked bread. It reminds me of a home I've never had.

I glance up. At the peak of the hill is a lone figure. I recognize her even with her back turned. Her hair is longer than it was in life, cascading in black waves to her waist. Her flowing bell-sleeved dress makes her look like an angel, or perhaps a ghost.

I snatch up the skirt of my dirtied gown and run toward her. My feet sink with each step in the soft, spongy ground. I do not take my eyes away from her. I'm scared she will vanish if I don't.

"Evie!" I shout. "I'm here."

She doesn't turn around.

My steps falter. "Evie?" I whisper.

Her silver bracelet weighs heavily on my wrist.

At last, her head inclines in my direction. Her brown eyes are heavy with sadness. "Alice. You're a Queen now."

Unbidden, my hand goes to my crown.

"Evie..." I trail off. I don't know how I can apologize to her, or vice versa. It's easier to say nothing, but I don't want to fall into that trap again.

"This game never ends, does it?" my sister muses. "One move after another, and the sides are still evenly matched. We can't win."

"Yes, we can. Chess has one victor."

"That's not what I mean." Her lashes flutter shut. With a jolt, I realize tears are shining on her face. "When will that victory not feel hollow? All of this was always pretend. You, Mom, and Dad were right. I was naïve. I acted like a child."

"No, Evie!" I exclaim. "I said that because I didn't want to admit you were right. Because I was scared and insecure about my future, I took it out on you."

"I didn't know what you were going through because I didn't ask. I forced you to deal with everything alone."

"I understand why you did. You felt freer in Meer."

Her shoulders sag. "I didn't want to die, exactly. I just didn't want to be on Earth anymore. So I created an illusion to live inside, because I needed to matter somewhere. I guess it worked. Meer is failing without me."

She points ahead. For the first time, I notice that the white hill we are standing on leads to nothing. It is more like a cliff than a hill, overlooking an endless chain of clouds.

"Look." Evie closes her hand into a fist. The clouds drift apart, revealing a sight that makes my breath catch.

Meer is not arranged like a chessboard. Instead, it is a continent, which I can't take in all at once.

I begin with the Red Castle: a spectacle of ruby-encrusted towers directly beneath us. To the east, the round Labyrinth coils in on itself like a snake. Beyond it, the Nacre Coast carves a crescent-moon shape into the continent that resembles the yin-yang symbol. In the shallow milk-white waters, I make out the shape of the abandoned *Minnowshark* ship.

My eyes drift to the Nameless Forest. It is a phalanx of dark trees that borders the giant Hamwishbone's house and guards the Pins & Needles Inn. The lights in the inn are dull; no smoke rises from the chimney.

I glance to my right. Evie is studying me. Her head tilts to the side.

"I think you're the only one besides me who's ever seen Meer from above," she comments.

"It doesn't look anything like a chessboard," is all I can think of to say.

"It's not about chess. It's about us—how we were pieces in Mom and Dad's games. I used to wonder how to win. I guess you came closer to finding that out than I did."

I wince at the bitterness in her tone. An apology springs to my lips. I bite it back—not because I'm afraid to say it, but because something tells me I should listen, rather than speak.

My sister gazes down at Meer. Tendrils of black hair whip across her cheeks. "I created Meer to learn why I didn't belong on Earth," she says at last. "Here, I wasn't the one outcast. I couldn't be singled out, because everyone was a little mad. Some more than others. I never meant for the Red Court to become as powerful as they did."

"Some of the figures in the Red Court seem to be based on real people," I say carefully. "Hamwishbone, the giant, is like Mr. Hammond. And the Knightleys…"

Evie's face closes. "I'm sorry. I don't want to talk about it. All I'll say is that some figures in Meer are based on people I know. I didn't intentionally cast anyone as the villain. But when you're in pain, everyone might as well be guilty."

I nod. Perhaps it is better that she does not confirm who the Knightleys were inspired by, although I think I could guess the answer. The specter of Mrs. Knightley's smile still haunts me.

I try a question that feels a little safer. "Have you been watching us from up here this entire time?"

She sighs. "I've tried. The Beyond is not affected by Time. That makes it harder for me to influence Meer. I could only reach out to you when you were in the Elsewhere. Once, I managed to do a little more. I warned you about the Knightleys in the Pins & Needles Inn."

"So you *were* the ghost," I say. "Did you leave me the other messages, too? The ones that were…"

I trail off, unsure how to describe the barrage of belittling, ominous phrases that followed me around the inn. YOU'RE TOO OLD TO CRY. DON'T BE UNGRATEFUL. SOON, IT'LL ALL BE OVER.

No; I do not think I need to guess who the Knightleys represented.

"No," Evie says immediately. "Those were the tricks of the inn. I wouldn't have said something like that to you. I wouldn't have had the energy, anyway. It was all I could do to send my presence from the Elsewhere."

I study the pearlescent clouds that ripple through the Beyond. They are the same color as Evie's dress, which shimmers as she clasps her hands together.

"Did you bring me here from the Elsewhere?" I ask. "I didn't see you."

She shakes her head. "That was you, not me. You're a Queen now. You can manipulate the Elsewhere. Mikayla can't. She's still there right now."

At the mention of Evie's best friend, my jaw clenches.

"There's something you should know about Mikayla," I say. "Many things, actually."

I explain the fallout of her attempted—and actual assassination—of the Red Queen.

Evie listens intently, her eyes fixed on me. She does not interrupt. When I stop talking, she presses her lips together. She looks more resigned than angry.

"Mikayla doesn't think before she acts," she replies. "She believes she's doing the right thing until reality catches up to her. That's what happened after she gave you that forgetting potion. Years went by, and…well, I never would've found out if not for the Sheep."

I bow my head. I'm choked by the thought of all the heartache that could have been avoided without Mikayla's intrusion. Maybe Evie and I would have been closer for much longer. Maybe I would not have tried to grow up as fast as possible.

It seems impossible that once, I walked through Meer at Evie's side. When I seek the memories of long-gone games of pretend, they slip out of reach, scattering into oblivion.

"I owe you an apology, Alice," my sister says. "All these years, I thought you rejected me and Meer. I blamed you for something that wasn't your fault."

A lump forms in my throat. I don't know how to reply.

She forges on. "I need to tell you something about Mikayla, too. When I died, she made a wish. I heard it from the Beyond. She said, 'I wish Meer would die with Evie.'"

I peer beyond the clouds, tracing the forests and shorelines of a world created from nothing but a desire to belong.

"She's to blame for Meer's destruction," I say.

Evie lets out a brittle laugh. "You give her too much credit. It didn't take much after my death. It was like toppling a house of cards. When I first met you in the Elsewhere, I was scared to say her name. I'm not scared anymore. I know I can't stop the end from coming."

My head whips toward her. "What do you mean?" I blurt.

Her warm brown eyes, brimming with fresh tears, meet mine. "I was afraid to leave Meer. Now, I understand my soul will rest if I do, and Meer will no longer exist. You won't suffer hallucinations. Your lives will go back to normal."

I'm half-listening.

If I lose Evie for a second time, what do I have left?

I grab her hand. "I can't leave you."

"Oh, Alice." She squeezes my palm, then startles. She unfolds her fingers from mine, revealing the Red Queen's signet ring.

"How did you get this?" she asks, lifting my hand to examine the ring more closely.

I give a helpless shrug. "Primera stole it from the Red Queen and gave it to the Sheep, who gave it to me. I don't understand why Primera would help us. She's the enemy."

"People change," Evie says simply. She rubs her thumb over the ring. "I haven't seen this in a while."

I study the round, engraved surface of the ring. Its weight is cool. Familiar. In the recesses of my mind, a memory stirs.

"Didn't Dad own a ring like this?" I ask.

A brief smile rises to her lips. "This *is* his ring."

"What? That's—" I almost say *impossible*. "—odd. How did it get into Meer?"

"I lost it during a game of pretend when we were kids. Years later, I found it in Meer, in Shepherd's Landing. My token turned up there, too, after I died." She points at my wrist, where her silver bracelet gleams. "Before I went Beyond, I took off my bracelet. That was how I became trapped between worlds. I had nothing to anchor me to Earth."

The memory of finding my sister inside her mirror makes

me list sideways. I force myself back to the present and fumble with the bracelet on my wrist. "If I give your token back to you, maybe you can return with me to Earth—"

She gives me a watery smile. "I've been without it for too long. You can still go back, but I can't."

"No!" My voice frays. "There has to be another way. I can figure it out. I just…I need time."

"Listen to me, Alice. Not all fantasies last forever. You can't save Meer. You can't save me. But dreamers are resilient. I still have dreams for you. For my friends." She swallows, looking down. "For our family," she finishes quietly.

"Mom and Dad miss you," I say. "Dad keeps pictures of your paintings on his phone. He scrolls through them every day. Mom hasn't taken away the fourth chair at the dinner table. Both of them come home later and later."

She inhales a shuddering breath. "I miss them. I'm sorry that things ended the way they did."

I can't think of the best way to tell her that I was wrong this whole time.

"I'm sorry that you felt so alone in our house," I say. "If I had noticed that you were in pain…"

The white sleeves of her dress billow as she holds up her hand. "Stop," she says gently. "Didn't you always tell me that hypotheticals are useless?"

Those are the words I would have told myself once. I'm not so sure I believe them now.

"Evie?" I say.

"Yeah?"

"I never hated you."

"I know."

"No, you don't understand. I hated that I could never refuse Mom and Dad."

"And I hated that even when I refused them, I felt guilty," she confesses. "I couldn't stop caring. I understand what it's like to torture yourself with what-ifs. Don't do that, Alice. Promise me you'll forgive yourself. Not for my sake, but for *yours*."

"I'll try." I clear my throat against the sting of tears. "I don't know if I can do this without you, Evie."

She rests her hand on my shoulder. "Yes, you can. You are the first and last Queen crowned by Meer itself. I'll send you and Mikayla back to the Red Castle, but after that, you don't need my help. Only you can end this game."

"How—" My voice breaks. "How am I supposed to say goodbye to you?"

"Hmmm. I prefer 'See you later' to 'Goodbye.'"

"Will I see you later?"

She tilts her head. A little of her old smirk returns to her face. "Maybe. With any luck."

I give up on words. I hug her, burying my chin in the crook of her neck. She smooths my hair. She smells like the earth after a storm: sweet and whole.

At last, I pull back. I memorize the freckles on her face, the dreamy flicker in her eyes, and the easy grace with which she holds herself.

My sister, the way she used to be.

My sister, the way she is.

Evie's lips brush against my forehead. "See you later, Alice. I love you."

The Beyond melts into a whorl of color, prying my sister from my arms.

"Tell me one thing," I manage. "Is this a dream?"

I can hear the laugh threatening to break free in her response: "Why do you ask me? You're the dreamer."

CHAPTER 39

I NEARLY FACE-PLANT onto the red-and-white checkered floor of the Red Castle.

I stagger to my feet. Mikayla stumbles beside me. We are roughly three yards away from the vortex between the thrones of the Red King and Queen. The air crackles with tendrils of maroon electricity.

"What happened?" Mikayla mutters thickly. Her forehead has a sheen of sweat. She clutches her stomach. "How did we get back?"

I close my fingers into fists, surveying the scars that cross-hatch my hands. My sister's bracelet gleams silver on my wrist, overshadowing the Red Queen's signet ring.

"I found Evie," I answer.

Her mouth falls open. She spins toward me. "You saw her? What did she say?"

My eyes sting. I rub my thumb along my sister's bracelet.
Will I see you later?
Maybe. With any luck.

I swallow hard, my voice rough. "We need to leave Meer as soon as possible."

"Alice! Mikayla!" Khalil yells.

He dashes in our direction, then skids to a stop. Confusion gleams in his dark eyes as his head jerks between us. "Wait. Didn't you two disappear just now? Am I seeing things?"

Evie was right about time not passing the same way in the Beyond. Only a few seconds seem to have elapsed since Mikayla and I were caught by the vortex.

"No," I say.

My heart aches, but I can't spare the time to dwell on it. I think I know what I have to do.

I walk toward the bloodred thrones.

Mikayla grabs my sleeve. "Alice, you can't! You'll get sucked back into—into *that*." She points at the vortex, still as wide as the maw of a hungry beast. Its gravity pulls at my clothes and hair.

I don't dignify her with an answer. I yank my dress out of her grip and walk forward at a careful, stately pace.

The Red King watches me from behind the vortex. His scarlet pupils follow me. A smirk plays on his lips. Electricity arcs between the spires of his crown.

"It is too late to parley, White Queen." His words carry to me over the sound of crackling energy in the room. "Will you surrender on behalf of your Court?"

My crown weighs down my head.

Evie told me to end the game. She didn't tell me to *win* it.

"No," I say. "I request a draw."

"What?" Mikayla says loudly behind me.

I ignore her and focus on the Red King.

His black brows angle down. He tilts his head. The vortex dulls, its edges shrinking.

I raise my voice. "It is not worth continuing this game.

Both sides have suffered losses. Our time runs short. I will honor a draw. Will you?"

The King leans forward on his throne, steepling his fingers. "I did not expect this proposal. It intrigues me. *You* intrigue me, White Queen. You are willing to walk away when you are so close to victory?"

I think of sleepless nights sacrificed for an endless string of tests and exams, words of hard-won praise committed to memory. I defined my entire life by the first letter of the alphabet. But I failed to see what—or rather, who—mattered most.

"Some things are more important than winning," I say at last.

He smiles. It is an odd expression, stilted. I cannot tell whether his tone is more admiring or grudging when he says, "Check, checkmate...none of it came to pass, as I believed. Very well. I will accept your draw, White Queen."

I scrutinize him, my heart in my throat. Can it be so simple?

He leans back against his throne. His eyes drift shut.

The vortex sputters, then coils in on itself. The air shudders as it dissolves in a shockwave of sound.

The force knocks me to my knees. My ears ring. I cradle my head in both hands, willing the world to stop spinning. An eternity passes until I gather the strength to stand.

The King's body is as rigid as the Red Queen's sand-covered corpse. His chest no longer rises and falls. A knowing smile lingers on his lips. It looks strangely triumphant.

For a few precious seconds, the Red Castle holds its breath.

Then, a shadow stirs behind the thrones.

The four of us stiffen.

A tabby cat with a bow-shaped collar wanders into the open.

Dinah surveys the motionless monarchs and the debris littering the throne room. Her black-smudged ears twitch. She licks her paw.

"So," she says, "what did I miss?"

We stare at her.

"What?" she demands. "Are you statues, too, like them?" She flicks her tail at the unmoving rulers.

Nobody replies. No one has time to.

A chasm rends the royal hall in two, erupting from the foot of the thrones and shaking the foundation of the Red Castle. At the sound of shattering quartz, my limbs go numb. My vision tunnels, then fragments.

No. I push away the memories of Evie's death. My breaths are thready, uneven. I can't break down now.

Khalil scoops Dinah into his arms. My cat burrows her nose into his shirt.

"What's going on?" he calls to me.

I wish I knew the answer. The Red King agreed to my proposed draw. His knowing smile flashes through my mind.

A groaning sound emanates from the ceiling. A pillar plummets at the far end of the throne room, toppling into the one beside it. One by one, the columns tumble toward us. Thick clouds of dust surround us as the castle continues to disintegrate. Hailey screams.

Anger smolders in my gut. This can't be how this ends. I refuse.

Suddenly, white light explodes through the air.

I throw up a hand to shield myself until I realize it's the same light that I saw in the dungeons. No—it is the same light I *summoned* in the dungeons. Rays of white pour from my palms.

Hesitantly, I push my hands forward. The radiance carves

through the smothering dust, illuminating a path toward the thrones. It reflects off the mirrored dais.

An idea occurs to me.

From what I know of Meer, it is at least plausible, if not possible. If it does not work...No. It has to work.

"Follow me!" I shout, breaking into a run. I don't wait to see if they listen.

I race toward the thrones, keeping my path parallel to the chasm that splits the room in two. My eyes burn. Quartz crunches under my feet. Clouds of dust rumble on my heels, threatening to suck me inside. Still, I push myself forward to the mirrored dais.

Then I collapse to my knees.

I behold my reflection. Soot stains my pale, scared face. My mouth tastes of copper and ashes. Around me, the white light is fading. I shiver. Why is it so cold now?

Footsteps slow behind me.

"What do we do?" Hailey asks, then breaks into a coughing fit.

Right. This was my idea. I have to see it through. I extend trembling fingers to touch the mirror.

My knuckles knock against the glass.

Instinctively, I reach for the guiding warmth of my compass. It is not there. It has been absent since we reached the Red Castle.

We have nowhere else to go.

"Alice, snap out of it!" Mikayla shouts. "What's going on?"

"We need a portal," I say numbly.

Otherwise, we'll be buried alive.

My vision swims. I'm not in the collapsing castle anymore, but trying to get to my sister from the other side of a mirror.

This time, *I* am the one who is trapped—pressing my fingers to the glass as if I can claw my way through it.

My arms fall to my sides. I slump forward.

At least if I die here, Evie and I will not be worlds apart.

A hand settles on my shoulder. Its weight draws me back to the present.

Khalil's curly black hair is dusted with rubble. There are new furrows in his forehead that I haven't noticed before. He looks as though he has aged years in the span of a few minutes.

I swallow the lump in my throat. "I've failed you all, haven't I?"

"Don't you dare give up now, Lee." The steel in his tone startles me out of my trance. "You are a Queen. Act like one."

I look down at my hands. They are hands that scribbled a thousand essays. Hands that shattered a mirror in seconds.

With time, perhaps the scars will fade.

I remove my crown. The pearls are stained. The diamonds are dull.

I press it against the mirror and place the full weight of my belief behind a single command. *Open.*

Then—

Blue smears my vision.

The sound of shattering quartz vanishes. So does the Red Castle.

I drift on my back, weightless. My hair floats around me in tendrils. Silence whispers in my ears. I'd think I am underwater, but when I exhale, no bubbles stream out from my mouth.

Beyond the surface of the water, I make out indistinct shapes. Murmurs encircle me.

I am overwhelmed with the desire to reach higher: to once again emerge into air and light and life. I have always known—although knowing is a different thing from understanding—that I don't need to suffocate myself for my own sake. The human instinct is to breathe. Why should I suppress it?

With a furious kick, I swim towards the light.

CHAPTER 40

IN THE TIME it takes me to break the surface, I watch Meer die.

My vision turns kaleidoscopic. Fragments of visions whirl past me.

The Living Garden withers. The Labyrinth collapses into miles of broken branches and ivy. Hamwishbone's hut and Pins & Needles are swallowed by the Nameless Forest as it hungrily spreads its shadows across the land. Eventually, the remains of Red Castle crumble into the ground. The sky folds up like a picnic blanket, and the white ocean of the Nacre Coast devours the continent.

I sense conflicting emotions from my friends. Mikayla's guilt and relief clash in equal measure. Hailey's heart weeps for the loss of so much beauty. Khalil grieves the loss of the last living part of his friend.

But I am drawn most to Evie's presence.

Though I cannot see Evie, her warmth surrounds me. Her voice whispers, *I will see you again.*

I believe her.

Suddenly, my knees sink into carpet.

I keel sideways, bumping into the violet blanket draped over Evie's bed.

My sister's room is exactly the same as when I left, with the exception of the daisy-patterned lamp and the framed watercolor now lying on the floor. A new crack splits the lampshade. It takes me a second to remember that Dinah knocked it over.

A quick glance at my hand reveals that the Red Queen's signet ring is gone. So is Evie's silver bracelet.

Perhaps it is merely my imagination, but the mural of flowers above the bed blooms with fresh vividness. The petals of the roses and tulips seem to sway in an unseen breeze.

My cat nuzzles against my ribs, releasing an insistent meow. I hardly notice.

Behind me is the portal I took into Shepherd's Landing— the mirror, which I now know was a door, beckoning me to find the secrets hidden inside.

If I close my eyes, I can almost hear the faintest strains of an enchanted melody.

I turn around, expecting to find the crossed-over threshold of Meer, and all the horrors of my sister's life exchanged for the hope of the future.

My reflection stares back from the smooth glass.

CHAPTER 41

APRIL, TWO WEEKS LATER

I STAND IN front of the mirror in Evie's room.

I wait for something to appear in the glass besides my own reflection: the curiosity-covered shelves of Shepherd's Landing, perhaps, or the luminous pearls bottled inside the Nacre Coast. I expect to see the serpentine hedges of the Labyrinth or even the snarling, heart-shaped spires of the Red Castle.

Stretching my hand toward the glass, I will it to morph into a doorway of darkness.

My fingerprints smudge my frowning reflection.

My gaze drifts to the floral mural on Evie's wall above her bed. I trace the braid-like pattern of daisies, roses, and tulips. Observing the painting now, it is so obvious that it was inspired by the Living Garden.

In my peripheral vision, something flickers.

I whirl toward the mirror.

My eyes are large and round behind my glasses, and my lips are parted in anticipation. My hair, tied back in a ponytail, snakes over one shoulder.

As I examine the mirror, my adrenaline ebbs. My sister's room looks no different. Perhaps my mind is playing tricks on me.

I push my glasses up the bridge of my nose. They were once the token that marked me as someone of two worlds. Now they are nothing more than ordinary.

Every day for the last two weeks, I have peered into Evie's mirror. Every day, the only thing I see is my reflection.

Just as Evie promised, my hallucinations stopped. I should be relieved. I am.

Still, a part of me longs for the enchantment of Meer, impossible and nonsensical as it was.

My reverie is broken by the sound of the front door opening.

I stiffen. My nails curl into the scars on my palms.

"Alice?" my mother's high-pitched voice calls. "Are you home?"

I don't need to cast a glance at the alarm clock on the nightstand to know that she has returned early from work. Far too early.

"Hi, Mom," I say, poking my head into the corridor. "Is something wrong?"

"No," she says, entering the hallway. Her pin-straight hair, like mine, is pulled back in a ponytail. Her usual black handbag is absent from the shoulder of her blazer, which is the pastel-blue hue of forget-me-nots. I'm not sure if I've ever seen her wear this color before, but it suits the softness of her cheeks. Evie would have liked it.

My mother doesn't comment on the fact that I emerged from Evie's room. She clasps her hands over her stomach, rocking back and forth on her high heels.

"Do you have time to talk, Alice?" she says. The pitch of her vowels rises, making her tone sound tremulous.

I blink. She's never asked me that. Usually, she just initiates the conversation.

"Is it about school?" I ask. "I know about the A-minus in AP Calculus. I'm going to bring it up."

A strand of hair escapes her sleek ponytail. She brushes it behind her ear. "No, it's not about that. I want to say that I would like to split Dinah's chores with you."

"Oh," I say. "Okay. Um…is that all?"

She exhales a heavy breath, knotting her fingers together. Her words are stilted. "Well, I think I should help, because you're always doing so much. You should have more time for yourself."

I lean against the robin's egg blue wallpaper of the hallway. "It's no problem. I've always taken care of Dinah."

"No, you don't understand," she insists. "I feel like I leave you alone too many times, to deal with too much on your own. You never complain, so I thought it was fine, but your sister…" She swallows. Her dark eyes glisten. "Your father and I put too much pressure on you. Both of you. I'm sorry."

"It's okay," I murmur. I don't know what else to say.

She shakes her head. "No, it isn't. I can't stop thinking about what I should have said. What I should have decided. I would do many things differently now…not only with you, but also with your relatives."

"Like your parents?" I ask carefully.

Her shoulders hunch. She doesn't meet my eyes. "They didn't want me to move to America at all. They argued it was safer to stay in Hong Kong. I wanted more for myself. But when I came to this country, life wasn't what I thought it would be. I was young and pregnant, and I had to work as a maid. Even when I got better jobs, my parents told me to go back home before it was too late. I didn't. Then, they fought with me about how to raise you and Evie. They said I had turned too American. That was when I realized that everything I did was wrong to them. So I thought, '*My family will be American, if being American means being happy.*'"

My breath catches. I've never heard this part of her past before. I wonder how much courage it took my mother to confess this.

"I should have tried harder to keep them in your lives," she continues. "A person without a family is like a tree without roots. But they were stubborn. I was, too." A tear trickles down her cheek. "It's my fault they didn't come to Evie's funeral."

My heart is in my throat. The funeral was the last time I saw my mother cry. I want to reach out to her and help her, but I don't know how.

Facing her in the shadowed hallway, I remember something Khalil told me weeks ago inside the Pins & Needles Inn.

"People change," I tell her. "We can apologize. We can try again."

She brushes another tear from her face. "Your father and I fought for this life in America for so long, we forgot to be satisfied with it. We kept chasing after more, more, all the time. Then we asked you and Evie to do the same. We should not have expected so much of you. I'm sorry."

I remain silent, unsure how to respond.

"I'm probably telling you this too late," she admits. "But I hope you listen when I say I want you to be happy, Alice."

The unexpected sting of tears rises in my eyes.

She barrels on. "You don't need to say anything right now. I just couldn't go longer without telling you how I feel. I hope you understand—"

I fold my mother into my arms.

CHAPTER 42

MAY, ONE MONTH LATER

STANDING IN FRONT of the multicolored chalkboards of Yuzu Deli, I decide to try something new.

When I rejoin my friends after ordering at the register, Khalil's jaw drops in feigned shock. "Alice, are you all right?"

"I don't know," Hailey chimes in. "We might have to check her temperature!"

I raise an eyebrow at her. "What are you talking about?"

"You didn't order strawberry-flavored boba tea. There's clearly something wrong."

I shrug, unable to suppress a smile. "I thought I would experiment this time."

A couple of minutes later, we retrieve our boba milk tea: mango for Hailey, taro for Khalil, and lychee for me. I take a sip. While I still think strawberry is the best flavor, I like this one. I might get it again.

The manager of Yuzu Deli, Mr. Wei, emerges from the kitchen and waves to me. I wave back.

"Do you like it?" he asks, nodding at the lychee tea in my hand.

"Yeah, I do."

"Good, good. Next time, try something else, huh? And tell your parents I say hello!"

"I will," I promise.

The three of us claim the best table, by the store's back window. It overlooks a small, flourishing garden of zinnias and tiger lilies. I imagine that these vibrant flowers are descendants of the Living Garden.

Hailey punches her straw into her drink. The sun sets her peacock earring alight. She still wears it even though we don't need tokens anymore.

"How did you guys do on your AP exams?" she asks.

Khalil heaves a sigh, tucking his hands into the pockets of his red varsity jacket. "I never want to hear the words 'AP' and 'exam' in the same sentence again."

She snickers. "Oh, come on. It couldn't have been that bad."

He flicks his straw wrapper at her. "Easy for you to say. You didn't take AP Calc!"

"Yeah, well, I don't see what you're worried about. You and Alice obviously aced it." Hailey pokes his shoulder. "Besides, *you* are done with AP exams forever. You're graduating."

"Don't worry, Zimmerman. I'll come back from New York to visit, if I feel nice."

"Will it be hard on your parents to have their children on opposite sides of the country?" I ask him.

Khalil twists his hands together. "I'm sure it will, but things are easier now that my brother is talking to them again. It's not perfect, but it's progress. He told me he's thinking of visiting Willow Creek for a couple of weeks." A soft smile touches his face. "My mother and father missed him so much. I did, too."

"I'm glad you're reconnecting," I say quietly.

Movement flickers in the corner of my eye. When my gaze snaps to the window, the flowers wave innocently in the wind.

"What is it?" Khalil asks.

I lower my voice so that the other customers in the deli don't overhear us. "False alarm. I thought it might be a hallucination."

"I don't get hallucinations anymore," Hailey remarks. "Sometimes Meer appears in my dreams, though."

"Mine, too," Khalil says.

I nod. "Same."

I used to dread sleeping because of the nightmares it would bring. Now, I wake up with a longing so acute that my breath catches—although my longing is not for Meer.

"Have you ever seen Evie?" I ask, almost afraid of their responses.

They shake their heads.

"Does she visit your dreams?" Khalil asks.

"No," I admit. "But in the Elsewhere, she said she would see me later. She never breaks her promises."

"Unlike a certain somebody," Hailey mutters.

When the three of us are together, we tend to avoid the subject of Mikayla. Khalil is more sympathetic toward her. Hailey is not. I still have no idea what to think.

A week ago, I was walking up the steps of my house while Mikayla was retrieving a stack of letters from her mailbox. She saw me. Her expression was terrible. It wasn't angry: just empty.

Mr. and Mrs. Wong are pressuring her to attend university. I know this because Mom and Dad sometimes let

Mikayla's name slip when they are gossiping and they think I can't hear them. A few weeks ago, I told my parents that I would no longer carpool home with her. "I don't feel comfortable," I said.

I have not told Mom and Dad about Meer. I don't know how I would, unless I dressed up the truth.

I want to believe that I can forgive Mikayla. Right now, hoping she heals is the best I can do for her.

"Penny for your thoughts, Queen Alice?"

I startle at Khalil's question.

"When are you going to give up that nickname?" I ask him.

"As long as it takes you to get rid of me."

"Four months isn't a long time."

He stirs his straw in his boba tea. "You guys will miss me when I'm at college, right?"

"Obviously," Hailey says at the same time I reply, "Jury's still out."

"Ouch." He clutches his chest in mock hurt. "I hope this jury is fairer than Meer's, then."

"You'd better," I say, without any heat.

After a pause, Hailey says, "I still can't believe Meer is gone. If it hadn't been for Mikayla…"

"Evie said that Meer would have died, regardless," I remind her. "And…Meer still exists, in a way."

Khalil shoots me a quizzical glance. "What do you mean?"

I steeple my fingers. "Lately, I've been thinking about what *existence* means. I came to the conclusion that if something exists, then it has the capacity to change someone. Or, put another way: Meer exists in the people we've become."

He and Hailey consider this. Outside the window, the flowers bend toward the sun, drinking in its warmth.

"I like that definition," Khalil replies.

"Me too," I say.

Two hours later, when Khalil drops me off at my house, I'm struck by how much brighter it is inside.

I can thank Mom for that. As the weeks have gone by, she has hung Evie's paintings around the house. She did it quietly, without consulting anyone. Although the vibrant colors sometimes clash with the robin's egg-blue wallpaper, they make the house feel a little less empty. On my way to Evie's room, I pass watercolors of tiger-lilies, roses, and bluebells.

Although my hallucinations have stopped, I still circle back to the place where I discovered—or rather, rediscovered—magic. It is as if I am following my long-gone compass.

I walk to her mirror. The glass does not ripple into darkness when I set my palm against it.

I lock eyes with my reflection. We sigh in unison.

I half-hated and half-loved Meer. All the same, I wish I hadn't had to let it go.

Or, more accurately, I wish I hadn't had to let *her* go.

Dinah saunters into the room and rubs against my leg. *Mrow.*

My cat doesn't talk anymore, but that doesn't mean she's any less insufferable. I scratch her behind the ears.

When I hear Mom's footsteps in the hall, I glance at the alarm clock on Evie's nightstand. Mom has returned from work two hours before dinnertime…which is part of the plan.

She and I have had many more long, heartfelt conversations since that day in April. Now, with my father, we are coming to a better understanding of our family and a better understanding of Evie. It can be uncomfortable at times, but more often, I come away encouraged. Hopeful.

"Alice!" Mom calls. "Are you busy? I need help carrying these bags!"

"Coming!" I say, scrambling out of Evie's room.

When Evie and I were younger, before Mom was promoted at the bank, the Lee women used to make dinner together. Mom and I recently decided to start this tradition again.

Mom folds the dumplings. I help even though she tries to shoo me away. "Don't re-injure your wrists," she says, swatting me on the arm.

My father arrives home when Mom and I are bringing the food to the table. In early May, he began covering earlier shifts at the hospital. Now, he comes home in time for dinner more often than not. Mom jokes that he craves home-cooked food too much. He doesn't correct her.

His face is creased with tired lines, but he smiles when he greets us. "It's good to see you two. Is that dinner? It smells delicious."

Mom smirks. "Of course it does."

I'm unused to the simple tenderness of these familial routines, and I savor them as much as I can. Some small part of me fears that everything will fall apart again. A louder part of me believes that we will only continue to grow stronger.

It is another few minutes before the three of us set the table and take our customary seats. Although it has been almost exactly four months since Evie died, her chair remains at the table, reflecting the yellow-hued kitchen lights.

My parents have a good-natured argument over which newspaper crossword is the best. They began doing crosswords to improve their English years ago and never stopped.

"The New Yorker is hard," Mom complains. "Too many clues I don't know."

"But it's not the easy way out, like USA Today!" Dad counters.

The conversation shifts. Mom makes scathing comments about the frustrating clients she received at the bank. She is bewildered when Dad and I laugh so hard that we can't take a sip of water.

"What's the matter? I'm not trying to be funny," she says.

That sets us off again.

Dad stops laughing long enough to ask me, "How was your day?"

I tense a little at the question before answering, "It went well. I have two tests coming up on Tuesday. I studied my flashcards and the review questions that I made."

"Alice works hard," Mom says around a mouthful of rice. "Too hard. She should rest more. She could overwork herself."

"It's fine, Mom," I say. "The school year is ending soon."

She waves her chopsticks. "Ah, just be careful."

"Is there anything else?" Dad asks me.

I muster a smile and start to say no out of habit. Then my gaze goes to the empty chair across from me.

I picture Evie leaning across the table and giving me an encouraging smile. Her presence, even imagined, is effervescent. I can't help but be drawn to it.

Go on, Al, she says in my head. *Talk to them.*

I say slowly, "Well, now that I think about it, I had the strangest dream recently. It was like the imaginary games I played with Evie when we were kids."

"It was?" my parents ask in unison.

"Yes. She was in the dream too, actually."

"I would love to hear about it," Mom says.

Dad nods in agreement. They wait for me.

My eyes sting. I wish that Evie could have received this kind of undivided attention. It is what she deserved.

I still have dreams for you and for everyone else, she told me as we overlooked the world of her own devising.

I smile to myself. I don't know why I was ever afraid that I would forget my sister's voice.

"Well," I say, "we should probably put away the dishes first. To say that it's a long story would be an understatement."

ACKNOWLEDGMENTS

This book has been a journey of four years and there are so many people I want to extend my thanks to.

I would like to first thank my family for working so hard to give me every opportunity and for unconditionally supporting me through the process of writing and publishing *Pawn*. Thank you to my mother for inspiring me to self-publish; to my father and uncle, for their encouragement and generosity; to my grandmother, who has waited so patiently for this book; and to my brother and sister for defining my understanding of loyalty and love.

I have endless gratitude for Nora O'Neill, the ever-talented illustrator and cover artist of this book. *Pawn* is as much yours as it is mine. Your art breathes new dimensions into the story. I cannot express how much I value your initiative, your flexibility, and your vision for this novel. Time and time again, I'm stunned by how much you just *get* me. I couldn't have chosen a better artist to bring Pawn's curious characters and places to life. It is such a privilege to call you my illustrator and my friend.

Thank you to this book's first beta readers: Kat, August J. Rose, Sam, You Lin, and Maddie Kwan. Additional thanks to the second round of beta readers: Sophie T., Maya Al-Khzaee, Samantha Wong, Kay, Alya Solace, and Daisy Beckett. Your feedback was instrumental in shaping this book, and I am unbelievably grateful that you gave me your time and attention. I am also thankful for Eve, Sarah, Natalie, and Rebekah, who helped me revise the synopsis of *Pawn*.

Many thanks to Sarah Emmer, whose humor, encouragement, and insight helped me polish my story further.

I would also like to extend my deepest gratitude to the Instagram writing community. If I had not joined it in 2021, I may not have written, let alone published, this book. Thank you to Sarah, Grace, Lu, Abbie, Queenie, Liv, Sydney, Laurel, Amber, Eve, and anyone else who has ever said a kind word about *Pawn*. I have met so many talented and amazing people through this community, and I cannot wait to see all of our books on the same shelf someday.

These acknowledgments would not be complete without thanking my friends: you know who you are. Thank you for sharing my love of books. Thank you for being my personal hype team and telling me my writing was great (even when I was pretty sure it wasn't). Your support means the world to me. I love you.

Thank you to Alejandra for taking the best author photos I could ask for. You're an incredible photographer and writer, and of course, an incredible person as well.

Thank you to my college writing group, who believed in me from the start.

I am fortunate to know many excellent educators who encouraged my creative endeavors, from high school teachers to college professors to librarians. Thank you for indulging my book ramblings and for asking, "How's the book going?"

Special thanks to Mrs. Cooper: the joy you take in what you do inspires me endlessly.

Thank you to Lewis Carroll for giving Alice's adventures

to generations of children and adults. I hope I have matched the spirit of his tale.

Thank you to Howard Shore (*Lord of the Rings*), Danny Elfman (*Alice in Wonderland*), and Harry Gregson-Williams (*The Chronicles of Narnia*) for creating the movie soundtracks that provided much-needed inspiration during the lengthy editing process.

Finally, thank *you*, dear reader. For as long as I can remember, it has been my dream to share my stories with an audience. Thank you for helping me fulfill that dream. Thank you for staying until the end of this fairy tale.

ABOUT THE AUTHOR

Calliope More is a fantasy author from the Midwest, currently pursuing a degree in Creative Writing. *Pawn: A Fairy Tale* is her debut novel. She is passionate about weaving myth, magic, and fairy tales into her stories for young adults. When she is not wandering through distant worlds, she can be found on her Instagram @thewritermuse.

ABOUT THE ILLUSTRATOR

Nora O'Neill is an illustrator and painter who delights in fairy tales and the quiet beauty of the natural world. She studies chemical engineering in Michigan's Upper Peninsula and can often be found hiking, backpacking, or planning her next garden.